TOUCH THE FIRE

Grania Beckford

ST. MARTIN'S PRESS • NEW YORK

Who sees his true-love in her naked bed,
Teaching the sheets a whiter hue than white,
But, when his glutton eye so full hath fed,
His other agents aim at like delight?
Who is so faint, that dare not be so bold
To touch the fire, the weather being cold!

Shakespeare, *Venus and Adonis*

❈ Contents

TOUCH THE FIRE

1 ❃ *Dainties to taste*

Torches are made to light, jewels to wear,
Dainties to taste, fresh beauty for the use,
Herbs for their smell, and sappy plants to bear;
Things growing to themselves are growth's abuse.
Seeds spring from seeds, and beauty breedeth beauty:
Thou wast begot; to get it is thy duty.

VENUS AND ADONIS

I walked through the soft April evening from Jermyn Street to Berkeley Square. There were tulips in window boxes, and the trees in the square were filmed with a mist of young green. I felt a fool, a fish out of water, a frog in the wrong ditch. I was sick for my own green place on the West Coast of Ireland, where already the speckled trout would be dimpling the pools of the river, and the birds would be crying over the bog and over the purple rocks of the seashore. The streets of London were no place to be in the spring of the year—not for me, a young man with acres to cultivate and tenants to prod and wheedle into good husbandry, with fish to catch and horses to exercise, and all manner of great books to read in the smoke-scented evenings in the great library of my home.

But my great-aunts had said—all four of them—that I must show my face to the world and put a London polish on my manners, or I should deteriorate into a hobbledehoy with a mind in muddy gaiters. My eldest great-aunt, Lady Diplington, had showered the fashionable world with letters asking her old friends to be kind to me. And so they thought they were: for when I took up my quarters in rented rooms in Jermyn Street, I found dozens of cards requesting the honour of my company at balls and receptions and all the mummery of the London season; and I took myself to the tailor and the hatter and the bootmaker recommended by my single surviving great-uncle, and disguised myself as everything I was not.

I did it all partly out of family loyalty; and partly because my four great-aunts and my one great-uncle would have badgered the life out of me if I had refused; and partly because I had a small, nasty feeling that they were right. I was a provincial peasant, an Irish Tony Lumpkin. I could talk about cows but not concerts, pigs but not politics. My manners were awkward and self-conscious. I did not know where to put my hands, which seemed too large. I *was* degenerating into a hobbledehoy; my mind *was* in muddy gaiters. I had been born to obligations beyond my house and my estate, but until I could act like a gentleman I could scarcely fulfil them.

And everyone said that this season of 1906 was to be a vintage year, a glorious and memorable festival, owing to the number of fashionable hostesses who were laying themselves out to surpass each other.

I threaded the press of carriages and motorcars outside Casterbridge House and climbed the shallow steps to the great door. I wanted to jump up them, and then jump down them again. I wanted to do something, anything, active, violent, physical; but I disciplined myself to behave with the proper languor which I was learning from the fine gentlemen who were my new friends. I gave my shiny new top hat to one footman, and my new silk-faced evening overcoat to another footman, and my card of invitation to a third. He transferred me, as though I were a parcel of dubious fish, to a gorgeous giant in peacock livery who announced me in a voice like a tuba:

"Sir Mah-Wah Ah-Wah!"

"Matthew Alban," I interpreted to Lady Casterbridge.

"Oh, yes indeed! Sir Matthew! *How* good of you to come. Dear Serena Dippywhip's nephew? Great nephew? Of course, you know, there's nothing ill-natured in that nickname. Hallowed by antiquity! How it began I have no idea. Are you enjoying London? May I present you to—the king is coming in a minute, and if I seem *distraite* it is because—Oh, Lord Henry! You promised to come early to hold my handerina. Do you know Sir Michael Albany, who has come all the way from some dreadful boggy patch of County Whatnot—"

"Matthew Alban," I said, the third and fourth words I had uttered since entering the house.

"Henry Clinton. How do you do? Philomena Casterbridge is always thrown into a sort of soufflé when the king comes here. I don't know why

—he must have been here a great many times, winning money at baccarat from poor old Eldred. The champagne is over there, and so is Lady Bulbarrow—two excellent reasons for steering in a southwesterly direction."

Lord Henry was about thirty—half a dozen years older than myself by the calendar, a century my senior in polish and worldly wisdom. He had butter-coloured hair and a silky saffron moustache, a pleasant tenor voice and a cheerful smile. He knew everybody in the great rooms of Casterbridge House. He greeted even the most formidable dowagers with an easy friendliness which, by some magic I had not learned, combined familiarity with respectful deference. He was evidently popular. He evidently deserved to be. He was all that my great-aunts wanted me to become. I thought that if I must choose a model, Lord Henry Clinton was as good a one as I should find.

But a part of me did not want a model at all. A part of me said that I was best as my taciturn and graceless self.

I recognised a few faces, but only a few. I had not attended many functions of this kind, because my new dress clothes had only been finished the week before. The people I recognised seemed less than avid to recognise me. I had made as much impression, in my nervous London debut, as a wet feather on a swathe of seaweed. The trouble, I well knew, was that I had not talked. If you are silent, nobody carries away anything to remember you by. I was not blessed with glibness. I had no talent, like Lord Henry's, for a stream of easy chatter. I felt I had not learned the language of this strange, pampered, hostile, glittering tribe which I was supposed to be exploring.

I stood or strolled by Lord Henry's side, drinking many glasses of pink champagne. It was sweet, effeminate stuff, not really at all what I wanted. Lord Henry suffered me to attach myself to him. To be sure, I gave him no trouble. I did not talk too much. I did not talk at all. I might have been one of the marble pillars, or one of the boot-faced footmen who carried the trays of champagne.

I felt that my tie was crooked, my face red, my buttons undone. I felt miserably self-conscious. I was sure that people were looking at me and laughing. I felt increasingly idiotic, clinging to Lord Henry's flank as though I would sink without his support. He was kind enough to introduce me to a number of people, including some to whom I had been introduced on other occasions.

"What a disapproving face," said a high, clear voice beside me. "You look like Lot comtemplating the Cities of the Plain. Who is your tame Savonarola, Lord Henry?"

"Ah! You may well ask. He has been frightening me with that smouldering eye, too. Consequently I've been talking too much and too loudly, simply to keep my courage up. May I present Sir Matthew Alban? The Marchioness of Bulbarrow."

Of course I had heard of Lady Bulbarrow. Even in County Clare there had been word, at dinner tables and in smoking rooms, of this most blazing of the comets of Society. She was not notorious, so far as I knew; simply celebrated.

She deserved her celebrity. She was a great beauty, the first I had ever seen—an undeniable, unmistakable, authentic raving beauty. Not young. Not much under forty. But she outshone the pretty girls in the room like a flambeau among fireflies.

Her face was a pale and perfect oval, crowned with a cloud of dark hair in which glittered, with an almost barbaric vehemence, the biggest tiara I had ever seen. Her head was set wonderfully on a long, slender white neck; and her bare shoulders looked too sculpturally perfect to be made of flesh and skin. A rope of pearls slid coldly out of sight in the valley between her breasts, as though she had so many jewels she felt no need of displaying them. Her dress was of silver silk. There was in her eye something I had never seen in a human eye before—a silvery, icy quality which turned ordinary mortal blue into something other-worldly, mysterious, mesmeric.

Icy, yet without the least chill. This was the fascinating paradox of Lady Bulbarrow's appearance.

She smiled as Lord Henry introduced us. Her smile had a lazy, leisurely quality, as though it knew it had plenty of time. It grew and grew, and filled all her face with warmth. I felt myself smiling in response. It would have been impossible not to do so.

"And are you really so contemptuous of us all, Sir Matthew?" she asked. The smile was in her voice as well as on that perfect mouth and in those amazing silver-blue eyes.

"Certainly not!" I cried. "I can't imagine why I should have been looking angry."

"A young Ancient Mariner, a Jeremiah without a beard—I don't believe you have been having an amusing evening."

There was sympathy in her voice. With a half-smile she glanced round at the resplendent mob as though she were sharing with me a private impatience with it all.

"I am a new boy," I said. "I feel exactly as I did my first week at boarding school."

"I never went to boarding school, thank heavens, or to school of any kind. But I know just what you mean. I have been feeling like that, off and on, ever since I was brought out. I am not going to be specific about the number of years ago that was, nor will I welcome curiosity on the point."

"Oh no," I said earnestly. "You can't possibly know what I mean. I feel as though I had strayed in here by mistake, and if they looked at me properly they would realise it and have me thrown out into the street."

"People are looking at you and laughing cruelly? They are all talking in an unfamiliar language about subjects of which you have never heard?"

"Yes! Just exactly that! How did you know? How could you know?"

"As I told you. I have been there myself, often and often. All nice people have. Everybody should feel uncertainty sometimes. Someone serenely confident all the time would be odious. Insensitive, don't you think? Simply eaten with fatuous conceit."

"Oh," I said, trying to digest this. It struck me as extraordinarily comforting.

"I gradually got more confident," Lady Bulbarrow went on, "especially after I was married. A famous title helps; no doubt of that, unfair as it is. Clothes from Worth and Paquin help, and so do pearls like these. One gets to enjoy some parties. I'm enjoying this one, just at the moment. But I don't enjoy every one. Not by any means."

"I haven't enjoyed any," I said. "Until this one."

"Then why do it? Why bother? You're a sportsman, surely, an outdoor creature like my late husband. He *hated* London. You have that extraordinarily healthy look which I can only get out of a pot."

"My great-aunts accused me of turning into a peasant," I explained.

"An Irish peasant? From County Clare?"

"Yes," I said, startled. "How did you guess?"

"I didn't guess. I asked Philomena Casterbridge who you were. Don't look so startled. She denied all knowledge of you—denied ever having set eyes on you. But I persisted. I always do when I'm curious, and I'm quite often *very* curious. Yours is a new face, you see. A nice one, if not excessively pretty. Also I was intrigued by the ferocity of your expression."

"I hope it's softened," I said.

"Yes, it has. I hope I can claim a little credit for that. Will you come and call? I shall be in London from time to time most of the summer. The *Morning Post*, alas, will report my comings and goings. And we've had a telephone put in. A number of my friends have resisted it, but I resisted for only about three seconds. When I'm not in London I shall be in

Wiltshire. You might like to come and stay—a Friday-to-Monday? The trout fishing has just begun. I think I shall like you even better in a tweed coat and wading boots. Are you engaged the Friday after next? We meet the six o'clock train at Salisbury."

She smiled at me with amazing warmth and friendliness. My tongue should have loosened; I should have made at once a graceful little speech of gratitude and acceptance. But all I did was open and shut my mouth, like a frog; and like a frog I made a ridiculous croaking noise.

I was clumsier even than that. I grow hot even now to think how inept I must have seemed. I found that I was staring, helplessly, at the valley between her alabaster breasts, into the soft secrecy of which descended the magnificent rope of pearls.

Her smile broadened. It was not in the least derisive. I managed to stammer at last that I would come to Wiltshire in ten days' time.

An elderly man, immensely tall with long white whiskers like my grandfather's, bent to murmur in Lady Bulbarrow's ear. She was still smiling as she nodded. She glanced at me with an expression I could not read, murmured something I could not hear, and followed the old man across the room. People parted to make way for them, forming a sort of avenue down which they walked. The old man strutted. Lady Bulbarrow floated. She moved superbly—regal yet supple, the silvery silk of her dress flowing out from a tiny waist, her bare back an undulating area of the most perfect unblemished white.

At the end of the avenue of people stood a portly, bearded man with an expression of the most excruciating boredom. With a shock, I recognised the king. The gaunt lady who had been boring him curtseyed with a kind of angular despair. Lady Bulbarrow's curtsey was, in the most striking contrast, a smooth, infinitely graceful reverence. Boredom left the king's face. He smiled broadly and took her hand. They talked animatedly, and the king laughed.

I watched them unashamedly. I became aware that everyone else was watching them, too, but pretending not to. I became aware of envy, admiration, resentment towards Lady Bulbarrow. She was one of the king's circle of close friends—even in County Clare we knew that. She was the most beautiful woman in the room, the most beautiful woman I had ever seen.

She had asked me to stay. Her smile had said that she was my friend.

"Smitten, my boy?" said Lord Henry Clinton, reappearing at my elbow.

"Yes," I said.

We both laughed.

I came away from Casterbridge House with a new opinion about London.

The chambers below me in Jermyn Street were occupied by an aging, raffish bachelor called Rivington Trench—"Rivvy" to everybody, including the old woman who sold flowers in the street by our door. He had been a tremendous blood in his youth, a member of the Pelican Club, an intimate of actresses, pugilists, bookmakers and barmaids. He had a thick nose covered in broken veins, and little red-rimmed eyes almost invisible in pouchy lids. His jowls shook when he walked. He was still very dandified, in an antique fashion. I thought his boots were too small for his feet, and his high stiff collars for his neck. I was very sure his trousers and waistcoats were too tight for his paunchy body. He walked down the street with little mincing steps, twirling a cloudy cane, his hat doggishly aslant, a flower in his buttonhole. He was thoroughly kind-hearted, generous with his money, all too generous with his time. In a few days I had relived dozens of close finishes at Goodwood and Sandown races (he had always backed the horse just beaten by dint of a villainous conspiracy of jockey, trainer, owner, judge and Jockey Club), of Homeric rat-killing contests between terriers, of wild nights at the old Criterion and wild days on the river.

Because of his generosity and his tolerance, he numbered some very queer fish among his friends. He was too kind to snub them, and they sometimes provided the audience he needed. I daresay they sat through his stories for the sake of his brandy and soda. The very oddest was a great bull of a man called Desmond Dacre. Nobody but Rivvy would have tolerated him.

Although Rivvy lived mostly with low company, he was a great expert on the fashionable world. He had no contact with it and wanted none. He was totally unpretentious. I do not know *why* he was interested in the doings of the great, but one might ask the same question of millions of simple people who like reading of duchesses and drawing rooms.

"Another desperate tangle with the world of rank and fashion, laddie?" he greeted me the following morning in his high, hoarse voice. "Who did you meet? The Casterbridges, wasn't it? Your name ain't mentioned in the *Post*. Tum-Tum was there, I see."

"Who?"

"Your sovereign, laddie. King Teddy the Good, God bless him, and may all his two-year-olds win at Ascot. Presented, were you?"

"No, not this time."

"Slow feller you are. All you need is to fall in a faint at the royal feet—
Dammit, cried TumTum, *feller's fainted; restore his tissues with a drop of
B and S, then ask him to dinner at the Palace!* Who *did* you meet lad-
die?"

Rivvy really wanted to know, so although I did not much want to discuss my evening with him, I mentioned Lord Henry and Lady Bulbarrow.

"Clinton," he said immediately. "Ah yes. Dukes of Belgravia, of the second creation. Your pal is Victor Belgravia's second boy. Second? Second?
What am I talking about? Third. Third, of course. What stamp of lad is
he?"

"Friendly. He seems very popular."

"Sons of dukes are popular. Of course, they can afford to be friendly.
He won't inherit, though. Eldest son, Mountblaize, he's married. Children. Sons? Can't recall offhand. I'll look 'em up in the Stud Book presently. Like to get things clear. What does a feller like that do with his
time, I wonder? Allowance, I daresay, but not a fortune. Ought to do a
job of work. Every younger son ought to do a job of work. Army, bar, politics, church, diplomatic service."

I laughed because Rivvy himself, *not* the son of a duke, had never done
a day's work in his life. He had inherited a little money from an uncle
with a cotton-mill in Lancashire. The money was in trust. Rivvy only got
the income. It was a sore point. I had heard the whole story within hours
of meeting him.

"Lady Bulbarrow, now," Rivvy went on, with a new and reverential
note in his voice. "Widow of the third Marquess. Married him when she
was very young—eighteen, I believe. I remember it well. St. George's,
Hanover Square. Royalty present—not the old queen, God praise her
memory, but Tum-Tum and a parcel of princesses. He was much older.
What did they call him? Harry. Harry Bulbarrow. Senior Steward of the
Jockey Club. Remember the Bulbarrow Committee? No, of course you
don't. Stiff sort of feller, I believe. Grandee of the old school. Died half a
dozen years ago. People said she'd marry again, but *I* never thought she
would. Only direction you can go from her position is downwards. One
child. Girl. *Most* unfortunate. Shocking disappointment to Harry.
Speeded his demise—that and getting his feet wet at Newmarket. Title's
gone to a cousin. The place will, too. All entailed, of course. She stays
there for the moment because he's abroad, the present feller, the fourth
Marquess. Governor of some outlandish place. Burma? Bechuanaland?
Brazil? No, couldn't be Brazil. One fine day he'll come home and move

in. Out she'll go. Very hard, that. A damned fine woman. I've got two photographs of her. One I cut out of the *Sketch*. Framed it in passe-partout. The other one I actually bought. Hand-tinted. I consider it a masterpiece of delicate elegance. Couldn't resist those shoulders. Never seen such lovely shoulders on a woman. Did you notice her shoulders, laddie?"

"Yes," I said.

"Mark you, she's not welcome everywhere. I have it on excellent authority that she's not asked to Doncaster House."

"Why? What on earth—"

"Old Duchess of Doncaster is a stickler. A regular tartar. Never set eyes on her myself, and I wouldn't care to."

"Lady Bulbarrow seems a great friend of the king's."

"Oh yes, just his style—beautiful and witty and a tiny bit fast."

"*Fast?*"

"Shows a reasonable turn of foot, I fancy. Powders."

"Powders," I repeated blankly.

"Powders, laddie. Administers a fine white substance, known as powder because it *is* powder, to the neck and shoulders and so forth, by means of a piece of swansdown. At least I think that's what she'd use. Powders. I happen to know from an unimpeachable source."

"What source?" I asked, not thinking it possible that Rivvy could know such a thing.

"Erstwhile personal maid of a lady who made some of Lady Bulbarrow's underclothes; now the deservedly popular Hebe, or pourer-out of B and S at the Running Footman in Vigo Street. A mine of curious information, owing to her one-time mistress's entrée to the boudoirs of the great. I could tell you some things! I probably shall, not at this second but on another occasion which I promise myself shall be soon. Where was I? Powder. Yes. Not *comme il faut*, if judged by the rigid standards. Like having Jews and Americans to dinner. *I* would, but of course the question doesn't arise. Fancy not having Baron Meyer de Rothschild to dinner the year he won four out of five Classic races! But the Duchess of Doncaster wouldn't."

I thought it grotesque that Lady Bulbarrow should be denied entry to any house in the kingdom. I do not think so now, but I thought so then.

Nothing in my life had prepared me for Moreys Castle.

My own home, Albanstown, is neither small nor ugly. It was built by my great-great-great-grandfather, the first baronet, in 1753; a big, simple, squarish house on classical lines, like most Irish mansions of the time. The

stables could hold forty horses; the kennels had once held a pack of the
old white deerhounds. Great windows opened on the south and on to the
sea a mile away. The Trustees had sent me away to school in England, to
Eton, and afterwards to Trinity College in Dublin. Otherwise, I had spent
all my life in my own place, on my own seacoast.

It had been my own place since the year of my birth, 1882, when the
Land Leaguers shot my father in the back. He was on his way in a dog-
cart to Kilrush to give evidence in the court against a rick-burner. My
mother died soon afterwards, killed by shock and loneliness, as well as
threats against the both of us.

The irony was that my own sympathies lay with those bitter peasants.
They could build walls to fence their tiny fields and dig ditches to drain
them, working like animals to make a barely tolerable life for their wives
and children, and then be evicted without notice by the agent of an absen-
tee landlord.

Absentees we were not, and never had been. (My four great-aunts and
my single great-uncle would have preferred more absenteeism from us.) It
was a wild and poor country, but I grew up to love every stone and pool
and bog, and the holt of the otter and the sett of the badger, and to know
every tenant and storekeeper, every fisherman and tinker. We had fine
snipe-shooting thereabouts, and moderate sea-trout fishing, and a motley,
bobbery pack of "Sunday harriers." I made time for these, as Lady Bulbarrow had correctly guessed, but it was little enough time I had. My own
farms and the farms and cottages and problems of my tenants seemed to
occupy full twenty hours a day.

So had lived all my forebears for the five generations of Albanstown;
with the resulting risk, to which my great-aunts were so alive, of our manners being buckled hopelessly into those muddy gaiters. Our manners,
but not altogether our minds. By a stroke of the greatest good fortune—
and this was another irony—my grandfather had fallen from his horse
while foxhunting far north in Galway, and damaged his spine so that for
thirty years he was practically confined to a chair. Already a man of education (he had taken his degree at Balliol) he became a considerable scholar,
not of one subject but of a dozen. History, travel, botany, the ancient Cel-
tic church, medieval music, old firearms—these were some of the ill-as-
sorted regions he explored. The result was a magnificent library, to which
my own father added.

For the rest, Albanstown had good English silver, indifferent French
furniture, and truly execrable family portraits. We had low hills, deep

bohreens, continual gentle rain. And we had the rustle or thunder of the
Atlantic rollers swinging at us always out of the west.

None of which had prepared me for Moreys.

The six o'clock train from London was indeed met at Salisbury—met
with a vengeance, met by a fleet of vehicles drawn by a squadron of
magnificent horses. There were no motorcars in evidence. A troupe of ladies, hatted and veiled for the journey, were helped into closed carriages.
Their maids and their luggage went in wagonettes. For the gentlemen,
there were three open Victorias, and for their valets and bags a kind of
horse-drawn char-à-banc almost as big as a London omnibus.

Twenty people were met off the train, to be carried to Moreys Castle. I
alone of them all had brought no personal servant; I alone had only a single, awkward portmanteau.

There was no room for me in the Victorias. I went in the char-à-banc
with the valets, my portmanteau under my feet.

We travelled about six miles along a river valley, the heavy vehicle
going unhurriedly between the hedgerows. It was a countryside of extraordinary, disciplined richness, in the sharpest contrast to the rock-strewn wilderness I was used to. Everything was tidy. The hedges were cut-and-laid
or clipped. The pastures were full of ewes and lambs and the arable fields
of young corn. Beyond the river rose swell upon swell of downland, with
beechwoods giving way to turf, and a sky full of larks.

As we went, the valets exchanged news. Most were old acquaintances. I
had a dampening effect on their gossip for a mile or so, but they became
used to me, or correctly deduced that I was not very important. They
talked not of themselves but only of their masters, as though they had no
lives of their own, no friends, families, ambitions, or even ailments. They
said "we" in a sort of reverse of the royal fashion: "We are asked to stay
with His Grace for Goodwood this year. After that, we are engaged to go
to Homburg for the cure."

The main road bent to the south, but we went straight on by what was
not a smaller but a larger thoroughfare. We passed between two lodges,
identical, Palladian in style, with columns and cupolas. They were exquisite, the weathered stone and the perfect proportions seeming to belong to
the landscape as comfortably as the trees and bluebells.

"Nasty, damp, unhealthy billets, those are," said a thin manservant in
elastic-sided boots. "Our sister's maid bin an' married Percy Jorkins, under-
gardener as was, an' they put 'em in one o' those lodges."

"Miss Rossiter, would that be? Which maided the Honourable Christabel?"

"That's her. Consequent I went an' took tea with them, bein' virtual in the family, so to say. Damp crawlin' up the walls so they couldn't get the wallpaper to stick."

The drive wound through a park of undulating, close-cropped grass badged with enormous elms. The river described great loops in the folds of the ground, intermittently visible, enriching the prospect. Inside a high iron fence a herd of fallow-deer was grazing, the evening sun on their dappled backs.

"There was roast venison on the table in the Servants' Hall last time we stayed," said the valet in elastic-sided boots. "Nasty greasy stuff. I couldn't hardly stummick it."

Beech woods now hemmed the drive, which curved between the smooth grey columns of the trunks. A sharper bend took us out of the beech wood and into a sudden full view of the façade of Moreys, half a mile away. I gasped. It was immense—no castle but a palace, part ancient, most built about 1700. There was a great tower in the middle and smaller towers, cupola'd, at each corner. It was as tall as a cathedral, story upon story. I had a dazzled impression of thousands of great windows, every pane giving back the evening sun. Terraces descended, like some immense petrified waterfall, to a thirty-acre lake. The lake had a wooded island in the middle, and a Grecian temple on the island. At a corner of the lake, a bridge in the Chinese taste spanned the exit of the river.

My first numbed thought was: I shall get lost in there; once I leave my bedroom I shall never find it again.

Then I thought, more worthily, how splendid the state rooms must be, how magnificently they must display the celebrated Moreys pictures—the Holbeins, the Vandykes, the Gainsboroughs. I thought how grand must be the view from the terraces over the lake to the beech woods, with the swell of downs beyond that. I felt, as I think any inexperienced stranger must, abashed and excited at the prospect of being an inmate of such a place.

"The stairs in this billet," said the man with elastic-sided boots, "is crool to the feet."

I keenly looked forward to seeing Lady Bulbarrow again. If her beauty was worth contemplating, her smile was worth treasuring. She would not have asked me if she had not liked me.

There were swans, dabchicks and wild duck on the lake. The drive encircled the water, passing close to the Chinese bridge. From the distance, I had imagined this to be a folly—a single wall only, to be looked at from the house and the terraces. But it was a real bridge, humpbacked, with mossy steps. As we trundled by, a figure emerged from a thicket of shrubs and climbed the steps of the little bridge. None of my fellow passengers saw her. She was a young girl with a pale face and a cloud of pale hair. She was very slim, and wore a white dress. She carried a hat as big as a cartwheel, and a book bound in blue. I had the ridiculous fancy that she had come out of the water, like a nymph. I was not close enough to make out her features clearly, but I thought she was beautiful, with great eyes in a small, pensive face. She did not glance at the char-à-banc, but gazed out over the lake.

I was touched by a wilting quality about her, a tender defencelessness, yet an utter purity. I was full of curiosity. She looked sad. I thought of doomed maidens in the poems of Lord Tennyson, of *Elaine the lily maid of Astolet*, of *Mariana in the moated grange*.

I wondered if I should meet her. I had a great dread that she would turn out to be a little milliner from a London suburb, come to stay with her aunt, the Moreys' housekeeper. That would have been a suitable circumstance for Jermyn Steet, for an adventure in the company of Rivvy Trench. It would not do here. At least life at Moreys seemed rich in promise. I wished I were invited for more than three days.

"A weekend is amply sufficient in a barricks like this," said the man in elastic-sided boots. "Give me Grosvenor Street, where *we* spends all day at the club and don't give no trouble."

My bedroom was at the end of a long corridor at the top of a lot of stairs. I followed an underfootman who carried my portmanteau; I made a serious effort to remember the route.

The footman said he was called Ernest, and that he was to valet me as required.

The room was far from splendid—half the size of my bedroom in Jermyn Street and no better furnished. The window gave inwards onto an area of leaded roof the size of a bowling green. The single picture was an engraving, after Henry Alken, of a group of foxhounds with a terrier. The single light was a candle in a squat porcelain candlestick. There was a brass bedstead, a chest of drawers, a wardrobe with a door that could not be made to close, a writing table, a washstand with a cloudy looking glass, an armchair, a bootjack, and an Indian rug.

On the writing table was a leather frame with a gilt coronet tooled into it. In the frame was a printed card with an embossed coronet at the top:

WEEKDAYS: Post Arrives 8:30 A.M.   4:30 P.M.
Post Leaves 6:00 P.M.
SUNDAYS: Post Arrives 8:30 A.M.
Post Leaves 5:00 P.M.
Carriages for Church 10:30 A.M.

Luncheon 1:30 P.M.
Dinner 8:30 P.M.

There was a stack of writing paper, coroneted and thick as parchment, in a coroneted leather box. The inkpot was full. There were three new pens in a brass tray. There was a coronet on the lid of the inkpot. I thought the ink itself would have carried a coronet if a means could have been found to engrave the design on the liquid.

Ernest brought me hot water and a second candle. He recommended the bathroom for the morning, owing to the number of gentlemen now requiring it. I washed as well as I could and dressed as well as I could. I examined myself dubiously in the unhelpful glass. It was all too easy to understand why the fashionable world had not, with a few blessed exceptions, made a pet or a lion of me. My silence apart, I did not *look* distinguished or interesting. Few more ordinary faces can have looked out over a white tie and a boiled shirt. Healthy, yes. Lady Bulbarrow had remarked that I looked healthy. It was not much, but it would have to be enough.

A girl in Dublin once told me I had nice blue eyes. They were blue, certainly. I could not tell if they were nice.

I supposed the company assembled a little before dinner. Perhaps at eight o'clock? But I had no idea where. Ernest had disappeared. All I could do, I thought, was to prowl about in the immensities of the place, listening hard for a buzz of conversation. I must hope I found the party before it went to the dining room, for how should I find that? Suppose dinner was not in the dining room but in the banqueting hall?

Who would I take into dinner? Who should I find beside me? What should I make conversation about?

Heartily wishing myself back in my native bog—or even in Jermyn Street—I ventured shyly out into the corridor. I went along it, all the way along it, towards the first of the flights of stairs. Another bedroom door opened and, to my joy, Lord Henry Clinton came out. His butter-coloured hair shone; his face shone; he was whistling a music hall tune. He clapped me on the shoulder with the greatest good will, and we went arm in arm towards the Venetian Gallery. It was there, he said, that we foregathered for dinner.

"What they should give you in a house like this," he said, "is a map. Or better, a native guide. He should be equipped with tin whistles and little mirrors and toys in case one fell foul of hostile denizens who might want to pop one in a cooking pot. My revered parent lives in tolerable state, but this! It's simply an exaggeration. You came down this evening? I was awfully glad to hear you were an entry. I came down yesterday, myself. I always travel on a Thursday—train's so beastly crowded on Fridays, with the whole world flooding out to house parties. My God, these stairs! We ought to be roped together like fellows in the Alps. But here are lusher pastures. The fat lowlands. Quite a different feel underfoot, I think. Best Wilton in these parts. And there's a fortunate inhabitant—Gareth Fortescue. They do him well, don't they?"

I looked my question.

"Old family friend, baronet like yourself, racing man; said to be a very fine shot, said to go well to hounds, house in Harley Street, house near Newmarket. Once dropped a bowl of trifle in the king's lap. Wife's a chronic invalid, never goes anywhere. How's that for a living portrait?"

Sir Gareth preceded us down the broad stairs we had now reached, all unconscious of Lord Henry's disrespectful commentary. He was a tall, grizzled man with broad shoulders and a high colour. From the look of him I guessed that, like some of my Irish neighbours, he drank a lot but took a lot of exercise. He carried no excess weight, or else his tailor was a genius. It was easy to picture him on the race course, or in the hunting field in one of the flying countries, or killing mounds of pheasants at the great shoots in Norfolk.

"When I marry a house like this," Lord Henry murmured to me, "I shall treat fellows who leave their wives at home like bachelors. After all, as far as the house is concerned they're single men like ourselves. It's a question of fairness, pure and simple. If Gareth Fortescue stays with me, he shall be in bedroom like mine or yours, in unexplored wastes where no civilized foot has ever trod. But he emerged from the grand corridor, no? I have never even seen one of those bedrooms, not in this house. But I'll lay the bathroom's less than a hundred yards away."

The Venetian Gallery at Moreys was, that evening, closely similar to the Great Saloon of Casterbridge House ten days previously—many of the

same people, the same noise, the men identically dressed, the women more
or less so. The king was not there, but this was chance; he often *was*
there.

The best thing the two occasions had in common—the best thing in this
room, as in that other—was Lady Bulbarrow. She looked up from a big
red leather place board, saw me come in behind Lord Henry, and crossed
the room at once with hands outstretched. And it was me she was greeting, for she had greeted him the day before. I thought people looked at me
curiously, but I did not look back at them, because I was looking at her.

She was as beautiful as I remembered, and her smile as warm.

But she had no time to talk. She introduced me to a Mrs. Quilter whom
I was to take in. Laboriously I addressed myself to this lady, who wanted
to listen to conversations far away in the crowd.

We sat down, thirty-six to dinner. There were as many servants in the
room as diners. Mrs. Quilter, to her chagrin, was on my right. A Major
Fothergill was on her other side; she found common ground with him,
and made full use of it. A shrill person called Lady Babraham was on my
left. She was engrossed with her left-hand neighbour, a man of startling
appearance—thin, intense, like an El Greco saint. His conversation did
not seem to be saintly. He made Lady Babraham shriek with laughter.

"Horribilino!" I heard her gasp with shocked glee. "And did she, afterwards . . . ? How too deevy! May I tell Sylvia? You *have*? Spoilsport."

Offered the back of Mrs. Quilter's left shoulder and the back of Lady
Babraham's right shoulder, I devoted myself to dinner. I had heard, from
Rivvy Trench and also from my great-aunts, that the menus of the day
were shorter and simpler than those of the late years of the old queen. It
was hard to believe at Moreys. We had iced melon, a choice of clear or
thick soup, a choice of salmon, trout or whitebait; for the entrée, a choice
of soufflé, sweatbreads or cutlets, roast chicken, roast beef, a remove of
smoked Parma ham from Italy, salads from heaven knows where, fancy
fruits, ices, little biscuits, and finally a savoury of devilled sardines. We
drank sherry, white wine, red wine and champagne.

My clothes felt as tight as Rivvy Trench's, and my nose felt the colour
of his. I did not wonder that *we* went to Homburg for the cure, after a
few months of such meals.

At a quarter to ten Lady Bulbarrow rose, having "collected eyes" all
round the table. She looked as though she had eaten only fresh grapes and
drunk only fresh water. The ladies left in a parakeet flock. The men
closed up on one end of the enormous table.

Drinking port, I found myself next to the man like an El Greco saint. The similarity was increased rather than diminished by a closer inspection. I thought he was a little over forty. He might have stepped out from a huge, gloomy canvas under a wild Toledo sky and shed toga or cloak for perfect evening dress. I could never get my white tie to sit as his did; I would not have ventured such studs and cuff links even if I could have afforded them. It was curious to see a man with such a remote, ascetic face drinking port with unconcealed enjoyment. Thin hair floated mystically about an intellectual skull, yet it smelled of the most expensive scented dressing.

He had a pleasant voice, rather clipped and pedantic. He said he was Lord Whitewater. I had not heard of him, and I lacked the skill to hide the fact. He was not in the least discomposed, but smiled and said, "I am not a public man. I seldom go to the House of Lords and have never opened my mouth there. The difficulty would be to find people who *have* heard of me. For years my chief interest has been—I hardly like to tell you, since you may think it so odd—has been in old musical instruments, and how they were made and played."

"But my grandfather studied them, too," I said. "I have read all his books, except the ones in German."

"But this is wonderful. You can tell me how a shawm was played?"

"Of course. You blew it. It was a double-reed instrument, like an oboe, but with the reeds in a sort of hollow ball to make the resonance."

"You *do* know. A scholar among the philistines. How delightful to encounter you here, of all places."

So he and I talked of sackbuts and serpents for half an hour until Sir Gareth Fortescue stood up at a quarter past ten and said that it was time to join the ladies.

Of all imaginable conversations, it was the one I had least expected to have at Moreys. I remembered that Lord Whitewater had been just as engrossed in his scandalous gossip with Lady Babraham. It seemed that people were complicated, and Lord Whitewater more complicated than most.

In another enormous room almost everyone sat down to auction bridge. It was not a game which had reached County Clare. They made eight tables, each with candelabrum, boxed cards, scoring pads and little gold pencils. A kind of ferocity entered the atmosphere. These rich people were consumed with anxiety to win shillings off each other.

Four of us were left out, another man and two women. The man sat between the women on a sofa. I sat nearby, within range of their conversation, as it were, though not part of it, so as not to seem an isolated outcast. The three on the sofa kept their voices low so as not to disturb the desperate concentration of the card players. I heard most of what they said. It was exactly like most of the conversations I had overheard at Moreys and in London.

"I didn't see you at Florence's."

"Her parties are always horribilino. Cold rooms and warm fizz."

"Where are you staying for Ascot? Are you going to Cowes this year? Shall I see you at Millie's on Tuesday?"

"Have you heard Frank's story about Millie? Too deevy for words . . ."

I did not speak to Lord Whitewater again. He was playing bridge with a partner like an old she-goat. I did not speak to Lady Bulbarrow again. She was playing bridge with a partner like an over-dressed buffalo. I did not speak to anybody.

Towards midnight, people laid their cards down and began making calculations on their scoring pads. Some handed each other folded slips of paper and some handed each other a few silver coins. Some, it seemed to me, pocketed the little gold pencils on the card tables.

I followed them all on another leisurely journey to yet another immense room where long tables were covered with white cloths and the cloths were covered with plates of biscuits, trays of sandwiches, devilled chicken, devilled ham, devilled bones, fruit, eclairs, chocolates, whisky, brandy, claret, hock, champagne, lemonade and Vichy water.

It was as though none of them had had any dinner at all. A few more days of this, I thought, and I should have to go to Homburg myself, or at least home to Ireland to walk thirty miles a day.

Fortunately I found Lord Henry Clinton, and he guided me to my bedroom.

Ernest, the underfootman, called me at half past eight. He brought my shaving water in a brass jug, and on a brass tray a pot of tea, a rack of toast, and a plate of Marie biscuits. He helped me into my dressing robe and said that my bath would be ready in twenty minutes.

The bathroom was much bigger than my bedroom. A small coal fire flickered in the grate. The bath was big enough for a pony, and encased in mahogany. The air was steamy from the previous bather and reeked of his

bath-essence. I recognised the scent because Rivvy Trench used the stuff
—"Hammam Bouquet," too sweet and heady for my taste.
The water was not very hot.

All the men and some of the women came downstairs for breakfast. It
was as though they had had neither dinner nor midnight supper. On one
sideboard was a gigantic bowl of porridge which the men ate standing up.
On another were pots of Indian and China tea, each on a spirit lamp; the
pot of Indian tea had a red silk ribbon on the handle, the pot of China tea
a yellow one. On a third sideboard were kidneys, kedgeree, fried whiting,
little fishy messes in scallop shells, bacon, eggs, sausages, all on spirit
lamps. On the fourth and largest sideboard were joints of cold ham, beef,
mutton, a tongue, a terrine, a gallantine, and the corpses of various birds.
There was a great quantity of fruit. The table was covered in flowers and
toast racks. The room smelled of the spirit lamps and the kidneys, of Hammam Bouquet and the perfumes of the women.

Gentlemen were helping ladies to various titbits from the sideboards.
Conversation was general and hearty. I overate, for the third time in thirteen hours, because I had nobody to talk to.

I was to go fishing. I went fishing. The river was swollen and
discoloured. To tie on a dry-fly was purposeless. The water-keeper knew it
as well as I. I mentioned a worm. The keeper's eyes popped with outrage.
I came back damp and empty-handed.

Lady Bulbarrow had guessed that she might prefer me in a tweed coat
and wading boots, but she did not give herself the chance to put her guess
to the test. I did not see her till dinner time. I did not talk to her at dinner. I did not talk to her after dinner.

On Sunday morning I followed the rest to the great hall at twenty past
ten. Everyone was there, dressed for church, being sorted into groups to go
in the wagonettes, the landaus, the Victorias, the cars. Footmen hovered,
waiting to help the ladies into the carriages. The footmen wore tall hats
and long coats with gold buttons. The ladies wore hats laden with
artificial flowers.

Except one. A slim, pale-haired young girl stood silent in a corner. Instead of the fleecy cartwheel she had carried on the Chinese bridge, she
wore a little schoolgirlish hat of straw with a bow at the front; instead of

her blue-bound volume she had a prayer book. Her expression was as pensive, her pose as defenceless, as on that ridiculous bridge. She wore white again. It was the right colour for her. She was beautiful. She had a broad brow, a little straight nose, a small, well-cut mouth. Her eyes were large and grey. There was sadness in them. I stared at her, wondering why she was sad, wishing I could make her smile. As though feeling my stare, she raised her eyes and looked at me. Her eyes caught mine. They held them for a long moment. There was a message in her eyes. I was sure of it. There was an appeal. I could not read it. She looked down and away. A faint flush crept into her pale cheeks.

Lady Bulbarrow came by, her hat laden with flame-coloured roses. She took the pale child by the arm. They went out together. I followed, as though on a string. Lady Bulbarrow was handed into a carriage. A footman offered an arm to the girl in white. She disdained it, and jumped up, suddenly childlike, into the carriage after her mother.

Her mother. It was suddenly obvious. "One child—a daughter." No little milliner, not with that brow, those eyes. Lady Bulbarrow's daughter. The Lady Camilla Glyn. Fifteen, perhaps? Sixteen? Camilla. The Lady Camilla. Why was she sad?

I was organized into a Victoria, with three tall-hatted men. Each carried his own prayer book. I had not thought of that when I packed my bag to stay at Moreys.

She knelt beside her mother in the family pew at the front. I could see only the cloud of pale hair and the slim, childish shoulders.

We stood, sat, knelt; we sang, listened, prayed. Often the pale head and the little shoulders were hidden from my sight by a great flowered hat; but I glimpsed them when I could. I did not know why I tried. She was only a little schoolgirl, fifteen, sixteen. Such vulnerable sadness was affecting. I thought she was like a bird.

There was a low time, a dull time, between church and Sunday luncheon. The women all disappeared to repair the ravages of two hours. The men assembled in the library. The vicar, who had preached a sermon about continence was there.

Luncheon was in the banqueting hall at an infinity of little tables for four and six. The intention was informality; it made more work for the servants. The pale girl was there; it seemed she joined the grown-ups for luncheon, though not for dinner. Lord Whitewater was at her table with others I did not know. I saw that he talked to her; I did not see that she replied.

Expeditions were arranged for Sunday afternoon, since the weather was fine and the house party bored. Cars and carriages again assembled on the gravel sweep by the front door. Some people wanted to go to Wilton, some to Fonthill, some to Maiden Castle, and some to sleep.

Lady Bulbarrow was busily and good-humouredly organizing the parties into the vehicles. She joined none of them, but retired, having earned a rest.

Sir Gareth Fortescue, though he looked so particularly energetic, also said that he was sleepy and needed forty winks on his bed.

I saw the shrill Lady Babraham dig Lord Whitewater in the ribs. There was a smile of complicity between them. I could not tell if they were making a comment or an assignation. Lord Whitewater's El Greco face looked as saintly and intense as ever. The secret smile sat oddly on it.

Lady Camilla drifted through the hall and up the great stairs, a pale Tennysonian princess among her mother's high-coloured friends. Lord Whitewater watched her. The smile left his lips. Lady Babraham was whispering to him. I do not think he heard.

I said goodbye to Lady Bulbarrow in the hall at a quarter past ten the following morning. Carriages were to take a dozen of us to the train at Salisbury. She looked very beautiful. There was warmth in her smile and in her icy eyes. She smelled of lily-of-the-valley. She held my hand for a moment, but instead of replying to my stammered thanks she was calling farewells over my shoulder.

I thought she had forgotten my name.

I was put in the char-à-banc again.

As we followed the drive round the curve of the lake, I saw a frail, pale figure drooping over the parapet of the Chinese bridge. This time she turned her head. She stared at me. I felt again a kind of electric message, as though a humming wire were stretched between us. I wanted to jump out over the tailboard and run to her. That would have been absurd behaviour and I would have missed the train. I sat like a sack, bouncing up and down on the wooden seat of the char-à-banc.

We rounded the bend into the beech wood. Moreys disappeared from sight, and the lake, and the bridge, and the girl. I had not exchanged a word with her, nor come within three yards of her. But I thought I should have in my mind's eye forever that image of the slim, white figure drooping over the parapet; and of the little face turning under the cloud of pale hair and staring after me with an unreadable appeal.

"*We* bin an' spilled Mayonnaise on our trousis," said the valet in elastic-sided boots. "Spongin' don't serve. Thank God for London."

2 ✻ *A thousand honey secrets*

If thou wilt deign this favour, for thy meed
A thousand honey secrets shalt thou know:
Here come and sit, where never serpent hisses;
And being set, I'll smother thee with kisses.

VENUS AND ADONIS

"I've come to say goodnight, Mamma," I said.

"Oh—very well. I suppose you'd better come in, Camilla. Do keep out of my way and Prior's way and Miss Fordham's way when she comes, and *don't fiddle with the things on the dressing table.* It's difficult enough to do everything without—Never mind, just sit there in the corner—*not on that hat.*"

"I wasn't going to sit on all those artificial roses, Mamma," I assured her. "I'd be frightened of being stung in the behind by an artificial bee."

Prior, Mamma's maid, looked at me with her usual gloom. She was laying out Mamma's dress, a lovely one of ice-blue taffeta. I supposed she would wear the sapphires with it.

Mamma's room was enormous, with a view over the lake and my enchanted forest beyond. My Chinese bridge looked best from Mamma's windows, like a bridge on a willow-pattern plate. The Temple of Minerva on the island looked very well, too. I had all sorts of plans for that temple, for the beautiful uses I could put it to. But there seemed very little chance of *that* dream coming true.

A dressing room opened off the bedroom. There was a small private sitting room beyond with its own door on to the corridor. Off the dressing room was Mamma's own bathroom which no one ever used except her. This was extraordinary luxury but necessary to Mamma's peace of mind. I once heard her say to Cousin Dorothea, "Nothing is so disgusting as finding someone else's watch-springs in the bath." She had recently had the whole suite redecorated with French wallpaper and pink-and-gold brocade. There was a triple full-length looking glass in the bedroom, and another in the dressing room, and another in the bathroom. Of course, if you are as beautiful as Mamma, it is nice to be reminded of the fact.

Mamma sat down at her dressing table. She wore a fur-trimmed dressing gown and high-heeled slippers. She drummed impatiently on the glass of the table with her fingernails. Prior hurried forward with a sort of cape of cream-coloured satin which she draped about Mamma's shoulders. Mamma began opening the gold-topped pots on the dressing table and dabbing her face and neck with creams.

Prior meanwhile pulled hundreds of pins out of Mamma's hair, and it began to fall down her back. Out of the mass of real hair Prior extracted the "hedgehogs," the horrid little pads people wore to support the elaborate nonsense of their coiffeurs.

Mamma stared at herself solemnly, her face covered in cream. She looked like a kind of frozen pudding, the cream-daubed sort which she loved but never allowed herself to eat.

"Another Friday," she sighed, "and the place crawling with people. I don't know why I bother. Very few of them appreciate it. How I crave solitude sometimes."

I nodded, keeping a gravely sympathetic expression on my face. At least, that is what it was meant to be. When I caught a glimpse of myself in the full-length looking glass, my expression looked more like indigestion.

Mamma craving for solitude was like a cat begging to be drowned in a water-butt. She detested it. She preferred having even me to having nobody; and she did not much like contemplating me, because I reminded her how old she was.

"*Prior!* Don't tug like that! Do you want to pull my hair out by the roots?"

Sometimes, I thought, Prior wanted exactly that.

Miss Fordham, Mamma's secretary, knocked and came in. She was about Mamma's age. She looked like one of the cabhorses in the rank outside Salisbury Station, a nice horse but not a beauty. I always expected her to throw up her head, neigh, paw the ground, and deposit manure on the carpet. She had spectacles, a Wedgewood cameo worn like a medal for good conduct, and a gold locket on a chain. I used to wonder what she kept in the locket. A twist of hair? A tiny photograph? Of a cavalier? A lover? Could Miss Fordham have had a lover? Could she perform an act of passion? Did she even have the equipment?

"There you are, Fordy," said Mamma. "Have you got the plan of the table? I haven't had time even to think about it. I want Sir Gareth to take me in. No—put him on my other side. Lord Claybank had better take me in. I want to ask him about—Has the rest of it worked out all right? Who will look after Lucinda Babraham?"

"I have put Lord Whitewater next to her, my lady."

"Oh. He deserves better. Although I can never quite fathom—Who have you put on her other side?"

"Sir Matthew Alban, my lady."

"I can't picture him for the moment."

"You described him as a young Irish gentleman, my lady."

"Oh yes. I wonder what possessed me to invite him. He has nice blue eyes. I suppose I must have thought that was enough—Who does the poor boy take in?"

"Mrs. Quincey."

"Grizelda. He'll never come here again. Well, it can't be helped. I'll talk to him myself after dinner, to make up for it. At least, I suppose he plays bridge—"

"There is one problem, my lady," said Miss Fordham delicately.

"Oh dear, how helpless you are. Must I do everything for you? What is it now? I don't know why I pay you if you can't solve the simplest difficulty. *Prior,* are you trying to scalp me, like a Red Indian? One day I'll pull your hair, and you'll see what it feels like."

"It would be convenient, in view of all the rest of the arrangement," said Miss Fordham, "if Lord Henry Clinton took in Miss Carradine. But I was wondering if—"

"Pooh. I know he's had a quarrel with the girl's brother. People shouldn't play billiards if they get drunk. No doubt the chit takes her brother's side, but they must just make the best of it. If people can't behave in a civilized way—Besides, it would serve Henry Clinton right if she snubs him. It was very presumptuous of him to arrive yesterday instead of today."

"Uncle Gareth did," I said.

"Oh—are you still there, Camilla? Isn't your supper getting cold in the schoolroom?"

"It is a cold supper, Mamma."

"Quite right too, much healthier for you—Uncle Gareth is in a quite different position. He was such an old friend of your father's. He's practically a member of the family. Don't you remember how often he used to come to shoot?"

I nodded, but I didn't remember. Papa died when I was twelve. I was quite old enough to know who his close friends were. It was only afterwards that Sir Gareth began to come more often, and to become "Uncle Gareth" to me, and to be a prop and mainstay to Mamma.

Mamma wiped the cream off her face with a piece of silk which she dropped on the floor. Prior had by now heated the curling-tongs on a spirit-lamp. She tried them on her own cheek. If they had been too hot, I supposed, there would have been a scream, a sizzling noise, and a smell of roast flesh. Mamma would have been quite cross at the smell. The curling-tongs gave "body" to Mamma's hair, which was actually rather lank and stringy.

While Prior curled and twirled, Mamma decided that the dinner table must be entirely rearranged. Miss Fordham shuffled the cards about in the red leather holder; putting them into their slots in dozens of experimental combinations. At one moment Mamma had herself sitting between Sir Matthew Alban and Lord Whitewater.

Prior put the "hedgehogs" back into Mamma's hair and hauled it up and twisted and piled and arranged it, and began sticking pins through it into the "hedgehogs." Soon Mamma began to look herself again.

By the time Mamma's hair was finished, the dinner table was exactly back to the arrangement with which they had started.

"Once again," said Mamma in an exhausted voice, "I have had to do the whole thing myself."

Miss Fordham disappeared (I expected her to whinny, and curvet out of the door), and Mamma and Prior went into the dressing room. I could see them through the open door. Mamma sat down. Prior pulled her silk stockings very carefully over her feet and up her legs. Mamma opened her dressing gown, baring her legs, so that Prior could smooth the stocking over her calves and thighs. Mamma's legs were beautiful, smooth as egg-shells, shapely. Her thighs were thickening. Mine were better. Mamma stood up, letting the dressing gown fall to the floor behind her. She wore only a little chemise. Prior enfolded her in the opened-out mould of the stays, whalebone and satin and lace, and fastened them in the front. She clipped the suspenders to the stockings and then set herself to lace from behind.

A grim look came into Mamma's face. She was holding her breath and sucking her tummy in. Her determination, and the strength of Prior's arm, produced at last the twenty-one-inch waist. It looked even smaller because she padded herself out above and below it. I did not think she needed to, because her hips had broadened and coarsened, like her thighs, and her bosom was heavy. She stepped into her drawers and her petticoat and was at last ready for her dress. Prior held it. Mamma burrowed into it like a cautious badger inspecting a new hole in the ground. If the hooks of the dress had caught in her hair, the screams would have been terrible. But she safely popped out of the bodice at the top like a dabchick surfacing on the lake. Prior began to do up the hooks.

Powder, sapphires, fan. A searching self-examination in the long glass. She went out forgetting that I was sitting in the corner.

I heard the buzz of conversation from below as I went to the school-room for my supper. I could have been down there. I should have been down there. I was seventeen, nearly eighteen. I was to be presented at Court the following year, to "come out," and be an adult, and look for a husband. In some other houses (not all), girls of my age dined downstairs unless they were paralysed with shyness or covered in spots. But I was kept cocooned in childhood, protected from the world, from taint and terror and temptation.

I did not know how I would have responded to temptation. I had the gravest doubts about myself. But I had never been *subjected* to any.

I wore girlish white, chosen by Mamma. I wore little straw hats in public. I had only recently emerged, after successfully using storms of tears, from the indignity of *pigtails*.

Why?

Well, I had worked it out, looking at my reflection in the lake from the Chinese bridge.

I was an only child, a ewe-lamb. Mamma was widowed. I was her responsibility. In protecting me, she was doing her duty. In overprotecting me, she was simply exaggerating a bit, as she did about everything.

Then again, there was the question of her own age. Of course, the date of my birth was no secret. It was in *Debrett*, with the date of Mamma's marriage and of her own birth. But a figure in a fat red reference book is one thing; a visible grown-up daughter is rather another. It had to come. Mamma must have known that. She could not keep me in the schoolroom until my hips spread, my breasts sagged, my teeth went black and fell out, and my mind became unhinged from frustration. But she could have one more season of youth, freedom, a child still safe in the nursery.

She had an unselfish motive and a selfish motive. Sometimes, because she was my beautiful mother whom I worshipped, I was sure the unselfish reason was the important one. Sometimes, when her public mask peeled off in private, I was sure the selfish was the important one.

The schoolroom was full of white paint, floral chintz, Bowdlerised books and wishy-washy pictures of knights and damsels. When I read the expurgated books, I wondered what had been cut out. When I looked at the knights and damsels, I wondered what they did together, and how. If a knight rescued a damsel in a forest from a dragon, far from anywhere and anybody, he would naturally woo her ardently. At least, the damsel would have grounds for complaint if he did not. But in armour? Was there a hole in the front of all that steel? If so, what if a foeman's lance, by chance or design, slid in? The knight would never be as good again, it seemed to me. He might give up errantry entirely.

I once asked Miss Clayton, my governess. "Miss Clayton," I said, "if a knight ardently wooed a damsel in a forest, how *did* he manage to, hum, unless his armour had a hole in the front? And if it didn't, however did he manage to go to the, after breakfast I mean, go to the, hum, or did they have to take it all off, like when I wore combinations?"

I was sent to bed without supper that night. I knew, therefore, that the question was a good one, with an interesting answer.

There were a lot of pictures I was not supposed to look at, even though they were by the Italian master, on account of naked men. But somehow the statues in the library were not considered. They were, by me—very closely, from all angles. I did not bother much with the chubby cupids, who though sweet had only little thimbles in front, but rather more with a life-sized allegorical figure in white marble who carried a sword in one hand and a book in the other and wore no clothes at all. His hands being occupied, he was supremely shameless. What he revealed was distinctly puzzling. I thought at first (when I was *very* young) that the sculptor had simply let a whimsical imagination run riot. It was all so very unlike my own front, which I regarded as normal. Then other statues, pictures, book illustrations, and a little whispered information from little boys who came to tea—these rich sources convinced me that the sculptor had known what he was about. I thought it very odd; I could imagine no greater inconvenience.

Then I once saw two dogs coupling (to the horror of Miss Clayton), and once two ponies, and once a Jersey bull trying to play leap-frog with a cow. I began to understand the function of my marble friend's peculiar growth. But there was much I misunderstood. For instance, I assumed that people adopted the position of the dogs, and the ponies, and the cattle. All creatures seemed agreed on the point. No one told me any different. I never cared to consult a grown-up.

No book gave me the slightest information. The references in the Bible were unhelpful—"He went in unto her." In? Unto? There was a Tintoretto of Mars and Venus in the Great Saloon, but they had not got beyond the talking stage. If I asked little girls who were brought to tea, they shrieked or giggled or burst into tears.

There was a locked bookshelf in the library which I managed to force open with a shoehorn. I found thick books by a man called Rabelais. They were in French. There was a leather-bound book called *Droll Stories*. They began, "In the city of D---- there was a young student who became enamoured of the young wife of a prosperous merchant . . ." The stories did not seem to me very droll, and they were no more explicit than *Lamb's Tales From Shakespeare*.

I returned in despair to study of the allegorical man in white marble. I called him Bert, after the best looking of the younger footmen. A sort of curved finger, coming to a point, with two plums behind. Was it always stuck down like that? If so, what use was it? I tried to imagine it flesh and blood, but it was obstinately marble to look at and to touch.

There may have been other girls as ignorant as I in England at that time. There can certainly have been none *more* ignorant. It was terribly annoying.

You are not to think that I thought about such subjects all the time. Only about nine-tenths of the time. Especially in bed, and in the bath, and when I was riding my pony, and in church. My mind should have been on other things in church, and but for one thing I daresay it might have been. But the Moreys pew was at the front of the church, naturally, and I always sat there with Mamma. Only a few feet away was the lectern, a brass eagle with a huge old Bible on it. The vicar read the first lesson, and General Mauney read the second lesson. He always read it; he liked reading it. He was a tall man with a military bearing and tight, old-fashioned trousers of military cut. A little too tight, perhaps; just a fraction too tight. The buttons never popped, but they strained. This took place every Sunday of my life not five feet away from me on a level with my eyes. Behind General Mauney's trouser buttons lay, or lurked, just such mysterious matters as my marble Bert flaunted in the library. Unless they fell off with age. I thought not. The General's buttons strained over *something*. I was extremely curious about it all.

Of course Mamma knew what lay behind the General's trouser buttons. She learned, no doubt, when she grew up and married. I did not think I could bear to wait so long.

It may seem amazing, but the General's buttons, and marble Bert, were the point I had reached when I was seventeen. And I was still very vague about the use to which that strange curly finger was put.

I dragged my way to the schoolroom. And down below, in the great rooms, there were hordes of men; not men, simply, but gentlemen, *hommes du monde*—suave, experienced, fascinatingly cynical, groomed and glossy.

And some of them would be nice to me at luncheon, in an awful bantering way, and that would be no help at all. At best, I would simply wonder what lay behind their trouser buttons.

Emmy was waiting for me in the schoolroom, looking a bit peevish. She often did. I used to wonder if her discontent had the same cause as mine. If so, she was silly. She was two years older than I, and she had been in service at Moreys for four years. Quite enough time to make any number of experiments. There was Bert, the good-looking young footman; there were dozens of other lusty swains, indoors and out. She looked like a girl who might enjoy it out of doors.

I thought there was a knowing look in Emmy's eye, and had been for a year or two. An Experienced look. But I knew I could have been quite wrong about that. Her eyes were brown in a broad, high-coloured face. She was sturdy, big-busted, not fat but not a nymph like me. (In using the word "nymph" of myself, I am not being vain, but simply quoting Lord Claygate, whose jolly, bantering, patronising tone was enough to make me want to empty a bowl of fruit salad over his head.)

Emmy was to be replaced as my personal maid when I came out in London the following year. It was a pity. I liked her. She was good at ironing and needlework. But Mamma said I would need an expert hairdresser like her own gloomy Prior. My hair waved naturally, which was considered great luck in those days; but when it got damp it tended to go frizzy, as though I was a pickaninny in a photographic negative. To conjure elegance out of frizz was beyond Emmy, or so Mamma said.

I once tried, ever so tactfully, to coax Emmy into telling me about her experiences. It was a failure.

"Men all want the same thing, m'lady," she said. "Except those that fancy something different, unnatural beasts."

"And do they get it?" I asked cleverly.

"Those that ask don't get. And those that don't ask don't want."

"Nobody can get on with anything much, then, can they? If it's no good asking and no good not asking—I daresay actions speak louder than words, though?"

"Actions!" said Emmy scornfully. "I'll give them actions."

She sniffed and went back to ironing my petticoats and would say no more. She never did say any more. I came to think that she had had not just an Experience, but an Unpleasant Experience. I thought it was her duty to tell me about it, so that I could avoid the same trap. But she never would.

"Curiosity killed the cat, m'lady," she said.

It was enough to drive one loonerino, as Mamma's friends would say.

Emmy removed herself from the schoolroom, and I unearthed my new book from the bottom of my old toy cupboard. I had to disturb a lot of old friends to get to it—my dolls Nancy and Annie and Clarence and Piers and little Timothy, and my dear lion with one button-eye missing, and a wooden horse on wheels called Marshal Ney.

I will tell about Marshal Ney before I tell about the book, because I may never return to that toy cupboard.

One summer when I was small, Miss Clayton took me, with some maids, to a rented house at the seaside. I had been ill, and they said sea air was what I needed. What I liked best about the rented house was a big picture in the dining room of a man in a cocked hat riding a magnificent black horse. There had been a battle; wounded men in gorgeous uniforms lay about in picturesque attitudes, and other men leant on guns or swords. There was a lurid, stormy sky. It was like that in real life, too, nearly all the time we were at the seaside; so I got not so much sea air as rented-house air. I spent hours by myself in front of the wonderful picture. I made up stories about all the men. The ones who were wounded were all going to get better, go home, and marry their childhood sweethearts.

Miss Clayton said it was a picture of Marshal Ney. She said he was French, but he looked English to me. I made up stories about him, too—about his strength and beauty and courage and gentleness.

I took a long and affectionate farewell of Marshal Ney when we left at the end of our fortnight. I told him I would never forget him, and I never have. In the train going home, I said to Miss Clayton, as an afterthought of minor importance, "But who was the person *riding* Marshal Ney?"

Miss Clayton told this story to Mamma when we got home as an exquisite example of sweet childishness. But Mamma was busy with a house party and just said, "Yes, yes, yes."

Marshal Ney, who had lost one wheel, was resting on my new book. I put him back tenderly with Nancy and Annie and Clarence and Piers and little Timothy. I had found the book behind other books in the locked bookshelf in the library. It had a bright blue leather binding, completely plain, as though secretive and ashamed of itself. It was called *The Temptations of a Dancing-Master; and Other Scandalous Adventures*. I had taken it down to the lake meaning to read it on my Chinese bridge, but I got involved in racing two caterpillars across a chestnut leaf. So I embarked on it, with high hopes, at suppertime in the schoolroom.

"In the year 18-- there came to the town of B----- a young dancing-master. Though handsome and of good family he was poor, and was obliged to earn his bread by teaching the young daughters of wealthy merchants the secrets of the dance . . ."

My heart sank. It had a horridly familiar ring. The handsome young dancing-master would put his arm round the waist of a fair pupil, and she would melt and make an assignation, and so forth. Hum hum. The adventures would not be very scandalous, and there would be *no hard information.*

I ate my supper without a book. I was extremely hungry for food, even though I was also extremely hungry for other things.

I always had breakfast upstairs when there was a house party; I was not at ease in the midst of a hearty gathering among the chafing dishes. But I didn't have it in bed, like Mamma and many of the other ladies. In a way, I would have liked it in bed for the look of the thing—luxury, languor, one slim white arm emerging from a silken sleeve, then a discreet knock on the door. But I actually preferred getting up for breakfast on account of toast crumbs. They always got not just underneath me, but inside my nightgown.

I came downstairs at half past ten in time to see a strange man crossing the great hall. I mean that I did not recognise him, not that he was weird. He was not in the least weird, but rather ordinary. He was of moderate height, with unruly light brown hair. He was wearing knickerbockers and a tweed coat. He was not startlingly handsome, but, from the side, seemed to have a nice face. I only saw him from the side, and then from the back.

He went out. He was dressed to engage in something active and sporting. In April that could only mean fishing.

I wanted to go with him. Why not? It was our river. Every reason why not. He would not want me there. The keeper would not want me there. The river bank would be boggy and squelchy, as there had been heavy rain earlier in the week. I did not admire myself in large boots. He might not catch any fish, which would put him in a mood of sullen despondency. Worse, he might catch one, and it would flap and flop on the bank, helpless and terrified, until the keeper knocked it on the head with his priest.

I guessed he was the young Irishman whom Mamma had asked because —I had forgotten why. I thought she had forgotten why.

Uncle Gareth came across the hall, going in the opposite direction. His face was grim, as it always was in repose, owing to riding so many high-tempered horses in Leicestershire. He saw me and smiled and waved up the stairs. He had one of those immediate smiles which light up a face as when you turn on the electric lights in a London room. Mamma's smile came slowly, as when you gradually turn up the wick of a lamp. I could see the merit of both, and tried quick smiles and slow smiles in front of the looking glass. I was still undecided on the matter.

Uncle Gareth was also dressed in tweeds—very smart greeny-grey tweeds with a pale waistcoat and a high collar and a dark silk tie with a pearl pin, and almost incredibly shiny brown shoes. I would have hated to be his manservant, or his enemy. I was not his enemy, but his honorary niece. I did not hate that, but I did not altogether understand it, either.

"There you are, Camilla," he called out. He had a harsh, military voice which for some reason was attractive. It was a very masculine voice. He was very masculine altogether, though so very old. His hair was grey. I suppose he was fifty.

"Here I am," I agreed, since it would have been silly to deny it.

"And what are you planning this fine spring morning?"

"Nothing. I have nothing whatever in the world to do."

"That's bad. Thoroughly bad. Bad for anyone, but worst for the young."

"Yes, I know. I don't like it myself."

I came the rest of the way down the stairs and joined him in the hall. He smelled very expensive.

I went on, "I have given up lessons because Miss Clayton ran out of knowledge. And nothing has taken their place."

"It will."

"Next year. It seems a long way off."

"It seems damned close to me. That's the difference thirty years makes."

"Are you forty-seven, Uncle Gareth?"

"I could probably pass for it, in a bad light with a bottle of dye on my head." He gave his harsh bark of a laugh and went off towards the smoking room.

I went out onto the east terrace which was full of the morning sun. There were nearly three hours until luncheon. I had nothing to do. I could think of nothing to do. Mamma's friends would talk to each other; they could do it forever. I did not want to talk to them very much; they did not want to talk to me very much. They were all indoors, except the Irishman who had gone fishing.

I leaned over the balustrade of the terrace and looked down at the gravel path twenty feet below. There was a big white wrought-iron seat there. On it sat a man reading a newspaper, with his hat on the seat beside him. I could not see his face from directly above, but I recognised him. His hair was distinctive—bright butter-coloured hair as smooth and glossy as fresh custard on a cake. He was Lord Henry Clinton.

I liked him. He was friendly and made me laugh. I considered dropping a pebble on his head by way of greeting. It might hurt him. It might disturb that wonderfully smooth yellow hair. He was in disgrace—minor disgrace. Why was that? He had done something wrong. He had come to Moreys a day early. It did not seem very terrible to me. There was scarcely a shortage of bedrooms or of servants or food or linen. However, a rule had been broken. Mamma was annoyed. Perhaps I should *not* drop a friendly pebble on his head, in case I seemed to condone his crime.

He was an outcast. He had crept away to lick his wounds. Faces were turned away from his in derision and disgust. He was consoling himself with the *Morning Post*.

I leaned over the parapet (I spent a lot of time leaning over parapets; it was a pose which suited me) and looked down at his glossy butter-coloured hair. I felt deep pity for him. I, too, was a kind of outcast. I could feel for him. I could comfort him. It was probably my duty to do so. I did not want to drop a pebble in his hair. I wanted to stroke it. He was suffering. I could kiss the place and make it well. He had a very nice moustache, silky soft, a shade darker than his hair. He had a light, bouncy, happy voice. He was much younger than most of Mamma's friends, though by no means a boy.

He was deeply engrossed in the newspaper. Probably, like everybody else, he was looking for his own name. "Among those present were . . ."

I felt a little crawling sensation at the base of my spine. At first I thought it was an insect, and scratched the place. The crawly feeling moved to a spot below my left shoulder-blade, where I could not reach it without contortion. It was not an insect. The cause was electrical, or spiritual, not physical. I was being watched.

I turned, curious, a little nervous.

I *was* being watched. I was still curious, and still nervous, when I recognised the watcher. He was a man I knew only by sight. He had stayed at Moreys before, but I had never spoken to him. I had not wanted to speak to him. He alarmed me. He was said to be very clever, and very learned, and very witty, and very sophisticated. He was certainly very elegant. There was something strange about his face. He had suffering eyes. It was as though all the time he had a fever. He was tall and thin, and dressed in dove-grey flannel.

A breeze blew from the south, gusting round the corner of the house and along the east terrace. It tried to pluck off my hat. I put up my hand to save it. The breeze pressed in my springlike white dress against my bosom and against my hips and thighs, moulding the thin stuff to the form of my body. My position, clutching my hat to the crown of my head, was like that of a marble female in the library with an urn on her head and a hand steadying the urn—somewhat draped, but revealingly. I was draped, but revealingly, owing to the wind and to my position.

I would not have given the matter a thought—I truly think I would not have worried for a second about the wind pressing my dress to the curves of my body—but for the hot fevered eyes of Lord Whitewater.

That was who it was. He had been called Mr. Watkinson, but his cousin had died and now he had the title. He looked as though he wanted to lick his lips. They were thin, bloodless lips, which made a sort of agonized gash across a thin, bloodless face.

I was fully and decently dressed, and my dress buttoned almost to my chin. Yet I wanted to cover my front with my hands, with my hat. My dress clung to me as though it were wet. I felt myself blushing. I was acutely unhappy and obscurely frightened.

"My little ladyship," said Lord Whitewater in a clipped voice like a schoolmaster's, "you look as fresh as a daffodil, a dew-moistened flower under an April sky. You are made of birdsong and hurrying clouds."

Well, that was quite nice, though a bit silly. I could not at once think of a reply.

"I am told you haunt the Chinese bridge," said Lord Whitewater. "Keen observers of the local scene have reported as much to me. Will you be so very kind as to show it to me? It looks enchanting from a distance. Will you walk with me there?"

It was a humdrum and respectable idea. It would fill a bit of the yawning vacuum of time before luncheon. But I did not want to go. I did not want to walk with him, there or anywhere.

He crooked his arm and extended his elbow towards me, at the same time making a slight bow. It was an elegant gesture, old fashioned, stylish. I was to take his arm and float at his side along the terrace and down the steps to the lower terraces and so to the lake. I did not want to take his arm. I did not want to touch him, even through a thickness of dove-grey flannel. I did not want those hot eyes near me, or that thin mouth that looked as though it would laugh at a beetle on a pin.

"I'm sorry," I stammered. "There's a puppy I must see. At the kennels. I promised."

"I will come with you to the kennels. I am an amateur of kennel design. Did the builder follow Xenophon's plan? It has never been surpassed."

"Yes," I said. "Come any time. Another time."

I turned and ran away. It was meant to look like hurrying, but it was running. My hat blew off. I made a wild grab for it, but missed. It fluttered along the stones of the terrace like a drunken but determined bird, eluding me. In the end I jumped on it. I caught it. I heard it crunch. It was a silly straw hat. It was ruined. I jammed it on my head just the same, and fled round the corner at the end of the terrace.

I heard laughter behind me.

Well, it was all very silly and childish, and I did not know why I had got in such a fuss. Lord Whitewater was one of Mamma's friends; he was her guest in our house. He could not eat me. He could not so much as nibble.

I slowed, and stopped, and drooped under the great colonnade on the north front. I hoped nobody had seen me run away, like a ninny, like a baby, from a kindly old man of forty.

I did not know why I had run away. But I knew I would do it again.

I came down to the hall on Sunday morning, dressed up as though for my first communion in the girlish white Mamma chose for me. Emmy had stitched a new baby-blue ribbon with a baby bow on a silly new straw hat. I felt like an Easter egg.

I was seventeen, nearly eighteen, and they did this to me. I could have come out in London that summer. Other girls came out in the year of their eighteenth birthdays. I should be haggard with age and ignorance before I was even a debutante.

The hall was clogged with the usual Sunday morning mob. Some of the ladies were trying to get put into the same carriage as Mamma, or the old Grand Duchess, or the wife of the Swedish ambassador. Some of them were trying *not* to be put into the same carriage as the old Grand Duchess, who always asked everybody about their bowels. I let it all wash over my head as I stood waiting for Mamma.

In half an hour General Mauney's too-tight trousers would swim into my field of vision, five feet away, at eye level. I was not passionately interested in General Mauney (actually he was a very nice old man), but it would set my mind wheeling and waltzing away in speculation.

It was something I might write a poem about:

> Wheeling and waltzing in speculation,
> Concerning the facts of fornication—
> The General's buttons, they do not pop,
> But if a hand were to start at the top . . .

I became aware of being gazed at for the second time in exactly twenty-four hours. It was like something in the Bible—"There is a time to be gazed at, and a time to gaze." It appeared that twenty-five minutes to eleven was the time to be gazed at.

I turned to face the gaze, ready to cringe, smile, hide behind the old Grand Duchess, or continue to write my poem in my head. It was a gaze much unlike Lord Whitewater's. It was a pair of nice blue eyes in an unremarkable and totally unfamiliar face.

Wait! Stay! Not totally unfamiliar. I had seen this person about to go fishing. He had brushed his light-brown hair better this time; it being Sunday morning. He wore a Sunday suit. He did not quite achieve the aggressive masculine elegance of Uncle Garth, the glossiness of Lord Henry Clinton, or the lizardlike perfection of Lord Whitewater, but he was dressed well enough. Quite well enough. To be better dressed was to be overdressed. Most of Mamma's men friends were overdressed, and they overdid the scented stuff out of all their little bottles, too.

Yes, yes, the nice blue eyes belonged to the young Irish visitor whom Mamma had asked for reasons she had forgotten, or she had remembered and I had forgotten. I had forgotten his name, too. Sir something. He was too young to have been made a Knight, so he had inherited the title, if you could call "Sir" a title.

The hypnotic cadences of my poem returned to my head:

Across from Ireland came a Sir,
With nice blue eyes and mousey fur.
His eyes are sharp but his nose is blunt.
He wears breeks below, with buttons in front . . .

With rhymes chiming in my head (and somehow they kept returning to the same point), I found I was unconsciously staring at those nice blue eyes. Had they a message for me? They had, as far as I could see, *no* message for me.

Mamma swept me out, and we trundled away to worship.

A retired bishop, visiting the vicar, read the second lesson instead of General Mauney. He was shrouded in a cassock. I austerely denied myself any speculation about *that*.

Sunday luncheon was always an ordeal. At a little table you are conspicuous. There is no escape from impertinent curiosity or heavy banter. At the big dining room table I could have felt comfortable if safely wedged between friends such as Lord Henry Clinton and the Irishman with brown hair and grey eyes. (Grey? Perhaps blue.) I could have talked freely and with confidence, though not, of course, about truly interesting subjects.

But now we were dotted all over the place, to some extent obedient to a plan, to some extent fluid. There was a lot of hearty laughter and the scraping of chairs. I found myself at a table for six, beside Lord Whitewater. That was not my plan, but it was his plan. He did it by magic, sinister magic. One moment I was about to sit down near the old Grand Duchess, who was kind to me (even about my bowels), and the next I was sitting by Lord Whitewater.

The other people at the table were impertinently curious (the ladies) or heavily bantering (the gentlemen). They thought it their duty to talk to me, and it was the only way they knew how. Lord Whitewater was neither. He talked to me as a grown-up. He asked my views about the architecture of Moreys, the placing of the stable-block in relation to the house, the terracing, the artificial lake made by damming the river, and so forth. I answered as best I could. My answers seemed important to him. He wanted to know what I thought.

The four others were bored to the vapours by this conversation, but oddly enough they did not interrupt it. They sat chewing and sipping and wiping their mouths, in disciplined silence. They were like cowed, apathetic schoolchildren. Of course, this increased Lord Whitewater's resemblance to a schoolmaster. It was not a *great* resemblance. He spoke like one and sometimes had a teachy sort of mannerism, making a point with a fluttering hand. But his mouth was still agonized and his eyes feverish.

It was a funny luncheon, the oddest I ever remembered, because I enjoyed the conversation. It interested me. I realised afterwards that I had learned a lot, although he had not seemed to be teaching me. And I was flattered to be encouraged to hold forth. I am not in love with the sound of my own voice, but I do not *detest* it.

At the same time, there was a part of me that writhed and cringed away from those thin, fluttering, scented hands, those hot eyes, that bitter mouth.

He looked at me and licked his lips. As he was eating lobster mousse at the time, the gesture was innocent. But it did not *look* innocent. Not that lick. Not those lips.

Expeditions were planned to beauty spots. Carriages and cars crunched away. Guests hovered. Some went, some stayed.

Mamma, exhausted by organization, waved a vague hand and drifted upstairs for a rest. Many others did, too. But some wanted strapping walks.

For myself, I had no idea what I wanted. I was pointed in absolutely no direction. When I went upstairs to the schoolroom, it was out of the purest force of habit. I had no more to do there than anywhere else. Less.

I sat in the schoolroom and thought about my conversation with Lord Whitewater. I remembered the names he had mentioned—John Evelyn, Wren, Vanbrugh, Capability Brown. I found myself truly interested in the subject. I wanted to learn about it, about architecture and the design of landscape. I did not think we had books on the subject. I wanted to learn. I wanted a teacher. Why not?

It would be a good way of filling the next empty year. It would not be useful knowledge, precisely—nothing useful was any use to me. But it would occupy me and make me more fit to be an educated grown-up, wife of an educated man.

Yes, yes. The decision taken, act at once. Mamma must be persuaded. That should be possible. I would be kept amused, kept out of mischief. She complained about the way I mooned to and fro. (Not convincingly, because she mooned to and fro herself when she was alone. She had as little to do as I did.) The knowledge I was after was not vulgar. It could not be called middle class. Lord Burlington could be quoted (I had learned that name from Lord Whitewater).

Was Mamma actually asleep? Sometimes when she went up to rest she did drift into a doze, and then if she was woken up she was very bad-tempered indeed. But often not. If she wasn't asleep she was probably bored. She would welcome company. The whole thing could be settled in half an hour.

I went along the corridor where her suite was. The thing was to find out if she was asleep. I listened at the door of her bedroom. There seemed to be a rustling, a kind of grunting. That might be Mamma in her sleep. I tried the bedroom door, turning the huge brass handle softly. The door was locked. That was unusual but not amazing.

I decided to creep into the little sitting room, and so into the dressing room, and so find out if it was safe to disturb Mamma, without disturbing her. I turned the door handles gradually so as not to wake her if she *was* asleep. I crept across the sitting room and into the dressing room, and across the dressing room to the door of the bedroom. The door of the bedroom was ajar. I peeped in. The curtains were half drawn. Part of the room was in half-darkness, including the corner where the dressing room door was. I was pretty well invisible to anybody in the bedroom. But a shaft of golden afternoon sunlight washed across Mamma's great bed. It lit up everything there like a spotlight on a stage.

I almost screamed with utter dismay, with horror and amazement. I wanted to run away, but I was held, powerless, paralysed. I watched, my mouth dry, my heart thudding in my throat.

The first thing I saw was a pair of naked buttocks, hairless, yellowish, muscular, raised high up from the tumbled top of the bed. It was an absurd position; it put me in mind of a sea-monster. The thighs hinged from the buttocks were muscular too, corded with muscle; the skin looked like that of a plucked chicken, sparsely dusted with dark hairs. The sunlight shone on the polished ivory of the buttocks, and gilded the hairs on the thighs. The trunk sloped down from the buttocks, down towards the pillows at the head of the bed. I could see ribs and muscles and all the elaborate contours of a powerful body thrown into relief by the angle of the sun.

He was resting on his elbows, but his face was buried in the face below him.

There was a whole pale pearly naked body below him. Plump thighs were spread wide, wide, the knees a little bent. The knees were quite pink against the pallor of thighs and calves. At the top of the thighs, between them, was a plump round mound of thick black hair. I had never seen such a thing before. It was quite unlike the silvery fleece which I wore between my own thighs. The black mound was bisected, vertically, by a pink mouth. Sunlight glistened on that coarse black hair and on those pink vertical lips. There was a pearly belly beyond, then heavy breasts with proud purple-brown nipples. The face was invisible, buried beneath the grizzled head of the man.

Arms rose from a crucifix position, lazily, and encircled the man's neck. There was a moan in a voice I had never heard.

The man moved one of his arms. He was still resting on his knees and on one elbow. He put his free hand, his right, over the woman's left breast. He caressed the breast, kneading it like the floury dough of a cottage loaf. Then with his fingertips he caressed the purple nipple. It did not look like the little pink flowers which tipped my own breasts, but like a mushroom, succulent, the central knob standing up from the saucer that surrounded it like a chocolate egg on a breakfast table.

One of her hands moved, still lazily, and pushed his head away from hers, down, down towards the breast. His face came down at the breast. His mouth opened wide. I saw the glint of strong teeth in the sunlight. He sank his mouth onto the breast and onto the nipple. He sucked like a baby.

The woman's head rolled on the pillows as though disjointed from the neck. I saw a pale face with tight-shut eyes, with loosened hair like seaweed all over the pillows. She moaned again.

The grizzled head, the greedy mouth, went from the left breast to the right, and nuzzled and mumbled at it, biting and sucking with a small wet noise.

She moved her hands from the man's head and from his shoulder, and slid them down his back, down his flanks, stroking, towards the upreared sunlit buttocks. The white fingers, outspread, gripped the buttocks.

One hand groped round and below. The fingers closed on something I had never seen before, never imagined, never dreamed of. It was an arm, clublike, jutting from the belly of the man, from his island of matted hair. It looked hard, reddish, a little gnarled. The spherical tip was pink and smooth in the sunlight.

It was hard to believe that the gentle curved finger of my marble friend could transform itself into this great spear.

Mamma kept her left hand, splayed like a starfish, on Uncle Gareth's buttock. She pulled at the buttock, hauling it down towards herself. I could see the fingertips dragging at the loose skin of the buttock. Her right hand held the spear. It seemed to heave and throb with a life of its own.

As she pulled his hips down towards her own, the rounded head of the spear nuzzled into the black mound of fur. She steered it with her fingers into the pink lips which pouted out of the mound. They swallowed it, slowly.

He moved his face back to hers, and his mouth to hers. Her mouth was wide open, as though to inhale his whole face. Their mouths were glued together.

His buttocks went down and down, until he was lying flat on top of her, his legs between hers. She was swallowing up all that big pink spear. It seemed impossible that there was room, that she could welcome that whole great invading club.

Both her hands were now on his buttocks, pulling him hard, violently, scrabbling and clutching at his flesh. His hands went under her buttocks, lifting them. Her thighs spread wide, wide.

Now he was rising up and down, as though pumping, as though the piston of a steam engine. The spear pulled two, three, four inches out of the lips, then plunged deep into her again so that it quite disappeared and the two copses of hair were mingled.

Up went the buttocks again. Out came the pink cylinder. The sunlight caught it. I saw it clearly. It glistened, like the oily piston of an engine.

She began to shudder, her face under his face, her breasts under his chest, her buttocks in his hands, her thighs wide spread and swinging. She made wordless noises into his face. She moved her face from beneath his. I saw it. I scarcely recognised it. It was no face I knew. It was blind, lost, oblivious. It was contorted. It might have been in torture or in ecstasy.

He shuddered also, his legs twitching, his buttocks vibrating under her clutching hands.

She, mad, went madder. One hand clawed at his buttock, scratching, the nails dragging over the skin and leaving livid marks. The other snaked over his back as though searching for a grip, a salvation, and finding none.

His hips no longer lifted and plunged. He lay tight down on top of her. Their legs were intertwined like fronds of weed in the river. They were still. I could hear heavy breathing. Sunlight washed across his back. In the hollow of the small of his back, in a flue of short downy hair, I saw the sweat glisten.

I was sweating myself. I could feel it in the small of my own back and between my breasts.

Slowly one of her hands relaxed from its grip of his buttock, and the other from its clawing at his back. She wrapped her arms round his neck.

He pulled his hands from under her. He laid one on her breast, and with the other smoothed back the hair from her brow.

"Oh God," she said, "Oh God."

She had not opened her eyes. Her face was still lost and blind.

My knees were trembling violently. My whole body felt out of control. I was very near falling down. My heart was thudding so that I thought it must crack my ribs. I heard my own breathing, harsh and rapid. I thought the two of them, on the wild ruin of the bed, must hear my heart and my breath. My mouth was dry. I tried to swallow, but could not.

"Oh God," she said again, in a more normal voice.

That was Mamma lying there, my own mother. Her bare right breast was cupped in Uncle Gareth's hand. Her left breast was squashed into his chest. Her thighs lazily shifted, outside his. And that great club of his hardened flesh was still inside her. Of Uncle Gareth's flesh. It was deep inside her, Mamma, in the most secret, private, inviolate, unmentionable part of her. She had steered it there. Her hand had helped it there. Mamma's hand, which sometimes stroked my head, or retied the bow in my hair.

It was more than I could understand. It was more than I could bear. It was incredibly exciting, ugly and sickening, beautiful.

"I've got cramp in my foot," said Uncle Gareth, in his normal voice.

Mamma laughed softly.

They were people again.

The spell was broken. I clawed my way out of the web which had held me prisoner and crept away through the dressing room and the sitting room. I saw, for the first time, that Uncle Gareth's clothes were all over the dressing room. I thought I heard the accusing tick of his watch. I slipped out into the corridor. There was no one about.

I went to the schoolroom and sat in an upright chair. I found that my hands were trembling so that I could hardly hold a handkerchief.

Most of the party reassembled for tea in the yellow saloon. There were buttered scones in big silver dishes over spirit lamps. There were egg and paté and jam and fish-paste sandwiches, very small, with the crusts of the bread cut off. (I loved them because when I was small, I was made to eat the crusts so that my hair would curl. Perhaps it worked. My hair *did* curl.) There was bread and butter, and brioches, and Tiptree jam. There were dozens of sorts of cakes such as walnut and coffee and Dundee and Aberdeen and chocolate, and there were little ginger biscuits of a special kind that could only be got from Biarritz. Every hostess kept those biscuits because the king liked them, and one never knew when he might come to tea.

Everybody was given a little plate and a little knife with a china handle that matched the plate. The butler, the underbutler, and half a dozen footmen were busy with plates and cups and cakes. But they all went away when everyone was settled, because it was an entirely informal occasion.

I expected not to be hungry, but I was. I expected to be thirsty, but I was not.

Mamma was in the midst of her guests, where she liked to be, talking and laughing and wearing an afternoon dress of lacy lavender. She looked cool and competent and charming. Her manner was exactly as usual. I could see nothing in her face, absolutely nothing, of the lost, blind, oblivious, tortured, ecstatic, abandoned savage who had sprawled naked on her back with a naked man crouched over her; who had moaned, and clutched, and offered her nipple to his teeth, and steered his flesh into the secret corridors inside herself.

The sweat had dried and the eyes opened. The hair was rearranged and the stays relaced.

Uncle Gareth, now in tweeds, stood at the far end of the room, talking to the old Grand Duchess. His face was grim, as usual, until it exploded into its sudden smile. I heard his harsh laugh and saw him stir his tea with a tiny silver spoon.

His impeccable trouser buttons looked incapable of concealing what I had seen.

I had a seventh egg sandwich, but refused a cup of tea.

3 �֍ *The precedent of pith*

With this she seizeth on his sweating palm,
The precedent of pith and livelihood,
And trembling in her passion, calls it balm,
Earth's sovereign salve to do a goddess good:
Being so enrag'd, desire doth lend her force
Courageously to pluck him from his horse.

VENUS AND ADONIS

"May I come in and say goodnight, Mamma?" I asked.

"Oh—yes—of course, come in, Camilla, if you must. I'm late this evening, so keep out of Prior's way."

I glanced involuntarily at the bed. I tried not to stare at it, or to blush when I looked at it. It was so tidy, so perfectly made and splendidly covered, that it might have been kept to show visitors and never even been slept in at all. It did not look like a couch of illicit passion. Over it was draped Mamma's dress for the evening.

Mamma was sitting at her dressing table, the satin cape over her shoulders. Prior was in the dressing room, busy with underclothes. I wondered if Uncle Gareth had left any telltale clues behind. Mamma was dabbing the creams into her face and neck, turning herself from a society beauty into a cake for a children's party.

What a lot of different roles people play, I thought to myself in an adult way. Mamma is a society beauty, a private bully, a conscientious mother, a lecherous whore, and a cream cake. What else?

"I would like to study architecture, Mamma," I said. "And landscape design, and so forth. Lord Burlington did it, so it is not vulgar. Also Sir John Vanbrugh."

Prior came in and began taking the pins out of Mamma's hair.

"So do you think I might possibly have a teacher, Mamma?" I went on.

"Teacher, child? Whatever are you talking about? Miss Clayton has left. She has gone to—I recommended her to somebody. Do you want the address? Miss Fordham will have it, I suppose. She certainly ought to have it, but one can't trust anybody nowadays to do a single thing, however much you pay them. Here she is. Come in, Fordy. Have you got the table plan? I hope it's better than yesterday's. *Don't tug*, Prior."

"Good night, Mamma."

"No, I simply can't sit next to Lord Claygate again, Fordy, nor the Swedish ambassador. The bishop? What bishop? I met him this morning? Oh, very well, I can always talk to—*Yes, yes*, do stop going on and on about it. *Prior*, I shall go demented if you pull my hair like that."

I stole away.

I could not sleep. I lay in my bed, hot and cold, reliving and reliving the extraordinary quarter-hour after luncheon. It *was* only a quarter of an hour. That was one of the most extraordinary things.

I tried to put it out of my mind, just for the night. But I could not. It glared at me, every detail, every movement, brilliantly lit by that afternoon sunlight.

I knew now what happened. I had been pitchforked into the knowledge, but in it I was. One lay on one's back, with no clothes on, amazingly defenceless and vulnerable. One spread one's legs apart, amazingly shameless. One was kissed. One pushed his head down towards one's breast (perhaps that bit was voluntary). One took hold of his behind, if one could reach it. One took hold of his club, that astonishing and unpredicted presence, and somehow ate it all up. One moaned, and shuddered, and was lost and blind.

That was what happened. But what did it *feel* like?

I understood why Emmy would not talk about it, if she had anything to talk about. It was not really a subject for conversation. If you had such a conversation, you would avoid the other person's eye and never be quite easy again afterwards.

What did it *feel* like?

I lay on my back myself, trying to imagine it. I was trembling. The skin fluttered over my tummy. I pulled my nightgown up to my hips, and stroked the fleece I found there. I pulled my nightgown up to my waist; then sat up, and pulled it off altogether. I lay back, naked, pushing the bedclothes away with my feet. It was a warm night, and very dark in my bedroom. I shivered, but not from cold.

This was how Mamma had been. I bent my knees and spread my thighs. This was how Mamma had been.

It was time for a kiss. I tried to imagine a kiss. I had only ever been kissed on the cheek, the forehead, and the top of the head. I opened my mouth wide since, odd as it seemed, that was what they had done. I tried to imagine the feeling of someone's lips on mine. I kissed the back of my hand. That was what it felt like to kiss. I rubbed my lips with my fingertips. That was what it felt like to have a rubbing and a pressure on one's mouth. It meant nothing. I was no nearer imagining how kissing had meant so much to them, done so much to them.

It was now time for the breast. I stroked my own breasts. They were firm, high, not large, not at all like those I had seen kneaded and nibbled in the afternoon. The process would be the same. The sensation should be the same.

I began to feel the glimmering of the sensation, the first faint imaginings of what it was all truly about. I touched a nipple with my fingertips. It felt different. Usually it was as soft as an oyster. But there was a new sensation in that little pink peak. It seemed harder, a new shape. How did it change? Why should it change? Sensation was concentrated there, yet it had fluttering echoes elsewhere, too, and a strange warm wire of feeling seemed to be carrying messages from my breast to my belly.

It would all be very different, I thought, if another hand, not my own hand, were stroking and fingering the nipple. I did not immediately see how that was to be arranged.

It was not merely to be handled, but to be sucked and nuzzled too. I tried to imitate that puzzling process. I licked my fingers. I pinched the nipple, gently, between two wet fingers, to see if I could tell what it might be like.

I could not really tell. But I thought I might be near to guessing what it might be like.

Pantomiming what I had seen, I reached for imaginary buttocks, and pulled them down towards me. I tried to imagine the feeling of bare male skin, smooth hairless buttock skin, under my fingers. They would be quite different under my hands from my own soft flesh. I supposed there would be a sense of strength, of bone and muscle. That was an exciting thought. I liked that thought.

Now one hand was to grope down and round and under. It was to take hold of the club. The club came down, down, and the tip landed *here*. I touched the place with a fingertip, the midst of the little hill with the fleecy covering. It landed here, but I was to steer it to a new place. Downwards. *Here.*

I investigated, between spread thighs, in the darkness, on my back, naked, my eyes closed. Here were the lips, vertically bisecting the mound. They were closed and dry. They were not pouting out of the fur as Mamma's had done. Was that right? They did not feel as Mamma's had looked.

Above the lips, I found something I had hardly met before. (Indeed, I had not seriously searched there before.) It was a tiny finger, soft, a sort of miniature of what men had, a miniature even of the saucy thimbles the marble cherubs had below their bellies. My fingertips made its acquaintance. It liked them. I did not know what it was called, or what it was for. Now sensation was concentrated there—a feeling different from, yet somehow a cousin to, the feeling I had conjured in my nipple.

This was a strange voyage of discovery. I was a blindfolded navigator.

But I had been shown. What next had I been shown? The tip of the club was to be steered to those lips.

I drew my thighs up almost to my shoulders. There was a movement of the night air through my bedroom, stirring the curtains, sending a little shiver across my nakedness.

With the fingertips of one hand, I continued to touch and stroke the tiny thimble above the lips, because it liked it. With the fingertips of the other I investigated those lips. The club had gone *in*. Well, I knew it was possible, because I had seen it. At first it seemed impossible. A dry mouth, clenched shut, like the lips over the toothless gums of a cross old woman in the village. I coaxed one fingertip between them. It was possible. It became gradually easier and easier. The lips, all unbidden by me, went a way of their own. I felt dampness. My fingertip slipped easily, more and more easily, deep between the lips. I wiggled it about, exploring. It was amazing. I seemed to have a cave inside me, soft-sided, bottomless, warm and wet like a fox's earth after a summer flood.

My finger was too short and too slim. But the thought of anything bigger—of a swollen club like the one I had seen—was terrifying.

The sensation grew and grew, nothing I had ever felt before, and focussed more and more completely on that one small part of me. It felt not small but large, the only part of me that mattered. There was sticky dampness, too, on that little soft thimble above the lips. I though I detected a strange, sweetish, totally unfamiliar smell. Was *that* me?

It was terribly exciting. I felt guilty and squalid. My finger was sticky-wet. I could not understand the smell. I was disappointed, cheated. I was a million miles short of the abandon, the bottomless oblivion, I had seen in Mamma's face. Was I capable of that? Was I old enough?

I touched my breasts. The nipples were still there. They were not like oysters but like hazelnuts.

I lay back, exhausted. I was too tired and too ignorant to explore further. There was a long way to go, but it was a journey for another time.

I knew that there was more, much more—an ultimate sensation which was still beyond my horizon. I knew it because I had seen Mamma's face. I shivered. I was cold.

I put on my nightgown and pulled up the bedclothes. They were comforting. I was back in the warm cocoon of childhood, back from the strange, dangerous, guilty frontiers. I snuggled myself into a ball, and presently dreamed of Mamma's big pearly thighs, and of the hot red club in the sunlight, and of my dolls Nancy and Annie and Clarence and Piers and little Timothy, and of Marshal Ney the wooden horse with one wheel missing.

Everyone left on Monday morning. They were taken off to the train at Salisbury. It was a bad moment for Mamma, although she said it was a good one.

Mamma and I were cosily domestic on Monday evening, just the two of us. She said she liked it, but she didn't.

She left for London herself on Tuesday morning, going off with Prior and Miss Fordham and a footman in a landau to the station. They had a huge weight of baggage, for three nights, which went separately in a wagonette with another footman. Both footmen would travel with the baggage in a third-class compartment with Prior. Miss Fordham would travel in a second-class compartment. Mamma would be torn between wanting a first-class compartment to herself, and *not* wanting it to herself. One of the London carriages would meet them at Waterloo Station and take them to Bulbarrow House in Grosvenor Square. I had not been there very much. It was gloomily magnificent, while Moreys—many times the size—was full of sun and scent.

Mamma always spent at least three nights a week in London during the season, which lasted from early summer into July. It was supposed to finish with Goodwood races, after which everyone went abroad or to Scotland, or first abroad and then to Scotland. The summer seemed to me the very time *not* to spend three nights a week in a steaming city. But Mamma lived according to the rules (in public). It was no hardship for her. It was what she liked. Without the world, the round, she would have withered and died, crossly, like an old bantam hen caught in a snare. Of course it was nice for her to be a Marchioness and a celebrated beauty and a particular friend of the king's.

I knew I took after her in some ways. My colouring came from my father, they said, and my small bones. I remembered a wizened, gentle figure with thin white hair; but in his youth he had ridden steeplechasers, and been as fair as Phoebus Apollo. I do not know what else I inherited from him, but I knew what I got from Mamma. I was changeable and moody and hard to please. I tried not to be, but I was. I was ungrateful, and occasionally horrid. I *did* try not to be. I had a temper. That was why Marshal Ney was missing one wheel. When Mamma screamed at Prior or a housemaid, I saw a sort of enlargement of myself—a little tintype thrown huge and distorted and highly-coloured on a magic-lantern screen.

Of course, that cosily domestic Monday evening, I looked at Mamma with new eyes. But even though they were new, they saw nothing new. She was cross and bored having supper with me, and snappy with the servants. She looked very beautiful. It was all just as usual. She was opaque, like frosted glass in the window of a London bathroom. I could not see, through the ordinary surface, any glimpse of the person I had seen after luncheon on Sunday.

Except once. One moment. She was eating a piece of crystallized peach. She had not spoken for a minute or two. She seemed thoughtful. She raised a little piece of peach toward her mouth, but her hand paused. She had forgotten it. Her mouth was a little open to eat the peach, but it smiled instead—her slow smile, growing gradually, as when one turns the wick of an oil lamp. She was looking inwards, or over my head at invisible things. She was remembering. The smile faded, and she ate the peach.

I thought that remembering smile made up for almost everything.

I had three days to myself. I put them to no good use. I didn't know then, and I don't know now, what I was *supposed* to do with my time. I even missed Miss Clayton, teaching me about the population of Borneo.

Mamma reappeared on Friday afternoon, exhausted by her duties in London. A dozen people came to stay on Saturday. The king came to luncheon on Sunday. He stayed to tea because of the biscuits from Biarritz. I was presented by Mamma for about the twentieth time. I received, curtseying and fluttering, the usual impression of a bored, bearded face above a bulging, pearly-grey waistcoat. Of course, I was terribly loyal and full of patriotic sentiments.

I kept thinking about Mamma and Uncle Gareth. I could not get the picture of them out of my mind. I kept thinking of that slow, remembering smile. I kept putting the two pictures together—the spread thighs and clutching fingers and red club and mushroom nipples, and the remembering smile. *That* was what it was all about—not just the one, not just the other, but the two together. *That* was what it did to you. *That* was what I wanted.

It was so unfair. Mamma had had so much of her life. She was nearly forty. She had been married. I had nothing. She kept me cocooned in my ignorance and innocence, and yet, herself—Oh, it was unfair!

Sometimes, remembering that Sunday afternoon, I began to shudder with excitement. I investigated myself, remembering, imagining. It was not much good. I tried different things. In my bath one evening I discovered a new merit in soapsuds. I was washing my bust, soaping it with my fingers (after all, a bust needs to be clean) and I found that the slippery warmth of the soapsuds had a most agreeable effect on my nipples. I doubt if nipples have ever been more thoroughly cleaned. It was nice because it was unexpected. I lost myself in the sensation. Then I heard a noise behind me, and saw that Emmy had come in with hot towels. She must very nearly have seen me stroking my nipples, hard and happy pink hazelnuts under the soapsuds.

The following week, the last in April, Mamma reappeared from London on Thursday. She arrived from the train with Uncle Gareth and a few others. I was not surprised to see Uncle Gareth. God knew I was not. I was surprised to see Lord Whitewater, so soon revisiting Moreys.

I went to say goodnight to Mamma while she was dressing. She was in a better temper than usual. I guessed at the cause, and felt a little sick at the guess.

"It's funny, Mamma," I said, "Lord Whitewater coming again so soon."

"Funny? Why funny? He is a very clever man."

"Is he a great friend of yours, Mamma?"

"He is a friend, of course. I would hardly have invited him otherwise. What idiotic questions you do ask, Camilla. Gareth wanted me to ask him again, as a matter of fact."

"Are *they* great friends, Mamma? It seems odd."

"Odd? Why odd? No, they're not great friends. Yes, of course they're great friends. Why wouldn't they be? Do stop badgering me with your nonsense when I'm trying to concentrate."

She was concentrating on creaming her face and neck with the scented contents of her pots. Of course it was important, as she was getting old. I saw that. I stopped badgering her with questions.

Anyway, it was silly to ask her questions when she answered first one way and then the opposite way.

"And how was the puppy?" Lord Whitewater asked me on Saturday morning.

"What puppy?" I replied blankly.

"The one it was so urgent you should visit a fortnight ago. In the kennels, I think you said."

"Oh! *That* puppy."

"*That* puppy."

"*That* puppy is—simply a young dog, you know."

He laughed. His laugh was clipped and precise, like his speech, as though he did not have very many laughs available for everyday use and must be economical with them.

"I am fond of puppies," he said.

"Fond?"

"Of puppies. Besottedly fond. My friends will tell that if I have a weakness, it is my excessive affection for puppies."

He was trying to be flippant and amusing, but somehow it did not quite work. He was better at being serious. His eyes were too hot and his mouth too bitter for persiflage. It all seemed false and calculated.

He went on, "This morning I insist on being conducted to the kennels to inspect, or interview, this puppy. You will be so amiable as to take me, my little Lady Camilla."

There was nothing I could do about it. I was so obviously idle. I had been doing nothing for an hour. I could not invent an urgent errand. I had to go with him. I had to take his arm.

His hair floated about his head, rather strongly but pleasantly scented. He was beautifully dressed, as always, in very pale grey with a miniature rose in his buttonhole. I wondered where he had got a rose in April. His hands were thin and yellowish, long-fingered with big knuckles. There was something about his hands which made me think there was no hair anywhere on his body.

He talked continuously as we walked to the kennels. He talked to me as an adult, without patronising heartiness. He talked about the origins of the earliest breeds of dogs, of mastiffs and greyhounds and harehounds, and how primitive people had trained and bred them. It was a far more interesting conversation than most of the conversations at Moreys. It was actually about something, instead of being about nothing except last week's parties and next week's parties. He *was* clever. It was possible to imagine him being anybody's friend. Yet it was impossible to imagine him anybody's friend. He was friendly without being friendly. He was a person without being quite a person.

He interested me. Something about him fascinated me. I had never met anybody like him before among Mamma's friends. Something about him frightened and repelled me. He was like a false man, rubber stretched over a wire framework. The hot eyes belonged to an animal.

I might have thought he was interested in me, only that was impossible —he was over forty, more than twice my age. I was glad we belonged to different generations. I felt safer knowing that those eyes, at their hottest, would turn elsewhere.

In bed that night, memory and imagination were once again busy; and so were my ignorant fingers. I put faces to the fingers—the nice blue eyes of a young Irishman I had never spoken to, or buttered-coloured hair and a silky flaxen moustache. I tried to exclude Uncle Gareth's face. I did not want his teeth in my dreams.

I found myself with Lord Whitewater's face in the darkness above mine. I was furious that my imagination played such a trick on me. When I opened my knees, lying naked on my back in the dark, it was his imagined body that somehow pressed between them. When I touched my nipples, it was his bloodless lips that mumbled at them. Try as I might, I could not chase his face away. It stuck to my mind's eye like flypaper. It was a horrible intruder into my fantasies.

But not into my real life at luncheon the next day. I expected him to capture me to sit beside him. I flattered myself. I was dreading it. I expected him to touch my hand on the table, and I knew his hand would be as cold as a snail in a graveyard. But he had gone away for the day. He had left a note for Mamma which we found when we got back from church. He was visiting an old servant of his family. He would be back early in the evening.

I was relieved. But I had a much less interesting conversation at luncheon.

It was another fine afternoon. It was a time for expeditions. Cars and carriages went off in various directions. Mamma, exhausted by arranging it all, floated away to rest.

Uncle Gareth, without a word, also strolled off upstairs.

The last thing I wanted to do was to repeat my peeping. The idea disgusted and appalled me. She was my mother. It was unutterable that I, of all people, should spy on them. It was not something I should see, or wanted ever again to see. Since I had seen it, I could not stop remembering it. But I must not see it again.

I felt very clear about this, very strong in my mind. I thought that I should be sick, or scream, if I saw that forbidden scene again. I thought I might be struck blind, and that I would deserve to be. I went firmly up to my schoolroom.

I went firmly up to my schoolroom, so I do not know how it was that I found myself slipping, very furtive and mouselike, into Mamma's little sitting room and into her dressing room.

The door was ajar, open an inch. I could see well enough—better if I crouched down, because of the flounce of Mamma's dressing table.

An invisible rope had dragged me there. An invisible net held me there. I squatted, trembling, wildly excited, disgusted, my heart thudding and my mouth dry.

Uncle Gareth was lying on his back. His stomach was flat and muscular with a line of dark hair running down from the button to join the big rough clump below. From the clump rose the round-ended club, a little-curved, with a prominent vein running down the side. I was once again aghast at the size of the thing. There was much I still did not know.

Mamma lay on her side. One heavy breast hung and swung just over his chest. She took the club in one hand and began to play with it. She was like a child playing with a toy. With her other hand she played with the plumlike lumps which Uncle Gareth had in a drooping bag of skin at the base of the club. I did not know what these were called or what they were for. I was keenly interested to see them, after my disappointing examinations of the marble men in the library. I had not supposed that the plums moved so freely, that the bag of skin could be lifted this way and that so easily. Mamma was very busy and happy, and smiling her gradual smile.

"My juggernaut," she said softly. "Old juggins. Juggerino. Jug-jug."

"For God's sake stop," whispered Uncle Gareth harshly. "I can't hold out against that."

"Poor old jug. Mustn't waste it."

She let go of him and lay back, letting her legs sag apart. His hands became busy. He caressed the mound and the lips that bisected the mound and the little thimble, like mine, at the top of the lips.

My own hands became busy. I could not stop them. Squatting, watching, I slid my hand under my skirt and up my leg and under my underclothes. I tried to do to myself all the things Uncle Gareth was doing to Mamma at the same moment. I probed and stroked as he did. One finger sank deep between the lips, two fingers, three. The fingers went in and out. I was hurting myself. It was unimportant.

Mamma moaned. I moaned at the same moment. My sensation was heightened by sharing it with her. I was beginning to feel what she was beginning to feel. My fingers were wet with the warm, odd-smelling moisture which I somehow made inside myself.

Uncle Gareth got onto his knees, between Mamma's thighs, so that he faced down at her. He sank onto his elbows. She took the club and steered it. I saw it probe into the wet lips and sink deeper and deeper between them. My own fingers, three, probed into myself. In and out went Uncle Gareth, slow, fast, plunging deep. In and out went my fingers.

Any excitement I had felt before was nothing to what I felt now. If a regiment of soldiers had come into the room I could not have stopped. The feeling grew and grew, almost intolerable, exquisite.

"Oh God, oh my God," moaned Mamma.

"Oh my God," I moaned under my breath, feeling the helpless gush of hot juice under my fingers, feeling transported and lost.

I had to go. I had to wash. I had to change. I could hardly walk. I thought my face was purple and my mouth wide open.

As I crept away across the dressing room, something struck me, something faint and unexpected. It was a smell. Over the sweet, acrid smell on my fingers, over the familiar essences and soaps Mamma used in her bath, over the cigars and hair oil I could just detect from Uncle Gareth's clothes, there was another smell. I had met it. I knew it. I could not place it. It did not belong here. It was a good smell, not sweet, something between cloves and sandalwood.

I thought vaguely that Mamma had a new sort of soap.

I went to my bedroom and looked at myself. My face *was* purple. My eyes were as bright as though I had a high fever. Between my legs there was a beautiful, tingling memory.

Lord Whitewater did come back in the evening. I did not see him. I saw him on Monday morning when they were all leaving. He shook hands with me. His fingers were as cold as graveyard snails.

As he turned away, I caught a whiff of the lotion he put on his hair. It was a good smell, not sweet, something between cloves and sandalwood.

4 ✿ *My smooth moist hand*

> My beauty as the spring doth yearly grow;
> My flesh is soft and plump, my marrow burning;
> My smooth moist hand, were it with thy hand felt,
> Would in the palm dissolve, or seem to melt.

VENUS AND ADONIS

My first thought was that Lord Whitewater had lent Mamma some of his hair lotion. That was ridiculous. He had lent Uncle Gareth some hair lotion. They were great friends (according to one-half of Mamma's answer to my question) and exchanged hair lotions, each trying the other's, as girls borrow each others' sashes and bangles.

Uncle Gareth had never smelled of cloves and sandalwood. He had not done so at luncheon on Sunday. I had passed close behind his chair. His stiff, wavy grey hair was well oiled, immaculate as always, and it smelled of pinewoods under the sun.

Lord Whitewater had visited the dressing room, then. A friendly call. He and Mamma were great friends. At least they were friends. At least he was invited to Moreys for the second time only a fortnight after the first time. He visited her *dressing room*? Of course he had not been asked to that holy of holies. He had not been anywhere near it. But he had. He was a special friend, then. Mamma had not one special friend, but two. Two lovers. Unknown to each other. Or, if they were great friends, known to each other. Was that possible? Could grown-ups manage their lives in such an extraordinary way?

Mamma had told me: Lord Whitewater was asked at Uncle Gareth's request. Asked the second time, that is. It was not her idea, but his. This made *no* sense in relation to the scent of cloves and sandalwood in the dressing room.

To talk to Lord Whitewater was one thing. He was clever and interesting, as everybody said, and he knew about all kinds of things seldom discussed at Moreys. It was even endurable to sit beside him, and to walk on his arm from a terrace to the kennels. He was so interesting, when he was serious, that one could begin to forget how horrible he looked.

But the thought of real physical contact with him—that was truly awful. His bare flesh on one's own bare flesh, his fingers, his bloodless mouth—no, no, no, that was enough to make you scream in your sleep with disgust. It must be so for Mamma, too.

So *could* Mamma . . . ? *Had* Mamma . . . ? If not, how did that scent of cloves and sandalwood . . . ?

I was completely puzzled.

There was another big house party the first Friday-to-Monday in May. The weather was fine and warm, the trees in leaf, birds singing, flowers opening.

Parasols blossomed among the parterres, and the croquet hoops were put out on the croquet lawn. Everything was full of life and vigour, except me.

In the spring a livelier iris gleams upon the burnish'd dove.

Very true. There is no denying it. Observation confirms it. The pigeons become quite vulgar, like parvenu ladies in satin.

In the spring a young man's fancy lightly turns to thoughts of love.

It may well be. I do not deny it. I did not then deny it. But I saw no sign of it. At least, not at once. Of the direction taken by a young woman's fancy, I was (of course) more aware. It turned to thoughts of love. Yes. Quite immoderately.

Uncle Gareth came again, powerful and effective and glossy and a bit dangerous. He reminded me of Mamma's new forty horse-power motor. His hair smelled of pinewoods under a hot sun. In this regard he was different from the motor, which smelled of oil and new leather and hot rubber.

Among all the faces which appeared on Friday, there was one which surprised me: Lord Henry Clinton. He strolled among the topiary yews on Saturday morning, glorious in white flannels and white buckskin shoes and a panama hat with a resplendent ribbon. It was really too early in the summer for those clothes, but I could see why he put them on. He looked like a knight out of shining armour, a Corinthian about to play a corking innings for the county.

It seemed that he was out of disgrace. Perhaps his disgrace had not been so very deep. I saw him walking with Mamma. They went into the yew alley at one end, and came out of it the other end quite ten minutes later. This was a slow rate of progress, since the yew alley is only fifty yards long. Five yards a minute (I think). Even the old Grand Duchess walked faster than that, even when she was asking someone about his bowels.

Mamma was exhausted after luncheon, perhaps by her walk in the yew alley. She disappeared for her rest. Uncle Gareth was exhausted, too, by smoking cigars and wondering whether to go fishing.

They had shut the door between the dressing room and Mamma's bedroom. It was not locked, but I did not dare open it. The keyhole gave only onto an armchair on which Mamma's stays and petticoat were lying. I heard movement and muffled voices. It was intensely aggravating.

I was disgusted with myself for even trying to watch them again. I was driven into a fever of excitement by imagining. I was wild with anger at three inches of mahogany and brass. I was ashamed of being there.

I wandered out of the house and down by the terraces. I was as purposeless as always. Here and there, in the pleasure grounds, I heard the gabble-gabble of Mamma's friends talking. They sounded like an aristocratic barnyard. Moreys was a palatial chicken coop.

It occurred to me that the difference between them and myself was that I was purposeless and realised it, and they were purposeless and did not realise it. Except Mamma. She at least had Uncle Gareth. That was enough purpose to be going on with. Most of the others were too old or too ugly or too heavily married.

I did not take my blue-bound book with me, or any other book. I had put them all back into the glass-fronted case in the library. They were not good. I could learn no more from them. I had learned practically nothing from them. They were a fraud. They had been sold under false pretences. My Papa or my Grandpapa had been cheated. I felt quite cross at the thought.

I wandered moonily towards my Chinese bridge, thinking it a pity that nobody was watching me. I could contemplate my reflection there better than anywhere else. The me that I saw looking soulfully up from the surface of the water was the real me, mysterious, enchanting, fatal.

But my bridge was already occupied. I heard voices—two men's voices. I heard a laugh and saw a puff of smoke. I saw a gleam of butter-coloured hair through the leaves. I heard another laugh—a light, bouncy laugh. He was still wearing white flannels and a splendid hat.

Without in the least meaning to, I thought of Mamma and Uncle Gareth rolling on the great bed. I thought of Mamma's remembering smile. I thought of my own wild jubilant discovery between my legs as I crouched in the gloom. I thought of Lord Henry's butter-coloured hair and of his silky flaxen moustache.

The hair on his body would be as fair as the hair on mine. How sweetly they would meet and join. Mamma did it. Why not me? She couldn't disapprove. She had no right to.

I leaned against a tree, panting, amidst the young leaves.

The two on the bridge came down the mossy steps and onto the bank of the lake. They were talking about the races at Salisbury. They passed close by me. With Lord Henry was a man I hardly knew—Captain Arkwright, an ordinary man. A very lucky man. He was with Lord Henry. He was in sole possession of Lord Henry's company. He did not know the extent of his good fortune.

They passed close by me on the path between the bushes which led from the Chinese bridge. Lord Henry seemed to look directly at me. His face showed nothing. He did not see me. I was in the shade, he in the bright sun. He had taken off his hat. The sun on his polished hair made it look like a golden helmet. He was a Viking god smoking a small cigar.

I watched the back of his head as he strolled away, and all unbidden came once again those scalding pictures, photographed on my mind, of the naked bodies clenched and trembling on the sunlit bed. My imagination was *very* feverish. It was something to do with the smell of last year's leaves, rotting on the bank of the lake under the hot sun.

I heard the *tock* of croquet mallets on croquet balls. I went to watch. It would fill the time until tea.

Lord Henry was playing, partnering the old Grand Duchess against Captain Arkwright and Lady Garston. Lady Garston was quite good, playing a vicious game, croqueting her opponents again and again and sending their balls far away into the borders at the edges of the lawn. Lord Henry

grew quite pink and ruffled at the humiliation. I thought that was undignified, but sweet. It made him young. He needed looking after. His
hand should be held.

The Grand Duchess called to me to take her place. She was too old for
the pace Lady Garston was setting. It would be good for my bowels.
Trembling, I took a mallet. Lord Henry had not affected me like this before. Mine was the red ball. I played brilliantly, and saved our side from
annihilation. It was deeply satisfactory. I was proud and happy. Lord
Henry was proud and happy, too, as well as grateful. Captain Arkwright
and Lady Garston were generous in defeat. I was generous in victory.

I thought that I would have tea by Lord Henry's side, but it did not
work out.

I was lucky on Sunday afternoon. The door was ajar. I was unlucky. I
saw nothing new.

There was another miracle between my own legs, beneath my own
fleece, in my own hot cave. The sensation was almost more than I could
bear. It was like an itch, a beautiful, intolerable itch. I had no sense of
completion. It was not satiety. I needed more. I needed a different thing. I
knew what I needed.

I crept away in despair at my helplessness, at the squalid shifts I was reduced to.

It was not fair. It was *not* fair.

"Camilla! Great Scott, what a start you gave me."
I put a hand to my mouth, and goggled like a frog.
Lord Henry Clinton had turned a corner, round the great bole of a
beech tree, and we had almost bumped into each other.

I had found myself walking in the beech wood beyond the lake, a
soothing place. The smooth grey trunks of the beeches were like the columns of a gigantic cathedral. Their branches, far above, fanned like vault-
ing. The sunlight filtered down to the floor of the wood as though through
stained glass windows. Birds sang like choristers. The wood was carpeted
with bluebells. No one preached sermons or read lessons from the Scrip-
tures. There was nothing to remind me of General Mauney's trouser buttons.

Lord Henry seemed out of breath. The perfect gloss of his hair was
ruffled. I wanted to smooth it.

"I came for a walk," I said in a funny little high voice.

I had been used to him and easy with him. But something had happened. I was not used to him now, and I was not easy with him. I was shy and excited.

"I came for a walk, too," he said cheerfully, smiling. "An extraordinary coincidence. I see the hand of Providence. Do you see the hand of Providence?"

"Yes," I said. "No."

"I was bored and lonely. You have put that right."

"Oh—I'm sorry you were bored."

"Evidently you like this wood, as you walk in it."

"Yes, I like this wood," I repeated stupidly, "as I walk in it."

"I didn't like it, not very much, until this moment. I thought it a sad and dull wood."

"Sad and dull." My conversation was becoming no more sparkling.

"Lonely and boring."

"Oh. Yes."

"Lacking magic."

"Ah."

"Now it has magic."

"It has magic?"

"It is radiant with a new magic. You have brought magic into the wood, Camilla."

"Have I?" I intended to say, but only a silly little squeak came out.

"You look more beautiful even than usual. I wouldn't have thought that possible, actually. You always look very beautiful. But when I suddenly saw you face to face with me, a yard away, utterly unexpectedly—I have never seen anything so beautiful, so bewitching in my life."

"Oh," I said. It was as stupid a reply as could be, but I was in no state to be clever.

"Hair," he said, very softly, standing close to me in the dappled light and shade of the beechwood. "Brow. Eyes. Ears. Nose. Mouth. Your mouth is a miracle of perfection. Classical without coldness. Passionate without weakness. Can you smile at me, Camilla?"

I tried to, but my face was not working properly.

He touched my hand. I jumped as though stung.

"Did I frighten you, dear Camilla?" he murmured.

"No! Yes. This is strange—"

"Yes. I feel most strange. I feel a new emotion, like a great orchestra inside me. I feel like a bird, like a lion. I feel frightened."

"You?" I stammered. "Frightened?"

"Frightened of the strength and tumult of my own feelings. Frightened of frightening you. I don't want to frighten you, darling Camilla. But I do want—"

"What?" I croaked.

"I do want very badly to kiss you."

I looked at him helplessly, my hat in my hand. He stepped up to me so that the front of his jacket touched the front of my dress. He put his arms round my waist, very gently, holding me loosely. I dropped my hat. My fingers were powerless to hold it.

It was happening. Something was beginning to happen. When I needed it most, wanted it most, by utterly extraordinary and miraculous chance, here we were.

He was two or three inches taller than I. I thought that exactly right. His face loomed down at me. I shut my eyes. I felt his lips on my brow, the tip of my nose, my cheek. I felt the silky caress of his moustache. I felt that one of my arms had gone round his neck, and then that the other had. He held me tighter, tighter. I felt the buttons of his jacket pressing into my breasts. There was a danger that his moustache would tickle my nose so that I would sneeze. I felt his lips on my lips. I felt his tongue. For a moment I was startled, perturbed. I remembered. I opened my mouth. His mouth was open. We pressed our mouths together. Our tongues met. I was dizzy with excitement. I felt drunk. I would have fallen, but for his arms gripping me and mine gripping him.

We were no longer standing but sitting among bluebells. I never knew how this change happened. His arm was behind my shoulder, supporting me. I still clung fast to his neck. I felt another hand, his other hand, on my arm and on my shoulder. It crept down from my shoulder, as though furtively, to my breast. I pressed my breast into the hand. The hand squeezed my breast through my clothes. Fingers, through my clothes, explored my body.

"You are so beautiful, so desirable, so exciting," he muttered into my cheek. "I love you. I adore you. I want you. I need you. I am going mad because of you. The thought of you makes me ill with joy and misery—"

I sobbed. It was ridiculous. I was beside myself with joy. His words were beautiful and perfect. I felt my own tears.

He kissed them away. His lips met mine again. He kissed me with a kind of tender violence. I was close to swooning. Wildly I took my hand from his neck and with it pressed his hand to my breast.

He muttered, "We must go back separately."

"We must go?" I wailed.

"I want to come to your room. Please let me come. I beg you, implore you, beautiful, miraculous Camilla, my darling love. May I come?"

People would say that I should have said "No." Mamma would have said "Yes." If she did, I could. I said, "Yes."

"When?" he murmured. "Now?"

"When you like. Yes. Now."

He raised me to my feet. We stood at arms' length, holding hands. He looked very dishevelled and abandoned and adorable.

He gave a sort of sob himself, and pulled me violently into his arms. I embraced him passionately.

"Before I go mad—" he gasped.

I felt the same. I did not want to leave him. I could not bear to let go of him. I was holding him, my own, my love, for the first time; I did not want to let him go. But he was right. We must go back. Separately.

"Now," I said, certain, aghast, delirious.

We kissed goodbye. Somehow I made my way back to Moreys. I went in through a little door under the north terrace. I did not want to meet anyone face to face. It would have been disastrous, because my emotion, my excitement, my guilt, must have been written all over me, and I could not stop my hands trembling.

I went to my bedroom. It was full of the afternoon sun. I drew the curtains partly over the windows.

I stood undecided, suddenly and appallingly aware of my ignorance. My clothes? What was I supposed to do? What did he expect? What about the brocade cover on the bed? What was the proper thing? How blatant should I be? Was I absolutely certain that he had meant—Could I possibly have misunderstood?

The door opened softly. He was there. He had smoothed his hair. He smiled. He looked serene. No doubts or fears assailed him.

I stood facing him nervously. There were hazards ahead.

"Your maid?" he asked softly.

"Away. Visiting her grandmother. In Wilton. Her grandmother has shingles."

I found it difficult to talk. But he was pleased with what I said. He locked the door. Then he almost bounded across the room to me and took me in his arms.

We were standing up, and then we were sitting on the bed, and then we were lying on the bed, embracing, our bodies touching all the way from our mouths to our toes, but still with all our clothes on.

I wondered anxiously, again, if Henry's position in the whole matter was the same as my own.

I need not have worried. At least, not about that.

He pulled away from me suddenly and peeled off his jacket and tie and collar and shoes. He gently pulled off my shoes and laid them side by side under the bed.

I sat up. My hands were trembling again, no longer with excitement but with nervousness. What next? The practical problems were daunting. The thought of my suspenders jumped into my head. Did I undo them, or did he? Did he know how to? What was the procedure?

I had not been shown this part. I had had no instruction in it. I had been too late at my lessons. I bitterly regretted my lateness by the crack in the dressing room door. I felt like an actress in the center of the spotlight who had not been shown her lines or rehearsed in her part.

There was something tentative and uncertain about Henry, too. It did not seem that he was well instructed in this phase, which, if merely a means to an end, was nevertheless crucial to that end.

I was wearing a white blouse with leg-of-mutton sleeves, and a tie, and a biscuit-coloured serge skirt, and petticoats under that, and a chemise, and white silk stockings, and silk drawers. The skirt did up at the back and the blouse did up at the front and the tie, of course, did up at the knot.

Lord Henry, I mean Henry, answered some of the questions in my mind by attacking the knot of my tie. I sat like a fool on the bed, my eyes downcast. His hands were trembling almost as badly as mine. I hoped it was just excitement. He tightened the tie, I suppose by mistake, instead of loosening it, and nearly throttled me. I croaked and pawed the air. He mumbled an apology, rather a formal apology, and presently took off the tie.

Then he began to unbutton the buttons of the front of my blouse. That *was* exciting. The backs of his hands nudged my breasts as he struggled with the buttons. They were big buttons, mother-of-pearl. The blouse was stiffened and shirred. When he had undone the buttons to my waist, he was able to slip the blouse off my shoulders. He put his hands on my bare shoulders. He kissed me.

That was better.

I tried to put my arms round his neck, which had been such a success before. But because of the new position of the blouse, my arms were imprisoned by the sleeves. I was like a lunatic in a straight jacket. It was discomfiting.

Well, we achieved it in the end, with untold gruntings. He spoke never a word. I did not like to speak. Part of the time I had to stand up, and part turn my back to him because of the hooks-and-eyes of my skirt. He had trouble, as I expected, with my suspenders. When he peeled my stockings down from my legs, he kissed my thighs. That was very good. When he bared my breasts he touched them nervously. They were not nervous at all. I was not as shy and bashful about my nakedness as I had expected to be. I wanted him to see me and to touch me. It seemed right and proper, and it was what I wanted.

His clothes came off quickly and easily. I was entranced. His sock-suspenders struck an unromantic note. His legs were not as muscular as Uncle Gareth's. His behind and tummy were plumper.

He was bashful.

I lay on my back as I had seen Mamma lie. I spread my legs a little apart. I felt superbly vulnerable. I looked down at myself. I thought I looked nice. My thighs were slim and my tummy flat and my breasts high and firm.

He took off his last garment, his own silk drawers. I was agog. But he kept his back to me, then shuffled to the bed and lay beside me, face downwards. He wriggled into a position where he could kiss me. He did so, his hands on my shoulders. He kept his front firmly buried in the bed-clothes. It was not the procedure I had expected. He had been to a different school from mine.

I was determined to be a good pupil. Also I was devoured by curiosity. I made him turn over. He was dreadfully reluctant to do so. He folded his legs over each other, but I unfolded them. I lay on my side, in the excellent position I had learned from Mamma. I inspected his spear, or club. It was a bit of a disappointment. It was about half the size of Uncle Gareth's, pinky-white, with a little drip by the little hole at the top. I took my courage in both hands, and the club in one hand. It was extraordinarily hard. I felt a vein along the upper side, and a sort of ribbing like the spring that keeps a door shut. The skin moved easily up and down. It was not attached to the spring at all except at the top and bottom. I found this most odd. The bag of twin plums was soft and floppy, the skin loose and curiously wrinkled. It looked like part of a very old man. I found that part mysterious and rather ugly.

He gasped and pushed my hand away and rolled over onto his front again. He attacked me passionately. But he was still following different instructions from mine. He kissed my mouth, which was correct, but when I tried to push his head down to my breast, as I knew I should, he resisted.

I pushed harder. He still resisted. He squeezed my breasts with his hands, rather painfully. He hurt my nipples, pinching them. I had the curious and unnerving impression that he thought they were blackheads and he was trying to pinch them out. He was not doing what I wanted.

I felt his hand on my fleece and his fingers on the lips in the fleece. This was truly and wildly exciting. A finger jabbed in. I felt the beginning of trembling dampness. He was a bit rough. He ignored the little thimble. His one idea, it seemed, was to push the finger in as far as it would go, to prove what a long finger he had.

He continued to kiss me from time to time, and squeeze and squash one breast, and keep that finger inside me. He seemed to have exhausted his ideas. Or else he was waiting for something. Of course he was waiting for me. It was my move. I remembered Mamma. But he was in the wrong position. I could do nothing until he lay on his back or knelt over me. Yet he was determined to lie on his front, in useless bashfulness and safety. I was baffled. The situation was becoming farcical. His finger seemed to have died.

"Buck up," I said, despairing of his ever again moving.

Galvanized, he slid on top of me. I opened my legs to enclose his. I had thought this movement would be easy and pleasant, and it was. It was lovely to have him lying on top of me, except that he did not rest his weight on his elbows, in Uncle Gareth's method, but rested it all on me. I was nearly squashed. I felt like dough under a rolling pin. But it was exciting to feel, for the very first time, naked flesh pressed against mine all the way down my body.

I knew the next step. I remembered so clearly. I had imagined so often. With one hand I grabbed at his behind. I pushed the other under him, over my own thigh, and took hold of his club.

Steering it had looked so easy. Really it was very difficult. Either it, or he, was perverse, or clumsy, or reluctant. It was a long time before I manhandled the bulbous tip of the fleecy mound, and longer before I steered it to the lips. And then it seemed to be at the wrong angle.

Then it really did hurt. He jabbed in. I felt it all the way. Something seemed to stretch and stretch and at last to split. I had hurt myself a little with my own fingers, but nothing like this. He was ruthless. He had forgotten me. His face was turned away from mine. His hands were nowhere touching me. He plunged in and out, inside me. Uncle Gareth had done this bit, but slowly, gently, only later fast and furious. Lord Henry, I mean Henry, was fast and furious at once, and all it did was to hurt me.

He cleared his throat. It was a pity he had to do that.

Then he stopped moving. Something had happened. I did not know what. Nothing had happened to me. He lay still, his face always turned away from mine. I could feel his chest going in and out with his breathing; otherwise he might have been dead, until he cleared his throat again.

I smelled cigar smoke in his hair.

What now? Had we paused for a rest? Was there more? There had to be more. I knew what was promised. It lay ahead, some way ahead, unreached but surely attainable.

"Get on!" I wanted to shout.

But I lay silent, puzzled, still excited, in a little pain, yearning.

I lay cheated.

He pulled away from me. There was a nasty little sucking noise. I felt like a bottle uncorked by an underfootman. He jumped off the bed. I heard him scrabble at his clothes.

I turned over onto my face and burst into tears.

He said, "Oh God."

Then he said, "Lock the door after me."

"Yes," I snuffled into the pillow.

I heard the door open and shut. He was gone. I got off the bed at last and picked up my clothes from the floor. I put them on a chair. I had to crawl under the bed for one of my shoes. He had kicked it there while he was dressing.

I collapsed on the bed again and cried myself to sleep.

The next thing I knew was that Emmy was standing by my bed in her outdoor clothes.

"Have a nice nap, m'lady?" she said. "That's nice, then."

I wondered how she had got in, if I had remembered to lock the door.

I thought, long and long, about the afternoon, sitting with my chin in my hands at a table in the schoolroom. I was more and more aghast.

Henry was widely experienced—he must be, a man of his rank and age and manner and popularity. Therefore I had miserably failed. I had been ignorant, girlish, nervous, silly. Oh God, I had been so silly! I should have —I should have—I did not know what I should have done, and there was no one in the world I could ask.

I went to look for Henry. I did not want to talk to him. I did not dare to talk to him. I did not dare to talk to anybody. I just wanted to see him. He was not to be seen.

I went forlornly back to my schoolroom and sat until the sky darkened. I did not go to see Mamma while she was dressing. I was sure guilt was written in scarlet letters all over my face.

Emmy had gone out again. A housemaid brought my supper. I hid my face even from her.

I found that I was in love with Henry. It was a new and horrible experience. It made me feel sick.

I know now why this happened, but I did not know then that there was any reason. It was simply an illness I had caught. Through an endless, empty week I was sick with wanting him. But if he had come into a room when I was there, I would have run away from terror of talking to him.

I wrote him long poems. Some were in the manner of Lord Tennyson, some not.

I began an intimate diary of my inmost feelings. But when I read what I had written, I tore out the pages and burned them out of embarrassment. It was like looking at someone sitting on a chamber pot.

I asked Mamma on Friday evening, ever so casually, if Lord Henry was to be invited again.

"Henry Clinton? I doubt it. Why ever do you ask?"

My face felt crimson, and I could feel my mouth twitching. I turned my face to hide.

"He—He was interested in a puppy."

"In buying a puppy?"

"Yes. Buying one."

"What puppy?"

"A small young dog. In the kennels."

"I don't understand a single word you're saying. If he wants puppies he must go elsewhere. Does he think this is a pet shop? No, he will *not* be coming here again. He annoys people. He is rather a puppy himself."

I felt sick. I knew I was going to be sick. I ran out of Mamma's room. I was sick.

There was nothing wrong with me. It was only love.

> She only said, "My life is dreary,
> He cometh not," she said;
> She said, "I am aweary, aweary,
> I would that I were dead!"

Well, no. Not quite. But I felt very low. I cried from time to time, sometimes easy tears that just spilled out and ran down over my cheeks, sometimes horrid dry sobs that hurt my chest.

He ought to come. Even if he were not asked to stay at Moreys, he should come to see me. He could come secretly and send a message from one of the villages. It was cruel of him not to come. He must want to come? Of course he must. Something prevented him. Illness. He had been in an accident. He had been run over by a bus, or fallen out of a train. He was drowned.

Another week went by. It was the middle of May, the most lovely and promising time of the whole year.

> But most she loathed the hour
> When the thick-moated sunbeam lay
> Athwart the chambers, and the day
> Was sloping toward his western bower.
> Then, said she, "I am very dreary,
> He will not come," she said;
> She wept, "I am aweary, aweary,
> Oh God, that I were dead!"

No, not absolutely to that point. But it was very lowering, having a broken heart.

He came. I saw him. It was Sunday. The fine weather held. The house was full. Most people were out. There were cucumber sandwiches on the lawn, under big stripy umbrellas and awnings.

I was on the roof. This was forbidden. There were six acres of roof, of slates and stone and lead. Here and there it was frightening. I wanted to be frightened. I wanted to hurt myself. I wanted any strong, sharp sensation that drove love out of my mind. I wanted to be alone.

I had some opera glasses with me. I nearly dropped them over the parapet onto Lady Clanmangan's head. That would have been a dreadful thing. They were pretty, with mother-of-pearl and silver, and I would have been sad to break them.

I spied on various people dotted over the lawns and round the lake. Some were difficult to recognize from above, some easy. They were not doing anything interesting. It was simply amusing to watch people who did not know they were being watched. I watched a game of croquet. Colonel Vandaleur cheated. He moved his ball when the others were not looking. One can be diverted, even with a broken heart.

I saw Mamma. She was with Lord Whitewater. He had come simply to luncheon, not to stay. He had come to see his family's old servant who was failing. I had spoken to him, or rather he to me. Luncheon was not informally at the little tables in the banqueting hall, but formally in the dining room. The placement had been devised as carefully as for dinner. This was because some German royalties had come. Lord Whitewater spoke to them in German. He sounded very fluent and impressive. They were pleased. The fat Princess trembled with gratification, her jewels bouncing on her bosom. He backed away from them, bowing most gracefully, and crossed the room to talk to me.

I saw him coming. There was a funny dead grin on his face. He looked as though he had eaten a baby and enjoyed it. I wanted to escape, but he moved quickly and took my arm.

"All the time I was talking to their Royal Highnesses," he said in his clipped, schoolmasterish voice, "I found myself wishing I were talking to you."

"I don't understand German," I said stupidly.

"It would not suit you. I should prefer to address you in French, or Greek, or Medieval Latin. You look enchanting, as always—a nymph escaped from an oak tree, undine on an outing from a watery cave to hugger-mugger among mortals for a moment. Ah, we move to the board. Alas, I must station myself between two dowagers, on the infrangible instructions of your lady Mamma. But I will hope to see you after luncheon."

That was one of the main reasons I was on the roof.

The Germans were surrounded by self-appointed courtiers who probably hoped for minor medals. Mamma sauntered with Lord Whitewater by the lake. I wondered what they were talking about. The conversations he was best at were not the sort of thing she liked. He was as distinctive as she, in a broad-brimmed straw hat of Brazilian appearance. Mamma twirled a pale blue parasol with a frilly edge. They strolled towards the little boathouse by the lake. I was mildly surprised. Would they go boating? I could not picture either of them afloat. Perhaps it would suit Mamma well enough to loll among cushions, like a corseted Cleopatra, while someone heaved at the oars. It would not suit Lord Whitewater to heave at oars. His hands were for holding pens, or ancient books, or the delicate stems of precious wine glasses. Besides, his Brazilian hat would fall off.

Somebody crossed the rough park grass, from the direction of the beech wood, going towards the boathouse. It was someone in a hurry. He looked a bit furtive. I raised the opera glasses.

My heart jumped into my throat, then sagged to the pit of my stomach. I saw butter-coloured hair, unmistakable, smooth as custard. The opera glasses shook so much they were useless.

When I focussed on the place again, he had disappeared.

Had he joined them in the boathouse? Hardly. Mamma thought he was a puppy. I wanted him. I felt sick at seeing him and with wanting him. He was hiding, or else he had run very fast.

The truth came to me. This was the secret visit I had prayed for. Of course he had come. Of course now that he had come, he was lurking. Something had kept him away, but now he had come to me. He was looking for me, prowling about the pleasure-grounds like an Indian.

I went in through the tiny attic window which I had left open, then rushed down an infinity of stairs past the floors of bedrooms and the state rooms and the halls, on into the basements, out of the small door under the north terrace, and flew to where I had seen him.

He was not there. He was not anywhere. I searched until I was dropping. He had lost heart and gone away.

My disappointment was so acute that I sat down and howled. The old Grand Duchess found me. She said the trouble lay in my bowels, and recommended pills.

Mamma had one of her headaches that evening. Emmy told me about it, bringing a message from Prior warning me to stay away from Mamma's bedroom. Mamma had headaches when she could bear her guests no longer. It happened half-a-dozen times a year. She had scrumptious suppers sent up.

The party, I suppose, went on without her.

I could not eat my own supper.

I haunted the gardens and the lake and the beech wood all the following week. He would come again. I must be ready. We would meet. I might be sick when we met, but we must meet.

He was kept in London again. He had caught the plague. He was dead.

"Did you tell me Henry Clinton wanted one of our dogs?"

"Yes, Mamma. So he said."

"He must have changed his mind. He wants a dachshund."

"A dachs—?"

"He has gone to Vienna."

"What?"

"Quite suddenly. In the middle of the Season. The oddest way to behave. His uncle is ambassador—his father's younger brother, Lord Algernon Clinton. A very prosy creature. Henry has gone as Honorary Attaché. Many young men do it. He will be missed in London, I suppose, especially by the bookmakers."

"How long," I asked, as steadily as I could, "will Lord Henry be in Vienna?"

"Good gracious, how do I know? What strange questions you ask. Three or four years, I suppose. Do stop pulling such faces, Camilla. You look quite hideous sometimes. Have you caught some vulgar illness from the servants? Really you depress me. *Prior.* If you will pull my hair any more I shall give you notice."

5 ✿ *Sweet bottom-grass*

Within this limit is relief enough,
Sweet bottom-grass and high delightful plain,
Round rising hillocks, brakes obscure and rough,
To shelter thee from tempest and from rain.

VENUS AND ADONIS

"Down here, Lord Henry?"

"Down here, Lady Bulbarrow," I said. I smiled. I stopped myself smoothing my hair back. Gaby says I do it too often.

"But yews are so gloomerino. It's like going for a walk in a churchyard."

"Going for a walk in a churchyard with you," I said, "would be nicer than going for a walk in Buck House gardens with anybody else."

Sylvia smiled. Words did the trick, as they usually do. I took her arm, and we started down the famous yew alley at Moreys. There was moss all over the ground. I wasn't so keen on that, because I was wearing my new buckskin shoes and I didn't want green stains all over them.

There was a white wrought-iron seat halfway down the yew alley. They had them dotted all over the place so that a fellow who got tired could sit down. We were out of sight of anybody, which is pretty difficult to arrange at a big house party.

"Let's rest for a minute," I said. "You must be tired."

"I ought to be looking after my guesterinos."

"Please, Sylvia."

"I don't think you ought to call me that."

"Oh, do let me! Please let me!"

"You really haven't known me long enough."

"I've known you longer than your godparents had when they took the same liberty."

She laughed. It *was* a good joke, though not actually my own. I read it in a story by a fellow called Saki. I'd used it a few times already, and it always went down well. It nearly always worked.

Still laughing, she shrugged and sat down on the seat, and I sat beside her. Things were going extraordinarily well, as I'd been pretty sure they would. She had a special smile for me. If other fellows noticed it they must have been green with envy.

In fact I'd known her for a good many years, my Governor having been a pal of old Harry Bulbarrow's. So much so that I was named after the old boy, I believe. Of course she was married until I was twenty-five or thereabouts, very much married as far as anybody knew, and I never cast my eyes in that quarter. Then a spell in weeds, and then emergence as one of the peaks in the range. Lit by the sun of royal favour, too. All a bit out of my reach, actually, being a younger son kept on a very short string by the Governor.

So things jogged on for five years, she going her road and I mine. Of course our paths crossed. We were often at the same doings. To be frank about it, no big party was complete without both of us. But some rather smaller parties were complete without me. Of course, I couldn't cope with the really high baccarat, and I couldn't return the hospitality. Being a younger son is the very devil, a damned unfair arrangement of winner take all and devil take the hindmost.

Our paths crossed, and I certainly admired her. Everyone did. She was a damned fine woman, a peach *au point*, at the point of perfect ripeness. Everyone said so. I never saw such a figure or such a complexion. In my judgment she was the best-dressed woman in London, too—always with a dash of a style of her own, a tang of her own, like something in one of those American "cocktails" fellows pour out of silver jugs.

Then one evening in February I went to the Haymarket Theatre, one of a party, and Philomena Casterbridge took me along to her box. I sat down beside Sylvia Bulbarrow and we had a long chat all through the second act of the play. She was always friendly after that. Fellows began to tease me at the club—she'd taken me up, I was her new favourite, rot like that. Then I began to think it might be true. Then I realised it was true. Being witty is what makes the difference. Whenever she saw me, even across one of those great crowds, I got that smile—my smile, the one for me. I used to dream about it.

Then some time in April, Philomena herself gave one of her awful parties. She asked me to come early to help with the sticky nobodies who always come early. I promised I would because old Philomena has always been more than halfway decent to me. But when it came to the point, I couldn't bring myself to. I came at the proper time, an hour late. A fellow has to consider the impression he makes.

The first person I met, the very minute I got in, was a boy from Ireland with a very decent face. He had precious little conversation. I daresay in Ireland he had very few neighbours, and those illiterate. My Governor owned a fair slice of County Wexford, but of course we never went there.

The young Paddy went to an adequate tailor. He had a pair of shoulders I envied under his coat. I daresay, at home he was forever tossing hay with pitchforks. His tie was a mess, without the quality of studied carelessness. Mine had the quality of studied carelessness without being a mess. I could see—without the least vanity I could see—that I impressed him. Wherever I went he went, too, listening to everything I said. I'm not ashamed to admit that I was gratified. I appreciate admiration. Show me the man that doesn't! We need it as much as the women do. I put on my best performance for his benefit.

Looking back, I don't quite know why I troubled. He wasn't good for invitations, or even racing tips.

I introduced him to Sylvia Bulbarrow, who had come right across the room to talk to me. She was gracious to him. Then she had to go and amuse Teddy after old Amy Battersea had aroused the royal boredom. It was some time before I had a chance to talk to her. She smiled at me in the special way, and asked me to Moreys for the Friday-to-Monday after next. There was a look in her eye when she asked me.

I had been to Moreys before, quite a long time before, with the Governor and the Mother. That was one thing. This was another thing! Not only that I was going alone, but—the look in her eye! The look in her eye!

I went to Newmarket for the Craven meeting, staying with Buffy Fowler at his ghastly villa at Cheveley. We were a festive party, all men of course. I dropped rather a packet on a filly called Lady of Morris (I still maintain I would have been a fool not to back her) and another packet playing billiards at Buffy's. We all looked on the wine when it was red, as the fellow said. Of course, I can hold my fizz like a gentleman; but young Bertie Carradine got shirty over nothing at the billiard table. I didn't really make a foul stroke—I just wasn't thinking at the time. I thought it was bounderish the way he insisted on a strict observance of the rules just because we were playing for money. I thought the other fellows might have taken my part a little more firmly, too.

I had Gaby for a couple of hours after I got back. I needed comforting. She was a paragon of patience and understanding, that *petit morceau de patisserie*. No rot about modesty, no airs and graces. I could do it with her better than with most, because she knew how to help a fellow.

I had to give her an I.O.U. when I left. She wasn't best pleased about *that*. Women don't understand about racing and billiards, and the systems a fellow has to follow to get back his losses.

I went down to Moreys on Thursday, of course, sending a wire ahead of me. I knew that was when Sylvia wanted me, although she hadn't actually said so. One has an instinct. And that look in her eyes!

Gareth Fortescue was on the train to Salisbury. I saw him in time and kept clear. I'd have enough of him at Moreys, if that was where he was going. Fellows liked him, but I didn't. He was too much the athlete and roughrider for me. He thought he was some kind of marvel because they had him in the Jockey Club and he rode expensive hunters. I thought he was an arrogant nobody. Baronets are two-a-penny nowadays, all brewers and grocers and aldermen.

He *did* turn up at Moreys with two or three others. They were all much older than myself and *habitués de la maison*. I daresay they watched Sylvia pretty closely, so she couldn't show her feelings to me. She had to pretend to be distant. It made me laugh like a hyena in private.

I thought they might have given me a better room. I should think Cordle, my man, was quartered in as good a billet. Possibly all that sort of arrangement was left to the secretary. I knew Sylvia had a secretary. I'd spoken to her on the telephone in London, trying to get in touch with Sylvia. Another possibility was that Sylvia had put me in a pigeon-hole in the bachelors' wing in order to hide her interest in me.

I never had a chance to get Sylvia alone. She was always with the others or else creeping off to rest. She rested all Friday afternoon. I daresay she was tired, poor little thing. She lived life to the full in London. She was always out when I telephoned. Luncheon parties, matinées, charity teas. No wonder she needed a rest in the country. But I bided my time and made myself agreeable to the others.

I had a start when I saw little Camilla, Sylvia's brat. I'd thought of her as a little chit in the schoolroom in short skirts and a pigtail. But she was nearly grown-up, soon to come out, with her hair up. She was pretty, too, in a pale, washed-out way. She moved well, like a classic yearling. She got that from her dam, I suppose, although their colouring was so different.

The main body arrived on Friday evening. I never saw such a squadron of vehicles as pulled into the forecourt. I nipped upstairs before they all got in to make sure of my bath before dinner.

I bumped into the young Mick, Matthew Alban, on my way downstairs after dressing. I was glad to see him. He *was* a decent boy. He was like myself at the same age—no, he was like myself at about seventeen. My innocence departed early, what with Oxford and London and Newmarket. Rank has its privileges as well as its responsibilities, as my Governor used to say. Only he put it the other way about.

I knew nearly all the people who'd arrived. It was the usual crowd. There was one complete stranger, an odd-looking fellow. I was told he was Whitewater—Viscount Whitewater. I'd heard of a Whitewater, but the one I'd heard was an old recluse living in France. It seemed that one had died, and this was the new one. I talked to him for a minute when we were introduced. He talked like a clergyman, using damned long words. He could be amusing, though. At least he had Lucinda Babraham in stitches during dinner, and she was a clever piece of goods.

I moved opposite to him—just happened to—when the ladies left the dining room after dinner. He was having a heart-to-heart with my young protégé, young Alban. They had plenty to talk about. God knows what it was. Whitewater's clothes were a thought flashy—too many jewels, an exaggerated cut to the waistcoat—but he wore them well. He looked a bit of an eccentric. He didn't brush his hair flat like the rest of us, but let it float about. I knew an artistic girl once, in Maida Vale, who did that. She was awful. I thought Whitewater was probably awful too, judging by his cufflinks and the cut of his mouth.

He put away a deuce of a lot of Sylvia's brandy. But he held it like a soldier.

We sat down to bridge after dinner, of course. What did people do before it was invented? I lost twenty-six shillings. It's a damned imposition to be given a ghoul like Grizelda Quincey as a partner. She added insult to injury by saying I played my hands badly.

I lost more money on Saturday night and more on Sunday. Not great sums, but enough to pinch after a bad Newmarket.

Newmarket followed me in other things, too. Of course Phyllis Carradine had got hold of her brother's version of our dust-up. So everybody was telling each other the story as though *that* version were *true*.

When I went up to bed on Sunday night, I borrowed a couple of sovereigns from young Alban to tip the butler. He said, without my asking him, that he'd keep quiet about it. He said I could pay him back any time, and gave me his address in Jermyn Street. Fair address, better than I'd expected. He *was* a decent young chap.

When I went to bed I found myself wishing I were still like Alban. Still like my own younger self, before I started having drunken quarrels at billiards, and losing money, and seducing society beauties.

That I was definitely doing. Slow but sure. She pressed my hand in the hall on Monday morning and smiled, and said she was sorry she had not seen more of me. There was a wealth of meaning in her words, and more in her tone, and more still in her smile, and more yet in her eye!

"Please may I come again?" I murmured so that no one else could hear.

"I expect so," she said.

Of course she had to be cautious and utterly discreet. Her position was high—she was a public figure. People bought her photograph in shops. Naturally she was often mentioned in the newspapers—more often than I, more often than my Governor. As a member of the king's close circle of friends she had to be beyond reproach. Of course *we* knew—the privileged few knew—a little of the king's own *affaires;* and there was gossip about others only a rung or two lower on the ladder than he. But the gossip was confined to an inner circle. It was never—it must never—become public property. We closed our ranks against the world. The Great Unwashed mattered politically as never before. They were very shockable, all Methodists and Presbyterians. They had strict rules for themselves, and they thought we had the same rules for ourselves. The established social order depended on their going on thinking so. I'd heard fellows talk about hypocrisy, but to my mind it was a question of the national interest. Secrets *had* to be kept. The great *had* to look respectable. We *had* to be a bevy of Puritans as far as the world knew.

Sylvia more than most—a Marchioness, a friend of the king's, a leader of society, a great hostess, a widow with a young daughter. I saw all that clearly enough. I was not precisely a beginner in the ways of the world.

So she had to say no more than, "I expect so," when I begged to be asked again.

Waiting for me in London was another letter from my Uncle Algernon from H.B.M.'s Embassy in Vienna. He had the same old roll in his pianola—would I go out there to assist him, in an unpaid capacity, with the parties and receptions and so forth that he had to give and didn't like.

My Governor put him up to it, of course. Uncle Algernon didn't really want me, but he had to do what my Governor said because of his income from the family trust.

I wrote back at once, very proper and formal. (There was a rumour that Uncle Algernon had the collars and cuffs of his nightshirts starched.) Very grateful, sensible of the honour he did me, convinced of my unworthiness of the trust he proposed to place in me, etc., etc. In fact, no. A fellow can't go leaving town at the beginning of the Season. It's practically unpatriotic.

In any case, if I'd gone abroad at that moment, people would have said it was because of my spot of bother with young Carradine at Newmarket. Speedy exile, admission of guilt. I would have looked like a damned fugitive.

Luckily the Governor was at home in Northamptonshire. I foresaw a sticky interview when he emerged.

The Season was beginning to creak into rapid motion—a sort of preliminary canter before the real "off" in May. There were lots of parties.

I saw Sylvia Bulbarrow pretty often, but always in a mob of people. It was impossible to talk to her privately. She was not at home when I called, or available if I telephoned. Of course her energy and sense of duty were tremendous. But I still got the special smile every time she saw me. I knew she liked me. I knew everything would work out in the end.

I saw young Matthew Alban a few times. A fellow put him up for White's and I signed my name. I wanted to talk to him because I liked him, but of course I didn't. You can't keep hobnobbing with a fellow you owe money to. I could have scraped up two sov, but it went against the grain, as it always does. It wasn't convenient, what with Cordle's wages and Gaby and playing bridge and going to the races at Sandown and Epsom.

I saw Whitewater a few times. Appearing from nowhere, having just inherited, he was bobbing like a damned duck on London waters. People seemed a bit dubious about him, as I was myself. Nobody knew anything about him. From what I heard, he could have gone about far more than he did; but he was a learned bird, and only gave half his energies to social life. I didn't think anybody even knew his Christian name—anyway, I never heard it used.

A curious thing happened.

I went to a biggish evening party of Lucinda Babraham's which everybody else went to too. There was hardly a soul there I didn't know, and hardly a soul I knew that wasn't there. What ever you could say about her in other respects, Lucinda's parties were always correct. Old Sybil Doncaster was there using her lorgnette like an edged weapon. (Not my own *mot*, but not bad.) I'd always been rather pally with the old dragon, able to get away with more persiflage than most fellows because she and my grandfather used to knock each other about in the nursery. But at Lucinda's she stared at me and turned away. Stared at me briefly through the lorgnettes and turned away in a pretty marked manner.

She was proabably a friend of old General Carradine's. They were cast in the same mould and probably sat on the same committees. A committee sat on by those two would never be the same again—the others would be flattened to the thickness of middle-class writing paper.

I didn't get a card from Doncaster House, either, when the Duchess gave a reception for the King of Bessarabia.

Young Matthew Alban did. I saw his name in the *Morning Post*. Fancy him being asked and not me! So I went round to Jermyn Street with two sovereigns in my waistcoat pocket. If he went to Doncaster House, he was not a fellow to owe money to. Alban was out, but I met an appalling bounder who called himself Rivington Trench, a bloated old masher with a burgundy nose and a bounderish white bowler hat on the side of his head. He said he'd take any message for Alban, who he said was an intimate pal. I didn't feel inclined to hand him two sovs. I didn't feel inclined to slide round to the corner to a pub for a spot of B and S, either. Somebody might have seen us. I got out pretty quick. My opinion of young Alban went down about eight notches.

Two days later Georgie Mourne came up to me in White's, just before luncheon, and asked me to support a fellow he'd put up for membership.

"Who?" I naturally asked.

"I'm sure you know him. A most amusing, gifted chappie. Maurice Whitewater."

"The Viscount?"

"You do know him? You must know him. Everybody does."

"I've met him, of course."

"Fine."

"But I've only just met him. No more. I can't sign my name for a fellow I've only just met. Rules are quite clear on the point. Look at the book."

Georgie went on about it, to the point of becoming a bore. I got the definite impression he was having difficulty scraping up enough signatures for Whitewater. Also that he'd promised Whitewater to do this for him, as though he owed him some kind of debt. Nobody likes being prodded, so I got a little stuffy and told Georgie Mourne I couldn't support his candidate and that was that. I simply didn't know him well enough.

"It's no more than that? You just don't know him well enough?"

"That's what I've been trying to tell you for half an hour."

"You haven't got anything *against* the chappie?"

"No, no. Absolutely not. I don't know him well enough to have anything against him."

"You haven't heard anything *against* him?"

"I haven't heard anything about him, for or against."

"If you got to know him better you'd sign for him?"

"Yes, I daresay—"

"Damn it all, Henry, you said your single objection to signing for him was that you didn't know him."

"Yes, but—"

"Are you dining tonight?"

"At the Clanmangan's.

"That will be small and early. You'll want supper later."

This was quite true. The same thought had occurred to me. I was considering taking Gaby to Rule's, but there was a small financial question mark over that project. Gaby had come late to expensive menus, but her attitude to them had the passionate enthusiasm of the convert.

"Join us at the Carlton Grill at eleven," said Georgie.

I accepted at once. Though it was still April, there was a good chance of asparagus and a smaller one even of plovers' eggs.

"Maurice Whitewater will be with us," said Georgie. "You can have a proper long talk to him. Get to know him, my boy. Then sign for him if you want to. No obligations. No strings attached."

All this was perfectly proper, but I felt that Georgie was somehow taking unfair advantage of my good nature.

Supper didn't change my mind about Whitewater—about his face, or his cufflinks, or his conversation. He was an odd mixture—he might have been bred by my Uncle Algernon out of Lucinda Babraham, being as much like m'tutor at Eton as Uncle, and as much like a wasp with a damned sharp sting as Lucinda. He was a prosing, preaching fellow, leaking facts all over the supper table, and a really catty gossip. Some of his stories were pretty good. I daresay they were true. I had to laugh at some of them. But I didn't think he'd ever be a pal, and I still didn't like his taste in waistcoats.

Nothing was said about White's. Subject never mentioned. He knew better than *that*. But he did say one surprising thing. He said, "You enjoyed, as I myself did, your recent visit to Moreys, Clinton?"

"Yes, of course," I said.

"I promise myself, and have been promised, a speedy repetition. You, I imagine, would like to be asked again, too?"

"Well, naturally," I said. "They do you pretty well."

"And are pretty themselves. Yes, yes, many things draw one there. I am not *absolutely* sure if it is in Lady Bulbarrow's mind to ask you to stay again this season."

"Why do you say that?"

"It is something I thought you would be glad to hear. Sorry to hear, of course, but at least not afflicted by that unfulfilled hope which, if deferred, maketh the heart sick, as Scripture assures us."

"She's not going to ask me—How the deuce d'you know that?"

"She told me. But I am sure I can persuade her to change her mind. I will use my best efforts on your behalf to that end, if you wish. You have only to say the word."

"As a matter of fact I *would* like—I *did* expect—I know what's happened. That damned bully Gareth Fortescue has been up to some of his mischief. Or else it's the Carradines. It's not Sylvia. I'm sure of that."

"As to that," said Whitewater smoothly, "you know best, of course. The fact remains. But if you would like to go—"

"I damned well would, as a matter of fact."

"Say no more. The thing is done."

"Oh. Well, thanks! Anything I can do for you in return, of course—"

"I can think of nothing. Certainly nothing I would dream of mentioning to you."

"I can give you the winner of the Two Thousand Guineas. Certainty. Had it from the trainer himself."

"Of scant interest to me. The Chinese remark, in that regard, that they have known for three thousand years that one horse can run faster than another, and view with tolerant amazement our continued absorption in the same phenomenon. They are not quite sincere since, when given the opportunity, they gamble desperately."

That was the sort of stuff he kept talking.

It was Georgie Mourne who pointed out to me afterwards that what Whitewater wanted was my signature under his name in the Candidates' Book at White's.

"I don't know," I said.

"But you do want to go to Moreys, dear boy, eh?"

So I signed. What's a signature? It wasn't like signing a cheque.

I found a note from Sylvia Bulbarrow's secretary two days later asking me to Moreys at the beginning of May. Cufflinks notwithstanding, White-water could certainly deliver the goods.

As a result of all of which, here I was sitting beside Sylvia Bulbarrow on a white wrought-iron seat in the yew alley, the two of us all alone and out of sight of anybody.

I took her hand. She let me take it. She was wearing silk gloves, the colour of milky coffee; I felt her fingers through them. I thought, though I was not sure, that they slightly returned the pressure of mine.

I was nervous. I'm not ashamed to admit it. Some fellows become practically professionals at this sort of thing, but I was a beginner. Of course, nobody would have guessed it—nobody *did* guess it—from the way I looked and talked and dressed. But in point of actually hard fact, dear old Gaby was the extent of my real experience. For some reason it had never been a success with any others. I tried quite a few, ranging in price from ten shillings to a fiver. That fiver was a beautiful girl, a dancer, and I gave her supper in a private room at Rosa's. Oysters, cold ptarmigan, cham-pagne! But it was no good. I had to go back to Gaby. It only ever worked with Gaby.

I knew it would work with Sylvia, even though she was a bit younger than Gaby. She had the same glorious shape and the same warm smile. I was passionately keen to try.

I said, "You know you're the most beautiful woman in London—I mean Wiltshire. The most desirable and adorable."

"Thank you," she said. Her smile was amazing. She liked hearing what I was saying. I was finding the right note. I repeated the message a few times with variations. I put my arm round her waist. She stood up imme-diately, not smiling.

I understood. I saw that I'd excited her. She was struggling to control her feelings. There was no more we could do on an uncomfortable wrought-iron seat. The next stage was for later, somewhere more comfortable and more secret.

I was sure she'd be like Gaby—warm, welcoming, understanding. She'd know how to help a fellow, if she liked him enough, and it was obvious she liked me very much indeed.

She walked rather briskly out of the yew alley. I understood why. My own heart was pounding. I was visualizing her magnificent body under those elaborate clothes. I felt ill with excitement. My first lady—my first *affaire* with someone of my own caste. Gaby with a damned big difference. My Freddie grew and grew at the thought, and I had to put my hand in my pocket to hide it. It was embarrassing when we met a crowd of people at the end of the yew alley.

Sylvia was tired after luncheon. She said she was, and she looked it. It was all that gaiety in London. Another twenty-four hours would make the difference. I went for a stroll with Charley Arkwright down by the lake. He had a couple of two-year-olds in training at Stockbridge, and I wanted to know when they were off.

I realised somebody was following us. It was little Camilla, Sylvia's daughter, looking quite attractive, though without her mother's marvellous hips and bust. She was following me. Well, she obviously wasn't following old Charley Arkwright. She was hiding in a sort of shrubbery to watch me. It was interesting. I don't think anybody had ever followed me like that before. I pretended not to see her, because I didn't want to embarrass her; and anyway Charley hadn't finished telling me about his nags.

I supposed she had a sort of infatuation for me. It was amusing. I was quite pleased.

We got nabbed for croquet by Ysobel Garston and a boring old Serene Highness. It's a damned stupid game in my estimation, and Ysobel played it in a damned stupid way.

Little Camilla was watching me again. She was following me about like a puppy. She did look awfully pretty, though too thin. She got pulled into the game. The Grand Duchess thought she was lonely and bored, so she pulled her into the game as a treat. It was rather a mistake. Camilla wasn't much good at the game, but we let her win. Ysobel and Charley let her win, which was decent of them. It takes away the point of the game, though. If you don't play to win, why play? Anyway, there was no money involved.

I'd had enough of Camilla by tea time and managed to surround myself with a group of fellows. It was flattering having her making sheeps'-eyes at me (she did have pretty eyes, by the bye), but she was dull to talk to.

I was at the end of a pew in church on Sunday morning, right on the aisle. No plan, pure chance. Sylvia went by me on her way out, right by the pew where I was standing. Her hand brushed mine. It was obviously deliberate. She didn't look at me. It was the clearest invitation I ever had. It was damned exciting. I had to put my hand in my pocket to control my Freddie. Looks bad, in church, but a damned great bulge would have looked worse.

I managed to sit at the same table as Sylvia at luncheon. I had to do some pretty adroit work with the elbow, but I made it. Of course she was careful not to show how pleased she was, with everybody looking and listening. I tried to press her knee with mine, but she pulled it away. She had to, of course, or we would both have become too excited. I *did* become too excited, actually, and I had to hide my Freddie with my table napkin.

She went off upstairs straight away after luncheon. She told everybody she was exhausted. She didn't look at me, of course. But I'd been given my cue. I gave her five minutes, then slipped upstairs after her. I tiptoed along the corridor to her bedroom. I knew which her door was, though of course I'd never seen inside. I knocked. No answer. I tried the door. Locked.

At that moment, to my absolute disgust, that damned sleek bully Gareth Fortescue appeared from nowhere. His face was absolutely black with anger. He was a much bigger, more athletic kind of animal than me. I'm not ashamed to admit I was scared at the expression on his face.

He said, in that ugly parade-ground rasp of his, "What the devil do you think you're doing, you insolent young puppy? Lady Bulbarrow has already been disgusted enough by your impertinence. She's been kind to you out of respect for your father. I respect your father, too, but that won't stop me whipping the skin off your back."

I thought he was going to attack me physically, there and then. He was quite capable of that sort of thing. He'd thrashed fellows before. I turned and ran. It was all I could do. There's no cowardice in running away from a fellow twice your size.

I went downstairs and out of the house onto one of the terraces. I was absolutely shaking at the crudity and vulgarity of that scene. In a civilized age you don't expect to be brought up against raw violence. Fortescue was a savage. He had no business in a respectable house with gentle people. Of course a big, self-assured, conceited, hulking great lout of a man could chase me away. He was as strong as an ox. He could insult me, too; talk in a most offensive way, because I didn't have muscles like a stevedore.

I got angrier and angrier with Fortescue the more I thought about his behaviour. I was even angrier with Sylvia. She'd been absolutely treacherous. She'd played with me. She'd deliberately encouraged me to think she liked me when all she wanted was damned servile flattery—from a younger man, a popular man, a good-looking man, a Duke's son. All she wanted was another toady. Well, she'd picked the wrong man. So she'd damned well find out. She'd bitterly rue the day she treated me like that.

I wanted to call Gareth Fortescue out and shoot him, if we still did things like that. But Sylvia deserved worse.

I walked about in an absolute fever of rage. Nobody could humiliate me like that and get away with it.

After a time—I don't know how long—little Camilla came out of the house by a side door. She seemed to be in some sort of state—as much of a state as I was in myself. She was usually pale, but she had a high colour and her eyes were wide and bright as though she had the grippe, and her mouth was a bit open.

She was obsessed with me. She was putty in my hands. Right! I'd show Sylvia. I'd nail her brat, her precious ewe-lamb. It was no more than poetic justice. It was the most perfect punishment.

Camilla walked off, in a fair hurry, past the lake towards the wood on the other side. I followed her, going cautiously. She set a good pace. When she got to the wood I made a circuit, running like Hades. I stopped to get my breath and smooth my clothes and get my blandishing manner in trim, and then I popped round a tree and came face to face with her.

She was absolutely overwhelmed by suddenly seeing me. She was very transparent, really. She almost threw herself at me. I launched into ordinary evening-party social chat, flattery and drollery, the kind of thing I did every night of my life. The idea was to put her at her ease, and to put myself at my ease, too. She was awfully slow in her replies, but I reminded myself that she worshipped me. I began to mix in a bit more strictly personal stuff—how beautiful she was, her eyes and nose, etc., etc. When I touched her hand she nearly had a fit. It was very unlike taking the silk-gloved hand of Sylvia's.

I put my arms round her waist and kissed her. It wasn't actually a thing I'd ever done to anybody before. (The Gabys of this world don't expect it. Why should they?) It was pretty easy. I must say I was a bit shocked by

Camilla. She was a nicely brought-up girl, and she should have resisted or pushed me away, or at least pretended to. But nothing like that. Just melted into my arms. Her hair tickled my face so that I nearly sneezed. I took a real good double armful and hugged as tight as I could. I'd heard that was what they liked. It did seem to be the right prescription, because she put her arms round my neck. There was nothing much of her—just a slip of a little thing. I couldn't help wishing it was Gaby I'd got hold of.

I remembered that a fellow told me—Georgie Mourne, I think it was—that the way to kiss a girl passionately was to do it with your mouth open. I couldn't imagine such a thing being popular with Gaby, but I thought I might as well try it with Camilla. It did work. We had a sort of boxing match with our tongues. It was quite a nice sensation in a way, but my mouth began to get a bit wet which was uncomfortable.

She sort of pulled me down onto the ground. Luckily the ground was soft, but I wasn't too happy about my white flannel trousers. My man Cordle says green stains never really come out. It was definitely shocking, the way Camilla behaved. She was just as forward as the crudest of the ten-shilling girls I used to try. She sort of found my hand with her bust and made me feel it through her clothes. It felt much too small. I wasn't sure what I was supposed to do with a handful of bust. It didn't come into Gaby's scheme of things. I just sort of squeezed it. Camilla seemed to like that, so I took it I'd guessed right.

Now what Gaby always did at about that point was to put a hand in my trouser pocket and feel my Freddie. I didn't think I could ask Camilla to do that. All the same, it was what I wanted—a little bit of encouragement just then.

I nearly lost heart, actually, but the thought of Sylvia's treachery spurred me on. I kissed Camilla some more, getting my face tickled by all that hair, and talked a lot of rot about loving her. They like that.

Then I said I wanted to come to her bedroom. Of course I expected her to say no, and we'd have a long argument and I'd persuade her in the end. But she said yes, straight away! Just like that. She really was a shocking little puss. Hardly out of the schoolroom and as fast as a Gimcrack winner!

Since we were committed, I definitely wanted her to feel my Freddie. But I was a bit shy about that.

Well, I went to her bedroom half an hour later, having tidied up the appearance on the way.

I don't know what I'd expected, quite, but I hadn't expected her to be standing in the middle of a big sunny room, fully dressed, with a cross ex-

pression on her face. For one thing I'd have felt a lot happier in the dark.
It was always in the dark with Gaby. It's more proper in the dark, and nobody feels awkward. You can do things in the dark you'd never do in daylight. She'd half drawn the curtains, but everything was still going to be
damned visible.

Then those clothes. What Gaby did was to go out of the room and
come back ten minutes later in a peignoir. That was the usual form with
the girls I'd tried. It avoided awkwardness. Also it gave one time to take
one's own clothes off, hanging up the coat and trousers so they didn't get
creased or baggy. There's no point in going to an expensive tailor and then
throwing your clothes onto a chair.

Kissing seemed a logical first step, so I tried it. She pretty well pulled
me over to the bed and then sat me down and then lay down. We stayed
like that for a spell, hugging each other, while I wondered what to do
next. Her hair was tickling my face so much I really was in danger of
sneezing. I had to sit up. I had to get clear.

Lying on the bed was doing my jacket no good. They get baggy at the
elbows unless you're careful. So I took it off. I took off my collar and tie as
well. My collar was definitely too tight for acrobatics on a bed. I thought
we had both better take our shoes off. You don't want shoes on a bed, or
any other furniture. That's a thing I was taught and it's quite true. A
spoiled chit like Camilla might not worry about putting her shoes all over
the bedclothes, but it went against the grain with me.

She was wearing a tie, too, a floppy sort of affair of blue silk. I was
going to suggest that she take it off, but I found I was doing it for her. It
was the first time I'd ever touched a woman's clothes like that—actually
taken hold of something and undone it. She made a sort of objection, but
I knew she didn't mean it. I felt the whole thing was taking an awfully
long time. A few minutes was plenty for Gaby.

After I'd got rid of the tie, I unbuttoned the front of her blouse. That
was a business. I can't imagine why they make buttonholes too small for
the buttons. When I'd undone all the buttons I could reach, I was able to
sort of peel the blouse back off her shoulders. There were just straps, narrow pink straps, on her shoulders. Otherwise they were bare. I was a bit
affected by them—they were so tiny, like a bird's. I put my hands on
them. That was flesh, bare flesh. It ought to have stirred me more than it
did.

I kissed her legs when I pulled her stockings off. They were amazingly
slim—skinny, really. I don't know why I kissed them.

Her bust was about as I'd expected. I was used to Gaby's, of course, and

Camilla's was as different as could be. They had pink in the middle instead of brown. They were wrong in every way.

It was pretty disgusting that she should let me look at them, bare, in broad daylight.

Her squirrel didn't look much like Gaby's, either. I wondered if it was arranged in the same way.

I was very embarrassed when I had to take my own clothes off. Naturally I kept my back to her—matter of simple decency. No fellow wants his Freddie stared at. I expected Camilla to look away, but she lay and watched me—deliberately watched me! I was never so embarrassed in my life. Of course I lay on my front on the bed to hide my Freddie. But she actually forced me over onto my back! She was much stronger than she looked, stronger than me. Of course I covered it up by crossing my legs over it, but she forced them apart! She really was shocking. She made me lie on my back with my Freddie sticking up in the air! I was absolutely crimson with shame. And then she actually took hold of it and rubbed it! Of course Gaby always did that, but the great difference was that Gaby did it in the dark. I could feel her hand, sometimes both hands, but I couldn't see what she was doing, and above all she couldn't see. A fellow's Freddie is pretty private, in my opinion, and nobody ought to go peering at it.

One thing, though—my Freddie was behaving itself. It didn't just wither away as it sometimes did. Camilla seemed besotted by it. Well she might be. Gaby, who ought to know, said it was championship material on its day. Of course, Gaby had never seen it, only felt it. Gaby did the same thing Camilla was doing, rubbing it up and down. It's a nice feeling. It's what fellows do to themselves at school. Camilla knew what to do, just as Gaby did, and it was obvious that she'd done it before. Must have done. She was a proper little tart. Must have been. So damned shameless with it, rubbing my Freddie in full view, in broad daylight.

Suddenly I could take it no longer. It was simply too embarrassing. I rolled over onto my front to hide myself. I felt better like that. I kissed the girl on the mouth, the proper place. She had some other idea—God knew what—but I wasn't standing any nonsense. It doesn't seem to me decent, kissing girls all over their bodies. I'd gone a bit far, kissing her legs. That was just because they were so thin and pathetic. I felt sorry for them.

I squeezed her bust. I knew she wanted that. And they like you to pinch the lumps in the middle.

Time was getting on, and I didn't altogether trust my Freddie. It had let me down too damned often. So I pressed on. I got my forefinger into her squirrel. It was dry and clenched up, but I got it better. I knew what to do with that finger.

She said, "Hurry up," or words to that effect.

I was absolutely thunderstruck. The ten-shilling girls talk like that because they want to get on with the next customer. But this little Camilla! It was really startling.

Anyway I bucked up. I got on top of her. It was nothing like getting on top of dear old Gaby, which was like lying on a feather bed. This was like lying on top of a little bird, or even an insect, a dragonfly. I could hardly feel her bust against my chest. Gaby's is like two lovely pillows for a fellow to snuggle between.

Then that demented girl took hold of my Freddie and tried to jam it into her squirrel! It was a struggle, actually. The thing was too damned tight. It was uncomfortable. Things shouldn't be such an effort. Going into Gaby was like getting into a hot bath. With Camilla it was like pulling on a hunting boot on a cold morning.

I shoved in and out as I did with Gaby, and it got a bit easier. Of course I didn't look at her. I would have felt embarrassed if I had.

Then the worst happened, the thing I'd been dreading. I realised my Freddie was letting me down. It shrank to nothing in just a few seconds. I couldn't even keep it in. I couldn't do anything. I might have expected it, Camilla being so skinny and unlike Gaby. I thought it would be all right because of the satisfaction of nailing Sylvia's brat, but that wasn't enough to keep my Freddie in business.

I just had to get off the bed and put my clothes on and leave. I don't know what I said. She'd turned her face away from me in contempt. I saw her shoulders shaking. I realised she was laughing.

So the damned family had humiliated me a second time.

6 ❋ *The pleasant fountains*

"Fondling," she saith, "since I have hemmed thee here
Within the circuit of this ivory pale,
I'll be a park, and thou shalt be my deer;
Feed where thou wilt, in mountain or in dale:
Graze on my lips, and if those hills be dry,
Stray lower, where the pleasant lie."

VENUS AND ADONIS

"Henry!" called Charley Arkwright. "Just the fellow we're looking for. Come and make up a four."

"Bridge?" I asked.

"Tennis, you owl. They've strung a net on one of the lawns and painted the lines, and the terriers are there to retrieve the balls you miss."

But I said I'd sprained my wrist, and escaped into the house. I didn't want to see people, any people, after what Camilla had done to me. I didn't want any people to see me. I just wanted to lie in a corner and lick my wounds. That's what it came to.

Besides, lawn tennis is a stupid game, in my opinion. So is the royal game, and so is racquets. Fellows think they're marvels just because they can hit a ball with a sort of spoon, and call you a rabbit if you miss. Women are worse. A good "eye" for ballgames is a pretty bounderish thing to have, as a matter of fact. Fellows who haven't got anything better to boast about ought to keep quiet.

I went all the way up to my room, the same rotten little room. I took off my coat and my collar and tie and my shoes, and lay on my bed. It wasn't what I wanted to do. I didn't know what I wanted to do. I wanted to blow up Moreys, and roast Sylvia and Camilla and Gareth Fortescue over a slow fire. I wanted Gaby.

I didn't want to face them all at tea. I could have done with a drink. I was at a pretty low ebb. The room began to get dark. Soon Cordle would come bounding in and it would be time to dress. I didn't think I could face them all at dinner.

There was a knock at the door.

"Cordle?" I sang out.

A housemaid came in. I couldn't see her very well in the half darkness. She did a sort of bow. It was meant to be a curtsey, but she hadn't been well taught.

She said, "Mr. Cordle's been took ill, sir—my lord."

"Oh?" I said. "What's the matter with him?"

"He did say as how he ate something that didn't agree, my lord, at noon in the housekeeper's room. It give him a fierce pain, he did say."

"I'm sorry," I said, actually a bit annoyed.

"So I come to draw the curtains and such," said the housemaid, "seeing there isn't a footman free."

She drew the curtains and then lit the lamp on the writing table. I was able to get a look at her. She was a peacherino! A very sweet round face, a little rosebud of a mouth, bright eyes, a small waist but a voluptuous figure above and below. She was about twenty, I judged.

It suddenly struck me that she was a younger Gaby. She looked as Gaby must have looked at the same age. But instead of Cockney she had a soft Wiltshire voice, like clotted cream.

The beginnings of an absolutely fantastic idea jumped into my head.

"It's an ill wind," I said. "I'm sorry about Cordle, of course, but it's very nice for me to have a beautiful girl like you drawing my curtains."

She smiled. I thought she blushed, but it was difficult to be sure in the lamplight. Her smile was very broad and sweet. She was the deuce of a lovely girl, especially when she smiled. There was something comforting in that smile. It may sound ridiculous, since she was so young, but there was something motherly in that smile.

I gave her some of the chat a fellow uses for barmaids in London. It's a pretty direct species of *badinage*, with a lot of heavy personal compliment. It just came out automatically, with no difficulties or hesitations. I'd never made advances to a housemaid before, but I judged they'd take the same piano-roll as barmaids and shop girls.

It worked even better and quicker than it usually did. Of course she'd never been subjected to really expert chat before—only the mouthings of a lot of peasants. It was a new experience for her, and she lapped it up. She giggled, and her smile grew broader and broader. She really was a peacherino, and she was damned friendly, too.

"What is your beautiful name, you luscious little sugarplum?" I said.

I know it reads like a damned silly way to talk, but I knew it was what barmaids and shop girls liked, and it was obviously what housemaids liked, too.

"Emily Brown, my lord," she said.

"Do they call you Emmy?"

"Them as I permits."

"You'll permit me, won't you Emmy, you adorable creature?"

It was exactly what I'd said to dozens of barmaids, and I got exactly the same reply.

"Oooh! Well, I can't say no to gentlemen like you."

"Then give us a kiss."

"My gracious, no!"

"Just a little one."

"Ooh, sir! You're taking advantage of a poor girl."

She pretended to be shocked and frightened, but the smile never left her face.

I kissed her. She didn't exactly respond, but she didn't scream or faint.

I felt like King Cophetua with the beggar maid. I kept my arm round her little waist and kissed her a few times. Her bust was wonderful. When I pulled her towards me, I felt it like a pillow through my shirt front. It was more exciting because I wasn't wearing a coat or shoes or a collar and tie.

"I'm ever so confused," she said. "I'm all atremble."

"I'll kiss the place and make it better," I said, suiting the action to the word.

Well, I conquered her. It was a glorious victory. I vanquished her fears, abolished her doubts, routed her scruples. It was, I fancy, partly my line in masterful London talk, partly the manly ardour of my advances. The two together crumbled her defences. Poor little helpless thing!

I could feel my Freddie growing and growing until it was quite uncomfortable against my trousers. Her hand accidentally brushed against it.

"Ooh, sir!" she quavered.

And then her hand was driven back, by some force stronger than herself, to feel it! Had she but known, it was just what Gaby would have done. Emmy felt it, with little frightened fingers, through my trousers. Of course I couldn't see what she was doing, as I had my arms round her.

That gentle, nervous, kneading of my Freddie was just what I needed. I was rampant then! I leaped to the door and locked it. I leaped to the lamp and blew it out.

Clothes tumbled. It wasn't at all awkward, being in the pitch dark. I didn't even hang my trousers up. Almost before I knew it we were together on the bed. It was pitch dark! I felt her body with my hands. Her bust and hips were big and soft and sweet. I lay between her breasts, snuggled up and comfy.

I felt her little fingers on my stomach and on my thighs—and then they fluttered to my Freddie! Oh, it was nice. Even Gaby never fondled it so gently. She rubbed and caressed it. I lay on my back, my legs apart, while she played and played with my Freddie. Up and down she rubbed, ever so gently, while her other hand fondled my cobnuts. I began to feel that marvellous urgent proper throbbing desire which I didn't experience so terribly often. I wasn't embarrassed, because it was dark. Besides, Emmy was only a housemaid. That made a difference too. The feeling in my Freddie grew and grew, gradually, inexorably. I became gloriously certain that it was not going to let me down, that it was going to work!

"Is that nice, dear?" the girl murmured.

"Yes! Yes! More!"

"And it's going to be a good boy for Emmy?"

"Yes! Any second now!"

"I thought so. There's a love."

I felt her in the dark roll over onto her back. She pulled me between her wonderful great legs and down onto her imperial bust. All the time she was still rubbing my Freddie. She never let go of it. The feeling there was mounting and mounting. The explosion was coming. I was sure of it.

She slid my Freddie into her squirrel. I nearly cried out! It was like a sponge with a hole in it, hot and wet and soft. It was amazing!

She pulled me in, all the way, right up to the base of my Freddie. Then she pushed me out again, until only the tip was inside her. Somehow she gripped that. She had muscles I'd never heard of. The sensation was electrifying. Most of my Freddie being outside, she began to rub it again with her fingers. It was wet now. I could feel the wetness of her fingers on it. She rubbed up and down, up and down, slowly and fast. It was her fingers that mattered, not the squirrel. Up and down they went, sliding and slipping, and the feeling grew and grew and grew and it happened!

I felt it jerk, with a sort of explosion of sensation, and I felt the all-too-rare gush of my manly juice.

She sighed and sobbed and pulled me deep into her. I'd done it. I'd won. I felt like a king. My Freddie felt as hot as a flambé banana.

"Good boy," she whispered worshipfully. "What a lovely boy. What a big, clever, *fierce* boy."

After a time we pulled apart. One does get restless. She handed me a towel from somewhere. I suppose she got that idea from being a house-maid. I gave my wet Freddie a rub, gently, because I was proud of it. We pulled our clothes on in the dark. It's better that way—not so awkward.

At last she lit the lamp again and smiled reverently at me.

"Ooh sir, ooh my lord!"

"Thank you very much, Nelly," I said.

"Emmy."

"I mean Emmy. I'd like to give you a little present."

"Thank you, my lord. Three pounds, if it's convenient."

Well, it wasn't, but I didn't really grudge it. Really I didn't. She was awfully like Gaby. But she was prettier than Gaby and twenty years younger. Gaby's a good sort, but she has her faults. She likes tripe-and-onions, and they do linger on her breath. She likes shouting matches with the waiters at Rule's. Her waist's thickening and she has spots on her back. Emmy had the same shape and the same warmth, and she most evidently worshipped me. She was better by far than any other young girl I'd tried. She knew how to help a fellow, but without being embarrassing. I'd conquered her with words and deeds, and crowned my victory! Three pounds was a bit inconvenient, but I didn't grudge it.

So a day that started badly ended beautifully. Triumph emerged from catastrophe. It shows what a bit of character will do. Of course, I had an ancestor at Agincourt.

What it came to, I decided as I dressed, was that some fellows were hard to please, selective, fastidious. To be able to explode into any little drab—that's nothing to be proud of. Quite the reverse. It's something to be ashamed of, actually, although to hear fellows talk you'd scarcely think so.

That night, very late that night, I lay awake thinking of Emmy. What a little peacherino, even at three sovereigns! Frankly, I'd more or less despaired of bringing it off with any young girl, owing to being fastidious and so forth. Emmy, all innocence, had unwittingly opened my eyes to my own powers.

My Freddie stirred against the sheets as I remembered those fingers in the darkness.

I wanted Emmy again, soon and often, even at three sovs.

Back in town I was still thinking of her.

I called round to see Gaby, but her niece said she was away. She'd gone to stay with her auntie in Worthing, the one who kept a boarding house near the station. The auntie had heart trouble, and Gaby was looking after her.

I thought of Emmy more and more, especially without Gaby to distract me. I was literally itching for her. Every time I thought of her fingers in the dark, slipping and sliding over the wet skin, my Freddie would start to grow. Right in the middle of big parties! I don't think anybody noticed, but once it was a damned close thing. I had a glass of champagne in one hand and a plate of curried prawns in the other, and there was nowhere to put either of them down, and I *had* to put my hand in my pocket to hide the bulge of my Freddie. It was a damned mortifying moment. All because I suddenly thought of those little fingers of Emmy's. For no reason, out of the blue!

So I did an unheard of thing. I slid down to Wiltshire by train on the Wednesday and got a station fly to take me to the nearest of the villages—Moreys Episcopi, they called it—and took a room at a pub called the Glyn Arms. Used an assumed name, of course. Called myself Mr. James Smith. Send Cordle with a message to the Servants' Hall at Moreys. What he thought I didn't enquire—I just buttoned his lip with a piece of gold.

So Emmy came to the pub, and came to my bedroom at the pub. It was sovereigns all round—Cordle, the landlord, the chambermaid, the boots, to say nothing of Emmy's three. Worth it! I'd hoped it would be exactly the same, and it was exactly the same. It was all either of us wanted, Emmy and I. It was heaven on earth. I felt ten foot tall.

All the way back to town in the rain next morning, my Freddie was itching and straining at my trousers. Luckily I had a newspaper to hide the bulge. Of course, it was partly the vibration of the train.

My Governor emerged from Northamptonshire because he wanted to bore the House of Lords on the subject of education. He was very hot on education, not realising the sort of things fellows learn at school these days. He summoned me to the presence, and he was pretty ferocious on the subject of my going to Vienna.

He'd been talking in Northamptonshire to somebody from Newmarket who'd heard about my little spot of bother with young Bertie Carradine. Highly unfortunate. He thought it was an extra reason for me to go to Vienna. I couldn't make him see that it was a damned good reason not to go.

Things were a little sticky in London. Invitations by no means dried up, but they came in a reduced flood. I held my head as high as I damned well could, and when some fellows hinted that I ought to resign from White's, I told them to go and boil their fat heads.

I saw Sylvia Bulbarrow, but not to talk to. I decided that she was getting a bit old to go about being a celebrated society beauty. Mutton dressed as lamb, even by Worth. Give me a country girl of twenty, I thought, who doesn't have to powder her neck and who never even heard of the damned Carradines.

On which subject, Emmy was properly under my skin, as the Americans say. I thought about her a devil of a lot. Gaby was still away. I thought of going down to Worthing, but where I wanted to go was Wiltshire. I went on the Saturday and the Wednesday and the following Sunday, the middle of May.

What I liked about her, among many other things, was her directness. There was no fiddle-faddle of the kind that creates awkwardness. As soon as she came into the bedroom in the pub, I knew why she was there and *she* knew why she was there and a fellow didn't get embarrassed. We'd lock the door and draw the curtains before we did anything else. Then I'd hug her a bit and she'd renew acquaintance with my Freddie. She picked up the trick of putting her hand in my pocket. The point of that was, the stuff a pocket's made of is much thinner than the stuff trousers are made of. She could feel it better through the thin stuff, and I could feel her feeling it. She liked that as much as I did.

She asked me for my address in London—just in case, she said, she ever wanted to go there.

"'Cos I knows you'll help me, dear, if ever I needs un," she murmured, while her fingers were busy in my pocket.

Much as I adored my little Emmy, I was hardly going to have her turning up on the doorstep of White's, let alone the family mausoleum in

Belgrave Square. I tried to think of a fellow I could trust, really trust. It wasn't straight away easy. There were plenty who were kind-hearted but couldn't keep their mouths shut, and there were plenty who could keep their mouths shut but weren't kind-hearted.

Suddenly I thought of young Matthew Alban. I didn't know him well, but somehow it was transparently obvious that one *could* trust him. He was the only one I could think of. That was remarkable, really, considering I was on nodding terms with everybody who was anybody in England and intimately friendly with hundreds of fellows born and bred in the purple. But so it was. I gave Emmy the number of Alban's diggings in Jermyn Street. She took her hand out of my pocket to write the address down.

On the Sunday, Cordle took off with my message as usual. But he came back saying Emmy couldn't get away. There was a very big party at Moreys, and the vassals were at full stretch. I felt quite shattered with disappointment. But things weren't quite as bad as they seemed. She *could* slink out for an hour at three o'clock in the afternoon. She'd meet me in the boathouse by the lake.

"The young person says it'll be quiet, my lord," said Cordle with a wooden expression, "the boating season not having properly commenced. There's boats of all descriptions—to wit, skiffs, punts and such, complete with cushions. I am repeating the young person's remarks, my lord. You can advance on the boathouse from the beech wood, my lord, out of observation of the windows of the castle, there being stands of timber placed appropriate."

It sounded all right—not perfect, but all right. It was better to meet Emmy in a boathouse than not to meet her at all. It would have been appalling to come all the way to Wiltshire and not see her. A ghastly waste of time and money, and a bitter disappointment. I wanted her badly. I needed her in regular doses, minimum twice a week, especially the way people were acting to me in London.

I borrowed a bicycle from the landlord of the pub and wobbled off towards Moreys. I hated the damned thing. It wasn't at all safe. But it was too far to walk from the village, at least in my new brown and white shoes from Tricker. There wasn't a cab or a carriage to be had in that dead little hamlet on a Sunday afternoon. There was a car, but that would have drawn too much attention to my arrival. Besides, what would I say to the chauffeur and where would he wait? The bicycle was the thing, but I hated it. They're not sensibly designed, in my opinion. They ought to have four wheels instead of two.

I toiled all the way to the west lodge of Moreys park, then up the drive to the beech wood. I hid the bicycle in a clump of young bracken and prowled cautiously through the wood. People might be walking there. Camilla walked there. The thought of meeting her was absolutely odious.

I made it safely to the far side of the wood. I took a look at my watch and saw I was a bit late. It was nearly half past three. I was aghast at the thought that Emmy might have waited for me, lost heart, and disappeared back into the house.

I came cautiously out of the wood, crawling like a fellow in a battle. There were trees between the boathouse and the castle, so I was out of sight of any windows. I could just see a lot of roof. There was nobody about. I legged it to the boathouse, praying that Emmy was still there, praying that nothing had stopped her coming.

The boathouse had a big door on the water side so that fellows could push boats out into the water, and a smaller door on the land side. The big door was shut, but the small door was open. I was overjoyed. It was open because someone had gone in—because Emmy had gone in. I tiptoed in. I couldn't see anything. You turned a kind of corner and there was a kind of canvas curtain over an arch. Inside that it was pitch dark. There was a smell of varnish and paint. I was nonplussed for a moment. I didn't dare sing out for Emmy, just in case somebody else was there, a boatman or a carpenter.

There was somebody there. It was a woman. She was weeping. I heard the sobs and sniffles. It was Emmy. She'd thought I wasn't coming. She was heartbroken. I opened my mouth to sing out the glad news, when—just the split second before I called—there was a man's voice.

"I had an idea you might show a visible reaction to my remarks," said the man. "That was why I suggested that we conduct out *pourparlers* in the seclusion of this edifice."

I knew the voice and I knew that prosy, preachy manner. Only one fellow talked like that. It was Whitewater.

I couldn't imagine why he'd made her cry. I'd never seen her cry. I was mad with anger. I opened my mouth to swear at the fellow, but just before I did so the woman answered.

"You can't have that," she sobbed. "It's not something I can give you. It's all wrong. Surely you see that."

I nearly fell through the floor of the boathouse. That was not Emmy's voice. It was Sylvia Bulbarrow.

I'd never seen her weep, either, or speak in any kind of emotional voice. She was usually so calm, supremely assured; sometimes she was laughing. It was extraordinary to hear her sounding so muffled, so wretched. It was totally unlike her. It was somehow disgusting.

"I predicted that response," said Whitewater, "though I can scarcely pretend to be flattered by it. But I am sure I can persuade you to change your mind."

"Never!" choked Sylvia.

"Oh yes. I am a man of many attainments, though I risk sounding vainglorious when I say so. Of all my accomplishments, that for which, perhaps, I am most remarkable is my ability to persuade people to change their minds."

"Not mine!"

"No? Bear with me a little further, then. I will endeavour to convince you by selected examples. I was, until last year, existing obscurely and penuriously as plain Mr. Watkinson, sustained in a remote place by a niggardly remittance from my second cousin Alfred Watkinson. He wished to be relieved of the embarrassment of my presence in London. He was himself heir to another cousin, the late Lord Whitewater. He stood, in fact, between me and that inheritance. I was concerned to change my cousin Alfred's mind on a number of issues, not least his perverse determination to go on living and to inherit, in the fullness of time, our noble relative's title and wealth."

"You—"

"I did not kill him, if that is the unworthy thought that has entered your mind. I did not touch him. I did not even meet him. There was no need. I simply wrote to him. I should explain that, while in Alexandria, I had become friendly with a widow, a lady whose principal attributes were Greek ancestry, Egyptian residence, and American dollars. I persuaded her to supply me with a quantity of the latter. That, also, is a tribute to my powers of argument; but I will not risk offending you by elaborating the details of my methods. Suffice it that they were effective. Thus financed, I was able to undertake some not inexpensive research. I have, as you know, conducted research into a number of fields of scholarship. On this occasion, my field was the *vie intime* of my cousin Alfred. I knew I should turn something up. One always does. I discovered that Alfred had once had an intimate relationship with—I really blush to reveal this episode—an Italian choirboy. I found that choirboy, latterly a grocer in Milan, and secured from him a written account of the affair. He was understandably reluctant to provide this document, but once again my powers of persuasion were successfully invoked. Thus armed, I wrote to my ill-judging cousin Alfred, mentioning a number of means of giving the widest publicity to my little discovery."

"You—"

"I beg you not to use whatever distressful word is bubbling to your lips, dear Lady Bulbarrow. Let us keep our conversation on a civilized plane. My cousin Alfred, in defiance of the teachings of Scripture, saw fit to blow his brains out, using, not that it matters, an army revolver. The Inquest declared that it was an accident, and the tragedy received little publicity. My noble cousin the Viscount shortly afterwards obliged me by himself dying. He was quite an elderly man, in indifferent health. I am not in a position to say whether this melancholy event was accelerated by the sudden and tragic accident to his kinsman."

"You can't—I won't—"

"You require more evidence? You shall have it. A half-wit called Mourne, doubtless known to you, showed a lamentable and inexplicable reluctance to perform a trifling service for me. To propose me, in a word, for membership of his club. I knew that Mourne's sister had committed an indiscretion when only twenty, and had spent as a result a period in a Swiss hospital. The child is now at school in Lausanne. My knowledge of this circumstance was what induced me to select Mourne as my sponsor for White's. He was quite amenable, once the thing had been put to him squarely."

Sylvia tried to say something, but through her sobs it was impossible to make out.

"That depressing young ninny Henry Clinton," Whitewater went on, "showed a silly reluctance to support my candidature. I bought his change of heart by the simple agency of a promise that he should be invited to your house. Sir Gareth Fortescue persuaded you to invite Clinton, did not he? And also to invite myself, the second time? We both know that he did, dear Lady Bulbarrow, but I doubt if you know why. The solution, to be brutally simple about it, is that I know about him and—yourself. Of course many people in our circle are aware of whispers, nudges, suspicions. I was early apprised of a theory as to the state of affairs—no more than a theory—by that well-informed source Lady Babraham. I set myself to turn supposition into certainty and to acquire evidence that would make the truth believed in a court of law or out of it. That I have done."

Sylvia gave a sort of despairing wail. I felt really and truly sorry for her.

"I would not have had the crudity to face you personally with this," Lord Whitewater went on with a sort of disgusting cheerfulness. "I would have continued to employ my lever, so to phrase it, on your friend. But my new project, which I may say is very dear to my heart, requires *your* consent. Indeed, your active assistance. On that, given all the circumstances, I feel sure I can rely."

"Never! I—I couldn't—"

"It is your amiable habit to address the—How can I put this with a proper delicacy?—to address an interesting part of Sir Gareth's anatomy as juggernaut, juggins, jug-jug, and similar endearments, while suiting, if I may so express myself, actions to those words. Come, come, Lady Bulbarrow, do you want the whole world to know that? The king? The whole of London society? The readers of the popular press? Your own servants? Really, you had better do as I ask. As I say, I have set my heart on this project. My affections are seriously engaged. Please let us have no more nonsense."

"All—All right—You devil," muttered Sylvia. She could hardly get the words out through her sobs.

"Good! Good!"

"It will—take time. I can't—overnight—"

"The end of the year. The announcement must be made by the thirty-first of December in this year of Grace, 1906. Agreed? Yes, to be sure; of course it is agreed. I knew we should come to a comfortable understanding."

I never did see Emmy.

7 ❀ *The heavenly moisture*

Till, breathless, he disjoin'd, and backward drew
The heavenly moisture, that sweet coral mouth,
Whose precious taste her thirsty lips well knew,
Whereon they surfeit, yet complain of drouth,
He with her plenty press'd, she faint with dearth,
Their lips together glued, fall to the earth.

VENUS AND ADONIS

"Emily! Emily Brown!" called Mrs. Collis the Housekeeper.

"Yes'm," I said, wondering what I had done wrong.

"You're to be her ladyship's personal lady's-maid. There! I'll be bound, that's a shock."

"Lady Bulbarrow's?" I gasped. It was a shock and no mistake. I nearly spilled the broth in the cheesecloth, as Bert says.

"No, you silly girl. Of course not. The idea! You're to be Lady Camilla's maid. Isn't that nice, now? It's a great honour for you. I said you're too young and green altogether, though a willing worker and nice enough mannered when you've a mind. But her ladyship insisted. Asked for you particularly. There now!"

I was pleased as could be, ever so proud.

I'd come to Moreys from the village four years earlier when I was sixteen. I secured the position because my Uncle Cyril Maiden had been head gardener. I started as an underhousemaid at nine pounds a year, but I went up the ladder quick, so to say, and I was a full housemaid at nineteen—twenty pounds a year, not carrying coals or doing the heavy scrubbing, eating in the stillroom, not so much as deigning to pass remarks with the poor little scullery maids.

Now this! A full-fledged lady's-maid! Tea in the Housekeeper's Room, supper in the Steward's Room, taken in by a visiting gentleman's gentleman! Lady Camilla's castoffs, too, only they wouldn't be much good to me, me having grown into a fine figure of a girl. That's what they called me, Bert and the others. A fine figure of a girl.

Of course my being Uncle Cyril's niece must have helped. Everything worked on a sort of family system.

I fell on my feet, not half! There wasn't much to do. Little Millie didn't need her own maid, truth to tell—just a pair of hands to iron and stitch and brush her hair. She didn't need help dressing or undressing, or want it. Compared to the life Miss Prior had, I was on velvet. Miss Prior was her ladyship's maid, and she had a time of it. All the lady's-maids had to wait up till their ladies came to bed, which might be one or two or later. How they all stayed awake I never did understand. Miss Prior once told me she jabbed herself with a hatpin to stop herself falling asleep in front of her ladyship's fire. Fancy if she'd been found asleep in her ladyship's bedroom when her ladyship came to bed! There'd of been a row like you never. She'd of been out of her place in a minute, even after twelve years. I was never troubled by any risk like that. My little Millie was always tucked up by ten.

I grew quite fond of her. She was a pretty little thing, only for being so skinny. It wasn't that she was backward, so to say, in the manner of growing up. It was having such very small bones. I didn't see how her ankles could support her, light as she was, or her shoulders take the weight of her head. Her eyes was the biggest thing about her. "Dainty" was a word you could use of her.

Her manner was gentle, mostly, and she was considerate when she'd a mind. She had a temper, though. She'd been a pickle as a tiny, so I'd heard tell, but by the time I was there she was more on the moony side. Dreamy. A lot of young ladies are like that, as they said in the Housekeeper's Room. Never me, to speak about, except at one period. I was more the active sort, a bundle of energy and looking for ways to improve myself.

I got an inkling what she was mooning about from the questions she started asking. But I wasn't going to divulge. Word gets round below stairs like you'd hardly believe. If mention reached Miss Prior or Mrs. Collis— Being Uncle Cyril's niece wouldn't have helped me then. Very, very strict, our life was. Punctual to the button, dressed just so, and behaviour correct as a gravestone.

It was unfair, really, when you think about her ladyship and that Sir Gareth. He was a fine strong gentleman, no doubt of that, and he'd funny like a bull. The other girls and me, we all agreed he'd funny like a bull, them as cared to discuss such matters when Mrs. Collis wasn't by. And it would have been a shame, her ladyship going to waste. But there was one rule for the rich and one for the poor, or so they thought.

Of course, myself, I started too young probably, and got a taste for it I never did lose. It was funny how I began. I was only thirteen, but already a proper little woman. Everybody said so, including Uncle Cyril. It was the way he looked at me made me realise it was true. My titties grew and grew, like vegetable marrows when they still have the flowers at the end. Great big lumps they were, but with flowers at the front. I did love them! And my welcome mat was like the horsehair stuffing when Uncle Cyril split the cushion in the parlour. It was that rich and thick! It all came on me sudden. In the winter I was still a little girl, seemingly, with a child's body huddled in a great parcel of itchy clothes. Then came the spring and then the summer, and I wore a cotton dress with bare arms, and I felt the wind on my arms and up my legs, and my titties pushed out the front of the dress; and my welcome mat, I do truly declare, pushed out the front of my dress, too, when the wind blew just so to press the cotton stuff against me. Of course, being only thirteen, and in the fiery heat of the summer, I didn't wear much under.

I seemed to feel the cotton stroking my titties and my hips and I seemed to feel the breeze and the heat giving me a sort of kiss, like, all over my skin. I was moony enough, then! That was time I was really a moony one. I never did a stroke in the cottage or the garden, or went for a walk or opened a library book, but mooned about all the time, thinking what come to my body.

Of course I knew what it was all for, so to say, being brought up as I was all among the labouring men and the animals and such.

One afternoon in August I took a message from Uncle Cyril to General Mauney. He was a fine gentleman, was General Mauney, but put out to grass long since. It was only half a mile to the General's, going over the fields behind the village. I mooned along, going gradual. The sun was hot, but there was a nice little breeze, just to stir the air. The heat and the breeze and my cottons, they felt almost like hands on my skin. It came into my mind they was hands. I seemed to feel hands, ever so gentle, stroking at my skin, at my titties and all up my legs. No wonder I was moony.

General Mauney was away for the day, but I saw Corporal Jewkes. Corporal Jewkes had looked after the General for ever so long, when they were both in the army and ever since. He polished the General's boots like you never saw. He was an even finer gentleman than the General, to my way of thinking, and a good sight younger. He was still upright and very strong, and there wasn't much grey in his hair or in his whiskers. He had fine big whiskers. He was every inch a soldier, was Corporal Jewkes, and every inch a gentleman. He'd always been kind to me, a special friend, with a pat on my head or my seat when I was a tiny, and chocolates or pieces of cake when I went with a message. He often kissed me when I was a tiny. I liked the tickle of his whiskers.

I give the message to Corporal Jewkes and he asked me in for some barley water. There was nobody about. The servants were all off for the day, excepting Corporal Jewkes. He wasn't really a servant, to my understanding, but more like an assistant.

I followed Corporal Jewkes into the kitchen. The air was warm but moving with the breeze from the open window. I stood in a sort of dream, looking at the little short hairs on the back of Corporal Jewkes's neck while he poured out the barley water. He turned and put the glass on the table and stood looking at me. I was like asleep, like in a trance.

"So little Emmy's big Emmy now," said Corporal Jewkes, "and as lovely as a band of military music. I used to kiss little Emmy whenever I saw her. Shall I kiss big Emmy?"

He marched across the room and puts his arms round my waist and kissed me. There I still stood like a dummy. He kissed me on the mouth, which he never done before. His whiskers tickled fierce. I liked that. All the while the heat and the breeze and my clothes was stroking at my skin, like hands. All the afternoon they'd been doing that, and all the summer they'd been doing that. It was like they was getting me ready for hands, for real hands, smoothing me and stroking me nice, so my skin would be ready for the real hands when they come.

So it wasn't any shock, nor even any surprise, when the real hands did begin stroking me. He was gentle. He stroked right inside my clothes, under my skirt and up my legs, under my drawers, over my titties, over the flowers in the middle.

I stood like a dummy with my arms round his neck, giving myself up to the lovely feelings.

We heard voices. The maids were coming back. All in a dream I drank up the barley water and walked home across the fields.

I saw Corporal Jewkes constant after that. There was lots of places where we could go to be private—barns full of the new hay, byres when the cows was out. Nobody saw us or guessed. Nobody went keeping an eye on Corporal Jewkes, of course, and I was just judged to be a moony.

He gave me a bob every time. A silver shilling! He was a real gentleman.

He kissed and he stroked me. Half a dozen times we met, and it was no more than that. It wasn't wicked. There wasn't nothing wicked about it. It was lovely. His strokings got more personal.

Then he took off my clothes. I didn't stop him and I didn't help him, but just stood in a dream in the warm air.

"By God," he said, "I'd like to. I'd give my pension to. But I reckon I'm too old."

"No," I said, my voice coming out of my dream.

He tried, but it wasn't no good.

"I am too old," he said in a misery.

"No," I said.

I remembered what cousin Tommy Maiden once showed me, when I was a tiny and he was fifteen. He rubbed his old rod up and down, and the cream, she jumped out like cake icing. I tried it on Corporal Jewkes.

"No, no," he says sharply. "Not in the daylight. It's not decent."

He was a gentleman, truly.

So another time we tried that in the darkness. That made it decent, said Corporal Jewkes. He kept a hand on my welcome mat, stroking and stroking gentle, and I kept a-stroking at his rod. He begun to shudder, and he give a sort of sob, and I felt the cream on my fingers.

We tried it proper again, next time in a hay loft, but it wasn't no good.

Then he fixed on a dodge he said might answer. He kept just the top of his rod inside of me (I was lovely and ready for him, after his stroking) and I made to hold onto it, just gripping with muscles I got there. I knew about those muscles from gripping at his finger other times. I rubbed the rest of it with my hand, the part he hadn't put in.

That did answer. And just as it answered, he pushed deep inside me. It was lovely. I never dreamed of anything so lovely. I was proud and happy because I give him that joy.

I tried it with others after that, different lads in the village. I didn't like it half as well. The cream come jumping out almost before they was inside me, so I didn't have time for my own joys. It was all in a scurry with the lads, like little dogs in the yard. My fancy was for doing it slow.

It was always best with Corporal Jewkes. I was proud and happy to give him his joys even when I didn't reach my own. I always had a present after. I kept the money saved in a sock behind the loose brick in our garden tool shed.

Then at sixteen I went to Moreys, and very pleased with the position. But you had to be ever so careful there, with the strictness and the whispers flying round.

That was why I wasn't going to tell Millie about Corporal Jewkes, or the village lads, or Bert and the others in the house. It was more than my place was worth, even to hint. I was sorry for her, though. She was brought up that protected she didn't know a tittie from a turnip. No wonder she was moony.

She began to get books from the library, naughty books, to learn that way. Where they kept them I never knew. I looked at them but I couldn't make head or tail. They were all in foreign countries in the olden days, and seemingly they managed things different.

She found a new one, in a blue cover, in the middle of April when there was a big house party. It wasn't any better than the rest. She kept it hid under her dolls in what they called the schoolroom. She didn't play with her dolls any more and she didn't have lessons any more. But nothing hadn't come to take their place. She had nothing to do but moon.

Being a big house party, we were a crowd in the Housekeeper's Room before dinner, all the visiting valets and lady's-maids. I wore my best dark blue with the brooch Uncle Cyril gave me. We was very formal and elegant. Mr. Hedges the butler gave his arm to Her Serene Highness, of course, she taking precedence of all the ladies; and the Earl of Clanmangan gave his arm to Mrs. Collis, he taking precedence amongst the gentlemen. Being the daughter of a Marquess, I was taken in to dinner by the younger son of a Duke, Lord Henry Clinton it was. His other name was Mr. Cordle, but of course we didn't take account. It was always "Lord Henry" and "Lady Camilla" and we took precedence according.

There was two Viscounts making a confusion, Lord Whitewater and Lord Claygate. Mrs. Collis looked them both up in *Debrett's Peerage*. There was always a *Debrett* in the Housekeeper's Room in case of such confusions. Lord Whitewater's title was the earlier creation, which give him precedence over Lord Claygate.

"And how was Newmarket, Lord Henry?" asked Mr. Hedges. Mr. Hedges was very interested in the horses. Mr. Mallinson, the head coachman, used to make a book on the big races. I used to have sixpence on my fancy myself, though Mrs. Collis didn't quite approve.

"We come a trifle unstuck on Newmarket Heath, I'm sorry to say," says Lord Henry. "A two-year-filly was the trouble, like so often."

He winked at me when he said this. He was a saucebox like a lot of the London gentlemen. It made a change from Mr. Hedges.

"The races," said Mrs. Collis, "were a veritable passion with the late Marquess. A veritable passion."

"With us, too," said Sir Gareth Fortescue. "But I think we do pretty nicely. Garry often has a bit on for me. He's very good that way."

"Sir Gareth is a very popular gentleman," said Her Serene Highness, "so they do all say." She would never have said "Garry," so disrespectful, but it was allowed to the valet himself.

"So is our Harry," said Lord Henry Clinton, "but that don't pay the bookies. We're talking about going to Vienna to keep out of trouble. His Grace is on and on about it."

"Would you accompany his lordship?" asked the Countess of Clanman-gan.

"Ho, yes, if I choose. I know far too much about our Harry to be treated arbitrary."

There was gossip all through dinner about the Quality upstairs. I didn't say much. There was no gossip to be told about little Millie. It was a huge dinner like I never saw until I became a lady's-maid. Mr. Hedges and Mrs. Collis was determined to impress the visitors. They done it for the honour of Moreys. It was very important to them. We even had champagne. I thought Lord Henry took a glass too many. I knew the signs from watching Uncle Cyril. He tried to squeeze my knee under the table.

On Sunday morning, between breakfast and church, I had to sew a new blue ribbon with a bow on Millie's hat. It was a little straw hat, a child's hat really, too young for her to my thinking. Her white frock was childish too. I don't know what she would have chosen. She didn't have no choice. They were keeping her a baby.

She did look sweet when she was ready. Moony, like always, with those big grey eyes. Suddenly I wanted to hug and kiss her like Corporal Jewkes done to me. I wanted to stroke her like he done to me. I didn't truly know what I wanted. I never felt like that before.

I saw Lord Henry Clinton for the first time in church—I mean the real one, not Mr. Cordle. What a difference! Mr. Cordle was skinny with a grey face and sticky-out ears and black hair so thin on top it looked like lines drawn on his skull with a pen. Lord Henry had hair like a daffodil. His moustache looked much softer than Corporal Jewkes's. His black Sunday suit showed off his colouring lovely. His face was nice, quite handsome—not so strong as Corporal Jewkes's, but happy and friendly.

I saw all the others, too, from our pew at the back of the church. Miss Prior pointed them out to me in the minutes before the service when the bells are still ringing and you can whisper without disrespect. The Viscount Whitewater looked ever so distinguished, like a martyr in the olden times in the *Illustrated History* Uncle Cyril had. There was one guest with light brown hair and nice blue eyes that Miss Prior didn't know who he was. Of course I knew Sir Gareth by sight, and some of the others. It was always funny seeing them in church. They seemed just like us.

Millie was moonier than ever in the days coming after. I knew in a general way what was making her so, remembering myself at thirteen. Poor kid, she was nearly eighteen. She went for moony walks and looked at herself for hours in the lake, hanging over the edge of the fancy bridge at the end like a dishcloth on the side of a sink. I thought there was a chance she'd fall in and drown, she was that dreamy and hanging so long over the rail.

Wednesday evening I ran her bath as usual, then went off for the towels in the airing-cupboard. I came back into the bathroom without her noticing. I watched her for a moment. She'd covered up her titties with soapsuds, and she was lying back in the water just squeezing and stroking her buttons with the suds. It give her the joys, to a mild extent. I could see that from the look of her face. Her eyes were shut and her mouth open.

I wanted to drop the towels and stroke her titties myself, but of course I never.

The Viscount Whitewater visited again, as I found by being taken into dinner by his valet.

"It is a pleasant surprise to have you with us again so soon, Lord Whitewater," said Mrs. Collis, talking as always like General Mauney reading the lesson in church of a Sunday.

"Morry's movements is unpredictable in a high degree," said Lord Whitewater, whose other name was Mr. East. "Here today and gone tomorrow at a fast rate of travel. I hope now we're settled in Charles Street, though, we won't be so restless as we been. It gets to be wearisome, a-packing up constant. And our Morry is a stickler about his clothes."

"You only recently inherited, I believe?" says Mr. Hedges. He knew quite well. He knew all that sort of thing as well as Mrs. Collis. It was just a remark passed by way of conversation.

"Last year," says Lord Whitewater. "I enlisted soon after, having previous assisted Mr. Schoonmaker, an American gentleman, in the identical capacity."

"We have entertained a number of Americans at Moreys, both ladies and gentlemen," announced Mrs. Collis. "Some of the young ladies have been sweetly pretty. From remarks let drop at this table, we understand there's grave risks of unconventional behaviour amongst the gentlemen."

"Not half as much as with Morry," said Lord Whitewater. " 'Unconventional' don't hardly begin to express some of his diversions. It all makes work, in the way of cleaning up. A high screw for heavy responsibilities, that's my situation—if the ladies will forgive my mentioning the sordid aspect of emoluments."

Mrs. Collis leant her head forward, solemn as the Grand Duchess (I mean the real one), to show she forgives Lord Whitewater talking of his wages. She wants to know urgent about the diversions. They all do. The stronger the meat the better in the Housekeeper's Room and the Steward's Room, as long as the expression is genteel.

"Sorry, all," says Lord Whitewater. "No go. I couldn't describe in front of ladies, specially young ladies," (he bows to me) "and my lips are sealed howsoever. I grant it's a shame, though."

He shook his head so that his cheeks wobbled. He was a fat man, not like his master, who looked like he needed port wine and pigs'-trotters regular to get him in condition.

Lord Henry Clinton visited us again at the beginning of May. Consequent I renewed acquaintance with Mr. Cordle. He offered to take me out to a tea shop in Salisbury, going both ways in a motor. He could get the time off if I could get the time off.

"Please, my lady," I said on Sunday morning, "my Gran is abed of the shingles in the hospital at Wilton, and the still-room has put me up two jars of calves'-foot jelly, and might I have the favour of the afternoon off, my lady?"

"Yes, Emmy, of course," says Millie. "I'm sorry about your grandmother. Would she like some grapes? You can get a bunch from the hothouses."

"Thank you, my lady," says I. I felt bad about that, she being so kind and thoughtful after I told the fib.

I wanted to look a fine lady, going to Salisbury in a motor. I wanted a hat with a veil like they all wore for the motoring. Of course, I didn't have such a thing. Millie did. I knew she'd lend me one—probably give me one —she was that generous. But I couldn't request. Who'd wear a motoring hat to visit their Gran abed in Wilton of the shingles? Having told my tale, I had to abide with it. So it had to be borrow.

I felt bad about that, too; but only a little bit bad, because no harm would come to the hat, and I knew I should have had it if I asked.

I saw Millie off for a walk a little after three, not so moony as usual, more striding with a purpose. She went beside the lake and off towards the beech wood. I didn't let her see me, seeing I was meant to be in Wilton. I started to nip up to her bedroom to find the hat I wanted in the cupboard. I pictured the one I fancied, navy with a coffee-coloured veil. On my way I encountered Mrs. Collis, who asked me to help her with some pillow cases. In the ordinary way she would have sent for a housemaid—it wasn't lady's-maid's work. But I obliged, of course. It's giving a helping hand as gets you on in the world. There was time enough to meet Mr. Cordle in the village.

So there I was in Millie's room, in the big fitted wardrobe, at half past three, looking for the hat.

In came Millie.

I had to hide. Nothing else answered. I felt bad about my fib and bad about the grapes and bad about the reason I was there. Millie would be hurt if she knew the whole truth. She did have a temper, too. She could make my life a burden. I had to hide.

I hid behind the dresses on hangers in the wardrobe. But I couldn't shut the doors on myself. It was only the summer dresses hiding me. If she looked at me direct she'd see me. She couldn't help herself. The room was full of sunshine. There was plenty of light, even in the wardrobe.

I thought she'd come in for a handkerchief or gloves. She wouldn't moon about in her bedroom. Her place for mooning was the schoolroom. I thought if I kept still and quiet, I'd be off to Mr. Cordle, nobody the wiser, in a minute.

Instead she went to the window and drew the curtains. It made the room not dark but a sight darker. I felt more easy. But I was puzzled. She wasn't one for drawing the curtains and taking a nap on her bed, not on a fine afternoon. But that seemed what she was bent on. What else was I to think? I hoped I could wait till she was asleep, and then creep out and away.

The door opened again. In came Lord Henry. I was struck all completely of a heap with astonishment. It was the last thing in the world I expected. Millie, with a man in her bedroom! No wonder she drew the curtains. But she hadn't drawn them enough. There was full daylight to see by, only not the direct glare of the sunlight.

Lord Henry looked lovely, no other word for it, dressed up summery and with that daffydown hair. If Millie had to pick someone, she picked right, to my thinking. She picked the one I would of picked.

He smoothed back his hair with his hand. It wasn't needed. His hair was as smooth as glass already. Smoothing it back was a nervous thing he did. It was obvious. He was as nervous as she was.

He asked where I was, his voice right husky with nervousness. She said I was visiting my Gran in Wilton. I wish I had been.

He locked the door. His hand was shaky. He kissed her. Neither of them was any good at that. I was taught proper by Corporal Jewkes, and I knew how it should be. Millie hadn't been taught by anybody, and Lord Henry hadn't been taught either, it seemed to me. They did a sort of dance to the bed, crossing the room while still trying to kiss each other. It was comical to watch. They sat down on the bed and they lay on it. They was as clumsy as wooden dolls, and making a mess of the bedspread.

I thought—that's all there's going to be, just cuddling with their clothes on. They'd have the room darker, else.

He sat up sudden and took his coat off. He didn't look happy about it. He frowned at his coat. He was worried for wrinkles. He shouldn't have thought of such a matter—it showed he didn't have his heart in the other. He took off his shoes and his collar and tie. He looked right silly with no collar.

Then he unbuttoned her clothes. She let him, her face looking a proper study. I could see her as clear as clear, but I couldn't guess what she was thinking. I thought it was already starting to be a disappointment. She wanted someone a lot more gentle. She wanted someone like Corporal Jewkes. Lord Henry was right clumsy with the bottons. I wanted to jump out of the wardrobe and do it for him. It was me had to iron the blouse after.

He took off the rest of her clothes. I don't know why they done it like that. It took a long time. It was obvious he'd never done such a thing before. What he wanted was for Millie to peel off.

I thought she'd be shy, but she wasn't. She lay on her back, as naked as a baby, in the light and in front of Lord Henry. He looked a bit upset.

He took his own clothes off as though he didn't want to. He was shy, unlike Millie. She might not want the room dark, but he did if he was going to take his clothes off. It was just the same like Corporal Jewkes.

Of course, he lay on his front on the bed out of shyness, the way Corporal Jewkes would of done if there was light to see by. Men are shy about themselves, always covering up or turning their backs.

Millie did surprise me then. She rolled him over and pulled his legs apart and began to play with his rod. It was a potty little thing compared to most I seen, not so much a sausage as a chippolota. It was nothing to be proud of. No wonder he was shy about it. It wasn't decent, the way she was fondling of it in the daylight. Where she learned such a hussy way to act I couldn't and can't imagine. It might do for some men, but it didn't suit Lord Henry any more than it would have suited Corporal Jewkes. I saw that at once. They was going all the wrong way about things.

He managed to roll himself over, but things wasn't going right. She was in too much of a hurry and he needed lots of help. I knew what he needed from what I done for Corporal Jewkes. But it wasn't my place to call out to Millie and tell her.

He got himself in, in the end, but I couldn't be hopeful. He was trying to do it normal but it wouldn't answer. He had Corporal Jewkes's troubles, for all he was thirty years younger. There was going to be no joys for either of them.

I was right. It didn't answer. His rod lay down and died. I saw it when it popped out. There was nothing of it.

His face when he pulled his clothes on was the saddest thing I ever saw. He looked like a little boy that couldn't reach the bird's nest. He had his face pressed to the shop window, but they slammed the door on him. All the joys escaped. It was worse than that—he was shamed. A man takes pride in being a man, and he'd failed. Of course it was her fault—he needed help and she never. Nobody had told her about that.

I felt truly sorry for him when he stumbled out of the room. I never felt so sorry for a gentleman.

I was sorry for myself, too. I was still hiding in the wardrobe, with cramp in my foot, and Millie crying on the bed. I was sorry for her, but it was her fault, and it didn't help me in the wardrobe. Time was slipping by, too, and I was missing my chance of tea with Mr. Cordle and going to Salisbury in the motor.

By and by Millie dropped off to sleep. It's funny how many do. I could tell when the sobbing stopped and the regular breathing began.

I climbed out from amongst the dresses and started to tiptoe across the room. Millie was lying on her tummy, still naked as a baby on the bed. She did have a lovely little arse. I felt I wanted to pinch it.

She woke up! I went a-crumble, creeping right by the bed. I passed an innocent remark and ran out of the room.

By and by I found Mr. Cordle. He was ever so cross. He'd waited in the village, where the motor-car was he'd borrowed, until there wasn't time to get to Salisbury and back.

"I'm truly ever so sorry," I said, "but it wasn't my error. I was caught by Millie in her bedroom and I couldn't get away."

There's many a true word spoken by way of a fib.

"I think you missed the chance forever, girlie," says Mr. Cordle. "From what I hear, our Harry won't be asked here again."

"Why ever not?" I said.

"I don't know precise. He got across her nibs, one way or another. We *are* in trouble, what with our fracas at Newmarket."

We exchanged remarks a little while longer, regretful of missed opportunity, and then, slow and careful, I said, "I done you a mischief, depriving of the outing, but maybe I can put things square by doing of a service."

"What's that, girlie?"

"Well! Along about half past six, I s'pose, you'll have to go to his lordship's room and do this and that for his comforts?"

"O' course. Harry can't be expected to draw his own curtains and light his lamp and such."

"*I'll* go along and do the needful. *I* don't mind. Then you can be free as air. It's just by way of making restitutions."

"*Is it indeed?*" Mr. Cordle looks at me particular. "I don't know. I sniff a little hintrigue. Are you that sort? Yes, I can see you might be. I don't know. There's valet's perks to be considered."

"Valet's parts?" I asked, not rightly understanding. I thought he had reference to sections of himself.

"Perks," he said. "When a lady of a certain sort visits our Harry, the gentleman's gentleman is entitled to a cut. Same like Tattersalls, when they sell a nag at auction, only at a higher rate."

I saw what he meant at last. He put a whole new idea into my head. I hadn't thought beyond the sadness in Lord Henry's face when his rod went into a wilted crocus and he bundled on his clothes and ran out of Millie's bedroom. Now I had a whole new idea in my head.

I thought, Corporal Jewkes always gave me a bob or two; Lord Henry could dig deeper than that.

I questioned Mr. Cordle about sums, not having any clear idea. He thought two pounds. I was all in a heap at the thought. Two pounds!

"Ten bob of that for me," he said, "for making straight the highway. Let's think, now. I ate a pasty in the Steward's Room at noon, seems to me. It afflicted me horrible with cramps below the ribs. I'm writhing on my bed, drinking stuff with a chalky flavour. So a footman looks after Harry instead. But there isn't any footman. No footman free. Why not? The Lord knows. 'Course He does, on a Sunday."

"There's no call to mock religion," I says, always being severe in the matter.

"No offence, girlie. Right—there's no footman free, so Mr. Hedges has conference with Mrs. Collis and they sends a housemaid, just to draw the curtains and light the lamp. You'll have to dress like a housemaid."

He was right. A print dress with an apron and a cap. I'd left that all behind when they made me a lady's-maid, but there wasn't a problem. I could dress myself so, like I used in bygone times, and slip up to the bedrooms in the east wing.

"About half past six he'll be there," said Mr. Cordle. "Don't forget my twenty-five percent."

All he did was talk. Talk, talk, talk; I never heard anything like it. Half of it I didn't understand, and all of it was silly.

I went in and drew the curtains and lit the lamp, and straight away he started talking. I tried to keep a straight face, like servants should, but I couldn't. It wasn't his talk that made me laugh, but the way he looked. He'd taken off his coat and his collar and tie again, and he'd been lying down on his bed. Consequent his hair was rumpled, and stuck up on the back of his head like a cockscomb with the terrors. He'd been crying. His eyes were red and his face had a pinched look like a child that's been stropped for stealing apples. Although I felt so sorry for him, I had to laugh, he looked that funny. I couldn't help myself. It didn't stop him talking.

It struck me he was talking to give himself courage. It wasn't for me, it was for himself. What he said didn't matter, so he heard his own voice. I thought we was going to be there till midnight. It was like being in a bedroom with a threshing machine blowing out the chaff—all stuff of no use or value, and liable to aggravate.

He said something about kissing me. I thought, high time too. But he was horrible bad at it. He could of taken a course of lessons from Corporal Jewkes.

I kept an eye on the front of his trousers, looking for signs, and after I given up hope at last I saw. There wasn't much to make a lump, I knew, but a little lump come. Of course I knew what to do to hurry things on. It took a bit of finding, it was that small. I hurried things on that way. He locked the door and blew out the lamp, and I slipped out of my housemaid's dress.

I mothered him, like you want to with the shy ones. I held him between my titties like Millie should have, only hers weren't big enough for that. He was a-feeling and a-fondling, which gave him courage.

I knew he had Corporal Jewkes's troubles, so I knew he wanted Corporal Jewkes's treatment. It was all depending on the darkness, same like Corporal Jewkes. That's where Millie went so wrong, making the poor man shy. I used both hands, cautious, just like I used with Corporal Jewkes. His rod stayed hard, for a wonder. I knew I couldn't rely, having seen it go to nothing with Millie, but I kept it hard with my treatments.

He said it was going to answer, so I popped it in the hole. I hardly felt he was there, poor little gentleman. I had to strain my muscles like I never to hold the little knob in the hole. I was still a-rubbing and a-fondling, of course, like I learned with Corporal Jewkes. It was that exhausting. I never knew it take so long before. I began to get cramp in my hand.

It answered at last. There couldn't hardly of been a teaspoonful. I never felt it, but I knew from his joys. I pretended to feel moony, like they like you to.

He needed a wipe after. It was easier for the laundry-maids, a towel than the sheets.

We dressed in the dark. It was awkward, but he was just as shy as ever.

I meant to ask for two pounds, but somehow it came out three. I did believe he would of give me ten. It was quite nice being able to help him, same like dear old Corporal Jewkes. But Corporal Jewkes made me feel like a queen, while his lordship only made me feel like a doctor.

I suppose there's joys in just helping, but I do like to feel *something*.

I gave Mr. Cordle his ten bob, though really it should have been fifteen.

8 ❋ The hot encounter

Now she is in the very lists of love,
Her champion mounted for the hot encounter:
All is imaginery she doth prove,
He will not manage her, although he mount her.

VENUS AND ADONIS

"It seems you've been and got yourself a follower, Emily," said Miss Prior on Wednesday afternoon.

"Who?" I asked, worried in case one of the village lads had been calling at Moreys, destroying at a blow the refinement I'd been labouring after.

"Oh, it's all right. Even Mrs. Collis can't disapprove. It's that nice Mr. Cordle, so to say Lord Henry Clinton."

He was there by the door of the Steward's Room, passing the time of day with Mr. Hedges. Of course, he could make himself welcome when he liked, being the younger son of a duke.

"Girlie," he said, taking me aside, "I can put you in the way of another two quid, on the same terms as last time."

"I'm agreeable," says I, thinking of my savings in the sock.

"He's waiting in a bedroom at the pub," says Mr. Cordle, "biting of his nails like a good 'un. What is it you done to him, girlie? I wouldn't mind a bit of it myself."

"Instead of your commission," says I, "you can have the identical."

I had a feeling Mr. Cordle would funny like a stoat. Those skinny little men often do.

He did, too.

I went to the Glyn Arms in the village, and Lord Henry was waiting in the best bedroom. It was all just as before. I got cramp in my fingers, but I didn't feel anything else at all. Instead of giving Mr. Cordle his ten bob after (which should have been fifteen bob), I took him to Farmer Martin's hayloft. There was hardly any hay there, it being Maytime; all last year's ate up and the new crop not in. We managed. It was nice. He gave me joys that his lordship couldn't.

Saturday they came again. What Lord Henry must have spent on the train! We drew the curtains and locked the bedroom door in the Glyn Arms, and all went according. Lord Henry took my hand and put it into his trouser pocket that time, which I saw the point of immediate. There was three shillings in silver in his pocket, as well as my hand. When my hand come out, the silver come too. He was too excited to notice.

Going downstairs with Mr. Cordle after, we run slap into Mrs. Venables the landlord's wife. Of course I knew her from a tiny.

"Ho," said Mrs. Venables, "Emmy Brown again, is it? And what may you be up to, a-visiting London gentlemen in my best upstairs?"

"Sewing, Mrs. Venables," says I. "The gentleman needs repairs to his linen."

"I don't believe it and I don't like it and I won't have no more of it in my house," says she, "I've always been a respectable woman."

"I *do* believe *that*," says I. "You never had no offer to be different, looking like a sow with the glanders."

She makes a gobbly noise, and Mr. Cordle and me proceeds to Farmer Martin's hayloft.

"That was a horror, girlie," says Mr. Cordle, "passing an offensive remark to the lady of the house. Which I hope you may not live to regret."

"The likes of her," says I, "can jump into the swill-tub and stay there. Like where old sows belong. She'd no call to virtual accuse me of baggaging."

"She knows who you are and she knows who Harry is."

"Mister James Smith or some such."

"Garn! She wasn't took in for two seconds, not after she looked at his pocketbook."

I didn't give the matter no further thought, what with giving Mr. Cordle his ten bobs' worth. He was right, though. It was an error.

Next week there they were again. Mrs. Venables saw me going into the pub. I didn't quite like the look she gave me. So when I was a-fingering Lord Henry, preliminary, I let my mind stray to the future. I thought, if I had troubles, he'd help me, because he knew how much I could help *him*.

He gave me an address in London. He said it was where he lived, and I could always go there in case of disasters. I felt safer, having that address. I knew a lord wouldn't lie to a poor girl. I went back to my fingering, feeling more cheerful.

The following Sunday I wasn't in the mood. Try as I might, I couldn't fancy any of it. I told Mr. Cordle so.

"It might as well be a pencil," I said. "He'd best give up trying, if you want to know the truth."

It wasn't only that, though. Corporal Jewkes needed just as much help as his lordship, but Corporal Jewkes was a man you could respect, a real gentleman. That gave it all a bit of meaning. I was proud to give Corporal Jewkes his joys, because he deserved them—the life he'd led, the medals he'd won, the way he looked after General Mauney. There was nothing to respect in Lord Henry, not really. I came to change my views about him. He was like a sort of custard, no body to him, no taste. It was funny, it struck me as funny, to think like that about the son of a duke. But when you get intimate with the Quality you don't always keep the respect you start with. I didn't respect Millie, though I was fond of her. I quite liked Lord Henry, but there was nothing in him to respect. Helping had got to be wearisome. And Mr. Cordle took a bit too much for granted.

"I won't go," I said to Mr. Cordle, "and that's flat. Apart from anything, there's Mrs. Venables."

"Don't go to the pub, then. Do it somewhere else."

"Farmer Martin's hayloft?"

"No."

"Why?"

"That's our place, girlie. I don't want to share it with Harry. It'd spoil my memories for me. I don't know if you know what I mean?"

I did. It was a nice thought. It come as a surprise.

"Tell his lordship I can't get away," I said to Mr. Cordle. "There's a big party here, and Millie needs her frillies ironed. It's not far off true."

"You can slip out for a minute. It's still two quid. Why not the boathouse? It's only two minutes from the castle."

"Rats and mice," I said. "It's full of beasties, a place like that."

"Garn. Nice soft cushions. Dark. I had a look in there when we stayed, always being fond of boats all my life. My old man was a waterman on the Thames, and I was brought up on boats. I was drawn to the boathouse like a magnet, but I had no profit. It's too dark to see, and nothing in commission this early. Next month, I suppose, or July they'll have the boats on the water. Meantime it's a lovely place for hassignations. Shall I tell Harry you'll be there at three?"

"Tell him what you want, Mr. Cordle," I says, "but I don't think I'll be there."

And I wasn't. I could have, but I wasn't. Even for three pounds I didn't want to.

Millie got moonier than ever. She cried more than previous. It quite upset me, seeing her so unhappy. I wanted to comfort her, but I couldn't do or say anything helpful, not without forgetting my place.

There was no more visits from his lordship. I found I missed Mr. Cordle, which I didn't expect. It was that nice thought of his, that Farmer Martin's hayloft meant something special to him. It didn't mean anything special to me—places come alike, to my thinking—and I'd been there with others. Not Corporal Jewkes—the ladder was too much for him—but Bert and the village lads. But it was nice, Mr. Cordle thinking of it particular. He had a bit of heart.

Then there was an awful evening, Millie in hysterics in her bedroom. She come from her ladyship's room where she used to say goodnight while her ladyship was dressing. Something was said or done—I never knew the rights of it. Millie couldn't tell me, the state she was in.

I could comfort her, without impertinence, when she was hysterical. I pillowed her head on my front and cradled her, rocking to and fro like a baby. She screamed and screamed, then shook with dry sobs. She was such a dainty little bit of a thing, I thought those awful sobs would break her apart. I thought her ribs wasn't strong enough to stand such violent sobbings. It was terrible, the noise she made and the way those sobs was shaking her. She burrowed her head into my front, and I held her like a baby, like a puppy. I stroked her hair. Her sweet little face was ugly with the misery and the sobbing. Her mouth was stretched wide open and her face was all twisted. It was terrible to see.

She fell into a sort of doze, by and by. I cuddled her still. I felt the warmth of her little body through her little thin dress. It was nice, sitting like that, with Millie like a warm puppy half on my lap.

"Emily Brown."

"Yes, Mrs. Collis."

"You are dismissed this minute. Pack your box and go. You've an hour to be out of Moreys."

"But—but—"

"Here's ten shillings. A week's wages instead of notice."

"*Why?*"

"*I'm* not to say anything, and nothing shall I say. The others are forbidden to speak to you, so don't go bothering them. Take your money, pack your box, and be off with you inside the hour. That's all. You may leave the room."

I burst into tears. I had to. Anybody would. I wanted to be dignified and brave, but I couldn't help myself. I stood with the tears pouring out in front of Mrs. Collis in the linen room where she'd called me.

She turned away from me and started counting pillow cases. I couldn't see her face. She wouldn't say any more.

My whole world just fell down in that moment, and every bit of it hit me on the head. I couldn't lift one foot in front of the other. I tried to ask more questions of Mrs. Collis, but I couldn't talk for crying. She wouldn't answer or look at me.

I got myself up to the attics to the little room I shared with two others. They were Maisie Burt and Phoebe Lavenham. No sign of them. They were forbidden to talk to me. I passed Miss Prior on my way up the attic stairs. She turned her head away and went down the stairs like a rabbit. I called after her, as best I could for the sobbing, but she never looked round or made a pause. She was forbidden. She wasn't going to risk her position.

After I packed my box, I tried to find Millie. She wasn't in her bedroom or the schoolroom. She wasn't anywhere. She was out, gone out with her mother in a carriage. So I couldn't see her ladyship either, even if I'd dared to try.

Mr. Hedges wouldn't talk to me. He shut the Steward's Room door in my face.

I carried my own box down and out of the door by the pantries. I trudged away down the drive to the village, carrying my box. Sometimes I cried and sometimes I boiled with anger and mostly I was numb, like a corpse.

I'd been happy at Moreys and doing well. I liked the regular life, all going according to plan, like a big machine, like the engine of a ship. I liked the dainty things, the silks and embroidered stuffs, the glass and silver and china and the lovely furniture. I liked the people, or had done— Mr. Hedges and Mrs. Collis, Miss Prior and Maisie and Phoebe and all the rest. I liked Millie. I knew I'd miss her very much. I'd miss all of it. It was my life, my whole life, and it fell on my head and nearly killed me.

I went to Uncle Cyril's. He slammed the door on me. He shut the window by the door. He made a face at me through the window, waving at me to go away. Since my mother and father died, Uncle Cyril's was the only home I had, except Moreys.

Word had been sent down from the great house to the village. The people there were all servants of Moreys as much as the folk in the house. Nobody would talk to me.

Corporal Jewkes would have helped me, but he was in hospital. It was an old wound he had.

I went to the garden shed at Uncle Cyril's and took out the loose brick where I kept my savings. Somebody had been there. The sock was there, empty. I only had the ten shillings, my next week's wages instead of notice.

What I did have, worth a thousand times more, was Lord Henry's address in London.

Ten shillings was enough to take me to London in a third class carriage on the stopping train from Salisbury. I got a ride into Salisbury on the tail of a cart. That carter hadn't heard the message out from Moreys that nobody was to talk to Emily Brown. He was stone deaf, which was maybe the reason.

I still felt sort of numb all the way to London in the train. There was no understanding what had happened. I'd done nothing wrong at Moreys. I hadn't done what I ought not to have done, nor I hadn't not done what I ought to have done. I saw the hand of Mrs. Venables, vindictive old cow, because I checked her. She'd reported something to Mrs. Collis. That seemed like enough. But they didn't *know* I didn't go to the pub to do some sewing, like I'd said, or that I didn't go just as a friend with Mr. Cordle. They might have suspicions, Mrs. Collis and the others. Then why not ask me? That's what anyone would do in the ordinary way—they'd say, I been given these suspicions, Emily Brown, now what's your story? That's what anybody would do. But they didn't ask nothing and they didn't say nothing.

It was right unfair. I was sick when I thought about it.

Millie being out in a carriage was my great misfortune. She'd of helped, surely, if she'd been by. But I was chased out with my box afore ever I could get to talk to Millie. That was my disaster.

I thought about it, round and round, all the way to London, trying to make sense of it, sick at the unfairness.

Salisbury was a city with a tall cathedral and the streets of houses. It was right large to my eye, being a girl from a little village. But that London! There was miles and miles of it before ever we got to it—miles of dirty, dingy spreading little houses and tall dark tenements and factories with dirty smoke, endlessly stretching in every direction before ever we got into London proper. I was filled with dismay. It wasn't what I expected, or what I liked. I heard a lady say they were the suburbs. I thought they were like God had been muck-spreading.

We run into a place called Waterloo Station, ten times bigger than Salisbury Cathedral, full of sad people and dirty pigeons. I asked the way to Jermyn Street. People was friendly enough, but I couldn't hardly understand the funny way they talked. They were like Mr. Cordle talking through the neck of a bottle.

I crossed the River Thames by a big bridge, and walked and walked and walked. It was a nice fine evening, still daylight. There were hundreds of clocks, on churches and such, but they all said different times. I was frightened in the streets, the buses and the motorcars and the great crowds of people hurrying along regardless. I was thankful it was fine weather—I didn't have an umbrella or any proper coat. My box was very heavy by the time I got to Jermyn Street.

The number of the house was plain to see, painted on the door. There was an iron ring on a chain hanging down the doorpost for to sound a bell for them inside. I put my hand to my mouth, suddenly wondering if I dared. Emmy Brown, a-ringing the doorbell of a lord! But the devil drove, so I put down my box and jangled.

The door opened. It took much longer than it would of at Moreys, for all there was a mile the footman had to walk. A female stood there, tall as a horse, in black bombazine.

She looked at me with a sneery look and said, "Well?"

Of course I was a right mess after travelling all day in a cart and on a train and on my feet. My clothes were all right—they had to be, for a lady's-maid at Moreys—but my box was a country box—not a Gladstone bag but a bit of leather on a wooden frame—and it looked a bit funny in Jermyn Street. My hair was coming down and there was dust on my shoes and dirt on the hem of my skirt. Of course I was a mess.

I cleared my throat and said very nervous, "Please, ma'am, is his lordship at home?"

"There's no lords in this house," says the female.

"Lord Henry Clinton," says I. "This is where he lives!"

"Be off with you. There's no one of that name here."

"But I—but this is the address he give me! Look!"

I showed her the paper. There it was, right enough—thirty-six Jermyn Street.

"Anybody can write a number on a bit of paper," says the female. "There's no Lord Henry Clinton here."

I suppose I looked as despairing as I felt, because she added, "You been and let yourself be deluded, my girl. Maybe there's such a person as you speak of, but he's not here and never was. I can't help you in any way at all. You'd best be off. I've gentlemen to look after and a hundred things to do."

She shut the door in my face. That was the third door shut in my face that day, and it was more than I could bear.

I sat down on my box and put my face in my hands and burst into tears.

Of course I was very tired.

Cars were going put-put-put both ways along Jermyn Street, and a few carriages and cabs. There were people walking, the men in straw hats and the women in frilly blouses and little embroidered capes and hats piled up with flowers. Some of them may have stopped and stared at me and some of them may have spoken to me. I was past caring.

Out of all the ruins of my lovely life that had crashed down on my head in the morning, there was one solid bit left for me to stand on. It was this number—this door of this house in this London street. The plank was rotten. There was no plank. I'd fallen through into nothing. There was no money in my purse. The only people I knew in London were Lord Henry

Clinton and Mr. Cordle, and they weren't here, and these people didn't know them, and I was fallen into a great black hole of nothing.

The door opened again behind me. I thought it was the female like a horse come to send me packing off her doorstep. I didn't blame her. It's not refined, having a weepy girl with a country box on your doorstep. I struggled to my feet, hiccuping, and picked up my box and started away up the street.

"Just a minute," called a voice. It was a man's voice, a gentleman's voice.

I stopped and turned. I brushed away tears with the back of my hand and looked to see who'd called. It was a young man, not half-a-dozen years older than me, dressed up very stylish for the evening, wearing a white tie and a tall silk hat. It seemed to me his face was dimly familiar, though I couldn't put a name or a place to it. He had nice blue eyes—that was what I thought I remembered. He took off his hat, which was a polite act to a draggled and blubbering lady's-maid just dismissed. He had light brown hair of the sort that's never quite tidy. I remembered that, too, but I still couldn't put a name to the gentleman.

The female like a horse in black bombazine loomed up in the door behind him.

"That's the young person, sir," she said, "what was asking for a Lord I-don't-know-what."

"We don't rise as high as lords in this house," said the young gentleman with blue eyes. "But we may be able to help in a humbler way. Which particular lord are you looking for?"

"L—Lord Henry Clinton, sir," I said, my voice not coming out as steady as I'd of wished.

"Oh." He looked at me, most surprised. "What made you think he was here?"

"This is the address he gave me, sir, faithfully saying he lived here."

"What a funny thing to do. What a strange fellow he is. Is he a friend of yours?"

"He's be—beholden to me, sir, for services rendered," I said, "and he said if I was in disasters, which I am, this was the door I was to come a-knocking at."

He glanced at the bombazined lady, saying, "This poor girl has been the victim of some kind of cruel hoax. Have you any money?" he asked me.

I shook my head.

"You're up from the country, by your speech. Are you new to London?"

I nodded.

"Just arrived today, to look for Lord Henry Clinton?"

I nodded.

"I wonder what possessed the man to give you this address."

"Do—do you know Lord Henry, sir?" I asked, hardly daring to hope.

"Yes. Not very well, but I know him."

"Can—can you direct me where to find him?"

"I can't help you to reach him. With all the goodwill in the world that, I'm afraid, is beyond me. I can tell you where he is, though. He's in Vienna."

Well, I knew very well where Vienna was. At the other end of Europe where an old Emperor with whiskers sat amongst orchestras and horses.

So I put my box down on the paving-stones, and sat on it, and buried my face in my hands, and burst into tears again. I was hungry as well as tired.

"As an acquaintance of his lordship's," said the young man to the bombazine lady, "I feel a certain responsibility. The poor girl's penniless and a stranger, and she's here through no fault of her own. She has no one to turn to except a grossly unreliable man who's a thousand miles away. We can't turn her away, Mrs. Huxtable."

"What would you have me do with the young person, sir?" asks the bombazine lady in a terrible voice.

"Give her something to eat and somewhere to sleep for the night. Put whatever's right on my bill. We'll tackle the whole problem in the morning. I simply cannot stop now, even in a case of crisis like this one."

"You can't, sir," says the lady, "with the King of Sweden waiting at Doncaster House for the pleasure of meeting you."

"Have you been reading my letters, Mrs. Huxtable?"

"Certainly not, sir! The idea. Only the cards, what you prop on the mantelpiece. I can't avoid a glance when I does the dusting."

The young man laughed. To me he said, "Mrs. Huxtable will look after you tonight. Tomorrow we'll work something out. I want to hear your story, but I really can't stop now. Is that all right? No more tears. We'll sort something out tomorrow."

He turns and jumps into a motor which is waiting there a-chugging with a man at the wheel. He waves at me cheerful as he drives away down Jermyn Street. His smile is as nice as his eyes.

As the motor drew away it left behind a gentleman who must have been standing the other side of it. He must have been bending down talking to the chauffeur. The motor had hid him, but when it chugged off he showed plain.

Plain? I never saw such a splendid gentleman. I couldn't help staring like a gowk. He was a big tall powerful man with a fancy waistcoat and a beautiful satin tie with a big jewel in the middle of it, and a pale-gray bowler hat and a red moustache and twinkling pale-blue eyes. He was a finer gentleman by far, to my thinking, than Lord Henry Clinton or even Sir Gareth Fortescue. He was more in the style of Corporal Jewkes, but only thirty-five or thereabouts. I thought he was likely a Captain or a Colonel, not a Corporal.

He called out in a big deep strong bass voice, "Evening, Mrs. Huxtable. I believe Mr. Trench is expecting me."

"That's as may be, Mr. Dacre," says my bombazine lady. "Go on upstairs, if you please, and you'll find Mr. Trench in his sitting room."

"And what have we here," booms the splendid gentleman, "a damsel in distress?"

"Sir Matthew asked me to look after the young person," said the lady, "and we're to see what's best to do in the morning."

"Dashed sporting of Alban. Typical of the chappie, who's a great friend of my own. Right, Mrs. Huxtable, lead on with your fair protégée, and I'll nip up and beat a tattoo on Mr. Trench's hospitable door. But wait! The box—allow me."

He picked it up like it was a matchbox and carried it in after us.

"Thank you, sir," I says. I was right grateful. That box had got heavy with the carrying.

"Men were created, little missie," he said, "to relieve beautiful young ladies of their burdens."

He took off his hat with a flourish and bounded up the stairs three at a time.

"That Mr. Dacre," said bombazine, "is a merry gentleman, so to say, at all times. Now you follow me, girl, and I'll find a cut off the joint. Cold mutton it is. Mr. Trench is having it upstairs with pickled onions."

"Ooh," I says, hoping there'd be some of them to spare for me. It's funny how misery does give you an appetite.

She led me down steep stairs into a kitchen which was as dark and deep underground as a coal mine. There was a cook and a kitchenmaid. The maid was hardly fourteen, I reckoned, and nothing like me at that age. She looked like a potato sprouting in a cellar—thin and white, with no strength or health. I couldn't of borne to work in such a place.

I told them my name and where I come from, but no more of my story. The cook was Cook, and the little girl was Doris. They gave me cold mut-

ton and cold mashed potato, but the pickled onions was all gone upstairs
to the gentlemen. A page-boy and a valet went in and out, despondent.

I couldn't make out what sort of house this was.

Cook explained, "The late Mr. Huxtable was butler in a great 'ouse in
Cavendish Square, an' 'e put by 'is money an' 'e bought a lease of this."

"What's a lease?" I asked.

"When yer buys the right to live in a 'ouse without actle ownin' of it.
Blimey, that Wiltshire of yours mus' be like pagan parts, yer never even
'eard of a *lease*. 'E died, but the Missus still 'as the lease, see? So she lets
furnished chambers to single gentleman wot pays by the month in advance."

"Oh." I thought about this. "What a funny way to live."

"Not for them as never sees the daylight. There's a bit of pink blank-
monge lef' over from Sir Matthew's lunching. 'E et 'is, but Lord Whitewater didn't."

"Lord Whitewater?" says I, very startled. "Why, I know him."

"You *wot*?"

"I mean I seen him."

"We all *seen* him, dearie. It's the third time 'e come to see Sir Matthew.
Wot they talk about dear God on'y knows. It's not talk like Mr. Trench's,
but all ancient learnin's. I 'eard 'em when I took in the savoury. An' that
Mr. East, 'e 'ad to lug a parcel of old books upstairs from 'is lordship's auto.
The mess! Dust everywhere, leakin' out of them old books, gettin' all over
the tablecloth where they was perusin' of 'em. Sir Matthew apologises
nice, like 'e always, but that don' do the laundry."

"Nor do you," says little Doris. "I do."

"Shut yer mouth, imperance, 'fore I clips yer lug."

I didn't blame Lord Whitewater not fancying that pink pudding. There
was never anything as nasty in the Steward's Room at Moreys. I felt I had
to eat it, though, the way Cook was staring at me.

I forgot how tired I was while I was eating, but when I finished it hit
me. I almost nodded off at the kitchen table. The others noticed, and
Cook said it was time I went to bed. They were kind folk really. But there
wasn't a bed for me—the house was completely full. Little Doris had a cot
in the kitchen as it was.

"It'll 'ave to be a sofy somewhere," said Cook. "An' the on'y one is the
one in Mrs. 'Uxtable's sittin' room. 'Ceptin' them upstairs in the gentlemen's rooms, in course. Mrs. 'Uxtable 'asn't lef' no hinstructions, an' she
bin an' gone out. We'll 'ave to wait."

Soon after, the manservant comes in with a message from upstairs. Mr.

Trench just heard I was looking for Lord Henry, seemingly, and being a friend of Lord Henry himself he wants to talk to me to see if he can help.

I didn't want to climb a lot of stairs. I didn't think I was capable. But it seemed like an order. And if the gentleman was a friend of Lord Henry, maybe he would help me.

I made myself a bit tidy in a bit of looking glass in the kitchen, and trudged upstairs after the manservant.

He had a nice sitting room, did Mr. Trench, with windows on the street. It was full of knickknacks and shells and cigar boxes and pictures of horses and photographs of ladies. The first thing I saw when I come into the room was a photograph of her ladyship—of Lady Bulbarrow. Mrs. Collis had the same identical photo, framed in pear wood, in the Housekeeper's Room at Moreys. I was brought up with it, so to say.

"Good gracious," I said, "that's her ladyship."

"Come and sit down, little missie," boomed a great bass voice from the window. "If you don't mind, Rivvy?"

"Not a scrap, laddie," says a hoarse voice. "The filly looks gone in the wind and a trifle shin-sore. Have a pew, my dear."

The two of them was sitting at a table by the window, cracking walnuts and drinking port. I sat down reluctant—I'd never sat at a table like that with quality before. I was able then to see them proper, in the light of the candles they had on the table. One was the splendid gentleman I knew with the red moustache and the fancy waistcoat. The other was much older with a red nose and watery eyes. They were Mr. Dacre and Mr. Trench, as I already knew. They give me a glass of port. I took it reluctant, but it was welcome. It wasn't in a class with the port we drunk in the Steward's Room at Moreys.

"We're both pals of Harry Clinton's," said the wheezy old man. It struck me he would of talked easier if his collar hadn't been so tight. "Desmond Dacre here knows him better than I do. The feller seems to have played a damned dirty trick on you. Can you read us the form book?"

"Eh?" says I, not very genteel. I was too tired to think clear.

"How did it come about Lord Harry gave you *any* address, little missie," says the splendid man, Mr. Dacre, "let alone a wrong 'un?"

"He was beholden," I said.

They asked me lots of questions, but I was too sleepy to understand rightly what they were asking or to know what I answered. I must of seemed a proper ninny, talking in my sleep. Mr. Dacre, he give me another glass of port.

How long all this went on I never did have any idea.

Mrs. Huxtable, the bombazine lady, came in and said I was dropping, which was right enough. She took me off to bed.

"We'll see you all right between us, little missie," shouts out Mr. Dacre. "You've fallen among friends. Your worries are ended."

I didn't know what I'd fallen amongst, but I was too sleepy to ponder. Mrs. Huxtable lent me a nightgown and handed me an armful of blankets and showed me a little settee in a little dark sitting room with a desk taking up half of it. I was almost too sleepy to undress and spread out the blankets.

I didn't sleep well, for all I was so tired, because of the London noises—horses, cars, people shouting, all an inch from the window, which was on a level with the street. I cried, thinking of Moreys and Millie and all. But I did seem to feel I'd fallen amongst friends.

The noise was awful in the dawn, to me used to nothing louder than birds and underhousemaids—clanging of pans, banging of doors, chugging of motors, thundering of hooves, and all manner of shouting and merriment. I wondered whether it was that London folk got up so early or stayed up so late. There was no hope of sleep, so I pondered serious.

With proper references, wrote down and signed, I could of got a position anywhere, having given satisfaction at Moreys. But I come to London without a character. Nobody wants a lady's-maid dismissed out of hand, as it might be for stealing—not in a big house. I could of got a position in a little house, maybe, but did I want that? To be a kitchenmaid in a little dark underground kitchen? A housemaid in a little tall house, all stairs and London grime? I'd grow backwards, I thought, and shrink into little Doris.

I was good at ironing and needlework, and dusting and sweeping and serving; but I was good at other things, too. Mrs. Collis and Miss Prior taught me one lot of lessons, and Corporal Jewkes taught me another.

But in London? Where would I go? How would I start?

Mr. Dacre, and maybe Mr. Trench, and maybe Sir Matthew, might find ways to help me. What ways? Gentlemen like that would think of finding me a genteel position. But me without a character? And them not able to give me one, none of them having clapped eyes on me before yesterday? Even with their help, I couldn't look higher than kitchenmaid or underhousemaid, and I couldn't look as high as a great house.

I couldn't go back to Wiltshire with all doors barred against me. I didn't have any friends anywhere else—there wasn't a soul in the world I knew to talk to except at Moreys and in the village, and a few in Wilton and Salisbury, and the new friends I made yesterday.

I tried to choose between different roads and plan which road was best. But I was brought face to face with the fact—there was only one road; I didn't have any choices. I had to take what help I could from Mr. Dacre and Mr. Trench and Sir Matthew, and then see what came. There was nothing I could do for myself. It was all up to them. I depended on them more than ever I did on Uncle Cyril.

They gave me a greasy breakfast in the kitchen.

"I've stretched a point for one night," said Mrs. Huxtable, "just to oblige Sir Matthew. But continue similar I can't and won't. There's no room for you here, Emily, as well you see for yourself. Where you'll go next I can't tell."

"When shall I see the gentleman?" I asked.

"There's no knowing as to that. Sir Matthew was up early, like always, to ride his horse in Rotten Row. There's no knowing when he'll be back. Mr. Trench is still asleep, like always, and there's no knowing when he'll ring his bell."

"And Mr. Dacre?"

"He went off home last night, of course. There's no knowing if he'll call here today. He's likely off to the races or busy somewhere. He keeps himself occupied, does Mr. Dacre. I don't suppose he'll have time to worry with the likes of you, all he has on his mind."

I nodded. I was to wait till Sir Matthew got back from riding, or Mr. Trench woke himself up. I could stay in the house till then.

But it was Mr. Dacre came, cheery and booming. I was glad to see him. He took a grip of my box and said I'd bother Mrs. Huxtable no more.

"But where are we going, sir?" I asked him.

"To find a spot of forage first, my little sugarplum. And over the manger we'll discuss your future."

I remembered Lord Henry called me a sugarplum. It came better from Mr. Dacre, somehow. He said it with more cheeriness. He could talk in that cheery way and it fitted with the rest of him. It proved what a real gentleman Mr. Dacre was, that he used the same words as a lord. He was wearing a different waistcoat, blue with spots, lovely. His hair was as glossy as Lord Henry's, only red. He took me to an A.B.C. shop (there was one in Salisbury where I would of gone with Mr. Cordle) and gave me macaroons and cocoa.

We chatted of this and that. He was ever so cheery and friendly. He made me forget our positions.

He said, "You may wonder why I whisked you away, Emmy."

"Mrs. Huxtable was eager I should leave, sir."

"Yes indeed. A dragon like that doesn't want a lovely girl hanging about in a house full of bachelors. Sets the cat among the pigeons, or the plump little pigeon among the tomcats, eh?"

He roared with laugher, showing ever so many big teeth.

"Fact of the matter is," he went on more solemn, "I didn't want you getting dependent on those other two. I'm not saying a word against either of them, mind. True blue chappies, both of them, and great pals of mine. But old Rivvy Trench—well, I daresay you saw yourself. He's asleep twenty hours of the day and he's tight three and a half hours, and the remaining half hour, which is when he first wakes up, he don't make any sense till he's got his teeth in. Not a word against Rivvy, mind! He's a first-rate sportsman and one of my greatest pals. But he hasn't drawn a sober breath after eleven-thirty in the morning since Persimmon won the Derby. The best fellow in the world—none better! But he's not the stalwart oak for you to lean on, girlie."

I remembered Mr. Cordle used to call me girlie. That came better from Mr. Dacre, too.

"What about Sir Matthew?" I said, because I'd felt I could trust those nice blue eyes and that smile.

"Irish," said Mr. Dacre. "Nothing but a Mick. A first-class fellow, mind, for a bog-trotting Hibernian, and a thorough sportsman. But rely on a Mick? I don't mean he'd do anything wrong. Never! But those fellows are stark raving mad. Tell you the sort of thing, so you'll see what I mean. I had an engagement to meet Matty Alban at the Cri, after which we were going down to Sandown. I turned up on the dot with race-glasses round my neck and a flower in my buttonhole, and wait, wait, wait—finally went away in disgust. Ran into him two days later at a party at the Archduke's. 'You're a fine one,' I sang out to him, 'letting a fellow cool his heels for two hours at the Cri when the horses were running at Sandown!' 'Couldn't help it,' he says, not a whit abashed. 'A fellow in Oxford Street had two cock-sparrows in a cage, fighting. Naturally I had a bet with a fellow about which one of them would win, and I had to stay and see the battle through.' Gospel. You see what I mean. Matty Alban would promise to do *anything* for you, and mean it—see fellows, write letters, spend money, even. Then something comes up, and he clean forgets the whole thing. See what I mean?"

"Then," I said, a bit glum, "I got to depend on you."

"Is that so dreadful, my little sugared almond?"

"Oh no, sir! I didn't mean it so. I meant, I'm a burden just to you, instead of spreading the burden, like, over three."

"You start worrying about that when I do. Now you listen closely to me. Lend an attentive ear."

Then he says a lot of things I thought of for myself already—how I couldn't get a genteel position without a character from Moreys; how I wouldn't like to spend all my days in an underground London kitchen; how I needed fresh air and sunshine and dainty things round, after the life I had at Moreys.

Then he says, "But you're wasted as a slavey anyway, pussycat."

I didn't rightly understand, not all at once, so he explains himself in a roundabout way, not looking at me direct while he talks. I got hold of his meanings eventual. What it came to was, I was so good looking and attractive to gentlemen that *that* was where my future road lay.

Well, the thought had crossed my mind, too.

"But I don't know how to begin or where to go," I said. "I don't know anything."

"I do," said Mr. Dacre.

He takes my hand and presses it.

"You've seen the great ladies," he said, "strutting round drawing rooms like fillies in the paddock before the Oaks. Seen their silks and their jewels and their furs, eh? Let me tell you this, my lucky little country mouse—you can have all that and more."

"Coo," I said, because he seemed so certain.

"You can move into my lodgings in Pimlico. Your own room, of course. Do what you like there. I'll buy anything needful. Pay me back when you can."

"Ooh," I said.

So that was my road. It was Corporal Jewkes's teachings, not Mrs. Collis's. It wasn't the life I would of chosen, considering everything, but if I had to do it I was getting the right start.

"Thank you, sir," I said. "I'll try to show myself grateful."

He took me to a place called Regent Street and into a shop as big as the whole of Wilton—as big as Moreys. They had everything! He bought me underclothes and stockings and such, and soap and a bottle of scent, and a real silk blouse and a skirt. He favoured nice strong colours, which I fancy myself. The quality wasn't what I was used to with Millie's things.

Then he took me to luncheon in a place the like of which I never saw before—not like a pub, nor yet a hotel, but a restaurant. I'd heard of restaurants, but I'd never truly pictured. It was lovely! All red plush and gilt, and little tables with flowers like the banqueting hall at Moreys. There was talk and laughter all round, and waiters, and a girl in a cage, like a songbird, taking money from the people for their dinners. I felt like a queen! Mr. Dacre made me feel like a queen! He was the first to do that since Corporal Jewkes.

He gave me ever so much wine and asked me lots of questions about Moreys, and who lived there, and who came to stay there. After all that wine, and a bad night, I didn't rightly know what he was asking or what I was saying.

We went a long way in a hansom cab to a little dark street with a row of little dark shops on one side and a dirty red chapel on the other.

"Not exactly Moreys Castle," said Mr. Dacre. "Not Jermyn Street, either. A poor place, but mine own. We're over the picture-framer's."

The picture-framer's was a lovely shop with a picture of cows in the window. I felt homesick for the village when I saw it. Beside the shop was a green door. Mr. Dacre unlocked it with a fiddly key. The door give onto a narrow passage with a flight of steps up and a flight of steps down at the end of it.

A woman came up the stairs from the basement as we came along the passage. She looked like a gipsy with the stomachache—blackish, with a miserable face. She wore a dirty apron and a black bonnet and was carrying a chamber pot.

"Ha, Mrs. Leach," booms out Mr. Dacre in his merry bass voice. "Here's my young niece from the country I was telling you about. I'll show her to her room. Don't bother to come up."

"Niece," says the gipsy woman, like it was a wicked word used in the way of anger.

Mr. Dacre led me up a flight of stairs to a landing. It was nice, with a window and a carpet and a picture of a horse, and a varnished wooden hat-rack and an umbrella stand. That brass could of done with a good polish, but that was someone else's worry. I put all that behind me, like Mr. Dacre said.

There was two doors on the landing, and another flight of stairs went up. The stair carpet was that worn the woodwork almost showed through. The stairs could of done with a sweeping.

Mr. Dacre opens one of the doors and makes a comical bow. I went into the first room I ever had of my very own. It was lovely! Comfortable, genteel, dainty and yet rich; not so big you'd get lost or lonely, not so small you'd get a stuffy feeling. There was a nice big brass bed with a yellow satin cover, and a small settee with plush upholstery, and a dressing table with a big triple mirror on hinges, and a stool in front of that with a brocaded seat, and a picture of a naked lady standing up to her ankles in water. She was covering herself up with her hands, but not very clever. There was a washstand and a wardrobe and a chest of drawers. On one wall opposite the bed there was a funny little door, like it might be for a dovecote, with a big glass knob.

"What's that?" I asked, never having seen such a thing.

"What they call a hatch," said Mr. Dacre. "A word borrowed from seamanship, an idea borrowed from the Borgias. They used to have meetings in here, very confidential discussions. No servants allowed to listen or observe. So their drinks were passed in from next door."

"Who had meetings?" I asked. I like to know what use a room's been put to.

"The Elders of the chapel over there," said Mr. Dacre. "They were rigorous temperance fellows, you know, so they always took their gin in teacups. Hence the hatch. Screwed up and painted over now. Do you think you'll be comfortable, dear?"

"Yes," I said. "Yes, I do. I'm that grateful, Mr. Dacre! I don't know what I would of done without you."

"Just what you're going to do with me, I imagine," says Mr. Dacre, "But possibly not getting off to such a good start. Now you'll want to unpack and get yourself settled, and then I want you to dress up in your new finery, and then we've got a call to pay. Don't be surprised by anything that happens."

I was surprised, though.

I put away my things very tidy in the drawers (that was something I *did* know how to do) and hung up my dresses in the wardrobe. They needed a lick of ironing after two days in the box. I put on my new clothes and put up my hair fresh and made myself look as nice as I could. I could never be as dainty as Millie, but there was plenty admired me.

Then Mr. Dacre took me in another cab ever such a long way to a big quiet street of very superior houses. He rang the bell in a funny way. He rang it, then waited while you might of counted twenty, then rang it three times quick. The door opened. A fat man stood there. I knew I knew his face, but I couldn't put a name or a place to it.

He didn't look at me, or only a passing glance. He didn't know me. He nods to Mr. Dacre.

"On you go, Emmy," says Mr. Dacre, and gives me a little push from behind. "I'll wait outside."

I didn't like that much. But I followed the fat man into a big hall ten times bigger than the Jermyn Street one with a marble floor and big pictures and a statue of a naked lady.

"This way, Miss," said the fat man, still seeming not to know me.

There was three big shiny doors off the hall, and there was a little one with green baize and brass studs. *That* didn't need polishing. I wondered for a moment how they polished the brass without getting the Brasso on the baize. But I put all that behind me.

The fat man led me through the little door. There was a white passage with doors off. He showed me through a door into a little white room, almost bare, with no window and a big electric light hanging from the ceiling. They were still a shock to me, those electrics, the idea not having got to Wiltshire. It was so bright as to be hurtful to the eyes. Most of one wall of the room was covered by a sort of screen, like a sort of plaited rushes. I couldn't see the purpose of that, nor why I was there.

I heard the door shut behind me. The fat man left me alone in the room. I looked and listened, puzzled, a bit scared. I couldn't make nothing of any of this.

Suddenly a voice come out of nowhere. "Turn round. Slowly."

I nearly jumped out of my drawers. It was a man's voice, not one I'd ever heard before. He sounded like my idea of a professor, only I never heard a professor talk. I turned round slowly, like he said, seeing no harm in that. I didn't know where the voice was coming from.

"Raise your arms above your head," said the voice.

I did that. I felt my new silk blouse tight against my titties.

"Lift your skirt to your knees. Higher."

I did that. It was more saucy, but I knew I had nice ankles and nice plump legs.

"That is all," said the voice.

That was all. A bell rang, and in a minute the fat man opened the door. He led me out to where Mr. Dacre was waiting with the cab.

"Well?" says Mr. Dacre.

"Bought," says the fat man.

"When?" says Mr. Dacre.

"Tomorrow at eleven," says the fat man.

"Done," says Mr. Dacre.

"Oh sir," says I in the cab, "whatever was that about? I felt like a pig in a pen at Wilton Market."

He laughed, which calmed my fears. "More like a yearling at the Newmarket Sales," he said.

I couldn't get no more out of him.

We got back to the rooms over the picture-framer's. While Mr. Dacre was paying the cabbie, I looked at the picture of the cows in the picture-framer's window. They were standing under trees in long rich grass that should of been cut for hay. There was a church tower beyond. It made me feel very homesick.

Upstairs, Mr. Dacre sits me down and talks to me serious. "You passed the inspection," he says. "That's the first fence jumped. Now about tomorrow morning—I don't want you to worry, but it won't be quite what you're used to. It may hurt a little—"

"*Hurt?*" I said, scared again.

"Nothing to show afterwards, and it's all the more for you. He won't draw blood or anything—he won't use a whip like Fred Archer's."

"*Blood?*"

"He can't damage you or bruise you where it shows. He knows he can't get away with that here, whatever he got up to in Egypt. Just what he'll fancy I don't know. Easty doesn't know either. A very whimsical gentleman, your first client under present management."

I didn't fancy the sound of "whimsical," though I didn't rightly know what it meant.

I was blindfolded.

Mr. Dacre did that. "Client's instructions," he said. "Don't fuss and don't touch it. And don't worry. You won't come to any harm."

I heard Mr. Dacre going out of the room—his feet always hit the floor like he was driving in nails. The door shut.

I sat on the side of my bed, wearing my lovely new clothes in a room full of morning sunshine, not being able to see so much as my nose.

The door opened. At first I thought Mr. Dacre came back, but then I heard breathing and smelled a new smell. I was puzzled for a moment—it was a smell I knew, but it didn't belong here. It belonged in a kitchen. It was cloves, like you put in an apple tart.

I heard the key turn in the lock.

"Stand up," said a voice I knew, the voice like I imagined a professor.

I stood up.

"Go to the head of the bed. Stand with your back to it. Raise your arms. Hold the rail."

I stood with my back to the bed-head, my arms up like I was being crucified.

I felt something cold on my left wrist. There was a little clang of metal hitting metal, and a click. The same to my right wrist. I tried to move my arms. I couldn't.

"Handcuffs," said the voice, with a sort of smile in it.

Then he began to feel my body through my clothes—my hips and my bottom and my titties, all through my clothes.

Then I felt a hand at the collar of my blouse. I thought—he's going to fiddle with the buttons. Instead I felt a great tug and heard an awful noise of tearing.

"Hi," I calls out, thinking with misery of my new silk blouse.

I felt a stinging slap across my face, on my cheek below the blindfold.

"Be quiet," says the voice, still with a smile in it, still like I imagined a professor.

He tore off all the rest of my clothes, my chemise and drawers and new stockings and all. I thought he had a pocket knife to help, but I couldn't be sure, and the clothes was all ruined neither more nor less.

I stood shackled up to the bed-head, naked as a baby. The brass was cold against my back and my bottom.

He felt me again, all over, pinching and tickling, slapping, prodding. I felt fingernails digging into my titties. I felt a patch of cold on my tittie, cold and wet. I thought—he's licking.

I heard movements, rustling noises, little bumps. It struck me he was undressing.

I heard clicks, and my arms came free.

"Kneel down."

I knelt, still with my back to the bed-head.

"Raise your arms."

I was handcuffed to the brass again.

I felt something against my face. It was skin. It was his skin. It was hard behind the skin. It was a big tube. It came to me what it was. He was pressing himself against my face. I felt the rough hair on my nose and on my mouth, and all of him squashed hard against my face.

"Open your mouth."

I didn't want to. He made me, pressing fingers between my teeth. Something went into my mouth, round, smooth, tasting a little salty. It came to me what it was. He pushed it into my mouth. He pushed so that it went right to the back of my mouth. I thought he'd throttle me so. I was frightened for my breathing.

He took it out and rubbed the end all over my face. It was wet from my spit. I tried to move my face away. He put a hand in my hair, took a handful, hurting. He bent my head back against the bed-head and held it still. He rubbed himself over my face, squashing it into my nose and mouth and ears. He was doing it harder and harder. He was hurting my face. I could hear him breathing, harsh like a dog.

There was a great rush of wetness all over my face, into my mouth and up my nose. He rubbed it into my hair and over my cheeks.

He wiped it off on my tittie. It was soft already, soft and wet.

I was crying under the blindfold.

I heard him dressing. I heard the key in the lock and the door open.

I was still kneeling, baby-naked, blindfolded, crying, handcuffed to the bed-head, with his juice all over my face.

"Not that again," I said. "Not him or anybody like him, ever again."

"All right, dear. I'm sorry it was beastly. He won't touch you again. You don't have to do anything you don't want to do."

And after that I didn't—just the normal, with normal gentlemen.

9 ❀ *The client breaks*

An oven that is stopp'd, or river stay'd
Burneth more hotly, swelleth with more rage:
So of concealed sorrow may be said;
Free vent of words love's fire doth assuage;
But when the heart's attorney once is mute,
The client breaks, as desperate in his suit.

VENUS AND ADONIS

I fixed on the name Desmond Dacre after finding it in a story in *The Crusader*. Grand yarns those stories were for a lad in the back streets of Battersea—all young bloods and dashing captains with names like Mervyn Fitzmaurice and Jack Peregrine and The Honourable Charles Harrington. I was Albert Fudge, and with my ambitions that didn't do. Desmond Dacre was a fellow in a story called *A Soldier's Honour*—Captain Desmond Dacre of the Bombardier Guards. I didn't risk the Captain often, except in company that wouldn't know any different.

I discovered early in life that what you need is style, confidence, a grand air, an expansive manner. Luckily I'm a big chappie, and clothes look well on me. I got lots of clothes. I didn't have to pay Mo Calman, the tailor, after I discovered how he got hold of his father-in-law's money. As time went by I paid less and less for more and more. A good trick, that! I even lived practically rent free after I found out about a woman who got rid of her niece's baby with an instrument. The niece died. A dreadful crime, that. So I moved into rooms over a shop in Collindale Road in Pimlico. Not the best address in the world, nor the best rooms, but I didn't expect to stay there for ever. Excelsior was the cry—onward and upward! Once I made myself into a gentleman, the world was my oyster.

It was happening damned slowly, though. I was looking out all the time for the big opportunity, but it never materialised. Little things, yes. A fiver here, a tenner there. But I was after bigger game. Trouble was, time the enemy, was against me. I was a damned fine figure of a man at thirty, not a whit worse than the fellows in *The Crusader*. But it couldn't last forever. I remembered my old man at the age of fifty—fat as a porker. Beer did that. I took the tip—never touched a thing except wine and spirits. I hated the thought of getting fat. My old man went bald, too. That did worry me. The old thatch was getting thin on top, and my moustache was going not so much red as a sort of dirty sandy colour. No style in that. So I touched it up with a bottle of stuff I bought for twelve bob from a chemist. Twelve bob! That was cash on the nail, too.

I went everywhere a gentleman does, looking and listening, sniffing for the big opportunity. I turned my hand to just about everything—sold tips at the races, played cards on race-trains, made friends with old ladies, kept a girl from Bermondsey and hired her out at a quid an hour—all good fair trading, hard work, kept the wolf from the door, but not the way to a fortune. I never stole to speak of, only from chappies so drunk there was no risk. I was never in trouble with Robert to speak of, only once or twice on the racecourse. But the really big thing seemed as far away as ever. And time was going by and I was getting thin on top. I put on a bit of weight, too, for all I never drank stout.

In 1904 I went down to Epsom for the Derby. It rained cats and dogs— I never got so wet in my life. I put my shirt—what there was of it—on the French favourite, which was nowhere. I was dismal and shivering when I got on the train after racing. A jovial old chappie in a white hat offered me his flask, saying I looked like a waif in a melodrama. He thought I had a nosebleed, but it was the damned red dye running in the wet. We got pally on the train and had a bite of supper together at Mario's in the Tottenham Court Road. Then he took me back for a spot of brandy at his digs in Jermyn Street.

It was a different world from mine. It was what I wanted.

The old chappie was called Rivington Trench—Rivvy to pals—and I stuck to him like a cornplaster. He wasn't a great swell himself—just an old boy around Jermyn Street—but he knew swells. He had something I hadn't got, which was a foot in the swell world. He was my ticket through a lot of doors. With him I could meet a different class of pal. With him I could find the big chance.

It began to happen in a small way, enough to keep hope alive. I began to get ponies here and there, instead of fives and tenners, for keeping quiet about things. But I wasn't making contact with the real top swells, lords and cabinet ministers and racehorse owners. Rivvy didn't know them. They were the birds I wanted. They *had* to keep their secrets.

In the spring of 1906 I'd known Rivvy for eighteen months, which made him my oldest friend. I saw quite a lot of him. A young chappie came to lodge for the season in the house where Rivvy lived—a Paddy from the bog, a baronet; plenty of this world's goods, *entrée* everywhere. I sniffed about. I reasoned that a lad like that was bound to have amusements on the side, like a bit of crackling from a milliner's shop. It seemed not. That horse wasn't an entry. The fellow led a blameless life.

"Your pal Matty Alban is a damned dull dog," I said to Rivvy. "He never gets up to any mischief at all."

"Not his fault," said Rivvy, who could always find some good in everyone. "Daresay he'd lead the devil of a life, wild Irishman with a pocketful of sovs. But the poor young chappie's in love." Rivvy sighed romantically. "It's a sad and beautiful story. Had it from the horse's mouth. He went and stayed down in the country and fell for a filly there. Angelically innocent, something out of a poem. Ever read any poems? Nor me. Stick to the *Racing Calendar*. Rummy thing is, the poor young chappie doesn't know what's happened to him. He talks about the filly, he broods about the filly, he dreams about the filly, and he doesn't know why. Keeps him on the straight and narrow. Good thing, I suppose."

"Who for?" I said sourly.

At the beginning of May I saw a spanking new De Dion parked outside the door in Jermyn Street. Chauffeur at the wheel, another vassal hovering. There was a crest painted on the side, so I guessed it was a real swell.

Rivvy knew, of course.

"We are honoured by a call from the Viscount Whitewater," he said. "Who turns out to be a pal of our pal Alban. He arrived with an armful of old books. Mrs. Huxtable says they've got them spread all over the table."

Whitewater was a new name to me. No loss, on the evidence to hand. If he was a pal of Alban's and went in for damned old books, he was of no interest to me.

He was, though. I passed him on the stairs. One glance was enough.

For one thing, he reeked of money. The diamond in his tie wasn't as big as the one in mine, but his was real. For another thing, there was something distinctly odd in the look of his eye. I wouldn't care to say exactly what it was. He just looked to me like a lad who'd have something to hide.

I sauntered on down the stairs and made pally noises at the chauffeur and the other valet. I could be as democratic as the devil when I chose. We were soon jawing away like old friends.

One of the chappies was new in the job, but the other had been in the billet for six months, since Whitewater came back from abroad. He was the lad for me. I offered him a drink. We went into the Blue Boar. He could see the car from the Saloon Bar and nip out when his nibs appeared. We talked about the gee-gees, mostly. I was still in the phase of softening up and getting pally. He drank gin so as not to smell.

I kept in touch with Stan East. Acquaintance ripened into friendship, as they say. I invested moderate sums. You have to do that. He began to unbutton.

Distinctly funny doings were recorded in the form-book, exactly as I'd twigged. Tastes acquired in Egypt. Stan couldn't give me chapter and verse. The Viscount didn't mess on his own doorstep. But he couldn't stop his valet guessing. Who can? What Stan did was to get hold of girls. It wasn't easy, because the girls were never to know who Whitewater was. That was sensible enough if he went in for oddities. Stan himself was never to see the girls afterwards. That must have been in case they told him things. Enough to set anybody guessing, that rule. Stan was sworn to secrecy about the whole thing. It was disgraceful, the way he was abusing a position of trust by telling me the little he knew. We had a drink on that.

"Most of the girls he sees he won't have," Stan told me. "He inspects them first, see. Very choosy, our Morry. I'm at my wits' end, sometimes, finding a morsel he'll fancy and making the dispositions."

A plan began to form in my mind.

"I can help you, Stan," I said, "as pal to pal. I know some girls."

"I bet you do."

"And I can provide premises. Comfort and discretion guaranteed."

"I'd never 'a thought you was in that line of business," said Stan.

"I'm in every line of business," I said. "Have another."

I pondered the matter. This was my big chance, and I didn't want to muck it up. I did have premises. I could get girls. I could get any girl on the streets of London. All it took was money. The worry was getting the evidence in a form I could use. It was no good my just peeping through a keyhole.

There was a difficulty here I hadn't met before. With Mo Caplan or Ma Leach or even the lads at Rivvy's level, a word to the wise was all you needed. "I know what you've been up to with little boys, laddie, but for a tenner I'll wipe it off the tablets of memory." Not that you do. One tenner follows another. Life must go on. But Whitewater was a rich, powerful man with rich, powerful friends. He'd spit in my eye and have me arrested.

Hard evidence from a girl? That was no go. They'd never talk. If one did, he'd set the Roberts on her. Besides, their own pimps would cut their tongues out.

I needed something in the way of a document, something I could sell him. "The contents of this envelope for a monkey, my lord."

The idea, when it came, was so obvious that I could have kicked myself for not thinking of it sooner.

I was in Rivvy's room drinking a glass of Marsala with a bit of morning cake. There was a female in a frame on his mantelpiece.

"The Marchioness of Bulbarrow," said Rivvy. "A damned fine woman. Captured for eternity by the magic of photography. Something to ponder, laddie."

He was right. Captured for eternity. Something to ponder. Christ!

I knew chappies who worked for newspapers and press agencies—a scrubby bunch that I didn't care to be seen with in the West End. There were portrait photographers, too—you saw their signs everywhere. But the more I thought about it, the less I wanted another party involved. He'd want his share. And he might object to what I was doing. There are chappies who object to almost anything.

I had to get hold of an instrument and learn to play it myself.

I was lucky there, getting the equipment and the instruction. The source was a little portrait photographer in Islington going bankrupt. I got the stuff away just ahead of the creditors. I learned how to make enough light with a magnesium flare, and how to put the plates into the camera, and how to aim the weapon and press the trigger. Some chappies would have found it beyond them, but I mastered the whole bag of tricks.

I'd already fitted up a room in my Pimlico digs for the Bermondsey girl I employed—damned elegant, too, no expense spared. I'd organized a peephole through an old serving-hatch just to make sure things ran smoothly. Now I fitted the camera to the peephole and moved the bed a yard so that everything that happened on it could be—what was Rivvy's phrase?—captured for eternity.

The lens looked a bit rummy in the wall, but it wasn't a thing a chappie would worry about in the middle of nailing a filly. The magnesium flare was another matter. I decided I could get away with it if the flare went off just as *he* went off.

The next thing was to come by a filly to enter in the Whitewater Stakes. I would have entered little Nancy Higgs from Bermondsey, but she'd caught a dose from a sailor and she was in no state to run. So I went to the old Metropolitan Music Hall in the Edgeware Road and lurked about in the Standing Room behind the stalls. Gloria and Maybelle and Gaby and Posie worked it as a regular beat. Gaby was the first I saw, a great sofa of a woman, a good sort but too old for it. Then I saw Posie and bought her a small brandy.

"But who is this gent?" Posie wanted to know. "I'm not going into nothing like what you describe, Mr. Dacre, without I know where I'm at."

"I can't tell you his name," I said.

"Then I'm not touching it. Thanks ever so much for the drink, but I got to know who my customers are."

"You don't know the customers you pick up here."

"I see them and I talk to them, don't I? I can tell what sort a gent is. I can smell funny business a mile off. You won't find a girl working regular who can't. We got to look after ourselves. I'd like to oblige, Mr. Dacre, reely I would, but I won't walk into nothing like this without my eyes open."

I couldn't budge her, even with another small brandy.

Finally I said to Maybelle (I bought her a gin-and-beer, "All right, I'll whisper the name if you promise to forget it. Just to prove it's on the up and up.

"Oh no," she said, when I'd whispered. "Not on your life. I heard things. Funny things. Remember little Hattie Beard? Drowned herself in the Paddington Canal last month. She had that Whitewater and found out accidental who he was. Hattie didn't tell me anything but she mentioned it by way of warning."

Gloria had heard of Whitewater, too. Nothing definite, but enough to put her off. She said all the good-class girls in London had heard the rumour. Word gets round, naturally, like with the bookies on the racecourse. I could see Stan East had problems on his hands.

That was the state of the race in the middle of May. The part I thought would be easiest turned out to be hardest. I began to wonder if my whole investment wasn't down the drain.

I was in the West End one evening and I bent my footsteps to Jermyn Street. I was on the point of crossing to Rivvy Trench's door when I saw there was a girl standing on the step. She had lovely big hips. She was talking to old Ma Huxtable. Ma Huxtable slammed the door, and the girl sat down on a box and buried her face in her little hands. It wrung my heart to see her. I can't bear the sight of a girl in distress. But of course a chappie has to be careful.

A motor stopped near the door. I recognised it as Matty Alban's. Alban himself came out of the house in evening dress and a topper. The girl had started to walk away, but he called out to her and stopped her.

He was picking her up—a little filly on the street!

I prowled closer to observe the touching scene, using Alban's car as a stalking horse. I couldn't hear what they were saying, but I got a proper look at the girl. A peacherino! I didn't blame Alban. She was a bit bedraggled, but she had a sweet, innocent face, and her figure was as good in front as it was behind.

Something Matty Alban said made her burst into tears again. You dirty dog! I thought. Is that the way you treat girls you pick up in the street? The brute laughed! Actually laughed! I could have wrung his throat. Then he jumped into his car and it roared away, leaving me standing like a fool in the street.

It seemed Ma Huxtable was about to lead the girl into the house. This struck me as damned odd after the way she'd slammed the door. I was intrigued. So I made myself agreeable and carried the girl's box indoors.

Rivvy didn't remember having asked me to dinner, which was fair enough, as he hadn't asked me. I convinced him he'd forgotten.

From what Ma Huxtable told us, the girl was nothing to do with Matty Alban. It seemed a rummy business. I persuaded Rivvy to have her up after dinner to answer a few questions. She *was* a peach under the gaslight. She was pretty sleepy after travelling all day, and a couple of glasses of Rivvy's port made her tell us her life story.

Shocking it was. It all came tumbling out. A dirty old man started her off when she was only a kid, and she'd done the rounds ever since. Lord Harry Clinton was her latest. I got the whole story out of her. Rivvy would have interfered, but by that time he'd gone to sleep.

It was absolutely infuriating to have the goods on a real tiptop swell like Harry Clinton and not be able to use it. Abroad! Enough to make you cry.

For all she was a tart, little Emmy Brown was as innocent as a newborn lambkin. It was bloody touching. Up from the depth of the country for the very first time, and no idea what time of day it was.

She was just what the doctor ordered for my pal the Viscount Whitewater.

Rivvy and young Alban would get her a job in a dressmaker's, all very respectable, forty-five pounds a year. I had to nip in before they talked in those terms. So I got her out of Ma Huxtable's first thing next morning and softened her up with a bob's-worth in a tea shop.

She looked at me with those big brown eyes and nodded her dear little head, trusting as a puppy. I was sure she was the goods for Whitewater. I took her to Swan and Edgar's and fitted her out. Her eyes were like saucers in the shop. It was a pleasure to give her things. Then I took her to Giulini's in the Marylebone High Street. We had a bottle of red wine for two bob, and her tongue ran away with her again.

She told me a long story about somebody called Millie, which didn't interest me until I realised who Millie was. Then I *was* interested. She sounded a funny mixture. And what a goldmine for a chappie would could get in and work it! Emmy said she had a beautiful little arse. I believed her. There's something about aristocrats.

From Giulini's I telephoned to Stanley East at Whitewater's house in Charles Street. Speaking guarded, I said I had an entry for the fillies' stakes. He told me to bring her round at five and gave me a code for the bell-pull. That was so he'd come to the door, and not one of the footmen. *One* of the footmen! I was chasing the right fox.

I was pretty sure Emmy would pass the scrutiny. And she did.

Rivvy and young Alban wanted to know what the devil I was up to, spiriting away their little innocent.

"Innocent!" I said. "You were hoodwinked by a wet handkerchief, Sir Matthew. Why do you suppose she was given the sack? Sticky fingers in the jewel boxes. If she'd stayed here another hour there wouldn't have been a gold watch left in the place. I took her off to a clergyman I know with a mission for fallen women. I believe I did the right thing, gentlemen."

Matty Alban didn't look too certain.

I went round the corner with Rivvy for a brandy and asked him about Lady Camilla Glyn. I knew he'd know, and he did. She wouldn't inherit the bricks and mortar, but she would get the devil of a lot of money. Her mother had the use of the interest, Rivvy said, but the capital was in trust. Lady Camilla's husband would be a very lucky man.

Or her gentleman friend, I said to myself, if she ever comes to London and I get her in my sights.

The chauffeur knocked on the door at eleven in the morning. Whatever little ways he had, Whitewater was punctual.

Ma Leach let Whitewater in, though she didn't want to. I wasn't going to let him see me. He might remember seeing me in Jermyn Street.

While he climbed the stairs, I looked through the camera to make sure everything was in the right place. Emmy was sitting on the bed with a scarf over her eyes like Stan East ordered. Most of the bed would be in the photo.

I heard Whitewater come into the room and lock the door. I heard Ma Leach's footsteps shuffle away. I heard clothes tearing and then the sound of a slap. There was a lot more ripping and rending. Wicked waste. Well, he'd be paying.

I heard a bonk-bonk of shoes in the floor, his shoes. Good biz, he was undressing.

After a bit I heard what I was waiting for—the panting of a chappie in the last half-furlong. He was roaring up to the winning post. I was sure of it. That furious breathing can't lie. There was a sort of shuddering sigh, and I pressed the lever that lit the magnesium and the bulb that worked the shutter of the camera.

I took the plate out of the camera so I could see through. Whitewater was dressing. He took as much time dressing as he had nailing Emmy. He had the whitest skin I ever saw on a man. There was no sign of Emmy. I saw Whitewater toss a big envelope in the bed. Money. He tossed something else there—a small bright thing I couldn't make out.

I nearly had a fit when I saw Emmy handcuffed to the head of the bed on her knees as though she was saying her prayers. It was such a surprise. The envelope was money. I checked that before anything. The bright thing was a key. I unlocked the darbies and took the scarf off Emmy's eyes. She was all right. She wouldn't say what had happened, but it was nothing dreadful.

He'd given her a little slap, but nothing that showed after half an hour.

The photo came out beautifully. It showed an empty bed. That was all it showed. Emmy and our customer had been out of the picture.

I got hold of Stanley East, saying we'd be glad to entertain his lordship on the same terms whenever convenient. It only meant moving the bed so the bedhead was in range of the camera. No problems. Emmy hadn't come to any harm—it was all hysterical nonsense.

But that horse wouldn't run.

"Our Morry never wants the same one twice," said Stanley. "He likes surprising them. It's got to be a new one every time."

"Christ," I said. "You're going to have a job filling the field."

"I am," he said. "Any further assistance gratefully received and acknowledged."

So I set out to look for another Emmy. It was a long time before I found one. But when I did find one she was the best there could be.

10 ❋ *Her face doth reek and smoke*

> And, having felt the sweetness of the spoil,
> With blindfold fury she begins to forage;
> Her face doth reek and smoke, her blood doth boil,
> And careless lust stirs up a desperate courage;
> Planting oblivion, beating reason back,
> Forgetting shame's pure blush and honour's wrack.

VENUS AND ADONIS

"Good morning, Camilla."

"Good morning, Mamma," I said, kissing her carefully so as not to disarrange her hat.

Her kiss was preoccupied. She seemed preoccupied altogether. I thought there would have been dark circles under her eyes if they had not been covered up by cream and powder. I thought there were new lines round her mouth, as though she had been tugging it down like the tragic mask on a theatre programme.

For ten days I had been dreadfully self-absorbed, thinking of Henry and myself and what we had done and what we had failed to do. I had not much noticed Mamma. But I did now, and I was shocked. She had aged ten years in those ten days. I did not think other people noticed. In public she wore the comic mask from the theatre programme.

I never saw her cry; I never had seen her cry. But I was sure she had been crying. She looked as I felt.

But she had not lost Uncle Gareth. I did not see how she could be as miserable as I was.

Looking properly about me for the first time in ten days, I saw that Uncle Gareth was as hard and glossy and confident as ever when anyone was looking. But when he thought he was alone, a sort of crumpled look came into his face. I once saw an old man in the village who had just been turned out of his cottage. He loved the cottage. It was all he had. But of course it was not his. He was turned out to make way for a new young gamekeeper. Uncle Gareth looked like that.

But he had not lost Mamma. He came to Moreys as before and took an afternoon nap when Mamma did. I did not see how *he* could be as miserable as I was.

A few days later a page boy came out to my Chinese bridge and said that someone had called to see me. I was surprised. Nobody called to see me.

"It's Mrs. Venables from the pub, m'lady," said the page boy. "Wants to see your ladyship most partic'lar."

I was full of curiosity. It took my mind off my own wretchedness. I did not know Mrs. Venables in the least, or anything about her. I could not imagine what had brought her to see me.

She was waiting in a little sitting room called the Outside Room, where Mamma saw farmers' wives. It was a gay little room with floral wallpaper and chintz chair-covers. Mrs. Venables was not gay. She had a black dress and a face of doom, and her stays creaked when she curtseyed.

"I'm right sorry to disturb your ladyship," she said in a clucking voice like a bantam hen's, "and I hope your ladyship will forgive the intrusion, specially as what I got to say to your ladyship is disagreeable and unpleasant and wicked sinful; and I do wish some other messenger could of been found to impart the communication to your ladyship, but my duty obliged me to disturb your ladyship, commanded by the voice of conscience. It's about that Emily Brown."

I am sure I looked as surprised as I felt.

"Seeing as how the baggage is your ladyship's personal maid, as is well known to all since she never stopped boasting about it ever since your ladyship thought fit to repose trust in sich a unworthy vessel, I thought it proper to relate confidential and personal to your ladyship the trolloping as has transpired in recent weeks."

"Go on, Mrs. Venables."

"She has come to my house repeated, which as all the world including your ladyship knows is as respectable establishment which me and Mr. Venables conducks according to the law in all regards and respects. She been visiting repeated a gentleman guest of the house in the best front bedroom over the taproom, which your ladyship will not of honoured with a visit, but which is a model of decorum in all respects and regards same like the Licencing Magistrates requires."

"The bedroom or the taproom?" I asked, becoming confused.

"Both, your ladyship, is conducted according. Your ladyship will understand and appreciate that we can't have trolloping baggages a-visiting gentlemen in the best bedroom, not if they was lady's-maid to the Marchioness herself."

"What gentleman?" I asked, thinking I'd get some facts from Emmy this time.

"He called and entitled himself Mister James Smith, your ladyship, which I was of thought and opinion was a halias assumed for purposes of licentious and wicked conduck. But I glimpsed of papers in a pocketbook which he left lying on a dressing table, a proceeding which I hope your ladyship will understand was prompted not by vulgar curiosity but by concern for the respectable conduck of my house."

"And?"

"The gentleman was his lordship the Lord Henry Clinton, your ladyship, which that Emmy Brown come a-visiting secret and sly half-a-dozen times if she come once. I did not wish to demean myself to a-peeping and a-spying, but I am sure your ladyship will understand that I had a duty to assure myself of proper conduck in my house; and in the strict line of duty, as commanded by duty and the Licencing Magistrates, I did observe sufficient to bear out my suspicions of wicked and lewd carry-ons such as are not permitted in my house."

"Oh," I said, hardly able to make any sound at all.

"I sees rage and disgust on your ladyship's face, identical such as I feels in my own heart, your ladyship."

She went on clucking at me. I did not hear another word. I wanted to scream.

I had been praying for Henry to come. And he did come. Dear God, he did come, again and again, secretly, to the pub, and made love to Emmy. That was what he liked.

Henry was safe from me. He was in Vienna. He was wise.

My new maid was called Grace. The name did not suit her. She was brisk and sour-faced and old. That was why I chose her. She would not steal any man I found.

She would have had no chance. I found no man. There were none in my life. None of Mamma's friends interested me. If I interested any of them, they would not have cared to show it. Mamma disliked her courtiers paying court elsewhere.

I felt squalid and dishonoured, making love to myself with my fingers in bed. The nights were very warm. Lust seemed to hang in the air like smoke. It reeked from the mock orange flowers and the lilies of the valley and the new-mown grass. It hummed from the mowers pulled by dapple-grey ponies over the lawns, and from the bees in the lavender and the bluebottle flies in the musk roses.

I was drugged by summer and by yearning. I fell into a state of utter lassitude. There was nothing to do. I had hardly energy enough to put on a hat.

At night I caressed my nipples so that they grew hard and urgent under my fingers. I loved that feeling. I truly needed it. I longed for other hands than mine to awaken those rosebuds into happiness. And I caressed the silky fleece below my belly. I became expert at it, fondling the little thimble, inducing the sweet-sour essence to moisten the lips, delaying the full thrust of my fingers until I moaned aloud with excitement.

Of course my mind's eye was crowded with pictures during those guilty nights. Henry was banished from my fantasies. He preferred fat servants. I found myself picturing nice blue eyes looking at me as I lay naked on my moonlit bed. I stroked my breasts and pictured a head descending to kiss them. The head had untidy light-brown hair.

I had never spoken to him. I had never been near him when he came to Moreys.

Mamma had asked him once. Might she not ask him again?

"I don't see why not," said Mamma, as her hair was being brushed by Prior.

I raised the subject again.

"I often see him," said Mamma. "He goes everywhere. He's no longer completely silent, but he doesn't talk too much. People like him. I imagine his time is fully engaged. Are we talking about the same man? You know the one I mean, Fordy?"

"Yes, my lady," said Miss Fordham, who was standing with the seating plan for dinner pressed against her gaunt bosom. She looked as though she wanted to snatch a mouthful of hay from a hay rack.

"Why do people like him, Mamma?" I asked.

"I don't know. Why does anybody like anybody? What extraordinary questions you do ask. He's said to be clever. Why are you interested?"

"I don't know," I said truthfully. "I just am."

Mamma turned so sharply to look at me that Prior could not help pulling her hair. After the tumult had subsided, Mamma said, "I would not advise you to become interested in this or any other young man, Camilla. We have—We are obliged—You know quite well that people in our position cannot always have—We must choose with—with a lot of things in mind. I can't discuss it now. One day we must have a proper talk about it."

She had been looking better. Now she was looking worse.

When I raised the subject a third time, Mamma said, almost furiously, "No, Camilla. I won't have you getting silly sentimental ideas about any young man. You must be guided. You must let me guide you. I know what is best for you. When the time comes, you will need someone older, able to take a firm line, someone with experience and knowledge of the world —Someone who—In fact, I—"

The fury left her. She flapped her hands at me, not knowing what to say.

"Alban's a very good fellow," said Uncle Gareth, surprised when I asked him. "Better manners than most lads of his age. Better informed, too. It's a pleasure to meet a boy who isn't a puppy or a waster. He hasn't pushed himself. He's become well known and well liked just by being the man he is."

It wasn't that Mamma wanted him for herself. It was that she wanted me not to want him. Why, since he was said to be so excellent in every way?

Mamma wanted me to want someone else.

Had she picked someone for me? Already? Why? Who?

I wasn't an Indian or a Royal Princess (not quite) to be forced into an arranged marriage. I expected to go onto the marriage market, like every other girl of my kind, when I came out in London the following season, and to catch the best I could. I expected the best I could catch to be the best available, not through special virtue but special luck. I was very lucky. I could think of flying very high. That, I concluded, was what was in Mamma's mind. She had visions of Archbishops, Westminster Abbey, gold state coaches, reception at the Palace—

I didn't. I had obstinate visions of nice blue eyes looking at me when I lay naked on my bed in the moonlight, and nice head of untidy brown hair tickling my breasts in the dawn . . .

I got his address out of Miss Fordham's book. I could see no conceivable use for it. I bought an address book of my own from the stationer's in Wilton and wrote the address down. It was the only address I wrote down. I could think of no one else in the world whose address remotely interested me.

At the beginning of July, Lord Whitewater came to stay again. He had been abroad.

"I wandered in the Levant, my dear little Camilla," he said.

He had taken to calling me Camilla. I could not object. Everyone could call me Camilla because until I was out, I was a child, so they thought.

"I retraced ancient footsteps of mine in those most ancient places," he said in that schoolmasterish voice, "looking for things which are not easily found in England."

"What things?" I asked, thinking he meant dates and oranges.

"Rich varieties of human experience, combining pain with pleasure, triumph with defeat, conquest with humiliation, which is good for the soul."

He had come on Thursday, which few people were allowed to do. It seemed to me that I saw him wherever I went.

I have said that none of Mamma's friends interested me or were interested in me. Lord Whitewater was a resounding exception. He did interest me and he did seem unaccountably interested in me.

Interest me? That is true, but inadequate. He *was* interesting in nearly everything he said. It was nice to have conversation after the interminable gossip of the others. But I did not feel easier in his company. He interested me—he fascinated and repelled me. He was a foreigner, a creature of another species. He was inhuman. He did not seem to be made of flesh.

I felt his eyes on me wherever I went. Whenever he came near he touched me. His hands felt like rubber.

Although he was interesting, I avoided him. At least, I tried to. I ought to have been able to in a place the size of Moreys. But wherever I went, there he was, as though he read my mind and knew where I was going before I knew myself.

"I'm glad you get on so well with Lord Whitewater," said Mamma. "He's wonderful company, isn't he? He's been to such very odd places— Nobody who saw a lot of him would have a dull hour. I envy the girl he marries."

I thought it was true his wife would not have a dull time. I did not envy her. The thought of being married to him was quite horrifying. I did not know why. It was just the person he was. He was like a sort of mad animal, with those hot eyes and suffering mouth, inhabiting the body of a corpse . . .

There was a fortnight of glorious weather in late July. The days were hot and sleepy, the nights warm and wakeful. I spent the days in languor and the nights in lust. Scented air drifted in through my bedroom windows. I writhed and moaned, dozing, dreaming dreams of piercing sweetness and sickening squalor, waking to find my fingers busy with the inexhaustible magic between my thighs.

At the end of July, Lord Whitewater came again, bringing with him the most extraordinary man I had ever met.

Occasionally Mamma had had artists and writers to stay. It was because they were being talked about. It was smart to have them, although they were not smart. When I was a child, I would have expected them to be interesting. But I discovered they were not. Some were just as patronizing and boring as other grown-ups, and some were too shy to talk even to me. Mamma and Moreys were too much for them. They hid in corners, escaping notice, and crept away like mice on Monday morning. I was sorry for them, but that did not make them more interesting.

Mr. Jasper Whittingham was completely unlike the furtive Royal Academicians who upset their glasses at luncheon through nervousness. He was not furtive or nervous. His voice boomed all over Moreys. When he laughed, the pictures almost fell off the walls. He was immensely tall with a mane of untidy black hair and a black beard which reached almost to his waist. He wore a short canvas coat with brass buttons, huge baggy trousers, and sandals without socks. His big toenails were the size of coffee saucers. Round his neck, instead of a tie, he wore a long red scarf which trailed into wine glasses and soup bowls.

"An incongruous figure here," Lord Whitewater said to me, "but so must Peter Paul Rubens have been at some of the courts he visited. Whittingham was the darling of the Slade a few years ago. Sickert and Roger Fry think the world of him. For once I agree with both. For my taste, he is the most original and accomplished painter of his generation. I expect you agree, being young."

I nodded wisely. I had never heard of Jasper Whittingham.

"To borrow a metaphor from my racing friends," said Whitewater, "he is bred perhaps by Monet out of Goya. He deserved greater success than he has achieved. That is why I suggested his visit here. Painting your gracious mother will bring him a measure of merited celebrity."

"Oh yes. Sargent did her just the other day."

"Yes, dressed up for a drawing room at Buckingham Palace, all silk and ostrich feathers. He catches a likeness, does our venerable John Singer; but in other respects his portrait of your lady Mamma is indistinguishable from six hundred others he has done at six hundred guineas a time."

Mamma had been very pleased with Sargent's portrait. It made her look about twenty-five. Mr. Sargent had come to stay. He was going to paint me when I was out.

You can see that although he was disquieting and disgusting, I did learn things from Lord Whitewater that nobody else told me about.

I learned something from Jasper Whittingham himself, too.

I was leaning over the parapet of my Chinese bridge on Saturday afternoon, studying my reflection, when the whole bridge seemed to shake, and the birds to burst in terror out of the trees. Mr. Whittingham bounded up to join me.

"Miladi Camille," he shouted, "la Dame aux Camélias, Ophelia athwart the brook! I almost wish I was one of those wretched pre-Raphaelites!"

"How do you do?" I said, which was not a properly artistic reply, but was the only one I could think of.

He kissed my hand, which nobody had ever done before. His beard tickled my fingers. It suited him, and so did his hair and his extraordinary clothes.

He was the exact opposite in every way of the detestable and treacherous Henry Clinton. All by itself that was enough to make him agreeable.

He looked at me with a savage frown, as though planning rape. I gulped. I was sure he had raped dozens of delighted shepherdesses, their gurgles drowned by his deafening laugh. He tugged his beard with one hand and put his hat on his head—it was black with a brim a yard across and a squashy top.

He said in a voice of formidable authority, "Look to your left. Chin up. I want the light reflected from the water on your cheekbones. A little towards me. Don't smile. Agh! It's too infernally pre-Raphaelite to touch. I must paint you twice. Before and after, innocence and experience. We'll hang them side by side in the Chenil Gallery, if Orpen and John don't hog the whole wall."

"Before and after what?" I asked, not daring to move from the position he had ordered me to take, although it was giving me a crick in the neck.

"Your awakening, my little faun, my anemone of the woods, my unplucked harebell. I'll paint you by moonlight. Agh—if it worked, it would be something after that old fraud Whistler. I must paint you in the nude, here on this ridiculous bridge. The textures! Agh—your skin like a white rose petal against the stone. Sentimental idea. I like sentimental ideas. You're a beautiful girl. Sit for me."

"In the nude?" I gasped.

"Not yet. Agh—let's promise ourselves. But not in this overblown palace of yours. The idea of living in that house is grotesque. What's the point of it all? A man needs somewhere to work and sleep and eat and make love, and wash and relieve himself. One room. More than that adds complication without increasing comfort. But I like this bridge. I like its uselessness. You cross, and then what? You cross back again. It's an exquisite example of the utterly purposeless. Like yourself. Like myself."

"But you," I said, "are a great painter—"

"I am a great painter. The fact cannot be too widely known, too firmly or frequently stated. What could be more useless? I create imperishable beauty. Who does it feed? Not me. Agh—to paint you as you stand now —to bring it off without sentimentality—that would be something. Don't move! Stay exactly as you are until next April. I want to paint you in the spring. I want to paint you very young and very old, so you'd better stand still until you're seventy."

He gave a great bellow of laughter. He had full red lips and big white teeth. Then he kissed my hand again and bounded away into the bushes beside the lake.

I found I liked being called "an exquisite example of the utterly purposeless." I liked Jasper Whittingham. He made a change.

I imagined him that night. An artist's hands would be deft, strange. I would pillow genius between my breasts. His beard would tickle.

"Will Mr. Whittingham paint you, Mamma?"

"Yes, it seems so. He wants to. He only charges fifty pounds."

I was delighted. He said I was exquisite. It is difficult not to be prejudiced in favour of someone who says you are exquisite.

He would paint me on the bridge in the time left over from painting Mamma.

"I shall go to his studio in London," said Mamma. "In ice-blue taffeta and pearls. He wanted to do it here, but it's out of the question. He doesn't fit in. I can give him more time in London. Here my time's not my own. I have to work and worry all the time, since none of the people I pay can be trusted to do anything without supervision. No, Fordy, I don't want Mr. Whittingham anywhere near me tonight. His laugh is too loud and his conversation is too—what's the word? It begins with O. Ob—something."

"Obscene?" I suggested.

"Go away at once and wash out your mouth with soap and water, Camilla. Obscure. He can take in the Grand Duchess, Fordy. Her sister used to do water-colours in the Alps. That will give them something in common."

Beyond the croquet lawn and the Temple of Flora there was a copper beech with a swing tied to one of its branches. I had often swung on it when I was small. Then I decided that swinging was childish. Then I decided that it was romantic. There were girls in drawings by Boucher and Fragonard in the Yellow Saloon, in big hats and panniers, on swings. One had lost her shoe. A very gallant young gentleman was retrieving it. He would slip it on her little foot while she smiled.

I saw myself as a Boucher girl, a princess pretending to be a shepherdess, dreamily swinging in the dappled shade. It suited my languorous mood. People came by and said how enchanting I looked. I was, perhaps, more inclined to use the swing when the house was full than when there was nobody to see me.

One afternoon I was sitting on my swing, barely moving, thinking it a pity that Jasper Whittingham was not by with his brushes.

A precise voice behind me said, "A push! If ever a young lady was mutely appealing for a push, you, dear little Camilla, are that young lady."

I did not want Lord Whitewater to push me. I could not see a way to tell him so. A swing invites a push. It is the function of swings to be swung.

Others pushed the wooden seat. But Lord Whitewater pushed me. I felt his hands through the cotton of my skirt. They felt clammy even through cotton. I swung forwards, backwards. I felt his hands on my behind. He gripped a moment before pushing. It was a split second, but he gripped. He did it again and again, not pushing hard, but squeezing my behind before he pushed.

It might have been so nice if somebody else had been doing it.

"Stop!" I said. "Please stop. I'm getting giddy. I'm going to be sick."

"Alas. *Mal de balançoire*. We shall arrest all distressing movement."

I might have foreseen that he would take this new opportunity. He caught me as I swung back, one hand on my behind and one on my thigh. He had an excuse. I had asked him to stop me. Anybody would see that he was doing as I asked. He was not. He was squeezing me through my clothes. It was more disgusting than anything Henry Clinton had done. His hands were furtive but unambiguous. I pulled myself away.

I really did feel sick.

I thought afterwards it was silly to have reacted with such nausea to a brief contact through my clothes. Especially as his conversation was still the most interesting I had any chance to hear.

At tea time he sat beside me and asked if I were better. His eyes seemed to squeeze me as his hands had done. I felt sick again. I could not eat my cake.

"Mamma, you may think this is silly, but I feel I'm being persecuted."

"What nonsense are you talking, Camilla? You have everything that anybody could want. I sometimes think we are far too generous and indulgent with you."

"Yes, Mamma, I'm grateful for everything, except Lord Whitewater. He—he dogs my footsteps, Mamma, and today on the swing—"

"You are extremely lucky that such a brilliant man takes an interest in you. You should be very flattered. It is extraordinarily kind of him."

"He takes too much interest in me, Mamma—If you see what I mean."

"He takes a keen and flattering interest in you, yes. He had told me so, very frankly and openly. You're extremely lucky to have aroused the—the interest of someone like that. Every girl in England will be jealous of you."

"But—But—" I was incapable of speech. What Mamma seemed to be saying was utterly incredible, utterly absurd.

"You've often said yourself how interesting he is, Camilla. Seeing you with him, I've often envied you. So has every other woman, let me tell you that."

"*But Mamma—*"

"What a fascinating life you'll have. All that travel! And everywhere he will know the best places to go, the best people to meet—"

"Forty!"

"What, child?"

"He—he's at least forty, Mamma! You *can't* be suggesting—"

"There's no need to fly into hysterics, Camilla. Of course nobody will make you do anything you don't want to do. But you're such a silly little thing in some ways. You need a firm hand and guidance. Of course you know you can trust me to put your happiness before anything, and to give you sensible advice—"

"You can't be serious!"

"It's simply too tiresome of you to take good advice in such a ridiculous way. I'm your mother, you seem to forget, and I'm naturally in a position to judge where your true happiness lies—"

"I'd rather die."

"Oh, don't cry about it! For heaven's sake, stop pulling such horrible faces."

Mamma was no longer being gently reasonable. She was back to normal. But she made a huge effort and said, "Of course it will take you time to get used to the idea. We all understand that. You must get to know each other better, and then—Of course, nobody is going to force you into anything, but I'm sure you'll see in the end that—At any rate, I want you to promise not to be silly, and to get to know Maurice Whitewater better, and be with him as much as possible; and then, you'll see, you'll find that you—I'm only thinking of your happiness, dearest child. Nothing else is of the least importance."

"Hap—pap—" I stammered, unable to believe anything I was hearing.

"And because I am only thinking of your happiness, I'm going to help Maurice all I can; and if you trust Mamma, dearest, you'll find that everything will—"

I thought Mamma had gone mad. She couldn't seriously be suggesting . . .

But she kept on at me about it, on and on, whenever she had a moment spare. Sometimes she talked about the joys of travel, sometimes about the bliss of learned conversation; sometimes she said how much happier I would be with the guidance of an older man, sometimes how attractive Maurice Whitewater was, how much he was admired by all the young ladies in London; again and again she said how envious every girl in England would be . . .

Always she said she was concerned only about my happiness. Nobody would force me into anything. I would come to see she was right. I was to trust her, because she knew best.

Of course he came to Moreys oftener than ever, all summer. His eyes seemed to tear my clothes off. His hands twitched and he licked his lips. Try as I might to avoid him, I was always finding myself alone with him. Sometimes he planned this, and sometimes Mamma did.

I would soon come to see that she was right, she assured me, because she knew best and she was concerned only with my happiness.

"No," I said. "I'm sorry to be disobliging, Mamma, but the thought makes me feel ill."

"In time," said Mamma, with a look of despair on her face which I had never seen there before, "when you know him better—"

"I've been with him for hours and hours and hours and hours, week after week after week after week. I've got to know him better and better and better and better, and I'd rather die. I truly would. *I'd rather die.*"

"In time," said Mamma wearily, "everything will come right. You'll see. You'll understand that we're right. We're only thinking of your happiness."

"Mamma, please listen this time. The thought of marrying Lord Whitewater makes me feel ill. I swear I would rather die. You can't make me do it. If you do I'll kill myself. Do you hear me, Mamma? Have I made you understand?"

I had never talked like that to Mamma before. I had never dared. I thought she would be angry. But she stared at me piteously.

"If you'd only trust us, dearest child—"

"Because you're only thinking of my happiness. You know best. Every girl in England will envy me. Mamma, I'll kill myself before I let him touch me."

The sun poured in through the open window of her little sitting room, bringing the sound of bees and birdsong, and the *tock* of croquet balls, and the distant shout of somebody playing lawn tennis. A fly droned round the warm air of the room.

Mamma looked at the fly, frowning, as though a fly were a new and disturbing thing. She turned back to me, and I have never seen such misery on a face.

Over and over again the same ghastly words poured out. I would be envied and happy. That was all that mattered to her. She knew best. I was to trust her.

"Mamma," I said, "must I go out and drown myself now?"

She said in a muffled voice, "I beg you, Camilla."

"*Why?*"

She began to cry. Her face became ugly and contorted. Tears spilled out of her eyes, streaking the powder on her cheeks. She began to sob with a harsh, painful noise. She covered her face with her hands. Through her hands and her sobs I could make out that she was begging me again.

"Whitewater is making you do this," I said, making a discovery so obvious that I should have made it weeks before.

She nodded through her sobs and through the wet fingers over her face.

"Whitewater can make you do whatever he wants," I said slowly, facing the truth which explained everything. "Even this. You'll even do this."

Then the most shocking and terrible thing happened. Mamma lost all that remained of her self-control, all dignity, all pride. She threw herself face down on the floor. She wriggled forward, her face in the carpet, and clutched my feet. Her wet contorted face was on my feet. She was kissing my feet in an agony of beseeching. I had never seen such naked misery, such passionate despair. It was disgusting.

Words came choking and broken out of the racking sobs. "Reputation. Newspapers. The King. Our name. Gareth. Jockey Club. His wife. Resign. Ruin. Abroad. Never show my face—How they'll laugh—"

I felt contemptuous and bottomlessly sorry for her. I could not bear another second of this shameless indecency, this grovelling.

"All right," I said. "I'll do as you wish."

Even as I spoke, I shuddered at the sound of my own words. But even as I spoke, I knew I had no alternative.

11 ❀ *These round enchanting pits*

> These lovely caves, these round enchanting pits,
> Open'd their mouths to swallow Venus' liking.
> Being mad before, how doth she now for wits?
> Struck dead at first, what need a second striking?

VENUS AND ADONIS

I said Yes. I say it was to die. I had no choice.

I had to do three things. Play for time. Pray for a miracle. Get away from Moreys.

My unspeakable interview with Mamma was at the end of July. My engagement to Whitewater was to be announced at the end of the year; not a day later, but not necessarily earlier. This was Whitewater's command. Mamma had to obey it or be destroyed; I had to obey it and be destroyed. But I had five months.

I would use them for praying for a miracle.

Meanwhile Moreys throttled me. Every room of the house, every inch of the garden and park, reeked of Whitewater. I wanted to get away from the reek. I wanted to get away from the memory of Henry Clinton. I wanted to get away from the memory of Mamma's degraded blubbering over my feet on the floor.

I wanted to get away from Mamma. Her gratitude was more distasteful than her despair. She kept bringing me presents I did not want and deferring to my wishes. She was frightened of offending me in case I changed my mind.

I might have expected to have enjoyed having such power over a grown-up, over my own mother. But I hated it.

I wanted to be among other people, in another place. Normally such a thing would have been unthinkable—I was a ewe-lamb; I was not even "out." But Mamma could not stop me. She did not dare, in case I changed my mind.

Whitewater himself was going abroad in early August. He came to say goodbye to me. Mamma contrived to leave us alone by the Temple of Flora. He would make some sort of advance to me. He was allowed to, expected to; he was my accepted suitor, approved by Mamma, and we were parting for a period of weeks. An embrace, a kiss, was almost mandatory on us.

I stood in a cold tremble waiting for his hands on my shoulders and his face on mine. I willed myself to be stoical, not to grimace or push him away.

I suppose my face showed my feelings. It always did, unfortunately.

He stood close to me. I smelled the scent from his hair, which would have been pleasing on any other hair. I did not look at him, but at the sunlight on the great trees. The sunlight said that the world was a good and beautiful place. It lied.

He said, "Dearly as I would like to take you in my arms, little one, I will postpone that joy until I return. Reunion will be celebrated by effusions denied to parting. You have five weeks, little Camilla, in which to prepare your lips for mine. Guard them well! Eat only raspberries and nectarines, think only loving thoughts, sleep sweetly at night, listen to Mozart and look at pictures by Botticelli. I would sell my soul to possess that sweet purity of yours! Alas, it was sold long ago, to buy other merchandise, and I am selling someone else's soul. Fortunately you have no idea what I am talking about. Goodbye, my very dearest."

He took my hand and kissed it. It was the second time this had happened to me. I remembered with a sudden nostalgia Jasper Whittingham's beard scratching my fingers, and his booming friendliness, and the nice things he said.

Whitewater's lips felt like graveyard snails. I pulled my hand away. I could not help it. He laughed softly. He did not mind my being frightened of him. He liked it.

"Of course you must go away, dearest child, if that is what you would like," said Mamma, making herself smile affectionately, making me ashamed for her.

I had seldom been "her dearest child." Now I always was. The words lost all meaning. They were an ugly joke.

This was the moment to exercise my new power. I said, "I will go to London."

"To *London?*" wailed Mamma. "In August? It is horribly hot and stuffy. No one will be there. The streets smell, you know, and everything is shut."

"I shall be there," I said, "and so will Cousin Dorothea. I shall stay with her. I am to look at pictures by Botticelli and go to concerts."

I understood Mamma's surprise. My choice was a thoroughly odd one. Everyone in her world left London just when I was proposing to go there. But, if I was to go, Cousin Dorothea was a thoroughly good idea. She never left London, as she found travelling tiring and vulgar. She was massively respectable. She had been a Lady in Waiting to the old Queen. She lived on a sofa, talking about banquets forty years earlier. She was kind. I liked her.

Mamma still showed signs of amazement and distress.

"Maurice Whitewater," I said, forcing myself to use his disgusting Christian name, "wants me to improve my mind, Mamma. He said so when he left."

"But in *August,* dearest child—"

"There will be so much to do later," I said obscurely.

Anyway, Mamma was pleased that I wanted to follow my suitor's instructions. It showed a change of heart, and she was concerned only with my happiness. Her objections petered out, and she wrote to Cousin Dorothea.

The reply came written crisscross on a sheet of black-bordered paper. Little Camilla would be welcome in Berkeley Square to stay as long as she liked; she would be company for her old cousin and could hear stories of the old days.

Mamma came with me to London. She looked with trepidation at the unfamiliar August streets. They looked safe enough to me, and not much different from the May streets except that more people wore straw hats.

Cousin Dorothea's house got all the afternoon sun. None was allowed in. She sat in stuffy semidarkness with her companion Miss Cole who was reading a newspaper aloud. I was surprised that Cousin Dorothea wanted to hear the news.

"His Royal Highness the Prince Consort," read Miss Cole in a voice like a piccolo with a sore throat, "today described his plans for a great exhibition of the scientific and mechanical achievements of the Empire."

The newspaper was fifty years old. It was what Cousin Dorothea wanted to hear.

Cousin Dorothea was small and plump with prominent eyes and a receding chin—very like her late royal mistress, but gentler. Her voice chirruped. She wore black silk dresses of an ancient style. She was the Dowager Countess of Hale. She had difficulty holding a fork, which was a grief to her, as she loved food. If she was like a plump September partridge, Miss Cole was like a midwinter sparrow. She felt the cold even in the heat. Her father had been a prebendary at Ely Cathedral. Cousin Dorothea paid her an enormous salary, every penny of which she gave to the Children's Hospital in Great Ormonde Street.

I was made very welcome and given tea. The servants who brought it in were as old as Miss Cole and nearly as old as Cousin Dorothea. The whole household seemed to move slowly, on tottering legs. Even the page boy was as gnarled as a walnut.

Mamma went off to Bulbarrow House after tea. She said there were a thousand housekeeping details to attend to. I supposed Uncle Gareth was in London.

I felt a sense of extraordinary liberation when Mamma's carriage wheels rumbled off. This is a dreadful way to speak of one's own mother, but when the footmen jumped away from the horses' heads, I felt as though a sack of flour had been lifted off my head. I felt like the children I had seen exploding out of the village school at noon, shrieking and turning cartwheels. I felt like the goldfinch belonging to the head stillroom maid at Moreys which I had let out of the cage, without anyone knowing, when I was nine.

I had an early supper with the old ladies. The dining room was stuffy and full of the smell of red cabbage. They had hearty appetites, but they ate slowly. They thought I must have a good schoolgirl appetite, too (which I did have, as a rule), and the old footman was constantly told to bring me more of everything, and especially more pudding. Cousin Dorothea loved pudding.

After supper Cousin Dorothea was helped back to her sofa. She must have been as full as a boa constrictor that had just swallowed a buffalo. After so much stodgy food on a hot night, I felt like a buffalo that had just swallowed a boa constrictor. Comfortably settled, Cousin Dorothea started on a story she thought would interest me. I began to feel very restless, but I was shamed by Miss Cole. She must have heard the story hundreds of times, yet she showed bright, unflagging interest and asked eager questions.

They said I was tired after my journey and sent me to bed at half past nine. I knew I had no hope of sleeping well in a strange bed in the stuffy London air with a noisy street below my window; especially having eaten too much and having had a perfectly comfortable journey. I had been sleeping badly even in the deep warm silence of the Wiltshire nights. I had been kept awake by despair.

People say that when you lie wakeful in the small hours, all problems seem more huge and horrible than they do by daylight. It is not so. My problems seemed just as horrible by daylight.

Grace helped me to bed and said that she would call me at eight. I lay back, sighing, expecting the ten hours to pass with excruciating slowness. Grace turned down the gas (Cousin Dorothea mistrusted electricity) and closed the door.

Immediately, the next second, she was standing by my bed with a tray of fruit and biscuits. The room was full of light. I was angry. Why did the silly woman disturb me and turn up all the gaslights as high as they would go? And, of course, it was morning. I had slept so deeply and sweetly that the night was abolished.

I embarked on a life of culture, guided by Miss Anabel Porter-Binfield. She had been a schoolmistress at the Cheltenham Ladies' College, recently retired; Miss Cole found her; she had gold-rimmed spectacles on a mauve silk ribbon, and an umbrella with a handle carved to look like a dolphin. I liked her. She tried to be strict and punctilious, but she was too absent-minded to be good at it. Had she been a dragon, I would still have felt liberated because I was away from the abject gratitude in Mamma's eyes. Of course, I had to have a chaperon.

When Miss Porter-Binfield had almost smothered me under the weight of the Italian Renaissance, I asked her about modern painting.

She wondered whether an innocent young girl should be exposed to such influences. "There are revolutionaries, dear, who are determined to *blow up* our artistic values! Mr. Wyndham Lewis—The Post-Impressionists—There is a young American called Epstein whose work you should certainly not—But, of course, Mr. Whistler, and that clever Mr. Sickert, one can contemplate their work in safety—"

"And Mr. Jasper Whittingham?" I asked.

Miss Porter-Binfield had not heard of Jasper Whittingham.

She took me, greatly daring, to an exhibition of the New English Art Club.

"There are no Whittinghams," I said, feeling cheated.

"Indeed there are not, my dear young lady," said a brisk voice behind me. It was a little man in tweed knickerbockers and Norfolk jacket in which he must have been very hot. "Whittingham is not a member of this Society, although his efforts to become one have presented an edifying spectacle, over many months, of unremitting labour and intrigue. If you are determined on a mortification of the spirit, you may adventure to the Chenil Gallery—that distressing money-grubber Willie Orpen's latest shop window for his daubs. He hangs Whittingham. I suppose his plan is to make his own paintings look better by contrast. He is right. They do."

The gallery was in the King's Road, Chelsea, near the Town Hall. Miss Porter-Binfield was dubious about adventuring into Chelsea, but she seemed reassured by the Town Hall. I had never set foot in Chelsea before. I had heard it was full of Bohemians and Apaches. They were all in hiding that day. The notorious King's Road looked like any other street, and the Chenil Gallery like any other house.

We entered demurely. It was a funny place. Downstairs there was a workshop smelling of chemicals. Upstairs there were two rooms full of paintings. They were not shocking. You could tell that a tree was a tree.

Suddenly I saw Whitewater. Not in the flesh—a painting of him by Jasper Whittingham. I thought this was an extraordinary coincidence until I saw that it was not a coincidence at all. We were here because of Jasper Whittingham whom I knew because Whitewater admired him. Nothing could be simpler. But it gave me a shock. I was in London to get away from reminders of Whitewater.

It was not really like Whitewater. But it was more like him than he was like himself. His real face was long and thin; Jasper Whittingham had made it impossibly elongated, like a skull run over by a steam roller. His real lips were thin and bloodless; Whittingham had given him a tortured gash for a mouth. His real eyes had a hot, inhuman look; Whittingham had given him live coals. The hands in the picture were as long as feet, with curved spread fingers like the tentacles of an octopus. They looked cold. There was an amazing contrast between the coldness of the hands and the hotness of the eyes.

Wherever I went in the room, the hot-coal eyes followed me. It was unpleasant. I did not like having Whitewater staring at me as he had done so often at Moreys. To get away from the eyes, I went into the other room. There was another strange portrait there: *Esmerelda, Number 23*, by Jasper Whittingham.

"That means, dear, he has painted the lady on twenty-two previous occasions."

I looked at her, speculating. It was an interesting face. Esmerelda had high cheekbones, heavy eyebrows, and a mass of straight black hair. She was standing in a sort of desert. She was wearing a peasant dress, kilted to show a red petticoat. Her feet were bare with a gold bangle round one of her ankles. She had a magnificent figure, like Mamma's, much fuller than mine. She looked foreign, a gipsy. She had an expression of wonderful, calm happiness.

I had seen that exact expression on another face. It had struck me vividly at the time. It was the expression on Mamma's face when she lay exhausted and flowerlike on her tumbled bed with Uncle Gareth, after the furies of passion.

Was that when Jasper Whittingham had painted his gipsy? Immediately afterwards? I wondered if she wore the bangle when they made love.

"I do not quite like that simpering expression he has given her," said Miss Porter-Binfield. "But the line is skilful."

"That painting is much admired, ma'am," said a man in a black cotton coat. "Still for sale, remarkably enough. A marvellous investment. Whittingham is certain to go up. Fifty guineas now, sure to be a hundred in a few years' time."

"Then Mamma has got a bargain," I said. "But of course he is painting her in his studio, not in a desert."

"I would not care to venture," said Miss Porter-Binfield with a shudder, "into the studio of such a man."

"It's a fair address, ma'am. Rupert Street, off Shaftesbury Avenue."

"Rupert Street," I murmured, a plan burgeoning in my head.

"Top floor, Miss, over a restaurant. Did I understand you to say that Whittingham was painting your mother?"

"Yes. Mr. Sargent did her last year."

"We do *not*," said the man, deeply offended, "mention that name here."

Miss Porter-Binfield refused to go to Rupert Street. I said that Jasper Whittingham was famous and respectable and had been to Moreys.

"Did I understand you to say, Miss, that Whittingham stayed with your family at a place in the country? In a country house, so to say?"

"Yes, certainly he did."

I found I did not mind being called "Miss," though it sounded strange, as I had been a "Ladyship" from birth.

"Where the gentlemen were wearing collars and ties and suchlike?"

"Yes, but—"

"And Whittingham, I'll be bound, was wearing sandals without socks, and trousers cut for an elephant, and a sailor's coat with brass buttons."

"Well, yes, but—How did you know?"

"Only clothes he's got!" said the man triumphantly. "His entire wardrobe."

Nothing would have induced Miss Porter-Binfield to Rupert Street.

"In any case, dear," she said to me, "he is certain to be away. Can you imagine an artist not taking advantage of this glorious weather in the countryside?"

"As a matter of fact, he's in London, ma'am," said the man. "Brought in some drawings last week. Lovely work, crayon and charcoal. Between five and seven pounds framed. A peach of an investment, ma'am, bound to appreciate."

We did not buy any drawings.

Never in my life had I done anything I wanted to do, anything I chose myself. The whole course of my days and years was mapped out for me. I lived on a lawn-tennis court with white lines and rules and umpires. It was worse than that. I was a passenger being wheeled along on rails. Well, I had got to London. I did choose that. But what was the point of being in London—to be trundled still in a perambulator, doing only what I was permitted to do?

If I was free I would be free. Not a "New Woman," with cropped hair and mannish clothes and cigarettes—I liked my hair as it was, and I had no intention of hiding my figure. I just wanted to . . .

The trouble was, there were no dashing, liberated things I did want to do. Music Halls, restaurants, taverns? I could not go alone. I did not want to. But one thing was possible. I could visit, as a friend, an interesting and famous man. I could do that. That was all there was. There was nothing else.

And he did find me exquisite. And he was a great painter, even if I did not quite like his paintings.

The key to escaping for an hour or two was Miss Porter-Binfield's absent-mindedness. I devised a stratagem of great simplicity and brilliance. I was to go shopping with Grace in Bond Street for gloves. Then I was to meet Miss Porter-Binfield at the Palafox Gallery. This arrangement was foolproof, except that Grace and I went to the Bruton Gallery instead. I peered at French water-colours for Grace's benefit until I saw her safely away up the street.

Then I went to Rupert Street. I walked.

I had never walked alone in London before. But people were doing it all round me. I enjoyed it. I was free.

Rupert Street was a little, dark, crowded, dirty street with a bakery and a Chinese laundry and a public house and a restaurant, and an old man selling bananas, and an old woman selling carnations, and a family selling fish from a barrow, and some grubby little boys in boots too big for them playing a game with a ball. The restaurant was called Carandini's. It had a single door with peeling green paint, so it seemed the studio was reached through the restaurant. I could not picture Mamma picking her way between the tables, dressed in ice-blue taffeta and pearls.

Since it was the middle of the morning, the restaurant was shut. The green door was locked. I peered through a gap in the curtains. I could make out white tablecloths and the gleam of cutlery and glass. There was nobody to be seen. From far above, I heard an unfamiliar musical instrument being played. There was no bell or knocker on the door. I knocked with my knuckles. I could not make much noise with them—they are small knuckles. My knocking was drowned by the noises of London streets. No one came. I hurt my knuckles, to no avail.

My dashing, liberated adventure had ended in utter anticlimax. I must walk tamely back to Bond Street to surrender myself to Miss Porter-Binfield.

Then a shocking thing happened, which might have been predicted. The little boys' ball crashed through Carandini's window a yard from where I stood. There was an explosion and a great tinkling of glass, and more tinkles inside. It was more effective than my feeble knocking. There were agonised shouts and pounding footsteps, and the green door burst open. A swarthy woman in an apron, her sleeves rolled up and her arms covered in flour, bounced out into the street.

The banana-man and the carnation-woman and the fish-family all began to shout and point. The little girls of the fish-family were laughing, which I wanted to do myself. The little boys had run away, sacrificing their ball.

The fat woman screamed in a foreign language. She looked this way and that, her face working with fury. She saw me standing by the broken window. She shook a floury fist in my face.

It was no longer funny. I was frightened. I wanted Miss Porter-Binfield.

"The young lidy didn't 'ave nuffink to do wiv it," said the banana-man.

The carnation-woman and the fish-family confirmed this.

"Oright," said the fat woman at last. "I believe. Why you not tella me?"

She forgave me for deceiving her, and I forgave her for suspecting me, and the banana-man and the carnation-woman forgave us for not having a battle, and only the little girls of the fish-family were really disappointed. It was no longer frightening, but funny. This was a better party than any I had seen at Moreys. The people were nicer.

I asked for Mr. Jasper Whittingham. The fat woman's face became dark with misery. She shrugged, and pointed to heaven.

He had died; No. He was upstairs.

"Can I go up?" I said. "I am a friend, and, um, a client."

She looked at me as though I must be mad and led me into the restaurant. There was a smell of oil and onions. I heard a lot of distant voices. My new friend led me through an archway into a passage. I glimpsed the kitchen, like a gipsy camp in a railway station. Uncarpeted stairs rose from the passage.

"Top, alla way," said my friend. She added, "Tart!"

I was startled, thinking she was being rude, until I realised that she was explaining that she had to get back to her cooking.

As I climbed, I heard the wailing and grunting of the strange musical instrument. It grew louder as I ascended. I went up three flights of stairs of dappled wood. Doors stood open, and I saw crowded little rooms with unmade beds. The smell of the kitchen climbed the stairs with me. The walls were covered with peeling paper. The paintwork was the colour of fudge. The windows were too dirty to see through.

The last flight of stairs ended simply in a door. From beyond the door I could hear the plaintive, barbaric music of the strange instrument.

This must be right, I thought, though it seemed so extravagantly wrong.

I knocked. There was no answer. The music continued. This was a day for knocking on doors and being ignored.

I knocked louder, with the side of my fist instead of my knuckles. The door was thin. It reverberated like a drum. Beating on it was satisfactory. I found myself beating on a fudge-coloured vertical drum in time to the music inside.

The music stopped, ending with a dying groan.

"You slut!" bellowed a huge familiar voice from beyond the door. "When I want an obbligato on the tom-tom I'll tell you. Come here with my clothes."

I opened the door and opened my mouth to announce myself, but I was so astonished by what I saw that no sound came out.

The room was the whole top floor of the house. It was full of cold white light from a big north-facing window. There was a raised platform, and on it a chair with a checked rug thrown over the chair. Facing the chair was a canvas on an easel. There was an unfinished painting on the canvas: a full-length portrait of the girl in the picture in the Chenil. She was nude. Her breasts were very like Mamma's. She was sitting in the chair with her bangle on her ankle.

In all the old-master pictures at Moreys, and the ones I had seen with Miss Porter-Binfield, ladies with nothing on were covered up, to a small but special extent, by a hand or a fortunate bit of drapery blown by the wind. Sometimes the bust was quite uncovered (though never painted with absolute fidelity), but not the fleecy Mound of Venus.

But Jasper Whittingham had Esmerelda lying back in the chair, half asleep, one arm behind her head, utterly relaxed, with her legs a little apart, and the copse of black hair in the fullest, plainest view, exactly in the middle of the picture.

That black hair was very like Mamma's, too.

Beyond the dais, by the wall, there was a table covered with American cloth, with plates and cups and pans, all very neat. There was another table with tubes and jars of paint, brushes, palettes, bits of charcoal, bottles and boxes, all equally neat. There was a pot-bellied stove with the stovepipe going out through the wall. Against all the walls were stacked dozens of canvasses. At the far end of the room there was a bed. Sitting up in bed was Jasper Whittingham. He was stripped to the waist and playing bagpipes. His long hair and beard were wilder than ever. His shoulders were broad but bony. I could see his ribs and the muscles of his stomach. The bedclothes were drawn up to his waist.

"Oh," he said. "The wrong slut. Who the devil are you?"

"Camilla Glyn," I said nervously, wondering if, after all, this expedition had been such a very good idea.

"The name means nothing to me, but the face is familiar. Ah! Ah! That idiotic Chinese bridge! Recollection floods back. I am delighted to see you. You catch me at a certain disadvantage. What in God's name are you doing here?"

I was prepared for this. "If you are going to paint my Mamma," I said, "who is fussy and rather elderly, and if you are going to do it here, then I must, um—"

"Inspect the premises? *Dieu de batailles,* another commission lost. You will report to your Mamma that you found the dauber in bed, playing the *musette—*"

"I thought they were bagpipes."

"Breton bagpipes. You will report that you found the master in the emperor's new clothes, because there are no artist's new clothes."

"Is it true that you only have one lot?"

"Of course. They are kept impeccably clean. When they fall, by the smallest stain, from the high standard I maintain, my handmaiden takes them away and causes them to resume incorruptibility. How, where, or by what miracle this is accomplished I have never inquired. Useless knowledge is as much a burden as useless property. Besides, I might be asked to pay."

"Is that your handmaiden?" I asked, pointing at the picture on the easel.

"That is one of my handmaidens, but not today's. The bearer of clothes is a different damsel. It's a curious thing, my little one—a moment ago I was cursing the tardiness of the bringer of clean clothes. Now I curse the certainty of her speedy reappearance."

"I wish you wouldn't call me your little one," I said.

"Is it impertinent? Shall I call you 'great one'?"

"No, it's not impertinent. At least, it is, but I don't mind that. But somebody else has been calling me his little one, and I don't want to be reminded of him—Why do you want your clothes not to come?"

"If you don't know the answer to that, you are too young to be told it. How beautiful you are. I must paint you."

"Like that?" I asked anxiously, pointing at the easel again.

"Like that, and in a thousand other ways. At dawn, at dusk, asleep and eagerly awake—But not here. In your native woodlands, or any damned woodlands, dew-wet, the cobwebs of dawn in your hair—*Dieu de batailles*, I'm getting pre-Raphaelite again. I want to entertain you for hours in a jocund place. But not today. When my clothes are borne back, the bearer will demand, as of right, entertainment and amusement. Will you come another time?"

"It is difficult. I'm guarded like a baby. It's so silly."

"You must slip your guards. We must plot. You are not dressed for plotting, and I am not dressed at all, but we must rise above appearances. Let me think." He sank lower in the bed as though better to think; his beard spread all over the counterpane like a dead gorse bush.

He made a plan. It involved telling several lies, invading a strange house, and writing a very strange letter. It was complicated and brilliant.

"I have done this sort of thing before, you know," he said, with something approaching modesty. "Either to escape creditors or in the course of a seduction."

"Which is it this time?" I gulped.

"Both, perhaps."

The essence of the plan was a false hostess who would apparently be entertaining me when Jasper Whittingham was entertaining me. She had to be lifelike and respectable, with a real name and a real address.

"A suitable address is the crux," said Jasper Whittingham. "I know so few. One, really—that of a man called Whitewater. Do you know any suitable addresses, where the residents are respectable but unknown to your guardians?"

The ones I knew, Cousin Dorothea knew too—Casterbridge House, Doncaster House and the rest. Did I know any others? There was one in my address book . . .

"Yes," I said. "We can go there as soon as you get your clothes."

"Why?"

"Why what?"

"Why do you go to these lengths to have a meal or an hour in my company?"

"Because everybody else I know in the world has been chosen for me."

"From all of whom I am sharply different?"

"Well, yes, you are."

"I am. By God I am. I understand a little, my shy warbler of the leafage, because I too have felt the need for rebellion in my time. I was not always as you see me now. For one thing, I usually had clothes on when I chatted to young ladies in the morning. I'm enjoying this, you know. It is a situation sufficiently grotesque never to have happened before even to me."

"Nor me," I said. "I'm enjoying it, too."

The door creaked open, and a big, beautiful girl came in carrying an armful of clothes. She had a squashy man's hat on her head.

"At last," shouted Jasper Whittingham. "The creature is called Topaz," he said to me. "Her mission in life is to look like Trilby. As you see, she is moderately successful."

"I want to be taken to Frascati's," said Topaz. "Who's this?"

"Her name is Io," said Jasper Whittingham, winking at me. "My favourite nymph in classical mythology, because she is the nymph with the shortest name. When written, it looks like the figure ten. I can't imagine what that has to do with anything. Divert each other while I put on my clothes."

I wanted to watch him dress, because I thought his methods and his underclothes would be unique. I was curious about other things, too. But he bellowed at Topaz and me to turn our backs.

She did not talk to me. She sneered at the picture of Esmerelda.

Jasper Whittingham sang as he dressed. He sang in French. I think it was French. His voice was gentle, a nice voice, quite unlike his speaking and laughing voice. But I liked that great voice, too. I liked everything about him. He was exciting. It was exciting being with him, and part of his wild artistic life.

"Wait for me here," he said to Topaz. "You will not be taken to Frascati's but to Carandini's. Io and I have an errand. I shall be back in an hour."

"With her?"

"Probably not."

"All right," said Topaz sullenly. She lay down, in her hat, on the bed.

"I expect she's tired," said Jasper Whittingham. "Come, little Io. I rather think you were turned into a heifer. I wonder why?"

He picked up an immense knobby stick like a cudgel, clapped his huge black hat on his head, and thundered downstairs. I pattered after him. Carandini's restaurant had opened. A few people were eating. I saw, in the light, what I had not seen in the dark—two more paintings of Esmerelda in the restaurant.

"Board and lodging," said Jasper Whittingham, pointing at them with his beard. "But I don't think I'll offer them the one I'm doing now."

He strode between the little tables. I thought the stiff pirate's coat would whisk everything off them, but he only knocked over one glass.

We burst out into the street. Jasper Whittingham bounded to the carnation-woman. He chose a pale yellow one and a red one. He gave the yellow one to me, with a comic bow, and pushed the red one into his own buttonhole.

"That'll be a tanner, dearie," said the carnation-woman.

Jasper Whittingham groped largely in the pockets of his trousers.

"*Dieu de batailles,*" he shouted, "I've come out without a sou."

I paid sixpence for the carnations. I had no idea what to do with mine. I thought of holding it in my teeth, but compromised by holding it in my hand.

Jasper Whittingham loped the short distance to Jermyn Street. I pattered after him, trotting to keep up. I felt like a little dog on a lead. This adventure was getting more ridiculous every minute.

We pounded to a halt outside the door of number twenty-six. I was nervous about the next bit. Not so Jasper Whittingham. He banged on the door with his cudgel. A grim woman in black bombazine opened the door. Before she could say anything, Jasper Whittingham swept off his hat and said, "Good morning, madame. We are enquiring for Sir Matthew Alban."

"Sir Matthew's off home to Ireland," said the woman, as we had known very well she would. "A month ago."

"Ah. We feared as much. Do you expect him back in the winter?"

"He might come, he might not. He's kept on his chambers. And what might your business with Sir Matthew be?"

"I am a painter, madame. Sir Matthew some weeks ago asked me to paint his portrait. I was unable to do so at the time, owing to weight of commissions. We did not conclude a firm arrangement, but left it that I should get in touch with him when my time permitted. I am anxious to do so now, if only as a gesture of courtesy to my friend Sir Matthew."

"He is a very pleasant young gentleman."

"Is he? I mean, he is indeed. There is no purpose in my writing to him in Ireland, since I cannot go to Ireland to paint him, owing to weight of commissions." He winked at me. "I propose therefore, with your permission, to leave a note for him here. He will find it on his return, and we shall renew negotiations."

"That do seem sensible," admitted the woman.

"We have, of course, brought no paper with us. May we beg a sheet of Sir Matthew's? And somewhere to sit, for a tenth of a second, while I write?"

"Yes, sir, that do seem reasonable. Are you bringing this person into my house?"

"This is my secretary, my strong right hand, my stout staff."

So the woman led us upstairs.

On the way, on a landing, we passed a fat, florid, elderly man with a purple nose and a white hat, who bowed to me in absurd way which I rather liked. Then he blinked little red eyes and peered at me.

"Have I not the honour of addressing the Lady Camilla Glyn?" he said, in a high wheezing voice.

"Well," I said, not sure of the best reply.

"Saw your photograph last month in the *Bystander*," he wheezed, "posed with your lady mother the Marchioness. Lovely pair you made, if I may say so. My pal Sir Matty Alban was always talking about you."

"*Was he?*"

"Waxed lyrical, my dear, I mean my lady. Well! Mustn't detain you. Honour to have met you."

Sir Matthew's sitting room was shrouded in dust-sheets, but the woman uncovered a writing table. Jasper Whittingham sat down, drew a sheet of embossed paper from the rack, dipped a pen in ink, and glanced at the woman.

She stood waiting. She was not going to budge.

"My dear Sir Matthew," intoned Jasper Whittingham, writing in a surprisingly small, neat hand, "Further to our conversation of some weeks ago, when you honoured me with the suggestion that I might try my hand at your likeness in oils . . ."

As he wrote this with his right hand, he slid half a dozen sheets of the embossed paper out of the rack and into his coat. He winked at me.

We left the absurd letter propped in a prominent place and went down in triumph to the street.

"Masterly in conception and in execution, my miniature rebel," said Jasper Whittingham as we came out into the sunshine.

I liked "miniature rebel." The whole day was one of the best days I had ever had in my life. I sniffed freedom and I liked the smell.

The fat old man in the white hat was standing on the pavement near the door. He bowed and swept off his hat, making me smile. With him was standing another man, big, good-looking in a flashy way, dressed to kill, with such a bright red moustache that I thought it must be dyed.

The fat man murmured to the flashy man, wagging his cane in my direction. I supposed he was telling his companion who I was. I could not see that it mattered. A lot of people knew who I was.

The flashy man seemed thunderstruck by what he was being told. He stared at me as though—as though I was in Esmerelda's position in Jasper Whittingham's new painting of her.

Jasper Whittingham bounded away. I trotted after him. At the corner of Church Place I turned and glanced back. The flashy man was still staring at me, his mouth slightly open.

12 ❀ *Sweet beginning, but unsavoury end*

> Here I prophecy,
> Sorrow on love hereafter shall attend:
> It shall be waited on with jealousy,
> Find sweet beginning, but unsavoury end;
> Ne'er settled equally, but high or low;
> That all love's pleasures shall not match his woe.

> *VENUS AND ADONIS*

"Why are you carrying that flower, dear?" asked Miss Porter-Binfield, panting with relief at finding me again.

"What flower? Oh." It was the yellow carnation. I had entirely forgotten I was carrying it. "I bought it," I said truthfully, "from an old woman. She looked so sad."

The last part was not true. The carnation-lady had looked anything but sad. She was drinking stout out of a bottle and chatting in the sunshine with the banana-man.

The whole strategy had worked. But it would not work again. I was back in bondage. My next breath of freedom must come with the letter from Jermyn Street.

The letter came three days later by the afternoon post. Miss Cole had a struggle getting the paper out of the envelope. The envelope did not fit the paper. Jasper Whittingham had forgotten to steal any of the matching envelopes.

The letter took the line we had discussed. Old Lady Alban found herself in London with no amusement since Town was out of season and empty. She was obliged to be in London because she was under the care of Sir Everard Horton in Queen Anne Street, the eminent heart specialist. She was occupying chambers in Jermyn Street. Her health did not allow her to go out. But she was well able to entertain. She would consider it a great favour if Lady Camilla should come and sit with her occasionally. Ideally, Lady Camilla should come in the evening, if Lady Hale could spare her then. During the day Sir Everard was apt to call, often without warning, if he were making other visits nearby in Mayfair. Lady Alban was particularly anxious to meet Lady Camilla and entertain her, as her own grandson, the present baronet, had been shown such kindness by Lady Bulbarrow earlier in the year. If Lady Camilla could be brought to Jermyn Street, Lady Alban would see that she was conveyed safely back to Berkeley Square by Lady Alban's own servants. She had the honour to remain, Lady Hale's most sincerely, Consuelo Alban.

Darlington, the aged butler, was sent at once for the *Baronetage*. He could hardly carry it. It was an old edition, completely out of date like everything else in the house. "Alban of Albanstown, Co. Clare," Miss Cole read out loud. There was a big coat of arms and a lot of family history in small print. The Alban family was established as a reality with a comfortingly long history and a reassuring number of quarterings.

"Do you *want* to go to Jermyn Street, dear?" asked Cousin Dorothea. "It is such a very long way."

It was five minutes' walk.

"Well," I said, "I think it would be a kindness to Lady Alban. Especially as she has a bad heart. She is bored and wants company. I would like to hear about Ireland. You will permit it, won't you, Cousin Dorothea? I can go once, you know, and if it is too horrid I can make an excuse and not go again."

"The miniature rebel fights again," shouted Jasper Whittingham. "The pocket Boadicea, the wee Washington, the baby Bolivar. Well done indeed, *petit Jacobin!*"

I laughed. I had much to laugh about—freedom, another beautifully successful stratagem, sitting alone in a hansom cab with a wild-bearded Bohemian artist.

"Where are we going?" I asked, not having had time to consider this in the excitement of escape.

"The Holborn Empire. Where else, on a Friday night?"

"A—Music Hall?"

"Of course! I love the Halls. It's a whole rich vulgar high-coloured world of uninhibited enjoyment. Not at all what you're used to, and it's time you saw it. There's more fun to be had in this world than you ever dreamed of. For a few penny pieces! People may envy someone like you, but I'm damned if I do. What do your millions buy you? Boredom. I saw enough of your life in that barrack in two days to be thankful to get back to mine. I want to paint the Music Halls. I want to paint the noise of the orchestra, and the smell of cheap cigars, and the 'oohs' and 'ahs' when a crowded house likes a little dancer—Here we are. How much, cabbie? *Mille tonnères*—one of my sluts has picked my pocket!"

I paid for the hansom.

"I reserved a box," said Jasper Whittingham as we went into the crowded foyer of the theatre. "You can't see the stage any better, but you can see the audience beautifully. Some foreshortened from above, some foreshortened from below, smoking cigarettes in the darkness, sweating and enjoying themselves. We pick up the ticket from the young lady over there." He began to sing: "She was only a bird in a gilded cage, a beautiful sight to see . . ."

The girl in the gilded cage handed him a ticket. She looked at him. He looked at me. I paid for the box. It was rather expensive. I did not mind at all.

People were standing in line outside for the fourpenny gallery seats. The doorman let a batch of them in. Jasper Whittingham towered over them all; he was as startling in that respectable crowd of clerks and shop girls as he was among Mamma's friends at Moreys. He waved his hat as though leading a charge; his beard billowed; I thought of Garibaldi and even of Moses.

The box was a little overfurnished room with one wall missing. Below us and all round us was the audience—more people than I had ever seen in one place before; Stalls, Dress Circle, Upper Circle, Gallery, and behind the Stalls a broad passage where people stood or strolled under a pall of cigar smoke like a thundercloud, with electric lights winking on huge mirrors so that everything seemed twice as large and the theatre receded into an infinity smoky distance. Everyone was clapping and shouting. Something had just ended. The stage, set with marvellous scenery, was empty. There were numbers in electric lights each side of the stage. A number 3 went out and a number 4 came on.

"Second house has just started," said Jasper Whittingham. "We've missed the first three turns. Probably a good thing. The great names come later."

But I was sorry to have missed any of it. I loved it. It was as new to me as Jasper Whittingham's bagpipes, or Mamma's tears . . . We saw bicyclists who kept falling off, and I howled with laughter like everyone else; we saw acrobats and clowns and jugglers and singers. All the audience joined in the choruses of the songs. Jasper Whittingham did so in his gentle singing voice. I would have done so, only I did not know the songs.

"You see why I must paint it, all of it," Jasper Whittingham shouted to me over the happy howling of the audience. "The way the smoke hangs, lit from below. A vision of hell! Merry hell. Inferno in the Holborn Empire. The souls of the damned having a good time. Look at all those faces, all turned towards Lottie Collins! Look at Lottie herself! Ta-ra-ra Boom-de-ay! Look how they love her! Look how they coo over her! I want to paint that coo . . ."

Then a man in a baggy swimming-suit was making the audience gasp with laughter.

"Dan Leno," Jasper Whittingham said to me. "The reigning genius of the Halls."

"Fancy," I said. "What a night. Two geniuses under one roof."

He laughed, but he agreed.

We climbed into a growler. People and motorcars and cabs were swirling about under the naphtha lamps in Holborn as the theatre emptied. It was still part of the show to Jasper Whittingham. My eye caught that of a man standing on the kerb by the stage door. He was staring at me. Not at Jasper Whittingham, but at me. This is not a thing you can be wrong about. I had had plenty of experience of being stared at when Whitewater came to Moreys.

I recognized the man. I did not think I had met him, but I knew I had seen him. I did not remember where or when. He was big, and flashily dressed. He had a moustache. It was impossible to be sure about the colour of the moustache, because the naphtha lamps had the same effect as moonlight, washing the colour out of everything. But I knew it was red, so bright that it looked as though it had been dyed.

The cab stopped near the bottom of Regent Street. I groped in my purse.

I gasped when I saw where we were. We were in front of a grandiose façade which I had often passed but *never* expected to enter. I had seen it by daylight. Now it blazed with its own brilliant lighting. Marble steps swept up to a tremendous door. It was the Café Royal.

Of course I had heard about it. Everybody had heard about it. It was the scene of orgies, where perverts and poets and actresses and courtesans drank champagne amid shrieks and witticisms. Wine glasses were flung as readily as insults, and ballet slippers flew through the air as thick as epigrams.

As soon as I had paid the cabbie, Jasper Whittingham hustled me up the steps.

"I can't go in there!" I cried.

"Why not? You won't get abducted, savaged, violated, robbed, or even seriously overcharged."

"But—um—I'm not dressed!"

"Alas, you are."

"Not properly!"

"All too properly. Come along, Io! You can wear what you like, say what you like, and within reason do what you like. Am I properly dressed? Yes."

I was wearing clothes for dining with Cousin Dorothea in Berkeley Square, or with Consuelo Lady Alban in Jermyn Street. My dress was dark blue silk reaching to the ground, and to the wrist, and to the chin.

At the top of the broad stairs, Jasper Whittingham paused, settled his huge hat at a desperate angle, threw one end of his trailing red scarf over his shoulder, took my arm above the elbow, and made an entry. It was quite as theatrical as anything at the Holborn Empire. The room was almost as big and almost as crowded.

I glanced round nervously for scenes of wild dissipation, for ladies in disordered clothing, satyrs, revolutionaries. What I saw were hundreds of normally dressed people eating and drinking at tables. There was a buzz of conversation and laughter, no different from the noise in the Banqueting Hall at Moreys during Sunday luncheon.

"Oh," I said with disappointment and relief, "they are just people."

Jasper Whittingham gave a great bellow of laughter which caused fifty heads to turn in our direction.

"Io," he said, "you are so sweet that sometimes I want to eat you, and sometimes—"

"What?" I asked, quite interested in the reply.

"At this moment, command us drinks. But, as you know—"

"Perhaps if I lent you some money?" I said. "I hope you will not be offended, but as a matter of fact I am very thirsty."

He said he would not be offended. I gave him five pounds out of my purse.

"I will pay you back when I paint your mother in November," he said solemnly.

By this time a little pink man in a tailcoat had come up and led us towards a table. It was all very magnificent, huge mirrors everywhere, gilt on everything, red plush, blazing chandeliers. Some of the women were beautiful. Here and there one could hear an insistent click-click-click. I thought people were eating noisily until I saw that they were playing dominoes on marble table tops.

Shouts and waves greeted Jasper Whittingham from table after table. Everyone knew him. Our journey across the room was a royal progress, finishing at last at a table against the wall with a red velvet bench instead of chairs.

I had never before sat on a bench to eat my supper. It seemed quite satisfactory.

Glasses arrived, full of a drink strange to me—bright green stuff over crushed ice. I swallowed some. It tasted of peppermint. Drinking it was like going back to the nursery. I was surprised that Jasper Whittingham had ordered a nursery drink. Would we eat beef-tea and milk pudding?

"*Crème de menthe frappée*," said Jasper Whittingham, "*bien vue*, if not precisely *de rigueur*. You will notice that everybody uses French phrases here as often as they can think of a suitable one. If they can't, they just sit saying '*Parbleu*,' or even '*Zut alors*.' That is because it is a café-restaurant of a kind familiar to Paris but otherwise unknown in England. We are all working hard at imagining ourselves on the *Rive Gauche*, especially those of us who have never been there."

"Why am I Io?" I asked.

"You must have some sort of name. You can't very well use your real one. You're not the first nobly born damsel who's used an alias while slumming here."

"I don't call it slumming. Who are the others?"

"I never bothered to enquire. They didn't interest me as you interest me. You've finished that beaker already? By an extraordinary coincidence, so have I. How well we agree together, little wood-nymph. We even drink the same beverage at the same speed. It is reassuring for me. Usually I have finished before the others have taken their first sip. Waiter!"

More frozen green peppermint arrived. I *was* thirsty. I was glad this was a harmless nursery drink to quench my thirst. More still arrived.

People stopped at our table, then moved on. Some sat down for a few minutes. I was introduced as Io. There was only one face I recognized, and that only dimly—a big, flashily-handsome man in sporting clothes, with a bright red moustache. The heat and the smoke and the constant movement of the people began to make me feel giddy. I was laughing almost continuously.

For a time we were having a conversation in the usual way. Then I felt less and less inclined to talk. When I tried, the words came out blurred and difficult to control. It was the smoke and the way the people kept moving about. If I talked less, Jasper Whittingham talked more. His voice rose and fell like the waves of a great sea. It made me feel seasick. That was it, I told myself; his voice was like the sea, so it made me feel seasick. I continued to laugh at everything he said, but I did not listen all the time. It was more restful just to sit and let the waves of oratory wash over me like a warm ocean.

Food arrived. Omelettes. I could not eat a mouthful, because of the smoke in the room. Jasper Whittingham ate my omelette as well as his own. He talked all the time he was eating, his mouth often completely full, yet he hardly once spat any omelette at me. Some, however, did get stuck in his beard. I could see that this was a disadvantage of being an artist. I looked at the eggy fragment, fascinated, as it twitched up and down in his beard as he was speaking.

Because I was staring at him, I did hear what he was saying. "I wish to put right, for your especial benefit, one of the commonest misapprehensions about love."

Love. He was talking about love. I set myself to listen, trying to ignore the way the room was beginning to swivel round.

"It is frequently supposed," he said, "that you love a person whom you need or to whom you are grateful. The exact reverse is the case. The person whom you most love is the one who needs you, who is dependent on you, grateful to you. You have invested in him. In a small but crucial way you own him. You view him *de haut en bas* with benevolent pity. Therefore you love him."

He raised one hand high above his head and began to declaim:

"A pity beyond all telling

Is hid in the heart of love . . ."

He stopped, looking crestfallen, and lowered his hand to scratch his ear.

"I've forgotten how it goes on. The brother of Jack Yeats, whom you met a few minutes ago, wrote that poem a dozen years ago. He is right. Remember those words, little Io. They are what you need to know about love."

I tried to repeat the lines: "A pity beyond all telling . . ." But the words came out in a jumble. I was too thirsty to talk, so I drank some more of the refreshing green peppermint. But I did remember the words. Oh God, I remembered the words.

I nearly fell over going down the stairs. There must have been a wrinkle in the carpet. I was cross at the stupid servants who left dangerous wrinkles in stair carpets, but then I forgave them. I felt too happy to be cross. I laughed to think how nearly I had fallen downstairs and how cleverly I had saved myself. Jasper Whittingham held my arm. It was comforting to be held by such a strong man who could talk for hours without a sign of flagging, even while he ate two omelettes.

He was still talking. We paused, halfway down the stairs, while he talked.

"Not forever," he was saying. "Just for two months, until the weather gets colder and the potential sitters scurry back to the rabbit warren. But think of it! Faithful Dobbin between the shafts. Little country lanes, at a walking pace. Turn the gipsy caravan off into a bosky wood or some quiet meadow spangled with dew-wet flowers. Are flowers wet with dew in early autumn? I want to take myself and my easel out, out, out of these streets and stinks. I've never painted landscapes. I've practically never *seen* landscapes. And in the evening the twinkling campfire, the sizzling sausage, the soft bed on the thymy grass. Or, if it rains, the snug bunk in the caravan. Dobbin eats as we go, nuzzling at his feedbag or cropping the lush grass of the wayside verges. I yearn for the expedition, little Io. But what the devil is a man to do? They want thirty pounds for the caravan and twenty pounds for the horse. I haven't got one tenth of that. *And* I owe fifteen pounds rent to the Carandinis, in spite of giving them paintings of genius."

"Oh," I said. It was all I felt inclined to try saying. I thought it would have to be a large gipsy caravan to accommodate Jasper Whittingham.

"*Nom d'un nom,*" he said, "what a gigantic nuisance money is. I'm not greedy, you know. At least, not very greedy. But, oh! *Gentil Seigneur,* for a day or an hour or a minute without the grinding awareness of not having any money!"

"Um," I said, wondering why the stairs were tipping backwards and forwards.

We went out into the street. Lights flared, cabs rattled, motors roared. I was delighted to see that an old friend of mine was standing on the pavement near the door. He was a beautiful big man with a beautiful red moustache. I had forgotten who he was, on account of the smoke and Jasper Whittingham's conversation, but I knew he was an old and dear friend whom I saw constantly. I waved to him. It was the least I could do. He took off his hat and bowed.

Jasper Whittingham, talking, did not notice. He helped me into a hansom.

Still he was talking. "One of the joys of life," he said, more quietly than before, "one of life's very great joys, is kissing beautiful girls in hansom cabs."

"Um," I said, pleased.

I felt his arm going round my shoulder. He pulled me towards him. I snuggled happily against him, feeling safe, feeling excited. His beard tickled my forehead. He took my chin in his other hand and tipped my face upwards. His fingers were very gentle. I could hardly see his face. It came down towards mine. I felt his lips. I felt his beard, too. I liked that. I felt his tongue. It shot right into my mouth. I felt as though I were eating a German sausage. My tongue met his, and it was very nice. I felt, without surprise, his hand on my breast. He squeezed my breast gently through the silk of my dress and my chemise. I felt his hand on my waist, my hip, my thigh, caressing, returning to my breast.

He moved his mouth away from mine. His mouth was wet from our kisses. I felt his wet lips on my cheek. I tried to find his lips again with mine. It was a safe and comfortable place for my lips to be.

"Oh God, how I do want you," he muttered into my cheek, his beard not scratching or tickling, but caressing like chinchilla. His lips tasted of peppermint.

"Um," I said, because I wanted him too.

His hand, feeling my body through my thin silk clothes, had woken up all the hive of wild bees which lived inside my breasts and my belly, and now they buzzed and swarmed under my skin. I wanted him. His fingertips, gentle as moths, caressed my nipples through my clothes. Desire grew between my thighs in instant magical sympathy.

"Yes," I mumbled. "Yes."

He gave a great groan, and kissed me almost violently. I felt myself being carried away by passion. I pressed his hand to my breast. I was in a whirlpool, going round and round.

Going round and round. He was. The cab was. I was.

"I'm going to be sick," I said desperately.

"Christ," said Jasper Whittingham.

He shouted to the driver to stop. He carried me bodily out of the cab and helped me across the pavement to some railings. I collapsed onto my knees, clinging to the railings. Nausea flooded up from my stomach into my throat, and I was miserably sick. He held my head. The smell was acrid and minty. I sobbed and retched. Tears poured out of my eyes. I felt terrible, racked by the spasms of nausea, choking, the taste of vomit in my mouth.

"Poor little beast," I heard Jasper Whittingham say. "Silly little wretch."

I stopped being sick at last. My stomach subsided and my sobs quietened. I felt a great deal better. I felt utterly wretched and humiliated. He wiped my face with the end of his long red scarf. My hair was coming down, and I had dirtied the knees of my skirt by kneeling on the pavement.

"Little idiot," said Jasper Whittingham. "Go back to the nursery where you belong."

I started crying again and I cried all the way back to Berkeley Square. He did not touch me. He did not even take my hand. I felt better. I felt quite all right. I was in despair.

We stopped at Cousin Dorothea's door, and Jasper Whittingham helped me down. Another cab came into the Square and stopped at the corner twenty yards away. Nobody got out of it. It stood waiting. I hoped that whoever was in it had not seen my exhibition.

Jasper Whittingham saw me to the door without letting himself be seen by the old footman who let me in. He murmured some kind of farewell. I was too miserable to listen. I kept my face turned away from him so that he would not see the shame and self-disgust on it.

The hall was lit only by one low gas-jet. The footman did not see the state I was in. I told him that I had had a pleasant evening, but that I was now very tired. I tried to keep my voice steady.

I wondered, as I lay in bed, how Jasper Whittingham had paid for the cab.

"No," I said at luncheon the following day. "I did not enjoy it, Cousin Dorothea. I'm afraid she is a vulgar old lady. She drank a lot of green stuff with ice in it, and ate two omelettes."

"Poor little beast. Silly little wretch. Little idiot, go back to the nursery where you belong." He had wanted me. I had wanted him. I could not bear to see him again, the see the pity and disgust in his eyes.

"Go back to the nursery where you belong." I writhed with the humiliation of it.

But he had reawoken the sleeping beehives of lust. His hand had stirred those sweet, intolerable sensations of desire which moistened the lips in the silky fleece between my thighs and hardened to hazelnuts the pink rosebuds at the tips of my breasts.

After an interval of weeks, my fingers were busy in the night, and I moaned at the brown London sky.

I wanted *somebody*. It was only fair. Mamma had somebody. Why not me?

I was buying some silver ribbon on the third floor of Carnaby's in Regent Street. Grace had come with me, but I had sent her to match buttons at the button counter. I lost sight of her. It did not matter. She would find me.

Meanwhile I was once again fleetingly alone in London. I had freedom. Much good it did me. I had nowhere to go and no one to see.

A man's voice behind me said, "Miss Io, surely?"

I was not pleased with the use of this name which brought back odious memories. But I turned. I had to. My ribbon was bought.

Standing there was a man I recognized. A big man, flashily dressed, with a moustache too red to be believed. I had seen him several times, it seemed to me, but I did not know quite where.

"Forgive my accosting you, your ladyship, but we were introduced at the Café Royal a few nights ago."

"Oh," I said. "Are you sure?"

"I would hardly forget," he said, with a sort of awful archness.

From a distance, I had thought him handsome. At close range he was still handsome, but his face was unhealthy and without strength. Physi-

cally, no doubt, he was as strong as a bull, but his eyes blinked at me nervously, and there was an anxious, pleading grin on his face.

He held himself in a swaggering, military style. He towered over me.
But he looked at me as though he thought I might bite. He was frightened of me.

This was quite unmistakable, and quite amazing. Why, in heaven's
name, should a great, overdressed bull of a man be frightened of a small,
light young girl?

"Why did you call me 'your ladyship'?" I asked, which was not exactly
what I meant to say.

"Oh, I know who you are. Of course, a lady like you is right to go
under a false name at the old Café. There's many do it when the high aristocracy goes slumming among the likes of us. But I happen to be a pal of
Sir Matty Alban's."

"Oh," I said blankly.

What he said was grossly unlikely. He did not look like a gentleman
nor sound like one. He tortured his voice into a sort of awful imitation of
refinement, but through it came the twang of the back streets.

"Sir Matthew has gone back to Ireland," I said stupidly, simply for
something to say.

"Back to the bog, poor old chappie. I had a bit of supper with him the
night before he left. 'Desmond,' he said to me, 'if ever you run into the
Lady Camilla Glyn, give her my respectful salaams.' 'That I will, Matty,'
said I, 'but how shall I know the lady?' 'Easy, dear old chappie,' said he,
'she's the most beautiful young lady in the kingdom. Eyes like an angel,
hair like spun gold, figure like a Grecian goddess. When you see a young
lady answering to that description, dear old laddie, you'll know it's Lady
Camilla.' Consequently, when I was presented to you by Lord What's-his-
name at the Café, I saw through the mask at once. 'Desmond,' said I to
myself, 'she may call herself Miss Io, and she may be called Miss Io by the
rag-tag-and-bobtail here, but it's the Goldsmith's Hall to yesterday's Pink
'Un that this is the filly old Matty was telling me about.'"

I looked round for Grace. She was nowhere to be seen. There were a lot
of people between me and the button counter. Matching the buttons
might be a long business.

Grace would rescue me from this vulgar adventurer who was trying to
scrape acquaintance with me because I was a lady.

Was that why he was doing it?

Was I to believe he had recognized me just from Sir Matthew's description?

It was a nice description. I did not see how it could be improved on.

"Of course, it's no business of mine, Lady Camilla," he went on, blinking at me like a puppy uncertain whether he was going to be beaten or given a bone, "but I don't like to see a very beautiful young lady like yourself alone and unprotected in a crowd. If I can be of service to you—carry anything, you know, or escort you wherever you're going—Be very happy, honoured, nothing but a pleasure. My pal Sir Matty would wish it; I'm certain of that. 'Don't let her come to any harm, dear old boy,' he said to me the night before he left, 'I trust you to do the right thing if need arises.'"

His voice was meant to be bluff, manly, reassuring. It came out like a sort of prayer, a desperate appeal. He was beseeching me to let him help me and protect me. I thought it was he who needed help and protection. His manner was meant to be swaggering, conquering, irresistible. It came out abject. It was obsequious. Why?

My puzzlement and curiosity grew. This was a *most* odd situation. I was flattered.

There was no sign of Grace.

Big and powerful as he was, I could come to no harm from this pathetic creature. That was quite certain. I had the feeling that one sharp word from me would cause him to dissolve in tears.

His face was pasty. I thought his health was not good. I thought he did not look after himself properly.

"If you've bought what you came for," he said, "may I have the privilege of escorting you to wherever you're going? You shouldn't walk alone, not in the streets. Deuce of a bad notion! Much safer to have a man's company."

"I'll have my maid's company in a moment," I said, "as soon as she's matched some buttons."

"Oh—" He looked infinitely crestfallen. I almost wanted to reach up and pat his head. He needed comforting. He needed somebody to tell him that he was a fine fellow, a good dog.

"You'd rather have your maid's company than mine, of course," he said abjectly. "I quite understand."

"I'm only going to Berkeley Square. I daresay my maid will be ever such a long time matching the buttons—"

I did not know quite how it happened; I do not now know quite how it happened; but I found myself walking with him along Conduit Street.

After all, Grace knew her way home. She had money enough to pay for the buttons.

It was not disagreeable to walk with him or even to be seen walking with him. He was certainly a fine figure of a man, as upright as General Mauney or his dear old servant Corporal Jewkes. You had to be a little tolerant about his clothes, but they were not much worse than some of the clothes worn by some of the gentlemen who came to Moreys. I felt that allowances should be made since he came from humble origins and was doing the best he knew how.

There was something pathetic and endearing about the worship in his eyes. I do not think anyone dislikes being worshipped. His eyes were like those of the spaniels in Sir Edwin Landseer's paintings (which Uncle Gareth loved)—moist, adoring eyes, which gazed at me as though I were a kind of god. Well, he had said I had a figure like a goddess.

He was trying to do something he did not know how to do, to be something he did not know how to be. I thought he should be given credit for the effort.

He kept up a flow of what I thought he thought was badinage. He reminded me of a bull trying to be a gadfly. He stared at me anxiously all the time, so that I was afraid that, from not looking where he was going, he would walk into a lamp post.

He said his name was Desmond Dacre, which I did not quite believe. He said he was a gentleman of leisure, with private means, which I did not at all believe. He said I was the most beautiful living creature he had ever clapped eyes on. I did not know whether to believe that part, but it was nice to try.

He begged to be allowed to see me again. He truly implored. It was touching. I was touched. A statue would have been touched, and I was much unlike a statue, except (according to him) in the matter of shape. It was impossible to disbelieve him when he said how deeply and devoutly he wanted to see me again.

I opened my mouth to reply without having decided what the reply would be. At that moment I saw Grace, pelting towards us with a distraught expression.

"Goodbye!" I said to Desmond Dacre, and bolted to Cousin Dorothea's door.

"I have said nothing to Lady Hale," I told Grace, "about your losing me in the crowd in Carnaby's. Anybody might have lost anybody. One could easily have lost an elephant. I am sure that it was not your fault."

"No, m'lady, I don't believe it was," said Grace with a look I did not quite like.

With Miss Porter-Binfield I contemplated an *Adoration of the Magi*, by —it is of no importance to the story who the picture was by. What struck one was the expression on the face of one of the Wise Men. "Adoration" hardly described it.

I know it is blasphemous to make the comparison, but that was the expression on Desmond Dacre's face when he looked at me.

I was not violently averse to the thought of seeing that expression again. After my humiliation by the railings, my spirits needed lifting and my confidence restoring. Adoration seemed a good antidote for self-disgust.

I had had admiring looks from Whitewater which I did not want to think about. I had had admiring looks from Jasper Whittingham which I did not want to think about. Adoring looks were altogether something else again. I did want to think about them. I thought of little else.

Was he an expert and experienced ladies' man, I wondered? Reverence would make him gentle; adoration would make him passionate; who could ask for a better combination?

Lying in my bed, in the hot London night, I thought: he would touch me *thus*, just here, and stroke me *thus*, just here . . . the touch would feel like *that*, and the stroking like *that* . . .

I excited myself, night after night, to trembling frenzies; and there was a new face in my fantasies, with pleading, adoring spaniel eyes . . .

We met again, briefly, in a crowded art gallery, behind Miss Porter-Binfield's prim back. I was surprised to see him in such a place. He pressed my hand, and murmured words of devotion, and gazed at me.

He pressed my hand nicely. He murmured nicely. He gazed nicely.

We met again and again, snatching moments of whispered entreaty from him and smiles from me. I should not have smiled at him. I could not help it. I liked those meetings. I looked forward to them. They had the charm of the forbidden, of the impossible. They were the only events in my uneventful learned life.

I realised, of course, that our meetings were not coincidence. He followed me about, lurking, and popped out of crowds or corners when he saw I was alone. He must, I thought, be devoting his whole waking life to achieving these few scurried meetings.

He squeezed my hand when he could. His fingers brushed my hips. He put a furtive, frightened arm round my waist once in the linen department of Craddock and Fothergill's.

My midnight fantasies built on these fleeting contacts. Instead of brushing my hip, his hand caressed it—*here,* then *here* . . .

I learned more about him from things he blurted into my ear in the midst of crowds. He lived with his sister in Pimlico in lodgings over a shop. His sister had a charming room. There was a picture it would interest me to see, since I liked pictures. The sister was away in Devonshire. He was interested in horses and racing, like nearly all the men who came to Moreys, except Whitewater.

He was magnificently unlike Whitewater, and unlike Henry Clinton. He would never make me sick by giving me too many green peppermint drinks.

He was like a soldier with very little hope, waving a brave flag in the face of the enemy. The brave flag was his falsely-scarlet moustache. The whole world was the enemy. I was his only friend. In some ways he was a very small boy. I began to feel responsible for him. Of course that was absurd. But I *did* begin to feel responsible for him. It was the first time that I had ever had to feel responsible for anybody. There was nothing I could do for him except smile. So I smiled. It was something, it really was, though it seems so little. To help someone, truly help someone, by smiling and being friendly, that is absurd. It is too easy; one should do more. But it was all I could do for him.

He had no confidence in himself because he was trying to be a gentleman without knowing how it was done. I tried to give him confidence with my smile.

Whitewater was a gentleman. Henry Clinton was a gentleman. There was much to be said for any man on the simple grounds that he was *not* a gentleman.

He thought he was not attractive to women. I showed that he was attractive by smiling at him and letting him squeeze my hand whenever he could.

Whitewater and Henry Clinton were sure they were attractive to women. There was much to be said for any man without that insufferable vanity.

I lay in bed, thinking with amazement that Desmond Dacre needed me. I pitied him.

Something came into my mind, something creeping timorously forward out of a fog of uncertain memories.

"A pity beyond all telling is hid in the heart of love."

Because he needed me, he would touch me *here*, and do *that* and *that*, very gently and respectfully, but passionately; and because I pitied him, I would touch him *there*, and do *that* and *that* . . .

"Please come. I beg you to come tonight. I'll kill myself if you don't come. Just to see the picture I was telling you about, and talk for a little while. I'm so lonely. I'm lonely and miserable. If you'll just let me hold your hand and talk for half an hour. They're all in bed by eleven? You can get out then? I'll have a cab at the corner of Bruton Street at eleven. Please! I beg and implore you! I'd go down on my knees if it wasn't for this crowd. Will you come?"

I was melted by the passionate anxiety in his eyes. I was flattered that he needed me so badly. I was excited by the pressure of his fingers on my arm. All the same, I was going to say no. Of course I was.

"Yes," I said, to my utter astonishment.

He was desperately respectable in the hansom. He stammered, and breathed deeply, and cleared his throat. He took my hand but let go of it again.

With any other man in the world, I might have been frightened.

This adventure, more than anything else I had ever done, would destroy my reputation utterly and permanently—even if we did just sit and talk for half an hour. Pimlico! A flashy "sporting gent" with a dyed moustache and a Cockney twang in his accent!

I was a good deal aghast at the rules I was breaking, because they were the social rules, which one was not allowed to break; not the moral ones, which one was, as long as nobody found one out. But I was not in the least aghast at being in Desmond Dacre's power. I was not in his power. He was in mine.

The room was a very ordinary little room, clean, garishly furnished. The picture he had spoken of was a sentimental nothing. It was a bedroom.

I was alone in a Pimlico bedroom, over a shop in a dingy street, with a big bull-like vulgar adventurer who adored me, in the middle of the night. It was grotesque. It was quite all right.

I sat on the bed wondering what we were going to talk about. He did what he had so often said he wanted to do: he fell on his knees in front of me. I did what I had so often thought of doing: I stroked his hair. He sank forward so that his head lay in my lap. His arms went round my hips as I sat on the bed, embracing me in a way I had never been embraced before.

"If you only knew," he muttered into my thigh.

"I know," I said. "There, there. Everything is all right."

To my dismay, I found that he was crying. I had never seen a man cry. He clutched at my hips convulsively with both arms and buried his face in my lap, and his shoulders shook.

It was moving. The top of his head was pressed into my stomach and his face was pressed into my thigh. A familiar sensation began to tingle below his face, inside my lap. I felt myself breathing more quickly. I stroked his hair and what I could reach of his cheek. He moved his head, burrowing into my lap. The sensation inside me sharpened exquisitely with his movement. He was arousing me by the pressure and movement on his head and face, and by the tears he was shedding.

Without any thought, suddenly, because I wanted to, I leaned down and kissed the top of his head. I held his head between my hands, in my lap, and kissed what I could reach of his cheek.

His hands, on my hips, seemed to go mad. They burrowed under my behind until I was sitting on the palms of his hands. His fingers were gripping my buttocks from below. I would have expected such a thing to be unpleasant. It was extremely pleasant.

All the time the beautiful itch between my legs grew more insistent, and I felt the warm moisture of my own desire seeping out from the magic caverns where it was distilled.

He raised his head. His face was puddled with tears. He looked at me with a kind of terror. It was wrong that he should feel terrified. If I could stop him feeling terrified, it was right that I should do so. I could. I did. I kissed him, his face in my hands.

His mouth, his tongue, were all that I had dreamed. He was gentle and passionate. His tongue in my mouth was like a little shy bird. It did not dare to thrust into my mouth. It had to be given courage, too, if I could do such a thing. I could. I did. I caressed the tip of his tongue with the tip of my own, welcoming it, befriending it. His tongue fell in love with my tongue and followed it into my mouth. He was passionate, but still gentle.

His hands pulled out from under me. I opened my eyes, which I had shut. I saw his hands hovering uncertainly near my body. *They* needed courage. I took his hands in mine and put them on my breasts. He moved his hands on my breasts. My breasts came alive under his hands. His head was between them. He pressed my breasts, under my clothes, against his temples.

The electric telegraph of desire was sending signals all over my body. I felt the current surge into my breasts as he fondled them, down my arms to my fingertips which stroked his head, down my legs to my feet and right into my toes. There was an urgent yearning between my legs now. I felt hot. He pillowed his head between my breasts. I fed him comfort and courage, as though I were a mother giving milk from her breast to her baby. It was a joyful thing to do. I was happy, soothing him, giving him strength.

One of us moved, taking the other, or perhaps both of us moved together—I did not know or care—but he was off his knees and sitting on the bed beside me, one arm round me, the other hand on my breast, kissing me with a new passion, but always gently. Together we sank back onto the bed and moved our legs so that we lay side by side. His hands were everywhere on my body. I put my hand inside his coat and stroked his chest through his shirt. I felt strength flowing from my fingertips to his heart. My legs were pressed together because I was lying on my side, and I felt the wetness above the tops of my stockings.

"Oh God," he muttered. "If you knew—Can I—Will you let me—"

I knew what he meant. He should not have spoken, just acted, but he was too frightened. I twisted over so that I turned my back to him.

"Undo the buttons from the top," I said.

I thought I would be able to talk calmly, but I was panting with excitement and my voice came out a little high, unsteady squeak.

His fingers were trembling. But he undid all the buttons, from the neck to below the waist. His hands came round me from behind, under the dress. I felt him kiss my bare back, above the chemise, where my dress was undone. His hands, under the dress, found my breasts. He squeezed and stroked them through the thin silk of my chemise. His fingertips explored the top of the chemise. They lost courage. I gave them courage. With my own hands I pushed his fingers inside the silk. Given courage, his fingers prowled like little crabs over my bare breasts. His fingertips touched my nipples, as gently as though he were holding butterflies.

I heard his breathing, harsh and uneven. My own excitement was becoming almost unendurable. I pulled his hands away from my bosom and scrambled off the bed. He stood up, facing me, his face uncertain. I kissed him quickly, standing on tiptoe and reaching up, and then let my dress slip off my shoulder and down to the floor. In my chemise I picked up the dress and tossed it over a little chair. I kicked off my shoes. He still stood staring at me, his hair rumpled, his face nervous, his eyes pleading and adoring, his hands hanging uncertainly at his sides.

I felt a wave of tenderness for him. He was the first person I have ever been able to help in an important way. I was burning with eagerness now, every nerve alive, the electricity making me tremble.

I reached up and pushed my hands under his coat, onto his shoulders, lifting the coat back off his shoulders. Galvanized, heartened, his own hands tore off his coat and waistcoat and collar and tie. He came to a halt again, dithering, scared. I pushed the braces off his shoulders and began to unbutton his shirt-front. I stroked his bare chest as I undid the buttons. I undid the top button of his trousers. As I did so, I felt, with the back of my hand, the stiff lump which distorted the front of his trousers.

He gave a sob, and turned down the gas so that the room was dimly lit. It was a good idea. We could see each other quite well, which was nice, but we could not see the garishness of the colours or the dreadful furniture.

We both finished undressing. I could see that his hands were trembling violently. So were mine. We threw ourselves, at the same moment, on the bed, and embraced as we lay facing each other. He was enormously big and strong. He dwarfed me. There was little hair on his body, but a great red clump above his club. We pressed our bodies together. I felt his hands on my behind, pressing me against him. I felt his club like an axe handle against my stomach. It felt enormous. I moved my hips so that my stomach rubbed against his club. I moved the upper part of my body so that my breasts rubbed against his chest. I was panting with excitement, hot and wet between my legs, happy to be doing for him what nobody else could do for him.

We began to explore each others' bodies with our fingers—two amazing, tender, simultaneous voyages of discovery. His hands had learned courage. I felt like a flower with each petal being gently lifted and examined in turn. His lips and tongue followed his hands, or went on delicate expeditions of their own. My skin tingled with the touch of his fingers and lips. I thought it must be glowing, luminous, it felt so charged with electricity. It felt not like skin but like electrified *soie sauvage,* crackling and reacting under his touch.

I was lying on my back, and I felt his lips on the tip of one breast and then the other. Sensations flooded to and from my breasts and belly. He mumbled at my nipples with his lips, gently as a baby. The sensation was unbearably exquisite.

Groping wildly, blindly, I found his club with my two hands. I rubbed the shock of stiff hair at its base, and cupped the bag below in the palm of one hand, and stroked the loose skin back and forth along the rigid bar of the club, and clasped the bulbous end.

His hand was between my spread legs. I felt his fingers meet the hot dampness there, and a finger slipped between the eager lips in the moistened fleece. I pressed his club to the place, telling it to have courage, to invade me.

He was above me, resting his weight on his elbows, his chest just touching my breasts, his club between my legs. I spread my legs wide and wider and steered the tip into myself. He was kissing me desperately. Our faces were wet with our kisses. I felt blind and demented. Everything, all my being, was focussed on the overmastering sensation between my legs as he went into me. He went in and in, deep, unbelievably deep. I felt him against the walls of the magic cave and against its soft back wall, deep inside me. It was miraculous to be inhabited by someone else, by him, so deeply and so gently. I clawed at his back and shoulders with desperate fingers and fingernails. The sensation inside me was like nothing I had ever felt before. Everything I had done to myself was the palest, weakest foreshadowing of this mounting ecstasy. The sensation mounted and mounted so that I was sure I could not bear it, that when the climax came it would kill me. He moved a little inside me, then gave a great shudder, and I felt a spasm, a sudden deeper thrust of his body inside mine. Still my own sensation was mounting towards the peak where the blinding explosion would come. I clutched at him, moving my own hips so that I rubbed myself, my hungry interior surfaces, against him.

And there was nothing to rub against. The club has lost its glorious bigness and strength and rigidity. It was a flaccid snake inside me. It was useless to me. It was less than my own midnight finger. On the brink of the revelation, I had been cheated. Oh God, I had come so very near, and all I was left with was a wild unsatisfied hunger.

He drew wetly out of me. I felt empty and lonely. He sat up, and sat on the side of the bed, shy now, hiding himself from me.

He said in a muffled voice, "You are wonderful—it's a miracle. Thank you, thank you, thank you. I never knew . . ."

I lay on my back feeling cold and cheated. The wetness on my legs was cold.

He began to pull on his clothes, keeping his back towards me out of shyness. I sighed, and dressed also. When we were both dressed, he turned up the gas. I turned my back to him so that he could do up the buttons of my dress. His hands were trembling again, and he made a long job of it.

I found that we were back in our original positions: myself sitting on the side of the bed, he on his knees in front of me.

"You'll come again, won't you," he said hoarsely. "You must! You must! Promise you will. Please. Oh please. Promise you will—you must!"

There was something abject in the adoration in his eyes. A man should not kneel in front of a young girl. He makes himself ridiculous. A man should stand up. He should be a man, not a Landseer spaniel. To ask is one thing; to beg and implore is unseemly. He was grovelling. To grovel is unseemly.

I did not want to look at the abjectness of his face. I looked away from him, round the room. It really was awful. It was much worse than I had realised. Everything in it was chosen for vulgarity, for a shoddy cheap effect. There was a pair of fluffy woman's slippers in a corner, and a sleazy woman's dressing robe hanging on a hook on the door. I had not noticed these hasty objects. No doubt they belonged to the sister in Devonshire. I did not want to imagine her. My betrayal, my screaming disappointment, had been on her bed. I did not want to think about that.

"Please promise to come again. Please. I beg you. You must," Desmond Dacre was babbling on.

I glanced at his face, and away again. He was shameless in his pleading. I was struck again by a feeling of familiarity. I had known his brother.

No.

It was not a man who had talked to me in this undignified way. It was a woman. What woman? Had I known his sister?

He clutched my feet, in an agony of supplication, trying again to get me to promise to come to this horrid little room.

This ridiculous gesture jogged my memory. It *was* a woman it reminded me of. It was Mamma.

His abjectness was as sickening as hers had been.

"No," I said. "I won't come again."

He wailed like a baby. He began to cry. Through his sobs he gabbled his appeals, abasing and debasing himself, losing all dignity. He lost all manhood. He lost all humanity.

My whole body was angry with him. He had used me for his own pleasure and cheated me of mine. He was a horrible reminder of Mamma.

"No," I said. "I only came here because I was sorry for you. You are pitiable and ridiculous. You have no idea how silly you look, blubbering on the floor like an idiot child. If you were a gentleman you would have more courage. But you are not a gentleman; you never could be. You are not even a man. You never could be. You are a silly, pathetic, blubbering slum-child, with a vulgar voice and a vulgar waistcoat, and you are no good at making love."

I should not have spoken to him like that. Even as I spoke, I knew it was not quite what I meant. But I was cold and tired, and I had been so cheated that I felt ill with physical hunger, and he was making a fool of himself, and he reminded me of Mamma, and the room was a nasty little room.

"I was sorry for you," I said, "but now I am just bored."

His face changed. His sobs ceased abruptly. He went very pale. He was still on his knees, as though he had forgotten his position.

He began to mutter, "I thought you were an angel, but you're a devil. You're cruel. You're a she-devil. I loved you. I worshipped you. I would have done anything for you. I followed you and met you as soon as I found out who you were. I wanted your money. But when I met you I didn't want money, I didn't want anything from you, I only wanted you. I thought you were a saint in heaven. Now I see what you are. No one talks to me like that. I'll show you. I'll show you. I'll teach you to talk to me like that."

His voice was so quiet that I could hardly hear him. It would have been better if he had shouted. There was something terrible about that whispered hatred.

His pride was in tatters. I had made a serious mistake. For the first time I was frightened. I was very far from any help, from anybody that I knew. I was utterly at his mercy. He was a very big strong man. His face was working with anger and hatred.

I saw that he was crying again.

He jumped to his feet and ran out of the room. I heard his feet clumping in the next door room. I shrugged to myself and stood up. I would slip out of the house and away. I would get a cab if I could, or walk. I would be in Berkeley Square before the servants were stirring.

I had just reached the door when he burst back into the room.

"Oh no!" he said, still softly, his face contorted. There were tears on his cheeks. "Oh no! You'll stay here. You're to be punished. I'm to be rich. Two birds with one stone. Ha ha! I'll teach you to treat me as you did, you devil, you torturer."

Before I knew what was happening, he pushed me back across the room to the bed. He threw me down on the bed. I struggled and tried to hit at him, but there was nothing I could do. He could have manhandled ten of me. I found myself flattened on my back on the bed, under his weight. I thought he was going to smother me, or rape me. I tried to scream. He clapped a huge hand over my mouth, hurting me, bruising my lip against my teeth. He took one of my wrists and forced it up to the head of the bed, to the brasswork. I heard a metallic click and felt cold metal on my wrist. He forced my other arm above my head. There was another click. My other wrist was shackled to the bedhead.

"Lucky he left these behind," muttered Desmond Dacre. "I thought they'd come in useful one day, but I never thought they'd be as bloody useful as this—By God, this is your day! By God, this is your day!"

He tied something round my head, covering my mouth. I was gagged. I could make no sound. He tied something round my ankles, and tied them to the foot of the bed. I could hardly move. I could turn halfway onto my side, but that was all the movement I could make. I was stretched out on the bed as though I was on the rack. I was as helpless as a pauper patient on the operating table.

"Lie here and stew for the night," he muttered. "In the morning I'll make the arrangements. He'll come running. By God he will! By God, this is your day!"

He turned down the gas and went out of the room.

I went through a period of utter despair—minutes, hours, I did not know. Then I recovered my courage enough to explore my situation. He had not hurt me, except for the bruising of my lip. With my fingertips I could feel the metal that manacled me to the bedhead. I could move my fingers but I could hardly move my arms. The gag was uncomfortable over my mouth, but not really painful. I could breathe quite well through my nose. The cord round my ankles was tight. It was not very painful. I tried to free my feet from it, but the knot held fast. Painful or no, I was as helpless as a corpse.

My skin crawled as I tried to look ahead. In my disappointment and contempt, I had flicked him on the raw. He was the more furious and vengeful for having crawled so low, for having made himself so humble at my feet. I had made a very great mistake, and it seemed I was to pay dear for it.

Pay how? My imagination reeled. I could not guess and dared not guess. I was very frightened.

I lay weeping, suffering, trembling, for endless sleepless hours. If Desmond Dacre wanted to punish me for what he called my cruelty, he had already done so a thousand times over by sentencing me to these dark hours of lonely misery.

I heard the noises of the waking streets. I saw the light of the sky, grey, then pearly, creep through the gaps in the window curtain. I was stiff and sore from my bonds, bottomlessly tired, frightened.

I railed at myself. I cursed my folly. I would have signed away every scrap of freedom, for the rest of my life, for the safety of my old prison.

Hours passed. Full day came. The street outside was full of noise and life. I heard footsteps in the house, Desmond Dacre's heavy footsteps, but nobody came near me.

Hours passed. I had time to think. God knows I had time to think. I regretted my outburst, not only because of its results, but for itself. Perhaps I deserved some punishment for speaking as I did. I had had the punishment.

In the middle of the morning, or the middle of the afternoon, the door opened. Desmond Dacre stumped in. He glanced at me. I stared at him, over my gag. He looked pale, tense, triumphant. His hands twitched. He was not abashed or cringing, but exultant. He did something I could not see, some delicate operation that took his full attention, by a sort of hatchway in the wall of the room.

"Ha," I heard him murmur. "Enough glare for the Eddystone Light."

I mouthed against the gag. I wanted to tell him that I was sorry if I had sounded cruel—that it was because he had reminded me of Mamma. I could only squeak.

He laughed nastily at my squeaks. "I'll teach you," he said. "This is your day."

Some time later—God knows how long—he came in again, hurrying. He carried a silk scarf. Roughly, fumbling in his haste, he tied it over my eyes, knotting it at the back of my head. I was blindfolded as well as gagged.

I was very frightened.

The door slammed behind him. Footsteps thudded in the next door room. Other footsteps approached, softer, prowling towards my door. The door opened and closed, and I heard a key in the lock. The footsteps approached the bed and stopped.

I heard a sharp intake of breath. It sounded like a gasp of astonishment.

I sniffed miserably, my nose sticking out between gag and blindfold. I caught a familiar smell. Unique, unforgettable—a mixture of sandalwood and cloves.

And then I knew what my real punishment was.

He said not a word, but I heard a long, happy sigh.

I felt hands on my body, touching, exploring, probing, through my clothes. Even through my clothes, I would have known that graveyard touch among all other hands on earth. A hand went up under my skirts, clawing up my leg to the bare thigh above my stocking. It tweaked and pinched at the skin. I shuddered, sickened.

My clothes were cut and torn away from my body—every stitch, violently rent and ripped away. I lay shackled by the wrists and roped by the ankles, naked on my back, gagged and blindfolded, with the tatters of my clothes about me.

He tweaked and pinched and licked my body everywhere, like a beetle, like a cockroach. I writhed in horror and disgust. The scent of his hair-wash filled my nostrils. I felt utterly degraded, as though I could never be clean again.

His hands and teeth went blessedly away. I heard rustling. He was undressing. I felt his bare arms and legs sprawling over my body. I felt his club, moistened, on my breasts and stomach and on my face. I was nearly sick into my gag.

I heard movements at the foot of the bed. My ankles came free. I could move my legs. They were too stiff and cramped to move. I felt as helpless as though I were still tied. Hands forced my legs apart. A hand tweaked the hairs of my fleece, and nipped and pinched at the lips within. These were not caresses, but brutal and degrading indignities. I felt myself shrink with revulsion. All was dry, hostile to his touch, clamped shut against him.

There was a click above my head. One of my hands came free. My arm felt too numb to move. It was still burdened with the weight of the handcuff, though the cuff was freed from the bedhead.

He turned me over, bodily, violently, so that I lay on my front. He put a hand under my stomach, and lifted it clear of the bed. With his other hand he thrust my legs below me so that I was kneeling, my behind thrust in the air, my face in the pillows. I felt him on the bed behind me. He forced my knees apart so that I knelt astraddle. A hand groped and probed at my backside. Not at the large opening, but at the small one behind. I gasped into my gag. I had never felt a hand there before, not my own or any other. It was dirty, disgusting, forbidden. I felt his body crush up against my behind, his hard club between my buttocks. Hands seized my buttocks, pulling them apart. I felt a shocking pain as he forced the tip of his club into the small opening.

This was not to be endured. Disgust and fury gave me strength. My freed right arm was weakened by cramp and burdened by the heavy metal handcuff, but I brought it up and round and back, and struck the handcuff, which dangled from my wrists, with all my force against the horrible thing which was defiling me. I hit it hard, as hard as I could.

There was a thin scream behind me. I heard such a noise from a hare, shot and wounded but not killed. The invader, the pain, disappeared. I struck again, wildly, with the handcuff, aiming for where I thought his most tender parts must be. There was another scream, high, girlish, vixenish.

I was all furious strength. Cramp, fatigue, misery were forgotten. I struck out a third time, connecting yet again with I knew not what. Hampered as I was by the handcuff, I pushed off the gag and blindfold.

Whitewater was crouched at the foot of the bed, whimpering and clutching himself. I had hurt him. I noticed, abstractedly, that he had extraordinarily white and hairless skin for a man. He hardly saw me, as he sobbed and nursed the hateful things dangling from the bottom of his belly.

I saw, to my joy and amazement, that in the handcuff which held my left wrist there was a key. I turned and released myself. I unlocked the other. I was free.

Whitewater would not whimper and nurse himself for ever. I was free, but I was naked and alone and when he had recovered he would overpower me. As I had reason to know, he was far stronger than he looked. I had a marvellous idea. I slipped off the bed, crept round behind him, and before he knew what I was doing, I had clapped a handcuff to one of his wrists and snapped the other end about the bar at the foot of the bed.

Then he woke with a start from his self-pitying trance. He saw me. He saw the manacle on his wrist. He began to gibber with rage like a rabid monkey. As naked as I was, handcuffed, squatting on the bed, he looked supremely ridiculous.

In triumph and relief, I laughed in his face.

But I was still naked, and I was still in this house of horrors.

I flew to a rickety wardrobe, praying that Desmond Dacre's sister had left some clothes, and that she was neither giant nor dwarf. The wardrobe was locked. I wrenched open the door with a strength I did not know I had. There were clothes there, awful clothes. I put on the first things that came to hand, anything, so that they covered me. Desmond Dacre's sister, it appeared, was the same height as me, but much more amply built. Her clothes billowed round me. There was room for two of me in her dress. I did not care.

When I was almost dressed, Whitewater suddenly spoke.

He was still crouched, naked and helpless and absurd, at the foot of the bed. But he had recovered control of himself. His face was rigid. His voice came out as clipped and schoolmasterish as I remembered.

"You have sentenced yourself, dear little Camilla, to a course of correction which I cannot flatter myself you will enjoy. I shall enjoy it, but not you. The entertainment on which I just now embarked, which you interrupted in a manner you will come bitterly to regret, is by far the least painful and undignified of the diversions to which, as soon as we are married, you shall be subjected. I have a score to pay now, little one, and my friends and my enemies will tell you that I always pay my scores. Always."

As I furiously tried to push my hair into a semblance of tidiness, he went on, "Another thing. I have decided to advance the date of the wedding. I was in a mood to be indulgent to your girlish hesitation. I am no longer in such a mood. The betrothal will be announced immediately, and the ceremony will take place within a month. Your dear Mamma will make no objection."

He was helpless and ludicrous, but he was frightening. He was more frightening, naked and handcuffed, than a hundred Desmond Dacres.

I opened the window, and threw the key of the handcuff far out into the street, amongst the crowds and traffic. I did not look at Whitewater, or say anything to him. I found my purse. The money I had had with me was still there. I unlocked the door of the room. I listened, tense, wondering where Desmond Dacre was. There was no sound. I ran downstairs and out of the house. The shoes I had borrowed were much too big for me; I lost one, and had to run back for it. After five minutes of walking I found a four-wheeler. I screamed at the cabbie and climbed in. He looked at me dubiously. I showed him that I had money.

"Berkeley Square," I said.

It was only then that I began to feel agonizingly sore, exhausted, cramped. I could not understand how I had done what I had done, and then walked for five minutes in the streets. Soon I should be back in

Berkeley Square, thankfully regaining my comfortable prison, with a tale of abduction or some such for Cousin Dorothea.

Berkeley Square? Whitewater would know I was there. He would come to me there. Mamma would make me have him. And then, and then . . .

The unspeakable things promised me, in that prim schoolmasterish voice, began to ring like electric bells inside my head.

"Driver!" I shrieked, "Driver! Take me to Rupert Street."

13 ✿ *Sweating lust on earth*

Call it not love, for Love to heaven is fled,
Since sweating Lust on earth usurps his name;
Under whose simple semblance he hath fed
Upon fresh beauty, blotting it with blame;
Which the hot tyrant stains and soon bereaves,
As caterpillars do the tender leaves.

VENUS AND ADONIS

I didn't much want to paint Whitewater, because I didn't much like him.
But a commission is a commission, and I needed the money.

I would have painted a Gorgonzola cheese, just then, for money, or
even for the cheese.

I thought I might get used to poverty, but I didn't. I thought I might get
rich, but that didn't happen either. The trouble was the way I'd been
brought up. When your father's a successful doctor among the twittering
old ladies of Tunbridge Wells, you get used to your comforts. Or at least
to security. Father did himself extremely well, but he believed in austerity
for the young. Cold baths, fresh air, hard exercise. They'd made a man of
him, he said, and they'd do the same for me. What they made of me was
a fugitive. I simply ran away when I was seventeen.

I ran away from the cold baths, the philistine boredom, the discipline,
the clockwork life. And the stifling security of gilt-edged securities piling
up at the bank.

I ran away from my sisters, too; all four of them, all older than I.
Queens of the Tunbridge Wells social scene? Who'd want to be queen of

such a dull, unimportant little provincial realm? They liked it. Tennis and amateur theatricals. May, the eldest, had recently married a solicitor when I ran away.

The oddity is, two of them at least were talented. Amy, the third one, drew better than I did when she was young. She limited herself to niminy-piminy water-colour sketches of the Pantiles. What a waste. It was something we inherited from our mother, long dead. Killed by boredom, I imagine.

My father wanted me to be a doctor. Failing that, a lawyer, or some other sort of professional man. This was rammed into me all my life at home in Tunbridge Wells and at school in Tonbridge.

Boarding school was like hell. Chapel, compulsory games, more cold baths and hard exercise and all that miserable character-forming piffle. I didn't want my character formed, not by them, not in the way they meant. They took little boys when they were still soft, like tallow and poured them into moulds. They all came out identical, perfect little English middle-class gentlemen, soul of honour, stuffed to the gills with decency, loyalty, etc.

I didn't want to be identical to all the rest. I wanted to be as different as possible. I didn't specially want to be English. I liked thinking of myself as Irish, Spanish, French, international, a citizen of the international country of Art. I didn't want to be middle class. Either a tinker under a hedge or a roaring, raving millionaire aristocrat. I didn't want to be lumbered with honour, decency, loyalty. Was Villon? I just wanted to paint.

So I took a handful of sovereigns from Father's desk and got a ride on a fruit cart to London.

I did a lot of different jobs. I lived in a lot of funny places. I learned my way about. I was often hungry. I kept in touch with the family. Father cut me off, but May and Amy and the others sent me money sometimes. That was how I managed to travel a little—not nearly as much as I wanted and needed to. I got myself drawing lessons, too, from an old Academician who needed money as badly as I did. He liked brandy. His drawings were good, very economical and exact. His paintings were terrible—huge, gloomy, "literary" canvasses—*The Fall of Icarus, The Judgement of Solomon, His Last Letter*. They always hung them at Burlington House, that morgue of all that is dead in painting, but nobody bought them. In drawing he taught me what to do and in painting he taught me what not to do. "Paint what you feel about what you see"—that's my rule. A painting has got to be rooted in physical reality, but it's got to be a personal vision of that reality. Otherwise why paint? Use a camera and be done.

Without my old teacher's help I would never have won my scholarship to the Slade. I acknowledge that debt. It's the only debt I do acknowledge.

We started by drawing marbles at the Slade, then graduated to life. That was the first time I saw a naked woman. The discipline was as strict as Tonbridge, but I began to get to know a lot of girls. I was intensely shy with them until I discovered the secret of bluff.

I was about twenty when I decided to be eccentric. It wasn't enough not to be identical to all the sober middle classes. I wanted to stand out in a crowd, any crowd. I became a sort of Parisian Bohème. That was before I ever went to Paris. It was amusing. I let my hair grow, and grew a beard, and fixed on a form of dress which was practical and comfortable—lots of pockets, no wasting time with collar and tie and studs and socks. It got me stared at wherever I went. That was good for the soul, and good for a lot of free drinks. It helped with girls, too.

A soldier dresses like a soldier. A Harley Street doctor, a parson, a bank manager, coachman, farmer, they all wear a sort of uniform that identifies them. Quite right too, people know where they are. I put on artist's uniform which I designed for myself.

I wore gold earrings for a time, but they were too bloody uncomfortable. One of my ears went septic. I gave them up.

Some of my friends were as untidy in their lives and their work as they were in their dress. That was a mistake I never made. I always knew where everything was—paints, pins, charcoal, crayon. Time spent looking for your tools under the bed or in a cupboard is time sacrificed uselessly.

The way to make money—the *only* way to make money—was portraits. Society hostesses, politicians, successful generals, debutantes. I never despised portraits. What was good enough for Holbein and Cézanne was good enough for me. I began to get a few commissions. Never enough to pay the bills. Some people liked the results, some not. Of course, some were better than others. I completely failed about once in four, and completely succeeded about once in ten.

The Bohemian role I played got me more business than it lost me, but it definitely lost me some.

This man Whitewater liked one of my Esmereldas and asked me to do him. I went to his house. It was interesting. The atmosphere of the house was strange; I never felt comfortable there. Everything was too perfect, in a chilly sort of way. But Whitewater was interesting to talk to and interesting to paint. He'd travelled a lot. I envied him his journeys in the Middle East and Africa. He hinted about some of the things he'd got up to. Girls, not like Alfred Douglas and his fat friend, but not like me, either. In that sort of thing I've always been quite normal. The shape of Whitewater's head and his usual expression made me think of some of the Grecos in the Escurial. So I did him with a sort of Greco distortion, elongating skull and neck and torso and fingers. I was painting what I felt about what I saw. It was good. He was intelligent enough to see it was good. He paid without a murmur. The money had to go straight out again, but it kept a few people quiet. It kept Esmerelda quiet.

I thought that, being a rich lord, he could be the cause of further commissions. I put this to him one day when I was varnishing the portrait. He suggested Lady Bulbarrow. I said I'd never heard of Lady Bulbarrow. He found this extraordinary, but I never read newspapers or met anyone in that world. I didn't give a twopenny damn about politics or wars or society balls. He said that everybody in England except me knew that the Marchioness of Bulbarrow was the most beautiful of all the celebrated society beauties. He said I could paint her any time I liked.

He more or less said that Lady Bulbarrow would do anything he advised. She had great faith in his judgement. He said he could take me down to her country place, called Moreys, in Wiltshire. If he wanted her to ask me, she would.

I said, "I can't go staying in a mansion with a lot of aristocrats. Can you imagine me in evening clothes? I don't possess a single tie, let alone a white one."

"You shall be a licenced eccentric, my dear Whittingham," he said, speaking just like my old housemaster at Tonbridge. "Wear your normal charming clothes, and do not comb your beard more than usual."

When I saw that place I was absolutely terrified. But I didn't let *them* see that. I invented a new way of talking—I was always doing that as the fancy struck me—and this one involved a sort of Teutonic exclamation— "Agh!" It gave me time to think and it established authority. I liked it. I used it for weeks, until Esmerelda said it gave her a headache. I painted her with the headache, but the picture was a failure.

I swaggered about Moreys, got lost all the time, made a lot of noise to keep my courage up. Nobody seemed to mind. I got the impression our beautiful hostess gained a bit of credit for entertaining a Bohemian. It was an *amusing* thing to do. They were a set of God-awful bores.

Lady Bulbarrow said she wanted me to paint her in London in the autumn. She was beautiful. Fine carriage, lovely shoulders. I would have

liked to see her stripped. It struck me that was a possibility. Not from anything she said, just the way she looked at me. She wasn't forty. Rather Esmerelda's build. For her, having a tumble with me might be an *amusing*
thing.

She had a daughter, a little thing called Camilla.

Now here is a curious thing. I was not frightened of Lady Bulbarrow.
At least, not much. At least, not after a few minutes. She was the first
Marchioness I had met (as Whitewater was the first lord) but she was
just a woman, very much a woman. A fine woman, friendly, with a look
in her eye. Once I got used to the extraordinary idea that I was talking on
equal terms to a Marchioness in her own palace, I managed to be quite at
my ease. At least, I managed to pretend that I was.

But the girl terrified me. She was hardly more than a child—hardly out
of the schoolroom—slim, slightly built, fine boned, pale haired, solemn,
perhaps sad. She shouldn't have been frightening. She should have been
anything but frightening. But all Saturday morning, and during the ridiculous festival they called luncheon, I tried to get up courage to go and talk
to her—and failed!

Perhaps shyness is a better word than fright. I've often seen grown men,
successful vigorous men, shy with children. This pale girl was not quite a
child—she was caught, like a butterfly in a cobweb, between childhood
and womanhood—but I was affected the same way.

I didn't want to leave the place without getting to know her. There was
only one way to approach her. Other people, her own lot, might simply
have gone up and started a conversation, but I couldn't do that. I didn't
know how to. The words would have jammed in my throat out of shyness.
I had to bellow and pose and roar and play the giddy goat, all to show a
confidence I didn't feel.

From one of the terraces I saw the girl stroll out to the lake and park
herself on a sort of willow-pattern bridge. (Rather a successful folly, giving focus to the prospect.) I strode out there myself. As I got nearer and
nearer I felt my courage ebbing away. It wasn't so very ridiculous that I
should feel like that. The girl belonged in this daunting palace—it was
part of her, as she was part of it. It was a very far cry from my own background. I imagined the ingrained, instinctive arrogance she'd have. How
could she help it? The estate stretching for miles in all directions—the villages all tenants, the peasantry forever bobbing and tugging their fore-
locks; the girl brought up to that kind of thing from birth—she'd have
the gift of showing contempt while being polite.

Well, I girded my loins and rushed up onto the bridge, bellowing some sort of complimentary nonsense. I kissed her hand. It wasn't a thing I'd ever done to any girl before—imagine Esmerelda's reaction to anything so fancy!—but it seemed in character.

She didn't say much. She looked at me with those great grey eyes, solemnly. Of course that made me talk more and more, perfect balderdash. I overused my new "Agh!" I said I'd like to paint her. That was true. She'd be difficult—delicate bone structure, only a faint colour in her cheeks, a cloud of golden hair. You can exaggerate the strength of a strong face, the age of an old face, the tragedy of a tragic face like Whitewater's —but how do you exaggerate the delicacy of a delicate face?

I had the silly notion the girl should be painted on silk, not canvas. Maybe ivory. An exquisite Japanese miniature. Not my cup of broth. In those days I was using big, free brush strokes and a fairly heavy impasto, and a simplified palette of strong colours. That suited Whitewater and it suited Esmerelda. If I painted this little porcelain creature, I'd have to go a different way about it. Learn a whole new technique. A good thing, too. Frontiers are meant to be extended.

I didn't make the mistake of staying too long with her. My monologue might have dried up. I kissed her hand again. It was a tiny hand, thin, small boned, perfect. Esmerelda had big, practical hands. I liked them, too. Lady Camilla's hand was cold. No doubt she was cold, an icy little virgin.

London seemed empty and flat when I got back on Monday after the amazing interlude in the Marchioness's palace.

I often thought of that perfect little face, delicate and solemn. I tried to do some drawings, just sketches, from memory. They were no good at all. Esmerelda got definitely waspish about them.

I wanted to get away, abroad or out into the country. After the beauty of Wiltshire the streets seemed more horrible than usual. Money was the problem, as always. My few sales at the Chenil almost dried up because of the time of year. There was nothing left of Whitewater's fifty.

I heard from one of the Soho shopkeepers about a family called Monger from Sussex. They were gipsies, not pure Romany but mixed. The husband was in jail for cutting off some poor fellow's nose in a fight. The wife needed money and had a caravan for sale with an old horse.

A magnificent idea came to me.

I went and saw the family and the caravan and the horse down in some awful southern suburb. They were pretty wretched. I was sorry for them.

The wife was a scrawny, illiterate drab with a swarm of grubby brats. The horse was better looked after than the children. The caravan needed a good scrub and a lick of paint, but it seemed sound enough.

The price came down and down during half an hour's conversation. But it didn't come down low enough for me.

There was nobody I could borrow the money from. Most of the people I knew who had any money were out of London. I already owed money to most of the rest. I thought of Whitewater, but a servant in his house said he'd gone abroad. He wasn't expected back until October. I thought of my sister May, but that was no good. She was expecting her third brat and there was none to spare.

Money, money, money! I couldn't see any way of getting any until the autumn, and I wanted the caravan at once while the fine weather lasted.

I could see the life so clearly. Go as you please. Stop where you please. Milk and eggs from farms. The horse grazing.

Esmerelda liked the idea but she never took it seriously. She knew bloody well there was no money and no hope of money.

I started a painting of her, a nude. I wanted to try something new, so I sat her facing me with her legs slightly splayed. I did the whole composition from the cunt outwards. Even the Post-Impressionists had never dared to do anything like it. It made Esmerelda giggle. She was proud of her bush. It was a fine one, too, like a blackamore's head, marvellously thick, rich hair. I wanted to paint the acrid smell of Esmerelda's cunt when she was excited.

I enjoyed doing the painting, but it didn't pay any bills.

Days passed, or weeks, one or the other. I was bored. I was desperate to get away. I found it difficult to work in the deadness and stuffiness of London. The heat would have suited me if the air had been fresh, but it was stale. I was so short of money that I had to give up Music Halls, the Café Royal, everything. The Carandinis fed us once a day and sometimes threw in half a bottle of their Chianti. It wasn't bad. It tasted like red ink with a sense of sin.

Esmerelda went away to stay with her married sister in Essex. She left me the address. I didn't blame her, although it was damned inconvenient. I'd never been so penniless, even when I first ran away to London.

Topaz moved in to look after me. She was making a bit of money, sitting for various people. (Esmerelda would only pose for me.) Topaz had a good, big, firm body. I wanted to paint her in the same position as the new

Esmerelda, but she jibbed. She had middle-class scruples, which was odd, as her father was a tobacconist in Tooting. I did some charcoal drawings of her head and some of her hands. They came out well. I took them down to the Chenil, and they said they'd have them framed. They knew I couldn't afford so much as a passe-partout.

Topaz was a bit exhausting in bed. She took too long to arouse. By the time she was ready, I was almost past caring. The weather was too hot for such bloody long sessions. When she was ready, she was too ready. It was too big, too loose a fit. I like being gripped tight, but inside her I flopped about like a herring in a barrel. Nothing to rub against. Esmerelda was rather the same actually, another big girl, but she did look after me well.

Topaz wasn't as tidy as Esmerelda, which sometimes annoyed me to the pitch of frenzy. I can't bear not being able to put my hand on something I want. It's worse in hot weather. You get irritated more easily, and it's more exhausting to search for something. I missed Esmerelda's housekeeping.

God, how I wanted to get away. The Monger family still hadn't sold their caravan. I went half mad thinking about it.

One fine day I was sitting up in bed playing the *musette*. I'd bought the pipes two years earlier for ten shillings from a baker in Frith Street. He'd had them in payment of a debt. I thought they added another Gallic touch to the *tout ensemble*. I enjoyed playing them. There's a lot of music I don't like, but I like Music-Hall songs and bagpipes. I had nothing else to do. I had to stay in bed in case old Mother Carandini came up. I had nothing to do in bed all alone except play the *musette*. There were no books in the studio. I never allowed books there. Esmerelda would have spent all her time reading. The place would never have been swept or the plates washed.

I'd told Topaz my clothes needed washing. She hadn't wanted to bother herself, but I was firm. Esmerelda had got me into the habit of cleanliness. So Topaz took everything off to the bagwash in Windmill Street after dressing up as Trilby in her idiotic hat.

There was a crash and a lot of shouting down in the street. Sometimes I used to run down and help when there were disasters downstairs. I didn't want the order and discipline of my life disturbed and I *did* want to keep in with the Carandinis. Their goodwill was absolutely essential to me, at least until I made some money in the autumn. But I couldn't do anything about the day's disaster, if there was one, without a stitch of clothing.

Peace seemed to fall, and I tried to play *Mon canard est tombé en l'eau.* Then Topaz, who sometimes had some very funny ideas, began to beat time on the door. I shouted to her to stop, because the door was no stronger than paper. She came in, but it wasn't Topaz.

To my absolute astonishment, it was the little golden girl I had admired in Wilshire—the Lady Camilla Glyn.

I felt the most abject idiot, squatting in bed in the middle of the morning with no clothes on, making quacking noises on the old *musette*. I had to make the best of it.

She came in, as solemn as I remembered her, and stared round with those great cool grey eyes. She looked cool altogether, which in the stuffy studio was quite an achievement. She was totally unperturbed by my distinctly *louche* study of Esmerelda.

I had to go into the booming, bantering, Bohemian routine, otherwise I would simply have sat in bed goggling with embarrassment.

I was very glad to see her in spite of feeling such an almighty fool. Apart from all her other advantages, I supposed she had plenty of money. I did want to paint her. It was very odd that she should be in London, and odder still that she should come all on her own to the studio.

She said she was inspecting the place to see if it was fit for her mother to visit. Of course it wasn't. There was no question of the Marchioness coming within a mile of Rupert Street. That must have been obvious to a cat. Therefore my astonishing little visitor had a different motive. She must have come because she wanted to see me!

She more or less said as much.

The devil of it was, Topaz was due back any minute with my clothes. There was nothing I could do to take advantage of a situation that ought to have been tailor-made for me.

Well, we had to re-create the situation. We had to have an assignation. This beautiful little creature, practically a royal princess, was not going to be allowed to drop out of my life by default. That was *quite* unthinkable.

So we made a plan, rather unnecessarily tortuous, which would let her escape from her chaperonage. She solemnly, seriously, agreed to everything I said. She was fully prepared to go along with the plan, weird as it was.

This was the thing about her which was truly amazing. She was a protected, coddled little aristocrat, with golden hair and delicate bones, and she was *fully* prepared to join in with my crack-brained scheme.

And then, if it worked, fully prepared to come out to dinner with me. She! With me!

I suppose aristocrats, if they're high enough, feel justified in committing any audacity. It's an interesting thought, perhaps not original: aristocrats and Bohemians have common ground, a common philosophy—audacity. A thing is permitted, by definition, if we permit ourselves to do it. We make our own rules; only the middle classes are compelled to obey other people's rules. Poor wretches!

Topaz came back. She didn't like the look of Lady Camilla. She wasn't expecting a beautiful young girl to be chatting to me. I thought I'd better keep Lady Camilla's name quiet, just in case of future jealousies and troubles, so I invented an alias for her—as, to be sure, I'd done for Esmerelda and Topaz herself. They could hardly be Gladys and Bertha, could they, meeting my friends at the Café Royal?

Of course the Café Royal was the place to take Lady Camilla; or rather, to put it more exactly, to be taken to by her. That was for another time. When the time came, even she'd be impressed by my reception there.

I dressed and we went off, leaving Topaz in a sulk. Lady Camilla bought me a carnation for my buttonhole. I thought that boded pretty well for the future.

Our tortuous plan worked well enough, although it meant I had to leave a letter to a man I never heard of, propped on his own chimney piece in Jermyn Street.

I was expecting a row with Topaz when I got back to Rupert Street. I expected right.

"Lah-di-dah little chit like that," she said. "She'd never take your dirty old clothes to the wash."

"Of course not," I said. "She's a client."

"Garn."

Words led to words, unfortunately, as they're apt to with somebody basically coarse-grained like Topaz. She was on the point of walking out—simply leaving me. I couldn't have that. I must have somebody looking after me, keeping the studio tidy, and I must have a model. Besides, she did have that bit of regular income.

I've no false pride about being "kept." A civilized society would pay artists richly, munificently. If it doesn't, somebody's got to keep them, however miserably. A painter's function is to paint, not to work in a shop or shovel coal. He enriches the world with his work. Topaz was serving the cause of art with her shillings. She had that privilege. She knew it as well as I did.

She shouldn't have kept on referring to that money, though, while we were arguing. It showed bad taste.

I pacified her in the end, but it left me exhausted and thirsty and late for lunch.

I wrote a careful letter on the paper I'd borrowed. It was a thing I was good at. For several years, writing letters had been my main source of income. Usually I was the impoverished widow of a missionary. Somebody found me out and I was nearly in trouble. I wasn't ashamed of that then, and I never have been since. Painters must eat like anyone else. If we starve or stop painting the world is the poorer.

The plan worked well enough and the evening started well enough. I did admire that girl's spirit and guts. For the first time, I saw her laughing. I'd seen her smile before, sometimes quickly, sometimes slowly, in rather an artificial, debutante way. (I call it a debutante way, but my experience of debutantes was and remains pretty limited.) Her laugh was natural and it was enchanting. There were a lot of qualities in that girl that had never had a chance to get out.

As a matter of fact, I thought it was a stroke of luck for her, meeting me. I thought it was a stroke for me, too, for nine-tenths of the evening. Not only because she had plenty of money with her, which enabled me to give her a thoroughly enjoyable night out.

She was agog at the Holborn Empire like a child at a Punch and Judy. She got caught up in the fun and mood of the place as I'd hoped. She was completely unselfconscious. That was nice. I stopped being frightened of her for the first time. The chilly aristocratic mask fell off, and there was an eager child's face laughing and humming and going "ooh" and "aah" with the rest of us, with the plebs and groundlings.

I wanted to grab her and kiss her then and there in the box, but I hadn't gained *that* much confidence. I needed a few drinks to get me to that point. I knew she was paying for them.

I was ravished by her delicate beauty and I admired her guts. Part of me, though, thought she was being pretty bloody silly. A girl in that position, with those advantages, enjoying a shop girl's treat! Slumming! Taking those risks! Putting herself at the mercy of a lecherous amoralist like myself!

Of course, I was agreeable. There are different rules for artists. There have to be. We couldn't paint or write or play otherwise. That's what my father and sisters could never understand, or my schoolmasters and schoolmates at Tonbridge, or any of the middle-class lemmings. Artists must *use* life, in all the forms relevant to them, in any ways they need. They must eat it, chew it up, spit or shit out what they don't want. Ordinary people beware—You're not our friends, you're our dinner.

We went to the Café Royal. I thought she'd be impressed by my reception, and she was. Talk about your royal duchesses coming into a ballroom! I never tired of that stir of interest, that roar of welcome. That was why it was so miserable, so intolerable, not having any money. I *needed* that visible approval, that welcome from my peers. All artists do. Some pretend otherwise. Sour grapes. But you can't be a lion over lager and sandwiches. Everybody knows bloody well you don't drink lager if you can afford champagne.

I thought of hock-and-seltzer, but I decided on something stronger. I didn't often go into the Café Royal with a fiver in my pocket.

I called her Io, for two reasons. It was sensible for her to have an alias, as I told her. But there was a silly reason, as well as the sensible one. I couldn't go on calling her "Lady Camilla." But I couldn't call her "Camilla." Who not? I didn't dare! Silly, isn't it? But I could call her "Io" quite comfortably.

We lapped up crème de menthe like kittens. I was thankful she was paying. I felt grand, on top of my form. It was a pleasure to be seen with her, a little frail, pale, raving beauty that nobody knew. It added to my triumph. In a dramatic sense she was a perfect foil for me. Some of the time I was holding court, some of the time tête-à-tête with Io. The evening was a perfect balance—public worship, private admiration.

There was joy in her face. It did me good to see her laugh. It was real, unselfconscious laughter, but it wasn't quite like anybody else's. Most people screw their eyes up when they laugh—almost close them. But she kept those great grey eyes wide open. It was as though she wanted to miss nothing. As the evening wore on, she never took her eyes off me. I began to feel supremely confident.

I wasn't getting drunk, mind—just banishing my nervousness, my shyness. Every so often I remembered that she was Lady Camilla Glyn of Moreys Castle. Then I had to have another drink, quick, to remind myself that she was just my little Io.

I kissed her in the hansom. It was grand. She liked it. She let me feel her body through her clothes. I was almost aghast at my audacity at that point. Stroking the arse of a Marchioness's daughter! What a superb little body she had, though. Firm, slim, active. Little bird bones, fleshed just right. I desperately wanted to see that flesh, paint it, caress it, kiss it, all of it, paint it again.

Desire was really hammering at me when I kissed her and felt her in the hansom.

Then she felt ill. She was ill. Too much crème de menthe. Perhaps I ought to have noticed it back in the Café Royal. But I hadn't. These bloody aristocrats have so much self-discipline they can get drunk without showing it. It's a kind of deceit.

I felt a bit sorry for her, but I was so damned disappointed I was furious. I'd really been aroused, hard as a broom handle, jammed against my fly buttons, that real urgent throbbing. You have to let it go after that or you don't get a wink of sleep. And all of a sudden the evening was over, done, dead. It was years since I'd been so let down.

I had a problem with the cab, too. I'd spent all the money on her bloody drinks, and a bit of supper, and a good *pourboire* for the waiters. (It's important, that, in regard to one's future reception.) My pockets were empty again.

I solved the problem neatly enough. The old trick. I'd done it hundreds of times. I took the cab back to the Café Royal, saying I'd left a portfolio behind. I told him to wait, then went in through the front door and out by the back. I was still so burning with disappointment I could hardly walk straight.

Topaz was in bed when I got back to the studio. She was no good to me —she was *souffrante*, swaddled in napkins. She saw the state I was in when I undressed for bed. The pole slipped its moorings and pointed at the bloody ceiling.

"Ah," said Topaz, laughing nastily, "so you never got to pushing it into Miss Lah-di-dah?"

"She was taken ill," I said.

"Poor boy," said Topaz, still unsympathetic, "you'll have to play with yourself, then, won't you, before you come to bed? Or you'll make a mess of the sheets."

"All right," I said, "but you do it."

"I wouldn't touch your barge pole with a barge pole," she said, "not when its stiff for somebody else."

"Whose bed are you lying in?" I asked.

"Mine. Anyway, it's me paying the rent for it."

"You do bring money into everything."

"One of us got to. *You* don't bring money into anything. Oh, very well. Pull off your drawers and come here."

I lay down on my back beside her. It bloody near touched my beard, the state I was in. It only took a matter of seconds, what with Topaz's hot damp hand and my memory of the feel of Io's little body.

I caught most of the mess in a handkerchief.

"Christ," said Topaz. "You built up a head of steam there, right enough." She began to laugh. "Some of it got in your beard."

It wasn't the way I'd expected the evening to end.

I decided not to try to see the child again. The whole thing had been a mistake. I'd been seduced by the magic of her background, by Moreys Castle and her title. And by the charm of her sudden appearance in the studio. And so forth. None of it was real. I was disgusted when I remembered her vomit on the flagstones. The aristocracy's stomachs and guts and kidneys are just like anybody else's. Their vomit and shit smell the same.

She was thoroughly undignified. Fancy her letting me kiss her in a cab. A waitress would be more fastidious than that. She needed a spanking. I felt quite middle class about it. Topaz agreed with me.

I put the little wretch out of my mind and tried to get on with some work.

But it was too hot and stuffy. And I was too poor for any of the diversions a man needs.

Lord Whitewater came to call. He brought me a box of fat Egyptian cigarettes. I said I was surprised to see him back in London so soon. He said something noncommittal about trouble in the Levant. At the time I thought he meant a local war. Later I thought he must have meant trouble of a personal sort—with the police, perhaps, or some girl's family or boy's family. From what I guessed of his habits, trouble was always a risk he ran. Probably money got him safely out of the country, but it wouldn't have saved him if he'd stayed.

I didn't try to touch him for any money myself. It was a struggle. I had to sit on my hands. He was my principal contact with the world of valuable commissions. I had to husband him. No good eating the seed in the fields. But I *did* have to sit on my hands.

Topaz said afterwards that Whitewater gave her cold shivers up the spine. I knew what she meant.

The cigarettes were excellent.

After that, suddenly, five or eight or thirteen days later, there was a timid little knock on the door of the studio.

It wasn't la Madre Carandini's knock. It wasn't Whitewater's. Topaz never knocked. Esmerelda was still away. My other friends were all avoiding me—they knew I was penniless and they'd got tired of buying me drinks. Selfish arrogant stone-hearted bastards.

I was doing a still life. Fruit from the restaurant downstairs. All gone bad in the heat, or the Carandinis would never have let me take it. Interestingly diseased look to it—oranges with a grey-green patina of mould, bananas blackened, white grapes a sort of sick brown, black grapes with patches of white fur. *Still Life in an Empty House.* (But if the house was empty, how came the painter there? When is an empty house not empty? Great conundrums of our day.) It was going well. I was pleased with it. Every brush stroke seemed to ring a distant cash register. The canvas reeked of putrefaction, decay, rottenness, even in primary colours. I distorted the form of the fruit, giving them a squashed, half-melting look. Putrid liquifaction. Ugh! I'd been working since half past ten when Topaz woke me up. It was noon now, maybe, or perhaps three in the afternoon. My only watch had been pawned weeks before. Small loss! Topaz was out all day, sitting for a sculptor in Charlotte Street. Small loss! I was working hard and happily and I didn't want to be disturbed. I kept quiet and said nothing, and hoped the outside world would go away.

But the door opened, inch by inch, and a nervous little head peeped round it.

Io, looking absolutely extraordinary.

Her face was always pale, but at that moment it was as white as the fur on the grapes. Her hair was coming down. She was wearing amazing barmaid's clothes—the skirt and blouse of a barmaid twice as big as herself, and a hat with a sort of artificial red cabbage on the top. It was a saucy hat—the hat for a bouncy barmaid on her evening off. Under it, dwarfed, was this solemn little white face, the mouth slightly open, the lower lip caught in little white teeth, the eyes enormous.

Without saying anything, she came through the door into the studio. One of her shoes fell off. They were absurd shoes, cheap and nasty, like boats on her little feet. She tried to put the shoe on by groping for it with her bare foot. She was wearing no stockings. The shoe skidded away from her over the floor. She had to bend down to put it on. When she bent down her hat fell off.

I wanted to laugh, but something in her face stopped me. She was fighting back tears. They almost won, but she won. Her lips were twitching, but she didn't cry.

She said, in a small voice, "Is that caravan still for sale? The one you told me about? With the horse?"

"Yes," I said, absolutely flummoxed.

"If I buy it, will you take me away?"

I stared at her, speechless with astonishment.

"Now?" she said, with a desperate urgency. "At once? This minute? I'll get some money from the bank. All the money you want. I must go away this minute. A long way away. I'll do anything you like. You can do anything you like. If you'll only get me away, far away, and I can hide."

"What from?"

She looked at me sharply. "I can't tell you. Not now."

"Don't you trust me?"

"You gave me too much peppermint. Never mind. *Never mind that.* Will you do it?"

My mind was lurching ahead like the fast train to Edinburgh. The Mongers' caravan and horse. I could paint and patch the caravan as we went. Her money, unlimited money for food, drink, comforts, every comfort. Deep countryside, late summer perfection. All nature my model.

All my prayers were answered without my even having prayed.

Doing the child a favour, earning her undying gratitude, and being paid for it. "I'll do anything you like. You can do anything you like." I was agreeable!

I searched quickly in my mind for snags. I saw dozens. Charge of abduction. What was she running away from? Was I going to be accessory after some ghastly crime? She was capable of crime—all aristocrats are, or they would never have become aristocrats.

"Why are you wearing those clothes?" I asked, partly to make time for myself to think, partly because I really wanted to know.

"I stole them," she said simply, as though it were the most natural thing in the world, as though it answered everything. "Will you do it? Will you take me away? I'll give you anything you want. All the money you want, or anything else. Everything else."

She looked at me solemnly when she said this, her lower lip caught in her teeth. I knew what she meant. She knew I knew.

"I must understand what I'm being asked to do," I said. "I must know what you're—"

"No. I can't tell you anything. Not yet. I can't talk about it. I won't. *Will you take me?*"

"Yes," I said.

She said, "Oh good," in a small, strange voice, and then fainted.

It wasn't dramatic. Nothing like the ladies in the melodramas who clap a hand to the brow and swoon with tragic elegance onto a *chaise-longue.* The child just crumpled, quite slowly, in a little heap on the floor.

I picked her up and carried her to the bed. I'd carried her once before, I remembered, out of a hansom to a kerbside where she vomited. This was a distinctly different occasion. She was as light as a little rabbit. I felt her thighs and her ribs when I carried her. She seemed to have nothing on under her extraordinary stolen clothes.

Stolen from a barmaid? Or even a fat drab of the streets? How in God's name had any of this come about?

Her eyelids fluttered after a minute.

"Oh," she murmured, "how stupid. It's because I'm so hungry. Is that fruit?"

"You need food and drink," I said. "And then—"

"And then first, I must write a letter to my Cousin Dorothea with a message for Mamma. To stop them worrying, you know."

"Will it do that?" This time I nearly did laugh.

"I don't see why not," she said. A very little colour had come back into her cheeks. She sat up and prodded vaguely at her hair. "I won't say I've gone away with *you*. I'll just say I've gone away, and I'll be well looked after and quite safe, and I'll come back when—"

"Well," I said, "when?"

"That depends. I can't tell. I can't see that far ahead. When I've written the letter we must go to the bank. I'll get as much money as you say and I'll leave the letter with them. They won't know what it says. They'll send a man round to Berkeley Square with it. Meanwhile we'll go straight to the caravan and buy it. And the horse. Then we'll start off straight away and disappear. I thought it all out in the cab coming here. Those are the things to do, in that order."

I was impressed again. Though she was in some sort of deep trouble, or thought she was, she had the guts to think and make plans on her way to me.

"You'll need clothes," I said.

"Later. Any time. That can wait."

"But you can't go into a bank dressed like that!"

"Yes, I can," she said. "I can do anything I like."

By God, it was true.

"There's one thing that's very important," she said slowly. "We mustn't be seen together."

"Why not?"

"If they think I've run away with you, they'll look for you. You'd be easy to find, wherever we hide ourselves."

I nodded. It was true—unless I shaved my beard and cut my hair. I didn't want to do that.

"We'd better not eat together downstairs," I said.

"No, of course we mustn't do that. Do you think you could be troubled to go down and get something for us and bring it up? I can be writing to Cousin Dorothea in the meantime, if you could kindly give me a pen and some paper."

"I can go down to the restaurant," I said, "willingly, but, er—"

She gave me a sovereign. Her little face was as solemn as a statue. It was hard to believe that I had seen her laugh, happily and whole-heartedly, at Dan Leno and the Five Silly Cyclists and my own jokes.

"The only writing paper I've got," I said, "is that stuff from Jermyn Street. You'd better not use that. Someone will go round there asking questions, and see my note to Sir Matthew Alban, talk to that landlady woman—"

"Of course I can use it," she said. "Have you got any scissors?"

I had scissors, naturally, though it took a few minutes to find them. Topaz had put them back in the wrong place on my work table. How maddening that is! Things must be exactly in the right place, all of them, all the time, or half one's life is wasted looking for them.

I found them. Io snipped off the engraved address at the top of one of the sheets. Nothing could have been easier. I simply hadn't thought of it.

I took the sovereign down to the restaurant, and la Madre piled up a tray with risotto and fruit and a carafe of their own Chianti.

By the time I got back, Io was waving the letter to dry it.

"What have you said?" I asked.

"Nothing. Just that I'm going away with a friend, and nobody is to worry, and nobody is to look for me."

"You can't stop them looking for you."

"I can stop Mamma looking for me."

"How?"

"By saying that if she does I'll change my mind."

"What about?"

"Something she wants me to do but I don't want to do. Never mind about that now. We must hurry."

"Why? The bank will be open for another two hours, and—"

"I want to get away. I must get away. I don't want to stay in London a second longer than I must."

"But you must eat before anything."

"Yes, I am hungry."

She attacked the risotto with a sort of dainty ferocity. I never saw food disappear so fast. It was as though she hadn't eaten for weeks. She told me she had missed breakfast, but she wouldn't say why.

I packed up an easel, an armful of canvasses, a packet of cartridge paper, paints, brushes, palettes, palette knives, turpentine, charcoal, crayons, pens and Indian ink, pins, primer, pipe and tobacco, *musette*, folding chair, umbrella, carpet slippers, frying pan, saucepan, knives and forks, glasses, plates, mugs, matches, corkscrew, towel, toothbrush, my one spare shirt, the remaining cigarettes in the box Whitewater had given me, address book, sticking plaster. If there was anything else I needed I couldn't think of it and I didn't own it.

While I was packing, Io polished off all the fruit I'd brought up.

I left a note for Topaz simply saying I'd gone away for an indefinite period. If Esmerelda came back, they could share the studio, or one of them could go somewhere else. Esmerelda might want to share the studio and the bed. I had an idea that her tastes lay that way, as well as with me. Topaz might like that, or she might not. It made no odds. They could please themselves. There was nothing of mine they could damage while I was away, because there was nothing of mine left in the place.

It's a great thing to be able to shake the dust of a place off your feet when the call comes and get out on the trail. To follow the gleam without a thousand hampering problems. The trumpet had sounded for me and I was off. It was a gigantic stroke of luck. I sang as I packed—*Mon canard est tombé en l'eau.* I felt in the mood for a French song, and it was the only one I knew.

Io looked a good deal more cheerful when she'd eaten. What she'd eaten would have fed a family of six. I made a mental note of that—the animal needs regular and copious feeding. What else she needed I'd discover soon enough.

I went out to get a cab, carrying the whole of my baggage. (I, of course, had no baggage. Nothing! She travelled even lighter than I did.) She was to follow five minutes later. Nobody in Carandini's was likely to know her by sight—it wasn't a clientèle that read the *Bystander*. But she insisted on this precaution. I consented. She had the devil of a strong will. Accustomed to instant obedience all her life. God in heaven, these purple aristocrats! What a way to live!

She was paying the piper. To a qualified extent she could call the tune, in minor matters.

Ten minutes later we were off to Pall Mall, going by the Haymarket and Waterloo Place. Io was in a hurry now, jigging in her seat as though she was trying to whip on the cabhorse by a sort of magic. She was in a terror in case the bank was shut. She was also in a terror of being seen, so she pulled her grotesque barmaid's hat down over her dear little face.

Parsloe's Bank was open.

"Now you must stay hidden," she said. "Sit back in the cab and don't move. I'll be as quick as I can."

She jumped down, not needing or wanting any help. She was as active as a cricket, as a schoolboy. Much more active than I'd ever been as a schoolboy. (Oh God, those organized games! The boredom and the terror!) She scuttled into the great solemn portals of the bank, attracting a stare of the most ludicrous amazement from the massive fellow on the door.

The minutes ticked by. I stretched out as luxuriously as the size of the cab and the length of my legs allowed. They're too long for a comfort, but they're a help in getting a man noticed. If a painter isn't noticed, he starves. Even if he is noticed he's apt to starve. But not me—not that day! I lit one of Whitewater's Egyptian cigarettes and contemplated the immediate future with a great deal of pleasure. I was vague about agricultural matters, but I imagined it was almost time for the harvest. I wanted to paint a field of ripe corn before it was cut, and the same view as it was being cut, and the same again as stubble. I foresaw a great triptych taking the whole of one wall of the Chenil, and Roger Fry's crit—

Io's head peeped out of the portals of the bank. She looked left and right, furtively, then trotted to the cab and jumped in.

I called to the driver to go to Mitcham. It would have been far cheaper to go by train, by the Metropolitan Line, but who the devil cared about *that*?

"I've got two hundred pounds," said Io, as calmly as though having two hundred pounds in cash was as common as to die. "And I've made arrangements to get as much more as we need, as we need it."

"But the Manager—"

"What about the Manager? He's quite a nice man, I think. He's called Mr. Coward."

"What did he think of this arrangement? What did he think of your clothes?"

"What does it matter what he thinks?" said Io. "He's only a sort of servant. I gave him my letter to Cousin Dorothea. He's sending it round by hand. I told him I was going to King's Cross Station to catch a train to Scotland. Can't this horrid cab go any faster?"

"I don't think it can," I said apologetically, though I didn't know why I had to feel apologetic about the cab.

It was four o'clock when we got to the bit of common in Mitcham where the Mongers' caravan was parked. It was five by the time the horse had been fetched from somewhere and put between the shafts. It was six by the time Io had paid fifty-five pounds to Mrs. Monger—thirty for the caravan, twenty for the horse, and five for the contents and some clothes.

Io took entire charge during this phase of the enterprise. Of course she knew about horses and understood what Mrs. Monger was talking about when she described the harness and feed and shoeing. It was all double Dutch to me. I sprawled about on the ground, feeling a bit useless, waiting, smoking my pipe.

Mrs. Monger's clothes would have been dear at sixpence, but Io wanted them. She was glad to get out of her barmaid disguise. She reappeared from the caravan in an ankle-length red skirt, a tight green blouse, and barefooted. She and the woman were much of a size. Io's ankles were the daintiest I had ever seen. She would have been well disguised, with Mrs. Monger's gipsy scarf round her head, except that her little face was unforgettable.

We found a shop open and bought sausages and coffee and bread.

At half past six we set off. Io drove. I sat beside her. We went southwest, towards Epsom. Io wanted to hurry. The horse did not. But we had started!

14 ❀ *Lovers' hours are long*

Her song was tedious, and outwore the night,
For lovers' hours are long, though seeming short:
If pleas'd themselves, others, they think, delight
In such-like circumstance, with such-like sport:
Their copious stories, oftentimes begun,
End without audience, and are never done.

VENUS AND ADONIS

"Have you ever driven, Mr. Whittingham?" said Io. "Can you drive?"

"Have I ever?" I said. "No. Can I? Yes, if instructed. And I think you'd better call me Jasper, as we're gipsies."

Her little face wrinkled into the first smile she had managed all that day.

She showed me how to hold the reins. It seemed easy enough. And how to flick old Bluebell over the rump with the whip which stuck out of a socket beside the bench we sat on. This seemed easy, too, but hardly necessary. Bluebell was content to walk forever, though not to go any faster than a walk.

We had trundled out of Mitcham on a road signposted to Epsom. The setting sun was on our right cheeks. Io said we were heading southwest. I took her word for it. The country was open but far from empty. All the cornfields were stubble. I had to revise my triptych idea. The stubble in the sunset was silver with a rosy flush. Not easy to paint without sentimentality. The sky and the hedges were full of birds. Io knew all their names, but she yawned deeply in the middle of telling me. It was a sudden yawn, which took her by surprise, and made her look very young.

"You're tired," I said.

"I'm very tired. I didn't get any sleep last night."

"None at all?"

"None."

"What in God's name were you doing?"

"Nothing. Lying on a bed. Nothing. But I couldn't sleep."

"You can sleep now," I told her. "We've dropped off the edge of the world."

"Not yet. I daren't sleep yet. Somebody may come after us. Then I must jump off and hide in the ditch."

"How could anybody come after us? They think you're going to Scotland. They think you're wearing a tart's hat with a red cabbage on it."

She almost laughed. "Wasn't it horrible, that hat? Do you think Mrs. Monger will wear it?"

"Who would come after you, Io?"

"I don't know. Mamma. The police. Or—"

"Or who?"

She shuddered. She would not tell me who.

People in carts and carriages and cars looked at us curiously. As far as I knew, none recognized me. Ignorant philistines. Of course it was just as well.

A milestone said we were three miles from Epsom.

"We don't want to go through a town," said Io. "Pull into that lane on the right."

Bluebell answered my signals, and we bumped along a narrow way between high hedges full of red and black berries. Io said they were blackberries and hips and haws and woody nightshade and elderberries. I planned a hedgerow triptych—deep dark greens, spangled with those brilliant berries. Io as a gipsy picking them. Io naked as the nymph her namesake . . .

She looked enchanting, infinitely endearing, as she sat beside me with her little hands folded in her lap. She looked tired, but there was an eager light in her eyes. I wondered if I had the skill to catch that eagerness on canvas. There was still a frightened, hunted look behind the eagerness. From time to time she leaned out to look backwards, to see if we were being followed.

She said blackberries were good to eat, and we might find mushrooms in the fields in the morning.

The sun was half hidden by a swell of hillside when Io pointed to an open gate into a big field of grass.

"Old pasture," she said. "The ground's hard. We won't do any harm."

I don't know how she knew the pasture was old. She took the reins and steered Bluebell through the gap. There were no houses in sight. There were no animals in the field. We had the sunset to ourselves.

Io sniffed. "Well mucked," she said. "Good place for mushrooms. They'll probably drive the cows back here in the morning. We'd better be gone by then. We must make a very early start."

"Then we must have an early night," I said.

She jumped down onto the grass.

"I'll deal with Bluebell, if you make a fire," she said.

She undid various belts and buckles and led the old horse out of the shafts. Of course she was still barefooted—she had no shoes. Her toes looked tiny, pink, vulnerable beside the big iron-shod feet of the horse. Although he seemed placid, I did not trust Bluebell at all. I did not trust any horse, or cow, or even sheep. I had no experience of them. But Io treated Bluebell with friendly confidence. She put what she called a halter on his head instead of the harness, and tied that by a long rope to what she called a wych-elm in the hedge. He began to nuzzle at the grass in a sleepy way.

She found a bucket in the caravan and went off to find water.

"We only need a little water," I said, "for coffee."

"Bluebell may need a lot. What we need is wood for the fire."

I jumped down, not as gracefully as she had jumped. I found, to my surprise, that the grass of the field was wet and cold. It tickled and chilled my toes between the straps of my sandals. Unlike me, Io had expected it. No doubt she had sometimes gone barefooted in the pleasances of Moreys. No—it was no good thinking in those terms. She was Io, not Her Ladyship.

I went off to find sticks and came back with an armful. I thought, as I laid the fire, how amazingly things had worked out. How idyllic this was. How my wildest dreams, back there in the reek of London, had miraculously come true.

Dream topped with dream, because Io was with me.

And nearly a hundred and fifty pounds, with as much more available as we wanted.

And the countryside beautiful, and time to paint, and new sights round every corner.

I thought I would not paint Bluebell. An equine portrait would be laughed off the walls of the Chenil. "Mr. Whittingham, seeking to emulate George Stubbs but without the latter's knowledge of anatomy . . ."

There was something wrong with my firewood. It had a malevolent quality which prevented it from catching light. It was dry. The paper burned gloriously. The wood obstinately refused to burn.

The sun went down. The sky darkened. It was still very warm. Io came back with a full bucket of water. She was limping. She said she had trodden on a flint and also spilled a lot of water on her skirt.

"All the way back," she said, "I was thinking—never mind, I'll get dry in front of the lovely fire Jasper will have made."

"I've only got three matches left." I said. "This wood's bewitched."

"Have you ever made a fire before?"

"No. Have you?"

"No."

"Like to try?"

"I'm so tired. I think I'll go to bed. I'm too tired to eat, anyway. It doesn't matter about the fire. In the morning we'll buy some—I don't know; I'm too tired to think."

"Firelighters," I said, remembering that Esmerelda had produced some for the stove in Rupert Street.

"I thought that was what you were," said Io. "Goodnight."

She climbed into the back of the caravan, and I heard her bumping about. It was almost full dark. We had no lamp or lantern. I was tormented with hunger. I prodded in the dark for the sausages we had bought, and the bread, and the coffee. I would have sold my soul for a pound of fried sausages and a mug of coffee. I ate some bread. It was dry, without butter. We had forgotten butter. I ate a whole loaf of bread. The sausages and coffee mocked me.

I smoked a last pipe, using my last three matches, in the dark by my little heap of blackened, unburned wood. I saw that there were problems I had not foreseen about the gipsy life.

Io was deeply asleep when I went to bed in the caravan. I groped for the other bunk. I tried to be very quiet. I heard her slow, regular breathing. It was tantalizing to have her so close. But she was very tired, too tired. It would have been cruel to wake her. Nothing was working out as I had expected. My bunk was as hard as granite, but bumpy, like a sack of coal. The blankets were rough. I wondered if they were verminous. It was not an aspect I had considered. I wondered if Io had gone to sleep in her clothes, or, if not, in what. I went to sleep in my shirt. At least, I tried to. I was as wakeful as she said she'd been the previous night.

Requirements listed themselves in my head. It was marvellous to have money to spend, unlimited money. Firelighters, those helpful little bricks soaked in paraffin. More matches, thousands of boxes of matches. Whisky. Also brandy and beer. (No crème de menthe.) Butter. More bread. A lantern. Two lanterns. Possibly pillows and a new mattress. Could one go into a shop and buy a mattress? "I'll take a couple of mattresses, please." It seemed an improbable conversation. Yet people acquired mattresses. Salt, pepper, mustard. Potatoes. How were potatoes cooked? The thought of roast potatoes nestling round a roast bird made me moan aloud with hunger.

A dry loaf, eaten rapidly on its own, is indigestible. I discovered this in the small hours of the morning.

I wondered what in God's name I had let myself in for.

I was homesick for the comfort and certainty of Rupert Street. Stuffy or not. Boring or not. Unproductive as I'd been there—at least it was easy to come by matches and hot water. At least no horses threatened to tread on my toes or bolt with me.

I slept fitfully on the hard bump mattress, afflicted by indigestion and hunger at the same time. Horrible combination!

I was wide awake when dawn began to filter in through the uncurtained windows of the caravan. Gradually the intense darkness dispersed. A few birds were clattering and chirruping outside. I had leisure, for the first time, to examine my new home. It was pretty comfortless. There was a kind of stove which I didn't trust with a stovepipe going up through the roof. There were the two bunks—the bigger one on which Io lay completely covered by a blanket, the smaller one about which I was urgently going to have to do something. A stool. Some bowls and buckets and oddments. A broom almost bald of bristles.

Well, it was all a challenge.

At least there was plenty of money—far more than I had ever had before.

Io shifted and mumbled in her sleep. One little white arm thrust back the blanket, revealing a mop of pale hair and one pale cheek. The rest of her face was buried in the pillow.

I felt a wave of tenderness and of excitement. She and I were off the edge of the world, in a little secret house on wheels, intimately together. She was very beautiful. She had chosen me for this adventure.

While she was deeply and childishly asleep, I could let myself think of her as the high-born, delicately beautiful Lady Camilla Glyn. I could let myself marvel at the extraordinary situation I was in. When she was awake and active she must be Io, the little fugitive nobody, or I would find myself undone by nervousness. But, for the time being, I was able to lie and gasp at the thought of the heights I was climbing.

The light strengthened. Io moved in her sleep again, and I saw a sleeve on her arm. It seemed a huge sleeve for such a little slim arm. I wondered idly what garment she had worn to bed. With a shock I realised it was my shirt she was wearing—my single item of clean, spare linen.

Then I saw that her skirt—Mrs. Monger's disreputable gipsy skirt—was flung over some pots on a shelf. And that her blouse—Mrs. Monger's strident blouse—was in a crumpled heap on the floor. Of course, my own clothes were in a heap on the floor. They were that sort of clothes. They were *designed* to be dropped in a heap on the floor when I took them off. Anyway, I was a man. Anyway, I was used to Esmerelda picking my clothes up. Anyway, I had gone to bed in the dark. But I'd never before known a woman who didn't fold up her clothes or hang them up. I had a slight feeling of uneasiness.

It came to me with a shock that Io—that Lady Camilla—had never in her life gone to bed without a maid being there to pick up the things she dropped. All her life she had simply let fall things she did not want. Somebody had scurried forward, picked them up, cleaned and ironed and mended them, and put them ready for her again.

The change in her situation was much greater than the change in mine. She had far more to learn about living as we were now living. I hoped she was stronger than she looked.

I fell at last into the deep sleep which had eluded me all night. I was awoken by the violent shaking of my shoulder, which, in my dream, was the work of a massive policeman. Probably the one who marched me off to the cells in Bow Street when I got drunk after Whitewater paid me for his portrait. I came slowly back to consciousness and saw that Io was shaking me. She *was* stronger than she looked.

She had put on her skirt, to my disappointment. She was still wearing my shirt. It billowed about her like a tent about a tent peg. Her hair was wildly untidy. There was a streak of dirt across her cheek. Her face was solemn.

"Wake up! Wake up!" she said. "You must help me with the horse. Then we must go. Now at once."

"Why?" I said. "What's the hurry?"

I had reason to suppose she had nothing on under her shirt and skirt. I was excited by the thought. One is often, I find, excited when one first wakes up in the morning, for no reason. It often embarrassed me at boarding school. Desire hoists itself like the gaff on the mast of a sailing boat. That's even when there's nothing to stimulate it. There was plenty to stimulate me there in the caravan—Io's firm little body inside those loose clothes, only a layer of thin cotton between me and her. She seemed to move as free and lithe as a snake inside those loose, skimpy clothes.

I wanted to reach out and hold her and feel her. But it was not the moment. She was not in the mood.

"We must get on," she said urgently. "We must go miles further on, to a place where we can hide."

"What time is it?"

"I don't know—late. Come on."

She jumped down from the back of the caravan. I pulled on trousers and sandals and picked up the blouse she had dropped on the floor. Most of her bedclothes were on the floor, too. I joined her outside as quickly as I could. I was faint with hunger and lack of sleep. The grass was soaking with ice-cold dew. It wetted the cuffs of my trousers and the hem of Io's skirt.

She was having a little trouble with the old horse. I was frightened for her bare toes and for my own. The horse disliked being backed between the shafts of the caravan. Io spoke to it in a tone I thought rash—very firm and dictatorial. I would have adopted a more wheedling note. But of course she was not frightened of the horse. Her methods worked in the end. She had to be pretty energetic when he tossed his head and tried to turn away. Her struggles confirmed, as far as I could tell, that she wore no underclothes. Under the circumstances it was difficult for me to help her.

I had no idea what buckles to do up, nor what strap to lead through what brass ring, nor what any of the pieces of leather and metal were for. I didn't suppose Io herself had ever harnessed a horse to a cart before—there were swarms of grooms and coachmen at Moreys, I imagined, to do that sort of thing—but she seemed to have an instinct about it.

She was dishevelled when she had finished and Bluebell was bitted and harnessed and blinkered and ready to pull us away. Her hair was a great wild aureole round her head, and her shirt (my shirt) had come partly unbuttoned. There was another smear of dirt across her face.

"I'm hungry," she said.

"We'll buy food and matches and firelighters when we come to a village," I comforted her.

"Yes."

"And you need more clothes."

"No."

"But that's my shirt."

"Then you need more clothes."

She put a bucket into the back of the caravan, which I saw was full of white billiard balls.

"Mushrooms," she said. "I thought this would be a good field with so much muck spread all over it. I picked them while you were still snoring."

"Was I snoring?" I said, abashed.

"You sounded like a steam engine."

We climbed up onto the front of the caravan. She bent down to pick up the reins and took the whip from its socket. This movement, with the undone buttons at the front of her shirt, exposed the creamy swell of one breast. I even glimpsed the pink nipple. She did not realise that she was exposing herself. She was pink with exertion. I hunched myself forward on the seat to hide my sudden and overwhelming excitement.

It was hardly fair that she should arouse me to such a point and then be in such a hurry to get on. It was almost as bad as vomiting.

"Oh my goodness," she said, "we're too late."

As she spoke, I saw what she meant.

A placid white face peered round the gatepost, ten yards from the caravan. It was a cow. Another pressed up beside it, then half a dozen more. Cows began to crowd in through the gate from the lane. They moved with a sort of awkward, hesitant strut. They were all round us. More and more came into the field. The caravan was an island in an ocean of brown and white cows.

A man came in with the last of them with a small boy.

If the boy was small, the man was very large, a typical beef-fed farmer, a mountain of brawn with a broad red face like an underdone roast and a voice like a bull. (I had never heard the roar of a bull, if they roar, but I imagined it like this farmer's bellow.) I could not understand what he said. He was shaking with anger. He brandished a cudgel like the one I sometimes carried myself in London as part of the costume. His was not part of his costume. It was for use. It was for smashing me, and perhaps Io and Bluebell and the caravan too.

Io's voice cut through the bellowings of the farmer and the contrapuntal squeaks of the small boy. Her voice was clear, high, hard, arrogant.

"Don't be ridiculous, please," she said. "You can see we have done no harm, and made no mess. You can't even see our wheel tracks."

This was hardly surprising. A hundred cows had just trampled over them.

The farmer bellowed something I did partly understand, about having the law on us.

At this, Io glanced at me. Under the icy aristocratic mask, there was a sudden and desperate look of terror in her face. It disappeared as quickly as it came. She turned back to the farmer.

"You will only make a fool of yourself if you bother the police," she said coldly and with perfect calm. "It would be more helpful if you got your cows out of our way and stopped talking nonsense."

It was extraordinary. There was much about Io (about Lady Camilla) that I was still not within a million miles of understanding. She looked the most completely disreputable urchin with her dirty bare feet, and dirty crumpled gispy skirt, and my huge, unbuttoned, almost indecently revealing shirt, and with her wildly untidy mop of hair, and with the streaks of a dirt across her little face. Yet she spoke like a duchess trying to be patient with a silly labourer.

The cows did begin to move on, driven shrilly by the small boy. They were amenable to going, though not in a hurry. The mountainous farmer still looked quite ready for violence. He did not get out of our way. Instead he came up to Bluebell and took hold of his reins, just by the bit.

"Ye made a fire!" He shouted.

"Rubbish," said Io. "Where is the burnt patch?"

Of course there was no burnt patch, because there had been no fire. There had been a useless blackened pile of sticks, but the cows had trampled them and quite obliterated any trace of my efforts.

"We have only been here for ten minutes," said Io. "We got out of the lane so as not to block. I should have thought that would have been obvious. How could you have driven your cows up the lane if we had been blocking it? We expected to be thanked, not to be shouted at."

"Ar," said the farmer savagely. But it seemed that Io had put a new thought into his head.

"Perhaps," said Io, a little more gently, but still like a marchioness talking to a slow-witted page boy, "You would kindly lead my horse out of the gate?"

And to my astonishment he did so.

"Thank you, my man," said Io.

She shook the reins, and tickled Bluebell over the backside with the whip. We began to bump away up the lane. I leaned out to look backwards. The farmer was standing in the midst of the lane staring after us with his great mouth hanging open. After a moment the little boy joined him and stared after us, too, with *his* mouth hanging open.

"People only need to be told what to do," said Io calmly. "They usually do it."

"By a gipsy girl with a dirty face?"

"Oh. I'd forgotten that. I was thinking I was—My feet, and so forth—Is my face dirty? There isn't a looking glass in the caravan. I expect Mrs. Monger preferred not to see herself. It's another thing we must buy. And a hairbrush and comb. I wonder if I shall be able to comb my own hair?"

I was still trembling from the altercation. Violence always upset me. That was one of the reasons I detested boarding school so much—the fights, the bullying, the rough-and-tumble of those horrible football matches. The way to be admired was to be stronger and crueller than the other boys.

All that had frightened Io was the threat of the police.

"What are you running away from?" I said yet again.

"I can't tell you. You least of all. You know—There's a good reason. Are you regretting this?"

She leaned forward as she spoke to scratch her bare instep. The billowing shirt sagged away from her front, and I glimpsed again the alabaster swell of her small high breast and the pink disc of the nipple.

"No," I said with difficulty. "I'm not regretting anything."

"We must get on."

"That farmer will remember you."

"Who am I? A gipsy girl?"

"Gipsy girls don't have golden hair. Or million-pound voices."

"Oh. I'll wrap that awful shawl round my head. And use a different voice. We *must* get on. We must get a long way away from that place. We must paint the caravan a different colour."

Io desperately tried to whip Bluebell into a trot. He would trot for a stride or two, so that the caravan bumped behind us like a little boat on a rough sea, and pots tumbled, and then relapse into his sleepy walk.

"We'll buy another horse," said Io.

I screamed internally for tobacco. I had tobacco. I had no matches.

We stopped on the edge of the big village which had half a dozen shops among the cottages round its green, and a tall church with heavy trees shading the gravestones, and a manor house of rosy brick just visible up an avenue of beeches. (Io said they were beeches.)

Shopping would make us both conspicuous. There was nothing I could do about that, short of cutting my hair and shaving. I had no scissors or razor. There was nothing Io could do about her bare feet or her delicate fair-skinned face, but she swathed her head in a greasy scarf and practised a gipsy whine.

We made an extensive list and went shopping separately. We thought we were slightly less likely to be remembered separately than together.

I still had not the slightest idea from whom Io was running, or why. The clink of her sovereigns in my pocket went far to calm my curiosity. So did those intermittent, stolen glimpses of her little white breast.

We bought nearly everything we wanted, including paint and paintbrush and whisky and all kinds of food and a shirt and matches and firelighters and lanterns and the other things on our list. Io bought a toothbrush and tooth powder. She said she did not want shoes or any other clothes. I failed to get brandy or a new mattress. No one had a cart horse for sale suitable to replace Bluebell. I was glad. I thought another horse was an extravagance.

We set off again. Io was desperate to keep moving. We kept to lanes and by-roads, and so saw little other traffic. The ways took us a twisty, corkscrew route, but Io said our general direction was westward.

I wanted to stop at midday for a drink, a cold meal, a smoke, and forty winks on a greensward under a tree. Io would not stop except to rest and water Bluebell for a few minutes at a time. We ate as we went, cold tongue and fresh bread and tomatoes. Io ate an astonishing amount.

It might be supposed that, since we were sitting side by side for hour after hour with nothing to do except steer a sleepy old horse, we should talk a tremendous amount and find out everything about each other. It was not so. Io was preoccupied. She did not want to talk about herself. If she had a secret life—and who has not?—she kept it secret. I did not want to talk about my own history to her, except in broad and somewhat misleading terms. It was so extremely drab compared to her life.

In the middle of the afternoon we passed a small hill with a knob of great trees on the top, casting a remarkable shadow over the broken and sloping ground. The effect was grand. I wanted to stop and paint it.

"We must get on," said Io.

"A quick sketch in oils."

"No. We daren't stop here."

"But—"

"When we're truly hidden you can paint all you like. Anything you like."

"Including you?"

She glanced at me. She gave, fleetingly, what I thought was only her second smile since we had started. It was only a little smile. Was there a hint of bashful invitation in it?

I glimpsed her breast as she turned to watch the road ahead, gathering up the reins. My blood pounded. I did not want to stop and paint, but to cup my hand over that breast. I wanted to make love to her there and then in the long sweet wayside grass.

But she said we must get on.

As the sun neared the western horizon, Io steered Bluebell off the road into a sandy, scrubby path of heathland with dry stony ground and prickly bushes and stunted trees.

As before, she dealt with Bluebell. We had filled buckets from a stream some miles back, which was as well, as there was no water near our camp. She gave him water, and some grain and bran in a bucket, and hay in a bag made of coarse netting. He was content. I was not. I thought that to-night I would kiss Io, and reclaim my shirt from her narrow shoulders
. . .

I collected wood and made a fire, careful not to set light to any of the small dry trees of the place. With my oily firelighters and plenty of matches, I soon had a good fire going, flaring and crackling, highly satis-factory.

Io said that she would cook our supper. She put a pan on the fire, and into it our sausages, some eggs, the mushrooms she had picked, and some bacon.

Over that supper I draw a veil. I learned later that when cooking things in a pan over a fire, you must have grease or oil in the pan. Io did not know this important fact. She had never cooked anything before. Nor had I. I had watched Esmerelda often, Topaz occasionally, cooking on the stove in my studio in Rupert Street; but I had not observed closely, or tried to learn. It had never occurred to me to do so. Io had never even *seen* anyone cooking. In her life, food was something which was brought by a footman.

We struggled to eat a little of the blackened and reeking mess which Io produced.

"There is something wrong with this frying pan," she said crossly. "We must get a new one."

"I don't mind," I said to her, almost truthfully, drinking whisky out of a tin mug. "I'll forgive you completely if—If I—"

I put a hand on her shoulder and started to draw her towards me.

"No," she said. "Not yet. Not tonight. I can't. Wait till we're hidden."

"But—"

"Anyway, I'm too hungry."

She slept in my shirt again. I did not touch her. I did not sleep much, either, tormented by hunger and by desire and by that mattress, in spite of another mug of whisky.

So for two more days.

I supposed that we travelled about four miles to the hour, and for about eight hours a day—a total of something like a hundred miles from our starting point. But far less as the crow flies, because our small by-roads bent us about in all sorts of directions.

A kind old woman in a shop in a village somewhere in Berkshire sold me another frying pan. She explained to me (as to a helpless man) that lard or dripping must be put in the pan before anything could be fried. I bought quantities of lard, and passed on this instruction to Io. Our second supper was edible. Io was pleased with herself. That gave me high hopes. But she said that I might not kiss her—or anything—until we were hidden away in a remote and secret place.

I wondered if she meant to go all the way westwards to Wales, or across the sea to Ireland to join our mythical friend the baronet's grandmother.

The countryside changed character as we went to a degree that astonished me. The change was gradual, yet very marked. By the third afternoon we were in an area of slow hills and very big, dense woodlands. It was far emptier of people and dwellings than the countryside we had left behind. The houses were of stone instead of brick, and some of the fields were divided by walls instead of by fences or hedges.

"I think we're in Gloucestershire," said Io. "But I'm not sure."

"We can surely hide here."

"Yes. I'm tired of travelling."

We found a deep and dripping wood on the side of a gradual hill. It was profoundly quiet. There was a stream at the edge of the wood. Two miles away there was a farm where Io said we could get milk and butter and eggs. Five miles away there was a village called Little Hennings with a single small smoky shop where we could buy almost everything else. There was a pub in the village, too. I had explored shop and pub when we passed through.

An overgrown track ran into the wood. I led Bluebell up it, dancing out of the way of his great feet, impaling my own toes on a thousand thorns and thistles. When we could go no further we stopped. We were hidden from every direction by the dense woodland all round us. We were even hidden from an aeroplanist above. We had unlimited fuel, as well as water.

Io breathed a great sigh and said it would do.

Tension and urgency, almost visible, left her face. She smiled at me and at Bluebell and at the surrounding trees.

"*Now* you can paint," she said.

"I want to paint you."

"Yes."

She cooked a better supper. She was quick to learn. I smoked a last pipe over the dying fire. She climbed into the caravan. I heard her movements and saw her fleetingly through the little window, lit by the hurricane-lamp hanging from the roof. I was breathless with suspense. I nearly choked over my pipe, and nearly bit the stem in half. I felt that my hands were trembling when I knocked it out on a stone.

She was asleep when I climbed in after her. Only the top of her golden mop of hair was visible in the rosy lamplight. I heard her deep, relaxed breathing. The blood was pounding in my loins, dragging my desire painfully up against the front of my trousers. But I could not wake her.

I awoke in the morning, from the deep sleep of early morning after a bad night, to find the caravan full of light, and Io sitting up in bed in my shirt.

Her hair was tousled and her eyes sleepy. She stretched luxuriously, yawned, and smiled.

"I feel safe," she said, in a husky early-morning voice. "I slept beautifully."

She swung her legs out of the bunk and stood up. Unlike me, she did not have to stoop in the caravan. The shirt of mine she was wearing was of the sort all men wore in those days—its tails came to my own knees, so on her they came almost to the ground. It was slit up the sides. I saw for the first time her slender calves. The cuffs of the sleeves came down far below the tips of her fingers, until she rolled them back as a pastry cook does. She looked ridiculous and adorable. She looked happy, because at last she felt safe.

"What shall we have for breakfast?" she said. "Fried eggs? Toast? Coffee?"

"I'll get a fire going," I said.

"No. I want to. I want to see if I can."

She could. She jumped out of the caravan as she was. Soon I heard dry twigs crackling and the sizzle of fat in the pan. I sat in my bunk, trying to think of breakfast, trying to tug my mind away from the thought of the body under that shirt, trying to calm the pounding of the blood. I pulled on my own trousers.

I found her crouched over the fire, a smear of soot across her forehead, enveloped in the huge areas of the shirt, happily absorbed. She was a little girl playing at being a Red Indian in the forest. She burned the toast.

When we had eaten, I smoked the very last of Whitewater's Egyptian cigarettes. I hoped it would calm me down. Perhaps it did. At least it gave my trembling hands something to occupy them. I did not want Io to see that my hands were trembling. She, meanwhile, wiped the plates clean with wisps of dew-wet grass. The movement revealed the swell of her breasts. No more. It was too much.

It was another glorious day—all our journey had been under clear skies and hot suns. Where we sat the mossy ground was badged with patches of sunlight and shade. A few birds were chattering in the depths of the woods around us. It was the most peaceful place I had ever seen. I thought it was the *only* truly peaceful place I had ever seen.

"Will you paint today?" Io asked suddenly, after a long friendly silence.

"Yes. I want to paint you. As you are. In that shirt."

"I must try to comb my hair, then."

"No. I want to paint it just as it is. Like a demented golden cloud."

I got my things out of the caravan—stool, easel, a canvas ready primed, palette and paints and brushes. I posed Io by the remnants of the fire, sitting with her hands clasped about her knees, looking down at the frying pan.

It started well, but it went wrong. The shirt was too large. It was grotesque. Her little ankles and arms and neck emerged from it in a way that should have been touching, but on canvas was simply silly. Usually it is possible to indicate the drawing of a body, its cohesiveness with proportion, even under voluminous clothes—just as the skeleton is implicit under the skin when a good draughtsman does a nude. But the shirt was too much. The ankles and arms and head did not belong to each other. I began to hate and resent the enshrouding shirt. Therefore I could not paint it. Because I was rendering what I felt about what I saw, the shirt was a dreary, boring enemy.

I was so intensely conscious of the little body inside the shirt. I wanted to paint that. I had to.

I wondered whether I dared suggest this to Io. I had mentioned before painting her in the nude, but only as a joke; as part of my performance, my rumbustious, Bohemian, no-respecter-of-persons. She had not seemed shocked or frightened at the idea, but that was simply because it *had* been a joke. I was frightened to do or say anything that threatened our relationship. We must remain on good and easy terms. She must continue to trust me, and to want to stay here with me. Not only for her own sake, hiding as she was from whatever it was, but for mine, too. I did intend to paint—and paint and paint—in this magic and secret place. But I had to eat. I couldn't, without her.

"Are you sure," she suddenly said, "you want to paint me in this shirt?"

"No," I said huskily. "I don't. I thought I did, but—"

"It's too big. Clumsy. Is that it?"

"Yes."

"It hides me."

"Yes."

"Shall I take it off?"

"Can you? Will you?"

"I said I'd be your model."

She took hold of the tail of the shirt in her fingers. She knelt up so that she was no longer sitting on the shirt. She began to draw it up her legs. When she had bared part of her thighs, just two or three inches above the knee, she stopped. She blushed and looked away from me.

"Am I to sit as I was?" she asked.

"I—herum!" I had to clear my throat shrilly. I could hardly hold my brush for the trembling of my fingers.

I had seen Esmerelda, and Topaz, and dozens of others, pose in the nude in a thousand positions. I had seen them step out of a chemise or dressing robe and suddenly reveal their nakedness. It was something I was well used to. It is part of any painter's academic training. It was part of my life. I was utterly unprepared for this excitement, this trembling and terrified eagerness, this suffocating suspense.

She knelt by the dying fire, the voluminous shirt halfway up her thighs. She looked at me wide-eyed, anxious, blushing.

I had never seen her blush before. I wanted to paint that blush.

In a shrill, unfamiliar voice, I said, "I think—one leg along the ground —the other knee bent. The right knee. Your right hand on the bent knee. The other hand on the ground, supporting you—Can we see how that looks?"

She gulped. She bit her lip. A look of resolution came into her face. She nodded manfully. She pulled at the tails of the shirt. It billowed about her hips and shoulders. She struggled inside it. Her head came clear, more tousled than ever. She threw the shirt away from herself, towards the caravan. She sat as I had told her to, her left leg, nearer me, along the ground, her right knee bent and raised, one hand on that knee, the other beside her left hip on the ground.

God in heaven, she was beautiful.

I could describe her in paint. Can I do it in words?

She was sitting in a patch of the warm morning sunlight which swam down through a gap in the curtain of leaves above us. It gleamed on the untidy gold mop of her hair and on the broth of silvery gold which, as far as her position allowed, she was hiding between her thighs. Her face was anxious, almost stern. Her shoulders were as delicate as a bird's. Her arms were slim yet rounded, and terminated in the slenderest wrists and tiniest hands in the world. He rib cage narrowed gently to a small waist, below which swelled sweetly rounded hips and thighs. The breasts which I had glimpsed now thrust marvellously towards me, high, firm, perfectly shaped, with nipples brilliantly pink in the morning sunlight against the perfect whiteness about them.

I write this romantical effusion about Io's body because in flat workaday prose I could not express its beauty, or the effect of its beauty on me.

"Is this right?" she asked, not looking at me, in a high and shy and childish voice.

Was it? I tried to think rationally, to drag my mind from flesh to canvas.

"You're a little stiff," I said, my own voice coming out no easier than hers. "You must relax."

"It's difficult."

"I know. Move your left hand a little away from your body. Lean more weight on it."

She did as I asked, obediently. She was still stiff. Some of the tenseness had returned to her face.

"Let me see if I can—" I began hoarsely.

I got up from the stool and crossed to where she sat.

She turned her head to look at me, solemnly. Her mouth was slightly open. I saw the gleam of little teeth in the sunshine and heard her rapid breathing. Her diaphragm, creamy skin between breasts and belly, was fluttering with her fast, shallow breathing.

I knelt beside her. She did not move.

I said, in a voice I did not know, "The head up—so."

I cupped her chin in my hand to lift her face. I could feel how tense she was, from the stiff movement of her head on her neck.

The thought came into my head, impertinent and all unbidden, that she would never make a good model. Esmerelda, when she sat, was relaxed and totally unselfconscious. She would slip easily into any position as I told her or as I pushed and pulled her about. Not Io. Instead of being something to paint, a dehumanised collection of planes and curves and angles, she was still Io, still obstinately a person—stiff, shy, staring at me in solemn alarm.

I had not meant to do it just at that moment, but I bent and kissed her. Her mouth was already open when our lips met. I felt myself drowning in the kiss as I knelt beside her. I felt her arms go about my neck. She raised herself to kneel facing me. I felt her breasts through the cotton of my shirt. I put my arms round her. I cupped her buttocks in my palms and pressed her against me. I felt my rod straining at my trousers, and her soft slim belly pressed against it.

She took one hand from my neck and slid it under my shirt. I felt her fingers wandering like mice over my shoulder and on my chest.

She freed both her arms and pulled at my shirt. She pulled it upwards. Once again she allowed how much stronger she was than she looked. She pulled my shirt up out of the waistband of my trousers in spite of the heavy belt I wore. Then her fingers were on my bare back and chest. She lifted the shirt further so that it was round my neck. Then her breast was pressed to mine. She rubbed herself against my chest so that her nipples caressed my skin.

I slid a hand between her chest and mine and cupped one of her breasts in my palm. It was wonderfully firm. It nestled into my palm as though the two had been designed to fit together. I cupped a buttock in my other palm and pressed her against me. My rod was as high and hard as a tree.

She pulled my shirt over my head and threw it away from us. Her fingers ran all over my bare back and shoulders. My own fingers found a nipple, which was outthrust and firm to my fingertips. With my other hand I stroked her slender back, going down the delicate ridges of her backbone to the base and to the soft swelling buttocks below.

Still our mouths were clamped together, and we devoured each others' tongues.

I felt her fingers leave my back. The skin of my back tingled with disappointment at the desertion. Her hands struggled between our bodies at the level of my waist. I felt them blindly busy. She pulled away from me a little to give herself room. I felt her undo the heavy buckle of my belt. I felt the sudden relaxation of the tightness of the belt. A hand went round my back and slid down inside my trousers. I felt it fluttering over my buttock, then slide over my thigh to the front.

She touched my rod with the tip of a finger. The effect was electric, devastating. But my trousers were too tight, too awkward for her. She pulled her hand out. I almost cried out with disappointment. Then I felt her fingers busy at the front again. She was undoing my buttons. It was still awkward. She pulled further away from me, and lowered her head so that she could see.

I opened my eyes and looked down at her back. Her face was invisible to me, looking down at the front of my trousers. I reached my hands down through her armpits, and found her breasts, and caressed them. They felt larger to my palms, because they were hanging down. The nipples felt larger and harder to my fingertips.

She undid every one of my buttons. She reached in with both her hands. My trousers fell down my thighs to my knees. I felt her fingers, like little moths, on my rod and my balls, and exploring through the hair of my bush.

She raised herself a little. She pressed her face against my chest. I felt that she was pressing her breasts into my loins. Her fingers were on my rod, and so, magically, was a nipple, rubbing gently against the tip. I felt my balls cupped in her other hand, and little fingernails nibbling at the loose skin.

My trousers were still round my knees, awkward and ridiculous. I wanted to get rid of them. The same thought seemed to strike her at the same moment. She took her hands from my parts, and put her arms round my waist, and leaned her weight sideways. I collapsed with her onto my side on the ground. She pushed me over onto my back. I felt the roughness of the ground under my shoulders and buttocks. She pulled my trousers the rest of the way down my legs, and pulled them off me. She threw them away. She wriggled up beside me. She leaned her breasts on my chest and her mouth on my mouth. I pulled her on top of me. She was as light as a bird, yet she felt firm and lithe. I opened my legs and raised my knees and pressed inwards with my thighs, imprisoning her. Her belly lay all along my rod.

Still kissing, she lifted herself off me. She lay beside me. She took her head from mine and laid it on my chest, looking downwards towards my feet. With eyes and fingers she began a minute, an almost surgical examination of my rod and balls and bush. She inspected and caressed every square millimetre of that avid flesh. I could only see the back of her head, but I could feel every movement, which sent electric shocks all over my body.

I wondered, fleetingly, where she had learned such extraordinary shamelessness.

She lowered her head, and I felt the nibbling of little mouse teeth on the tip.

She raised herself. She swung a knee over my chest and knelt above me. Her back was towards my head. She was facing my rod. She bent down over it. She fondled it, minutely fingered it, stared down at it. She lowered her breasts onto it. She put it between her breasts, and squeezed her breasts together, embracing it.

My sensation was mounting and mounting, so that I knew I must explode unless she left it alone for a little. So I stretched out my hands and cupped them over her breasts and pulled her back towards me. We lay now both on our backs, she on top of me, my hands cupping her breasts, her thighs clamped together about my rod.

I stretched down to her sex. I stroked the soft hair. Instantly her legs sagged apart. She was already wet, oozing, relaxed. I fondled her clitoris and lips, and pushed a forefinger inside.

She moaned, the first sound she had made.

I caressed her with the finger, in and out. Her legs spread wider. She took my hand with hers. She pushed my finger deeper inside herself. It was almost scalded.

She struggled off me. She lay, close against me, on her back on the mossy ground. I felt her hand on my rod. She pulled it. I understood, and followed where she pulled. I raised myself to kneel above her, my knees between her thighs. She raised her knees to her shoulders. Still holding my rod, she steered it down onto herself and into herself.

Very gently I lowered myself deeper, deeper. It was incredibly tight, hot, wet. Our lips and tongues met. I began to move in and out, slowly, slowly, slowly. I could hear the sibilant clicking of my moving rod as it was sucked at by the hot wet walls of her cave. Because she was so small, her cunt gripped me like a hand. I never felt anything so tight.

Her tongue was deep in my mouth. My hands were under her buttocks. Her hands tore and scrabbled at my back.

It was as I exploded, in a paroxysm of excitement, that I thought: dear God, this is the Lady Camilla Glyn, of Moreys Castle.

We lay for a long time, as I shrank and cooled inside her, and the sweat dried from my skin and my breathing and heartbeats became calm.

I painted her just as she was, lying naked on her back on the moss, her hands behind her head, her legs a little apart, one knee slightly raised, eyes closed.

I painted outwards from the cunt. I painted the scent and the wetness. The face was a good likeness.

It was good. It was the best thing I had ever done.

In the afternoon I turned to a different sort of painting. I began to paint the caravan—green and yellow, as I'd always intended, instead of a sort of dirty dried blood. Easy and satisfying to slosh paint over areas of wood.

Io was pleased, the caravan harder to recognize, harder to trace.

She herself set about clearing up the inside. Wearing just my shirt, she was dusting and scrubbing and taking things out and putting them back. She started happily but she got hot and cross. She did not spend long on the job.

I couldn't find the tea, or the firelighters, or the matches. Later, I couldn't find the whisky. We wasted a lot of time searching for them, getting in each others' way. The smaller the space where you live, the more necessary it is to keep things tidy, to know exactly where everything is. Io couldn't be made to understand this. She thought I was making a fuss about nothing.

Of course, all her life things had been where they should have been because a footman or a lady's-maid had put them there. If anything was lost, somebody else did the searching.

Dinner was not a great success. Edible, but greasy and leathery.

But the night was miraculous.

We went to bed at the same time, for the first time, in this kindly rosy glow of the hurricane lantern. Io pulled off the shirt—all she had worn all day—and stood naked, looking at me, smiling, the tenseness and anxieties of the morning far away. I took off my own shirt and sandals and sat on my bunk to take off my trousers. I unbuttoned them and slipped them off. Of course, the sight of her lovely nakedness had raised my rod almost to my chin. She reached down with one small grubby hand and took hold of it. She pulled it. She led me by it! She led me to her bunk. I walked the two paces bent almost double so as not to hit my head. She climbed onto her bunk, never letting go of me. She pulled me in after her. Steering me, controlling me, using my rod as though it was a tiller and I a boat, she laid me on my back. She devoted herself to my rod again. She seemed endlessly fascinated by it, as it was by her. She let go of it and began to crawl all over me. It was like having a puppy on one's chest. She sat on my chest, facing me, then lowered her breasts to my face and a nipple into my mouth. How sweet it tasted! She moved down me and sat on my loins so that my rod was pressed between her buttocks. She lay on top of me and wriggled up my body so that her whole body, from breasts to thighs, rubbed against my rod.

She knelt above me. The lamplight gleamed on her silvery fur and on the pink urgency of her nipples. She grasped my rod and steered it into herself, probing in, just the tip. The tip felt the wetness and the heat. She lowered herself onto me, impaling herself, sliding slowly down and down so that she was squatting on my loins with my rod deep inside her, tightly and wetly grasped as though by a mouth. Her eyes were wide open and her face solemn.

When I emptied myself, in a huge glorious gush, I heard a roar in my own voice.

We slept side by side, cupped together like spoons in a drawer. She felt tiny, slight, flexible, lithe as a snake, light as a bird. I lay awake for a long time, happily exhausted, full of tenderness, enchanted at the feel of her silky skin.

I woke in the dawn to find my rod, soft as asparagus, was nestled into her buttocks. Finding itself so, it stirred and rose, uncontrollably. Its movement woke her. She turned her head, sleepily startled. She groped for my rod and fondled it. It arched in her hand like iron. She guided my hand to herself. She was quite dry and closed to my fingers—and suddenly wet and open to them. Within seconds I was deep inside her, and within seconds I had shudderingly shot my load into her scalding passages.

So the day began wonderfully.

Later I thought I would try to paint trees in the morning sunlight. I wasted a lot of time finding the things I needed. Io had put them away and forgotten where she had put them. I had to keep a strict rein on my temper.

A man *must* know where his tools are.

I had to forgive her, because of the miracle of her little lithe body, and because she never in her life had to do anything for herself. And because, when I went off to the farm to get supplies, her sovereigns jingled in my pocket.

It did not seem to me that the caravan was any cleaner for the scrubbing and dusting she had done. I mentioned this to her. She said I was fussy and ungrateful, and if it was clean enough for her it should be clean enough for me.

I thought that our plates and pans and forks should be washed after we had used them. She said that it was quite enough to wipe them with grass. It was all she would do. Everything consequently became greasier and greasier with each meal.

The shirt she wore—my shirt—became sooty and greasy from cooking and from the fire, and dirty from the inside of the caravan, and daubed with streaks of green and yellow from the wet paint outside the caravan. She was indifferent. She would not change it.

I was not quite happy about eating food cooked by someone with such dirty hands. She would not scrub them on the grounds that they would at once get dirty again.

I painted her four times on four successive days. I painted her gipsy skirt and blouse, picking mushrooms in the early morning in the field beyond the wood. I painted her sitting crosslegged, like an Indian beggar, in the skirt only, with dappled shadows on her shoulders and breasts. I painted her twice in the nude, once sitting on the shaft of the caravan (whence she got wet yellow paint on her behind) and once standing against the craggy and pitted bark of an ancient tree. All the paintings worked. They were all good.

I tried landscapes, too. They were no good. I could not get on canvas what I felt about what I saw.

Io was content, I thought, because she felt safe. I was content because I was eating free, and drinking copiously, and painting well, and living in such fresh air as I had not met since the seaside holidays of my childhood, and sinking myself into that lovely little body every night, and most mornings, and some middays, too.

All the time, though, I waged an unceasing struggle to keep the caravan tidy. I even tried to dust it myself. I was no good at that. I simply moved the dust from one place to another and broke one of the lanterns. The plates and pans got so greasy that it was unpleasant to touch them.

It began to rain. Io would not go out, or even get out of bed. I tried to make a fire in the stove in the caravan; but the wood was so wet that, even with a stack of oily firelighters, I produced only reeking smoke, which made it impossible to see from one side of the caravan to the other. I realised that we should have collected a store of firewood while it was dry and made a pile of it under some kind of rainproof cover. I realised that we should have swept the birds' nests out of the caravan's chimney.

It rained for two days, weeping steadily out of a slate-grey sky. Io was apathetic. She was bored. I painted another nude of her, lying among the grubby blankets on the bunk. It was good in spite of the bad light I worked in. It was a painting of lassitude, of boredom. She did not much like it, but she was wrong.

I spent part of the two days in the bunk with her. But she expected too much. Women can climb the peak again and again. Men have limits. With all that she did with her busy little fingers, my rod was unable to raise its head after a dawn and a noontime and a mid-afternoon effort.

The caravan was cramped quarters when the weather kept us inside it. It would have been tolerable—amply comfortable—if only it had been clean and tidy. Io could not see this. Even if she saw it, she was incapable of doing anything about it. She dropped things and let them lie where they fell. She put dirty plates on the floor and dirty pans on the bunks. She dropped baconrinds among my paints, and eggshells on a half-finished canvas. It was enough to make a man scream with irritation.

She needed someone to look after her. We both did.

We could not go on as we were. Yet we had to. She wailed and clung to me when I talked about going back to civilization. And if lost her, I lost the best livelihood I had ever had.

Besides, I did not want to part from her. Her body, with familiarity, grew more rather than less exciting. She thought all the time of new things to do with it, and with me.

But we did need somebody to look after us.

The wind changed. The weather cleared. Io gave me a pocketful of sovereigns, and I set off through the dripping undergrowth for the village.

I went to the pub, and borrowed paper and a pen, and wrote to Esmerelda at the address of her married sister.

15 ❁ *Variable passions*

Variable passions throng her constant woe,
As striving who should best become her grief;
All entertain'd, each passion labours so,
That every present sorrow seemeth chief,
But none is best; then join they all together,
Like many clouds consulting for foul weather.

VENUS AND ADONIS

I started packing as soon as I got Jasper's letter.

"Now Gladys," said my sister Mildred, "you shouldn't come running whenever that man snaps his fingers. It cheapens you."

Mildred could never understand, living the life she did with a husband like hers. Poor old George! Clerk in a solicitor's office in Ongar. Their idea of art was robins and stagecoaches in the Christmas supplements of the magazines. But I'd learned to see things through Jasper's eyes. It was no good trying to explain anything to them.

Of course I was shocking to them, like a foreigner, a savage from Borneo. An artist's model, in our family! They never saw any of the nudes, only the gipsy ones, but they thought they were bad enough.

"There you are, wearing I don't know what, with nothing on your feet," said Mildred at the Chenil. They'd come up for the day on an excursion ticket from Ongar. It made me laugh to think of some of the ones Jasper had done of me. That last one, before I came away! I didn't mind. I was proud of my body and of Jasper liking it so much and painting it so often. He said my nipples were a beautiful colour, and so they were. He made them a bit more purple, usually. He said that was what he felt about them. I didn't mind.

I didn't really look so much like a gipsy. It was the way he painted me. I was more like an Italian, perhaps. It was odd how it came out in me. Father was English enough, a normal complexion. (He was a solicitor's clerk, too, until he caught the consumption and died.) Mother was half Welsh. Her mother came from Glamorgan. I don't know how she got herself all the way to Essex. My colouring came from her.

I was always a big strong girl. That did come from Father.

I ran away from home when I was eighteen. Well, it was scarcely running away—just moving out. Father had died. Home was with Mildred and George. They wanted me to stay because I made myself useful. I was nothing but an unpaid servant. I didn't mind that, except it was so dull. I had to get away or be suffocated. I went to London, of course. It was that or Chelmsford. I got a job in a café, cashier; not very grand but it did mean sitting down. I pitied the waitresses.

That was how I met Jasper. When I got off work, he took me to his studio to paint a picture of me! And paid me five shillings! I hated the picture at first because he made me look all dirty and common.

"It's an animal quality I see in you," he told me.

"Animal!" I shouted at him. "Thank you very much for nothing."

"Can you come again tomorrow?" he said. "I want to try something completely different."

"No," said I, "not till you get this place cleaned out. It's disgrace. No wonder you made me look dirty. I *am* dirty after sitting in that chair."

The upshot was I did go back, and I cleaned the place up for him. He did try to keep it tidy, I'll say that for him, but it was greasy and grimy before I started in. I went regularly after that, once or twice a week after I got off work, and did a bit of sweeping and scrubbing and washing. I didn't mind. He much preferred things to be clean and tidy, but he just wasn't good at making them so. A lot of men are like that, and artists more than most.

The first time he asked me to take all my clothes off, I flatly refused. It was months before he persuaded me. When it came to the point, I didn't mind. It was the thought of Mildred and George, as much as anything, that made me willing. Nothing that would horrify them could be so very wrong.

I didn't much like the picture, with those big purple nipples. But it was hung in a public gallery! My face, plain as day! Someone told the owners of the café. I was discharged without notice for giving the place a bad name!

Jasper asked me to undress again next time I went to the studio. I didn't mind. In a way he'd ruined me, but in other ways I was very grateful to him. Anyway, I had no choice. I needed what he paid me, little as it was. He posed me on the platform he had, pushing me this way and that. He hadn't done that before—only told me how to sit. I was startled, feeling a man's hands on my naked body. It had never happened to me before. Suddenly he wasn't posing me at all—he was just stroking me! He said my body was beautiful. He stroked my legs and said they were beautiful. I was proud of them. He stroked my breasts and said how beautiful they were. I liked that very much. I was shocked and frightened and proud. He stroked my legs and breasts and behind, and his hand went up between my legs and stroked the insides of my thighs. I liked it very much.

He kissed me. He led me towards the bed at the end of the studio. I could still have said no, but I didn't. I wasn't in love with him, I think, but I admired and respected him very much, and his hands excited me. It was flattering to be admired and praised and stroked by a great artist. My whole body was flattered and excited.

It was my first time. It hurt. I didn't like it. He said it would be better the next time, and it was. Then it got better and better. I moved in with him, having nowhere else to go except George and Mildred in Ongar. He said he needed me and it was true. I was proud to look after him. He said I was serving Art by looking after him, and it was true.

He had a woman come and cut my hair in a new way, and he bought me new clothes, very dashing and foreign. He began taking me about to Music Halls and restaurants and the Café Royal. He said I was Esmerelda. Gladys Brumby wouldn't do as a name, he said, for an untamed animal like me.

Untamed animal! That was a fine return for darning his shirt and taking his sheets to the bagwash. I didn't mind, though.

All the time he was teaching me. He explained why he painted people the way he did, pulling them out of shape, changing the colours. I began to understand.

Sometimes we had money, sometimes not.

He was very extravagant. I tried to make him sensible, but I couldn't. In some ways he was practical, in others he was a baby. If he had money, he bought everybody drinks at the Café Royal. He loved that. He loved being noticed and praised. It was always nice being with him, being the centre of attention with him, as long as he had some money. I got to know a lot of very clever people, artists and writers, at the Café Royal. I was Esmerelda to all of them. I was almost a bit of a celebrity myself.

The best of all was that I knew I was important to Jasper, necessary to him. And he was a great artist with a wonderful future.

A funny thing happened. The woman who had cut my hair came back to the studio. Jasper was away—she knew that. It was me she wanted to see. She was about thirty, fair, nearly as tall and well-built as I was. She had a strong face, good-looking, handsome rather than beautiful.

There was a painting of me, not quite finished, on the easel. It was a seminude. I was sitting on the model's throne, leaning back relaxed, with a towel over my middle. The feeling of it was that I'd just taken a hot bath and I was sleepy and relaxed after it. The hair-cutting woman stared and stared at it, and then at me.

I had an inkling straight away. I would have expected myself to be horrified, but I wasn't. I liked her. Her name was Louise. I remembered that when she had cut my hair to give me the gipsy look Jasper wanted, she'd almost stroked my head and neck, touched me in a way that was almost loving. I hadn't minded that at all. I'd liked it. It was soothing.

"I want to trim your hair again," said Louise. She sat me down in a chair and stood behind me. She snipped a little with her scissors. She stroked me as she had before, the top of my head, behind my ears, the nape of my neck. I was wearing a gipsy blouse, cut straight across, with bare shoulders. She began to stroke my shoulders, still standing behind me as though she was cutting my hair. She did it very gently. I liked Jasper's roughly manly ways well enough, but I liked this gentleness, too. There was something soothing and sweet about it.

She was talking to me all the time. First about my hair, how glossy and black and beautiful it was. Then about my shoulders and back. Then, with reference to the picture, about my breasts. She said how lovely they were. She began to stroke them. No woman had ever touched me like that before. I liked it very much because it was so soothing and gentle. I liked Louise. I trusted her. She said she loved me. I felt loving about her. She put her hands down inside my blouse, reaching down as she stood behind me. I felt her hands stroking my two bare breasts, her skin on mine. I felt her own breasts pressing on my head. I reached up and touched them. She took my hands and pressed them into her breasts.

She took my clothes off, all of them, gently, as though I was a baby. She stroked me all over. She stroked my body hair, and kissed me there.

She knelt between my legs and kissed me. I had never felt anything like that. She kissed my feet and my thighs and my breasts. I was excited. It was all new to me, this gentle stroking and kissing, new and lovely. There was something beautiful about the gentle touch of a woman's hands all over my body and between my legs.

She took off all her own clothes. She had a lovely body. We kissed each other standing up, like a man and a woman, with our breasts pressed together. It was an amazing feeling to me. I had only ever felt the hard flat chest of a man. It was amazing, lovely, to feel the soft full breasts of a woman, the nipples touching my nipples, hands exploring my body, gentle kisses.

We lay down on the bed together and she stroked me. She kissed me all over. Her finger went inside me, slowly, gentle as gentle. I felt myself beginning to twitch with excitement. I gushed beautifully over her finger. It was the gentlest thing that had ever happened to me. I did it for her. She went almost demented, rubbing herself against my finger. I was happy to make her so happy.

She was a parson's daughter from Devonshire. She'd come to London, to live in the world of London, because she liked girls rather than men. This was impossible in a Devonshire parsonage, but it was possible in London, with actresses and dancers and models like me. She became a hairdresser so that she would always be with women, touching them, stroking them. That was what she liked. Often, she told me, what started as a hairdressing appointment ended as we had just ended.

I did not see her often—perhaps once every six weeks. I did meet other women who liked the same things. Some of them liked men also, as I did. Some were even married. There were great jealousies among them.

If Jasper guessed about my new life he said nothing to me. It made no difference to him and myself. I still looked after him. He still painted me. I still enjoyed his lovemaking. I liked the contrast. After soft feminine breasts on mine, I liked to feel his hard flat chest. After fingers or tongues inside me, I liked to be filled up with the hardness of his flesh. And then, after a week or two, I would itch for the other again, and find Louise or another girl who would stroke me like a baby and share my happiness.

This life suited me very well as long as Jasper had some money. That summer he had none, in spite of a couple of commissions. One was a man called Whitewater, a real lord! He came to the studio once when I was there. I wondered how Jasper could have borne to paint him. He was horrible. He gave me cold shivers up the spine. Still, he paid. But the money was gone as soon as it came in. Jasper and I could hardly go out at all. London was very hot. He became bored and irritable. He started a new picture of me, a nude, which I hoped Mildred would *never* see.

He went away to a grand house in the country for two days in search of another commission. When he came back, he abandoned the painting and began doing dozens of charcoal drawings of a girl. He was drawing from memory. He would not tell me who she was. She was a beautiful girl, with a delicate face and big eyes. I became very interested in the girl, looking at Jasper's drawings. I wanted to meet her. I was sure that I would love her. Jasper said I never would meet her because she was practically a princess and lived in a sort of gilded captivity. That made me still more interested. I had to hide my interest in a show of indifference, saying that the girl had an ordinary and boring face.

This led to a quarrel, simply because we were both bored and fed up because of the heat and because we had no money. I said I would go away until the weather was cooler and he could afford dinner. I went to George and Mildred. They were quite glad to see me because I was useful in the house. I could make new curtains and new covers for the parlour chairs.

Then Jasper's letter came. It was a cry for help. He needed me. He could not paint unless I came to him. He did not say that it was my duty, but it was. He did say that he had plenty of money. For the time being, he had all the money we could want. He said he was in a beautiful place in the deep countryside. He told me to come to a village called Little Hennings, near Cirencester. He would meet me at the Red Lion in the village.

Mildred disapproved, but she lent me some money for the journey.

I had to cross London from Liverpool Street to Paddington, and change at Swindon for Cirencester, and then get myself carried out into the wilds. It was wild, too. The journey took nearly all day. It was half past five before I got to Little Hennings. It was a little grey village, very quiet. I felt strange there with silent people staring at me.

I found the Red Lion. It was the only pub. It was a low blackish building, very small. I started in, but the landlord hurried forward and barred the way. They wouldn't let me in on my own. I wasn't sure if they would have let me in even if I'd been with a man. The landlord was quite polite, though I could hardly understand what he was saying. His wife, standing behind him, looked as though she wanted to be quite rude. I felt lost.

Of course, the one thing Jasper hadn't said in his letter was when he expected me at the pub—what time, even what day. He hadn't given me an address—just the name of the village—so I couldn't write to tell him when I was coming. Anyway, he wanted me quickly, not after an exchange of letters. He needed me at once, he said. I suppose I simply assumed that when I arrived at the Red Lion, there he'd be waiting for me.

I wondered if he'd had an accident. He sometimes did trip over things and fall down and hurt himself. He could be clumsy. He didn't always look where he was going. He was a great one for striding along a street, shouting back something over his shoulder, and going slap into a lamp post. That kind of thing could happen in the country as easily as it could in London. I began to be worried for him, thinking of what might have happened.

I began to be worried for myself, too. They wouldn't let me into the pub, a woman alone. I had no money after the journey, even if they'd let me in. I had no money to pay for dinner or a bed or to get back out of this wilderness to London.

I said to the landlord, "Please, have you seen a tall man with a black beard?"

"There be a sight o' such as they," said the landlord. "Tall men wi' bearden."

Very slowly, in a grumbling voice, he began to tell me the names of all the tall men he knew with black beards. There was a farmer, a miller, a shopkeeper in another village, a blacksmith, and a man who sang in the choir in church.

"A stranger," said. "A man from London."

"Ar! Him. He do shout an' bang about, wi' a pocketful o' sovereigns an' a great thirst."

"Yes!"

"We seed he, a time or two."

"Where can I find him?"

The landlord scratched his head. He was still standing in the door of the pub, barring my way. He had no idea where to find the tall man from London.

"Out away," he said vaguely, pointing in various directions.

Out away. A cottage? A farm? How far? The landlord had no idea.

"Oh God," I said, in despair.

The landlord's wife nearly had a fit.

"A-do b'lieve," said a gentle voice behind me, "a-do b'lieve a-knows the bloke ye d'mean."

I turned. A small man of about thirty-five stood there with his cap in his hands. He had bright blue eyes in a small brown face, and untidy brown hair. He wore a patched coat and leather leggings. His features were neat and regular. He looked innocent, almost silly, like a child.

"Get away wi' ye, Tranter," said the landlord. "Us all *knows* the bloke. Question be, where's he to?"

"A-do b'lieve a-knows where he be to."

The small man had a voice like syrup, very sweet and slow.

"A-painting picters, all hours?" he said to me. "Be that your bloke, pretty lady?"

"Yes!" I said thankfully. "Can you show me where he is?"

"Ay. Sure-lee."

"Ye watch un, Miss," said the landlord. "This boy'll pench anythin' that baint nailed down, an' a sight o' goods that is. Keep a hand on y'bag, Miss, if ye ride wi' he."

The small man laughed. It was a noise like thick cream being poured out of a jug. He was staring at me with those wide blue eyes. I knew that look. A lot of men stared at me. My face was unusual and my figure was good. His stare was nice. It was appreciative. It was much nicer than the suspicious pig eyes of the landlord's wife.

The small man pointed to a cart twenty yards away with a tubby white pony between the shafts.

"Take ye a piece o' the way," he said. "Then 'tes a piece afoot."

"Thank you, Mr. Tranter," I said.

He smiled. He had a nice smile. He picked up my bag and carried it to the cart. He handed me up into the cart as though I had been a duchess. Jasper never did that. If you are a great artist, you need not do such things. They are done for you. So I was unused to it. I liked it.

When he picked up the reins I saw how neat and slender his hands were. They were like a girl's hands, but brown from the weather, like his face. I thought he hadn't done much manual work in his life with those hands. He might do delicate work, making little delicate things.

"A-baint Mister Tranter," he told me. "A-baint nothin', b'way o' name. No family, ye d'see, that's knowed of. Find I in a ditch, they did, parson an' doctor a-drivin' by in a gig, when I were a sennight old. 'Twere like that Moses, in they ol' bulrushes, 'cep I were swallowed up by orphanage. Tranter d'mean a bloke wi' a cart, semply, a-carryin' folks an' goods for silver shillin's."

"Oh," I said, "but I can't pay you! I haven't any money left at all."

"Nay, nay! A-ben goin' this road anyroad, for t'reach me dwellin'-place. 'Tes no extra. 'Tes a joy t'gi' a ride to a lovely lady."

He said his name was Bob. In the village he was called Tranter Bob, because of his trade as a carter, or Bob Tranter.

"It'd come both ways," he said. "Frontyways, or backsyfore. Makes no odds t'me."

He was not like anybody I had ever met in my life. He was not like anybody in London, or in Ongar. He was smaller and lighter than me, delicate looking. He was like a little wild animal, a very trusting and friendly animal.

I said I was Esmerelda, and I had no surname either.

"Esmerelda," he said, marvelling. In his slow, treacly voice the name sounded a yard long. It was nice, in his voice.

He lived in a small cottage, he said, which had once been used by a gamekeeper. The gamekeeper had refused to live there any more, because it was so remote. It was nowhere near anywhere or anybody. That was what he liked.

"*Do* you steal everything that isn't nailed down?" I asked him.

"Nay!" He laughed, that nice thick-cream laugh that wrinkled up his face like a walnut. "Jus' what a-d'need, yere an' there."

The pony plodded along a road and then a lane and then a smaller lane. It was very wild and empty country. Too empty for me. The sun was setting. It was warm and breathless. Flies buzzed round the pony's head. I wondered where Bob was taking me. I was homesick for London.

I was glad he was a neighbour. He was the best thing about Gloucestershire. I thought he was a sort of pet, a tame wild animal, like a rabbit.

We came to an enormous wood. It was dark in the wood. Bob stopped the pony and jumped down. I was puzzled. Had we arrived? He lifted down my bag, then helped me down. His hand was smaller than mine. My hands and feet are quite large because I am big and tall and have big bones. His hand felt strong. I wondered how such a small hand could be so strong.

He pointed to a track which led into the wood, uphill. It was full of deep shadows.

"A piece up-along," he said.

"Is there a house in the middle of the wood?"

"Nay! 'Tes a cart."

"A *cart?*"

"Ay, one o' they Egyptian housen. Follow ride up-along, ye can't mistake un."

"Where is your house?"

"On-along, half a mile. Ye go left by the liddle bridge, an' ye find I amidst trees and bushen."

He took off his cap, smiled, and jumped onto his cart. The pony plodded away, along the lane. It turned a corner, going out of my sight behind the tall hedge.

I'd wanted Bob to come with me up into the wood. Not because of the weight of my bag—because a big, silent dark wood was strange to me. There was nothing like it in the country round Ongar. That was all flat cornfields, full of houses and people. I didn't know what might not be in the wood, hiding behind trees, waiting to jump out at me. Though Jasper made me look like a gipsy, I wasn't one. I belonged in London, in streets, with lights and people. I felt small and uneasy, creeping up the path through that huge wood.

Cart? Egyptian house? Suddenly I remembered that Jasper had been talking about a gipsy caravan. That was when he wanted to go away, and I did go away. But he had had no money. How had he got money? "A pocketful of sovereigns," the landlord said. Jasper? He never had such a thing for more than a few minutes. But he had bought a caravan, and he had money in his pocket. Yet he needed me. None of it made the least sense.

Suppose he wasn't there when I found it? Suppose a band of gipsies had killed him and were waiting to kill me? Suppose I never did find it? Bob said I couldn't miss it. But Bob was used to big woods in gathering darkness.

I crept a long way up through the wood, hearing nothing, seeing nothing. It was getting darker all the time. There was a touch of chill in the air. The air felt damp. On and on I went, carrying my bag, with things clawing and catching at the hem of my skirt.

And then I saw a flickering light. And then I heard a man's booming voice. And there I was.

It was light enough for me to see all I wanted to see. I never in my life saw anything like it.

There was a gipsy caravan, very pokey and ramshackle. Part of it had been newly painted a horrid green and a horrid yellow. Part was still a dirty dark red.

Near it was a fire, burning on the ground. Just burning. There were a few little flames, and a lot of smoke. There was a big cheap pan on the fire, balanced on two stones. Something sizzled faintly in the pan, a dark mess, giving off a dreadful smell.

All round the campfire and the caravan there was mess and rubbish. Bits of paper, empty bottles, orange peel, banana skins, old empty tin cans with jagged lids where they had been opened. There were clouds of sleepy flies buzzing over the rubbish.

There were two people by the fire.

One was Jasper, drinking something out of a tin mug. He was in his shirt-sleeves. It was one of his two shirts. It was torn and filthy. He was filthy, too. There were all kinds of things stuck in his beard and in his hair.

To my astonishment, I saw that the other person was a child, a little girl. She was squatting by the fire, stirring the pan with a stick. She was wearing a sort of enormous dirty tent. It was slit up the sides, and I could see little skinny legs, black with dirt. The tent was partly unbuttoned at the front, and I could see a bit of dirty chest. She had a sort of scarf, black with grease, tied round her head. Her sleeves were rolled up. Her arms were bare. Her arms and hands were very dirty. Her face was very dirty. It was so smeared with dirt that it was impossible to make out her features.

What in God's name, I thought, was Jasper doing with a child? A filthy waif of eleven or twelve years old?

I jumped to the conclusion that she was one of the gipsy family Jasper had bought the caravan from. Perhaps he had brought her to cook for him, or look after the horse. I suppose they must have had a horse. Perhaps she had hidden in the caravan and travelled as a stowaway.

What in God's name was the child wearing? With a start I recognized Jasper's one other shirt. I had mended it dozens of times, and washed it hundreds of times. It was past mending or washing now. The poor little thing had nothing else to wear? No shoes, certainly. Perhaps, as a gipsy brat, she never had worn shoes.

Was I to be a mother to the wretched little thing? Was that why Jasper needed me so urgently?

I came forward to the fire at last. I said, "Hullo, Jasper."

He gave a great shout and waved his tin mug. Some of it spilled. I smelled whisky. He *did* have money. What money? Where from?

"Esmerelda!" he shouted. "Well met, indeed! We have need of you, Io and I."

"I can see you do," I said, looking round at the mess, and looking at both of them, and sniffing the nasty-smelling concoction in the frying pan.

The child he called Io looked up from the pan. I could not guess at her expression, her face was so dirty. She did not seem overjoyed.

"Esmerelda, this is my little Io," said Jasper heartily. "Io, you have heard of Esmerelda."

The child nodded. She stared at me for a moment. She had big grey eyes, surprising in that dirty little face, even in the gathering darkness. She said nothing. I wondered if she could speak.

"I've had a tiring journey," I said to Jasper.

"Ah, but what a paradise you have found at journey's end," said Jasper.

He did not ask how I had found him in this forest. He did not explain about the pub. He expected me to do what he needed or wanted, without having to bother himself about any of the practical details.

Artists get away with murder. It is their right.

"What are you cooking?" I asked the child.

"A *mélange* of this and that." Jasper answered for her. "It is the *specialité de la maison*. Every bite a surprise." He roared with laughter. I thought the whisky he was drinking was not his first of the evening. "No room for boredom."

I sniffed. "It smells to me," I said, "as though the fat's gone bad."

"Lard? Can it?"

"Easily, in weather like this."

"What can we cook with, then?"

"Bacon fat. If you've got any bacon."

"By your foot."

I found a wad of rashers wrapped in a piece of newspaper. Somebody had dropped the bacon in something dusty. I sniffed the bacon. "Bad," I said.

They had plenty of other food. It was all bad.

"There's nothing fit to eat here," I said. "You must keep things cool and clean."

I made a better fire, with more heat and less smoke. I emptied away the muck in the pan and cleaned it. I found some eggs which were all right. I scrambled them in some milk and butter which was only just on the turn. There was no salt or pepper. There was some stale bread which I toasted. We had scrambled eggs on toast.

I found knives and forks for Jasper and myself. They were encrusted with old food. I scoured them with handfuls of earth, then washed them. The child ate with her fingers. She licked them afterwards. I wondered what they tasted of.

"Civilization comes to the wilderness," said Jasper, giving a gentle belch. "Our lives are transformed, little Io."

"Hm," said the child. I didn't know what she meant. It was the first sound she had made.

I thought I recognised her face, but I knew this was impossible. I guessed she reminded me of one of the Rupert Street urchins who played football outside the restaurants. But she was much dirtier than they were.

Jasper gave himself a mug of whisky. He gave me some. I was glad of it, although I didn't much like the taste. He gave the child some. She did like the taste.

"My God, Jasper!" I said. "That's an awful thing to do!"

"Why?" said Jasper. "She's paying for it."

I thought he was joking. He often made jokes I didn't understand. I was really shocked that he gave a mug of whisky to a young child. But I was too tired to argue.

I took one look inside the caravan with a lantern. I shrank back. I truly recoiled. It was a slum, wildly untidy, filthy. I didn't see how the most primitive savages could have borne to live in such squalor.

"I don't know where to start," I said to Jasper. "You, or the child, or the caravan, or the mess you've made out here."

"Decide in the morning," said Jasper comfortably.

I had to agree. It was too dark to do anything, and I was too tired.

"I'll go to bed," I said. "The child should go to bed, too."

"We'll come in a minute," said Jasper. "Yours is the bunk on the left. The smaller one. I'm afraid it's a bit hard."

"Where does the child sleep?"

"She finds a nook."

I thought the hardest bed in the world wouldn't keep me awake, exhausted as I was. I was wrong. Sleep on that mattress was impossible. Also the caravan smelled. It smelled of mice, rancid butter, paraffin and Jasper's feet.

They were talking outside. At least, Jasper was. After a time they climbed into the caravan. They bumped about in the dark. I heard a little high giggle. It was only the second sound I had heard the child make.

I heard a deep sigh as Jasper got into the other bunk. I wondered again where the child slept.

I heard another giggle. It came from the other bunk. She slept there with Jasper! I almost choked with horror. I had heard of such things, in London. There were evil men who did such things. I had not thought it of Jasper. I lay, trembling, aghast at the dreadful things that might be happening a yard away from me.

Of course they simply, innocently, shared a bunk, to make room for me. Perhaps the child suffered from nightmares and needed comforting.

They were not sleepy. I heard them moving. I heard rapid breathing.

The worst was happening. My heart thudded with horror and with curiosity.

I heard panting, a child's excited panting. Jasper's breath was harsh in his throat.

I heard a little wet, sticky noise. Rhythmic. Unmistakable. I had heard that noise so often when I was in bed with Jasper myself. In and out, in and out, slow, faster. A sound like a kiss, like a spoon in a thick, eggy custard.

I found I was sweating, trembling, sick with disgust and with envy.

I slept at last and had horrible, exciting dreams. I awoke in full daylight to hear Jasper snoring in the other bunk. I looked at him with disgust and contempt. The child had disappeared. The inside of the caravan looked worse, far worse, in the merciless daylight.

I shook Jasper awake. He was slow to come to life, as always. He mumbled and belched. He tried to pull the covers over his head. Living in a caravan had not changed him.

"Get up, you disgusting animal," I said. "I must give this place a scrub."

I drove him, half awake, out of the caravan. He pulled on his trousers as he went.

I set to work. I took everything movable out of the caravan—the bedding, all the plates and pots and pans, stools, oddments of decomposing food. I told Jasper to get me a bucket of water. He complained at being treated as a serf, but stumbled off, still sleepy. He came back with a bucket of very clear, clean water from a stream. I found a scrubbing brush, and hard yellow soap, and set to work.

Jasper made a fire, but there was nothing to eat until the child came back from the farm.

I sent Jasper for more water. He went to the stream five times in all. I made him dig a hole to bury the rotten food and the bottles and cans they had left lying about the ground.

I think I was scrubbing for about two hours. The sun rose high. It was hot. It was stuffy inside the caravan. I was pouring with sweat, and filthy from the grease and dirt of the caravan.

"I need a bath," I said to Jasper, who had been sketching me in charcoal as I scrubbed the floor and walls of the caravan.

"One thing we didn't buy," said Jasper. "Not included in the contents."

"What about the stream?"

"I suppose you could bathe. There's a pool. Quite private."

I had brought a towel, soap, sponge, and clean clothes. I would never travel without those things. I set off with them through the wood, in the direction Jasper pointed out.

I thought he might come and sketch me while I bathed. But he had become engrossed by a tree stump. He was drawing the tree stump with pen and ink.

I found the stream. It was only a little one, five or six feet across. The water was clear. I put in a finger. It was cold. One bank was covered with trees and bushes. The stream was the boundary of the wood. The other bank was an open green field. There was a belt of trees beyond the field. There was nobody about. There were no sheep or cows in the field.

I took off my shoes, raised my skirt to my waist, and waded across the stream to the grassy bank. I walked down the stream until I came to the pool. It widened to ten feet, and the water was slow and deep. The grass sloped right to the lip of the pool. The bottom was pebbly and clean with a little bright-green weed in waving strings.

I looked round carefully. There was nobody to be seen. I thought there was nobody for miles. Once I was in the pool, I could not be seen even by someone in the field, because the level of the grass was much higher than that of the water.

I pulled off my dirty clothes, thankfully, and lowered myself into the water. It was cold but bearable. It was wonderful to feel the clean water after the sweat and the filth of the caravan. I sponged and lathered myself vigorously. I rubbed myself as clean as I had scrubbed the caravan. I climbed out and dried myself. I felt the sun hot on my skin.

I decided to wash my dirty clothes before I put on my clean ones—just skirt, blouse, chemise and drawers. Otherwise I could get my dry clothes wet in the stream.

I began to wash my skirt, which was dirtiest from the scrubbing.

I heard a small noise behind me, a little squeak. I turned, snatching up my clothes to cover myself.

The child stood at the top of the bank, looking down at me. She carried a basket. It was piled high with mushrooms. She was an extraordinary sight. She wore a tattered and filthy skirt, and Jasper's shirt, just as filthy. The shirt reached almost to the ground. It was enormous on her. She had a scarf tied round her head, hiding her hair entirely. Her face, arms, hands, feet, ankles and neck were dark with dirt. It was impossible to guess at her real colouring under these layers of dirt.

"It's time you had a bath," I said.

She shook her head.

I reached out and grabbed her ankle. She tried to pull away. Of course I was much stronger than she was. I was as strong as most men, and she was only a scrap of a twelve-year-old child. She hit out at me with the basket. Things flew out of. Eggs broke. She screamed. I took her other ankle, and pulled her down the bank. She dropped the basket, and began hitting at me with her fists. She could do me no harm at all—her fists were no bigger than little apples, and her wrists were as slender as pipe stems.

She fought and fought. She was very lithe and active, and stronger than she looked. I managed to pull the enormous shirt up over her head.

Of course I expected a little flat childish chest. I was astonished to see that she had fully-formed breasts. They had been quite hdiden in the great stiff folds of the shirt. They were beautiful, high and firm, with nipples of a marvellous clear pink. I pulled her skirt off. She wore nothing underneath it. She had hair on her body, like my own, though softer and finer, and pale yellow instead of jet black.

She was not a child at all.

I pulled the scarf off her head. She had a lot of curly golden hair. It was dirty but the colour was beautiful.

I pulled her into the water, though she screamed and struggled. Holding her with one hand, half in the water and half on the sloping grassy bank, I covered her with soap and scrubbed her all over with the sponge. She screamed when soap got into her mouth and eyes.

With the dirt gone, her skin was perfectly white, and so fine and smooth it looked transparent. She was utterly transformed from the grubby little slut I had seen.

I pulled her right into the water, to wash all the soap off. I pulled her out onto the bank. I wrapped her in my towel, and began to dry her.

It was then that I recognized her. With all the dirt scraped off, and with her hair in a golden tangle round her head, I recognized her. She was the girl Jasper had drawn, again and again, from memory, when he came back from the palace in the country.

"Who are you?" I said.

"My name is Io. I hate you. You've put soap in my eyes, and you've washed off my disguise."

"Disguise?"

"Now I shall have to rub myself all over with mud."

I had expected her voice—if she had one—to be a gipsy whine. I had heard that often enough from the drabs who came to our door in Ongar selling clothespegs or besoms. But it was a high, clear voice, an expensive voice. I had *not* heard that in Ongar, but I had heard it in the Café Royal, from the aristocrats who came slumming.

This girl was slumming with a vengeance.

She was trembling. I rubbed her with the towel. I felt the sun warm on my own bare shoulders and back. I thought she would soon be warm, too. I crouched behind her, squatting, rubbing at her wet hair. I dried her shoulders and her breasts. I was gentle. I felt her breasts, firm under the towel.

I knelt behind Io. I was in the position that Louise had been in when she trimmed my hair, and went from that to stroking my shoulders, and went from that to stroking my breasts. Io was sitting on the grass. She was shivering.

Louise's breasts had pressed onto my head when she leaned forward from behind me. I leaned forward from behind Io. My breast pressed into her damp hair. I stroked her little breasts with the towel, as though still drying them. But they were dry. I stroked them without the towel.

My hands had gone up to Louise's breasts, by my head. Io's hands came up to mine. Louise had been dressed. I was naked. Io's fingers found my naked breasts.

We stayed like that for a long time, my hands on her breasts and hers on mine. I could feel the excitement in her nipples, and I could feel the excitement in my own. She pressed my breasts into her cheeks.

I pulled her backwards against me. I felt her buttocks against my knees, and her back against my belly.

She let go of my breasts and put her hands down, and behind, and on my buttocks. She pressed them. I felt her little spine pressing against my mound. I rubbed myself against her back. The feeling was lovely. She was so slender and delicate. I felt like a mammoth, like a man.

Her legs were spread as she sat on the ground. I reached down and between them. She began to tremble again. She lay back against me. I had one hand on her breast, and one caressing between her thighs. She was excited.

I moved round so that I crouched between her legs. I lowered my face to her lovely golden fleece, holding her buttocks. She lay back on the grass, her legs wide. I kissed her thighs and belly, going round in a circle, going round in smaller and smaller circles. I was teasing her. I was getting closer and closer. I glanced up her face. Her eyes were closed. She had an expression of intense concentration. I knew what she was concentrating on. I knew what she wanted. I knew I could give it to her.

I put out my tongue. I licked her button. It tasted clean and sweet. She was trembling. I felt her hands on my head. She pushed my head down-onto herself.

At last I slid my tongue between the lips as far as I could. It was very nice. My tongue was happy inside her. She was happy too. I made her happy. It was exciting for me as well as for her. I felt her violent twitching and heard the long, happy sigh she gave.

I kissed her on the lips, as though I had been a man. She kissed me. She embraced me. I was very excited. I guided her hand to my own paradise.

"Roll over," she said in a strange, thick voice.

I lay on my back as she had done. She kissed me as I had kissed her. I saw the golden hair of her head nestled against the jet-black hair of my body. I saw her intent look. I saw her tongue come darting out of her mouth, like a little pink serpent. I felt it shyly lapping at me. I felt it on my button and on the lips. I began to feel a frenzy which was very rare for me.

The storm came quickly and violently. I felt myself jerking like a puppet. I thought she must be drowned in my flood. It was beautiful.

Then she lay in the crook of my arm, her head on my breast, one leg thrown over my legs, her body pressed into my side. She was the smallest girl I had ever made love to, the youngest, the most beautiful.

"Thank you," she whispered, "thank you."

"But doesn't Jasper—?"

"No. Never. He's always too quick. I only pretend."

"Why do you pretend, darling?"

"Because I must stay here."

"Oh—"

"It's only happened like that, ever, with you. With myself, my own finger, all by myself, and with you."

"Don't you like men, Io?"

"Yes. Yes, I do. I hope I will. Not yet. Nothing like that. They're too quick."

"Why are you hiding? Why do you need a disguise?"

"Don't let them find me. Don't let anybody find me."

"I'll look after you," I said.

I hugged her tight. She buried her little head in my breasts. She pushed my breast against her face, against her mouth. Her tongue came out. She licked my nipple, and then kissed it. She caught it between her lips, and then between her teeth. I liked that very much.

"I won't let anything happen to you," I said.

At the time I truly meant it.

16 ✿ *Ripe-red cherries*

When he beheld his shadow in the brook,
The fishes spread on it their golden gills;
When he was by, the birds such pleasure took,
That some would sing, some other in their bills
Would bring him mulberries and ripe-red cherries;
He fed them with his sight, they him with berries.

VENUS AND ADONIS

Of course, from that moment I made myself responsible for Io. She was as
helpless as a baby, poor little thing. It was something new to me, to find a
girl who couldn't do anything for herself. Men yes. My sister Mildred had
to do everything for her silly old husband George. I had to do everything
for Jasper. I was used to that. It's right. Nobody minds, or should mind.
We go through life picking up things our menfolk drop. But Io went
through her life as Jasper did—dropping things, relying on someone else
to pick them up.

I didn't mind. I liked looking after her. I washed her hair and combed
it out. I looked after her hands and fingernails. I liked it. She was so
beautiful, and looked so dainty and delicate. She was so affectionate. I
found I could make her cry with joy just by using my tongue. I liked that
very much. And after, everything I'd done to her she'd do to me. It was as
though she had a sense of fairness. Whatever I did, she'd do the same.

Of course, I took over the shopping as well as the cooking and cleaning.
Io gave me the money, all the money I wanted.

Jasper was working hard. He was painting well. I could tell that, and so could he. He was happy because he knew he was doing good work. He did a lot of paintings of Io, some nudes. They were very good, as good as anything he'd ever done. He sketched me, but no paintings. No nudes. It was just as well; I hardly had time to sit for him. Io had all the time in the world.

Since I'd scrubbed off Io's disguise, not knowing it was a deliberate disguise, she'd kept out of sight of anybody. That was another reason I did the shopping.

She still wouldn't tell me who she was or why she was hiding. She was frightened of being found, really frightened. Sometimes she showed it. Then I would hug and kiss her, to calm her down, like a baby. Some of our most beautiful times came after those moments.

She'd never done it, never done anything, with a woman before. She said she liked it very much. She wanted to like men, but she hadn't been lucky. I was shocked she'd even tried, so young and so well brought up.

Jasper wouldn't tell me who she was. He said it was her secret and he was bound to keep it. I knew he'd met her at that palace where he'd stayed earlier in the summer. But I'd forgotten where that palace was or whose it was, if I'd ever known. I was very curious about Io, as anybody would be—I wanted to know who she was and what she was hiding from.

I wanted her to come to bed with me every night, especially as I'd made a new soft mattress for my bunk. But she always went to bed with Jasper. I think they did it every night—certainly most nights. Jasper wanted it every night, as I had reason to know. He was a man who needed it. He was entitled to what he needed, being a great artist. He loved it. It made him feel manly. That was important to him. He needed that for his painting.

Io liked it all right, she told me, but there was no magic for her. She pretended there was, to please Jasper. She needed him. She had to keep him happy. That was because she had to stay hidden.

Much as I loved Io, I did want a change. I wanted a man. There comes a time when you do. I loved that little flickering tongue and those little exploring fingers, but I wanted to be filled up with a hard ram driving into me. There comes a time when you do.

Jasper said he couldn't, for fear of upsetting Io. She was paying for everything. If she got angry and left, went to hide somewhere else, he would have to leave too. He was painting so well he wanted to stay. Not just Io, but landscapes too. He was extending his range. It was important to him. He was getting together enough for a one-man show. Besides, he'd never been so comfortable before, he said. He'd never had so much food and so much whisky, because he'd never had so much money.

I got a cucumber from the farm. It was too dry. I greased it with butter, as though I was going to cook it. It gave me an amazing feeling, sliding in cold and slithery. I tried with other things, too. The cucumber was best. I gave myself some amazing feelings. But it wasn't really what I wanted. I wanted a man's hard warm ram driving into me, filling me up. I wanted the man attached to the ram, the person, his chest and arms and face, his mouth and teeth, all of him, his personality. A cucumber is lovely, but it has no face or personality, no warmth, no hair or balls.

The cucumber was a lovely cold slithery feeling. I was very glad to have discovered it. But still I wanted a man. And still Jasper said he couldn't do it; he couldn't risk annoying Io.

I went to look for the man who had given me a lift from the village in his cart. Bob. Bob the Tranter. I remembered him as very small, hardly bigger than Io. I also remembered the way he looked at me. I went to find his cottage. Down and out of the wood, on along the lane, left by a little bridge into another wood. I was a long time finding the place. I found it in the end, a cottage not much bigger than a shoe box. There was no garden round it, nothing, just the thick woods. The cart was there, his cart, the one I'd ridden in. There was no sign of the pony or Bob. There was no smoke from the chimney, or any sound. Bob had gone away with his pony but without his cart.

The cottage was all on one floor. It seemed from outside to have only one room. All one end of it was a huge chimney. There was a door the other end. I tried it. It was locked. There was one little window. I peeped through. It was dark inside. The cottage was empty.

There was no man at the farm where I went for eggs and milk. No man for me. There was a fat farmer and his fat son, both with fat wives. I didn't want them. I wasn't as desperate as that. They might have wanted me, but they weren't given a chance. There was nobody in the village, either, not for me.

It turned October. Summer was done, by the calendar, but it was still summery weather. The nights were cooler, but the sun was still hot by day. Sometimes there was a thick mist in the early morning, and everything was soaked in a heavy dew. I cleaned out the little stove in the caravan and swept the chimney. It worked well. It gave off a lovely heat, and I could cook over it. The caravan was very snug on those cool evenings. But it was crowded. With three of us in there, there was hardly room to move. Io didn't take up much room, but Jasper's legs filled the place.

I began to want to go back to London. But Jasper wouldn't hear of it, and the thought of being left alone sent Io half into hysterics. They needed me to look after them. Jasper needed me there if he was going to paint, and Io needed me there to look after her, just to look after her. All the same, I was homesick for Rupert Street, the smell of cooking coming up the stairs, cooking being done by someone else, the bright lights of the streets, the laughter in the Café Royal.

The weather turned. We woke up one morning to a black sky and sheets of rain. It was much colder. I lit the stove. Jasper refused to get up. He sat in his bunk playing his French bagpipes. The noise was awful in such a confined space. Io wouldn't get up either. She moved into my bunk.

I cooked breakfast. The caravan was full of the smell of frying. Both Jasper and Io wanted a big cooked breakfast even though they were staying in bed all day. After breakfast Jasper lit his pipe. The caravan was full of his smoke. I opened a window. Rain came in, Io shrieked. I had to shut the window again. The caravan got very stuffy. The stove smoked because of rain coming down the chimney.

Jasper asked Io to come back to his bunk. He put aside his bagpipes and lay down. He was wearing an awful cheap shirt he had bought and nothing else. Io was wearing his other shirt which I had washed and mended as best I could.

She glanced at me. She made a comic face. I did not think she was in the mood to go to Jasper. But she got out of my bunk and crossed to his. She got in beside him. They lay side by side. I saw his hands beginning to be busy under the covers. I imagined he was pulling up the hem of her shirt to the waist. I saw that her hands were busy too. I thought his shirt was also up to his waist. She glanced at me, then looked at the roof. I knew what her hands were doing.

She was bound to do all the things Jasper wanted. At least, she thought she was. She had to keep him contented so that she could stay in hiding with us. Really her money would have kept him quite contented, I thought. But she thought it was safest to keep him happy in every way.

It showed how frightened she was, of whatever frightened her.

I had done so often to him what her hands were doing. I had done so often to her what his hands were doing. It was more than I could bear, to stay and watch them. I went out into the rain. I set off to walk to the village. The rain was hard and cold. I was soon soaking, even to my drawers.

I could feel that my hair was plastered to my head with the rain. My shoes squelched in the muddy puddles. It was unpleasant, but it was better than the stuffiness of the caravan. It was better than watching Jasper and Io. I was shivering with cold as I walked, and I was shivering with desire and envy, too.

I came down to the lane and walked fast along it. Round a corner, through the noise of the rain, I heard a horse's hooves. It came into view. It was a fat white pony. It was Bob the Tranter's pony. Bob was riding it. He was as wet as I was. The pony was dark with the wet.

I was very pleased to see him. He looked very pleased to see me.

"Y'be still yere, then?" he said, his voice like thick honey. " 'Tes cruel weather for t'bide in a cart."

"Yes. But the others want to stay."

"Ay, an' they d'need ye for to coddle un? Y'needs a sight o' coddlen yersel', pretty lady. Y'be domp as a newt in a duckpond."

"So are you, Bob," I said.

He gave a very broad, surprised grin. I thought he was pleased and astonished that I'd remembered his name.

"Ay, Miss Esmerelda," he said, to show he remembered my name too. "But a-ben retarnen to a yuge fire in my house. A drap o' tea an' a drap o' whisky an' dry clothen an' a sight o' comforts."

That sounded nice. It sounded very nice indeed. I suppose my feelings showed on my face, because Bob said, "Ye'll cam' for t'be dry, Miss Esmerelda?"

"Yes!" I said.

He grinned again. He stared at me, grinning. I could feel that my soaking blouse was clinging to my breasts like a skin. I glanced down at myself. The shape of the nipples was clearly visible with the thin cotton glued to them with rain water—the central teats, stiffened by cold and wet, and the discos surrounding them. My skirt clung to my stomach and thighs. Bob saw, and liked what he saw.

"Jomp op ahind," he said.

I scrambled onto a bank. He steered the pony to the bank. I somehow got on the pony's back. I sat sideways on the pony's rump with my arms round Bob's waist. His waist was like a girl's, like Io's.

The thought of Io's little waist made me think of her and Jasper. I thought of him ramming himself into her, or of her lowering herself onto him. It was extraordinary to be sitting on the back of a pony, with my arms round a man's waist, thinking of a ram sliding into a slot . . .

The muscles of the pony's rump slid backwards and forwards, right and left, as he walked. I felt the movement vividly through my thin clothes. It was like a caress, a gentle caress by a giant. I felt myself becoming excited. I found I was tightening my arms round Bob's waist, and pressing my right breast into his back. It felt like Io's back to my breast, as slender and as delicate.

Controlling my voice as best I could, I said, "I wonder why I haven't seen you."

"Ah. A-ben away. A-ben stayen a piece, to Ziren. A-ben glad t'be home."

The rain was coming down as heavy as ever. It wetted me even more thoroughly, every stitch I was wearing, than when I was walking.

We came to the little bridge. Bob jumped off the pony, and helped me down. He took the saddle and bridle off the pony and put it in a small field by the wood. Carrying the saddle, he started up through the wood to his cottage. It was a strange feeling, to walk along with clothes glued to my body. My nipples showed more prominently than ever through my blouse. This was because I had been thinking of Io and Jasper in bed together, and holding Bob by the waist, and leaning my breast into his back, and because of the caressing movement of the horse under my thighs and buttocks.

Bob took a key from a crack in the cottage wall. He unlocked the door. He gestured for me to go in first, as polite as a lord. (Jasper would have charged in in front of me, to get out of the rain.) The cottage was all one room, as I thought. It was a cabin, rather than a cottage. It was dark. It felt cold and damp because it had been empty while Bob was away. One end was an enormous fireplace with a sort of open cooking-range over part of it. There was a bed, a table, two chairs, two cupboards, various utensils, pieces of harness, a cartwheel, tools, and various nets and poles and things I did not understand. Everything was perfectly tidy. And, though the cottage had been empty, everything was perfectly clean.

I stood dripping onto the rush matting on the floor. Bob peeled off his jacket with difficulty, since it was glued with water to him as my clothes were to me. He hung it neatly over the back of a chair. (Jasper would have dropped it on the floor.) He laid a fire in a twinkling and lit it. It caught and blazed at once.

"Y'be bes' t'tak' off they wet clothen," said Bob.

"Yes," I said.

He unbuckled his own gaiters and pulled off his boots and socks. His feet were small and white and clean. They were like Io's feet when I had scrubbed her.

He struggled out of his shirt. The skin of his chest and back was white, as white and fine as Io's. There was a line at his neck and wrists where the deep sunburn ended. The rest of him was as white as milk. He was slim and wiry, but not skinny. He was not at all frail or underfed. I could see the muscles in his arms and across his stomach above the belt of his breeches.

He found two rough towels in one of the cupboards. Perfectly clean, like everything else. He gave me one. He turned his back to me.

"A-baint looken," he said.

I began to unbutton my blouse. He took off his own breeches, his back to me. I should have turned round, but I watched him. His waist was slender, his hips narrow, his behind neat and muscular and white. His buttocks looked as smooth as peeled eggs.

I pulled off my blouse and my skirt, my shift and my drawers. I put them on a chair, I began to dry myself.

Bob wrapped his towel about his waist. I wrapped my towel round me, above my breasts. It came almost to my knees. I was dressed like a woman of the South-Sea Islands. I could feel the warmth of the fire on my bare shoulders and legs.

"Sit," said Bob.

I sat on the edge of the bed, since both chairs were covered with our wet clothes. Bob found a third towel. He bent down, and picked up one of my bare feet. He began to dry it, very carefully and thoroughly.

I could see a bulge forming in the towel below his waist, thrust outwards as he hardened.

He let go of my foot. It was quite dry. Suddenly, uncontrollably, I pushed it under his towel, and groped upwards with it between his legs. My foot found his ram, hard as a tree, under the towel. I tried to grip it with my toes. I raised my other foot under his towel. I felt his balls with my toes. I gripped his ram between my two feet. I rubbed it with my feet. I pulled his towel away with one foot, while I pressed his ram against his belly with the other.

He grinned. He was not at all bashful. He was proud of it. He was proud to be showing it to me. He was right. It was as big as Jasper's. I gasped when I saw it.

I was not bashful either. Because I had raised my two legs, my own towel was up about my waist. My legs were apart. I was showing him everything. I didn't mind. I was proud, too. He put one hand on the back of a chair, to keep his balance, and raised one of his feet between my legs.

He put it on my fleece. He began to caress me with his toes. He rubbed my hair, and found my button and rubbed it with his toes.

I reached out for his ram. He grinned, and came towards me. He put it between my breasts. He pulled my towel away, and laid his ram between my bare breasts. I played with it. I kissed it and licked it and bit it. I wanted to. I had been wanting this hard tube of male flesh, wanting it so badly, growing damp and hungry between my legs with wanting it.

He sat down beside me, and then we were lying down. The bed creaked with every movement we made. We made a lot of movements.

Then a strange thing happened.

He turned into Io.

He had no ram, no balls, but only lips and teeth and tongue and fingers. He kissed me, my lips and nipples and the top of my legs. He nibbled at my button, and his tongue slid into my hot cave.

He did everything I had done to Io, and everything Io had done to me.

I came to a shuddering wet climax on his tongue, and another on his fingers. I came on his toe. I was weeping with joy. I never before had such a succession of violent, beautiful climaxes.

He went into me at last, sliding in as easily as butter. My lips had never been so wide and wet and ready. I cried with joy to feel myself filled again. I felt it slide against the wet walls, and press against the back, filling me completely. It was a joy to have it there at last.

He lay still, filling me, deep inside me. I wanted him to move. I screamed internally for him to move. He began to move. He was slow. He drew almost all of it out, leaving just the tip inside me. I looked down and saw it, pink and glistening from my fluids, the brown curling hairs at its base moistened by my juices. He moved inwards again. It disappeared inside me, all of it. I felt the tip pressing against the back of my womb.

He moved his legs outside mine. He pressed inwards with his legs on mine. This tightened my passage round him, so that the effect of every movement was intensified.

He began to move more quickly. I was moving too, lifting my hips to meet his. The sensation inside me was almost unbearably lovely. I could feel it mounting and mounting, higher than ever with Jasper or with Io or with Bob's fingers and tongue.

When the explosion came, I jerked like a fish on the deck of a fishing boat. He exploded too, deep inside me, thrusting hard and deep.

He stayed lying on top of me, inside me, until it grew soft and small and slipped out. Then he lay on his back beside me, one arm under my wet head, the other hand on my breast. I played with his small soft ram. It was wet and red. I had never done such a thing before, afterwards, never with Jasper. I had not wanted to. Now I did want to. I felt happy and grateful. I felt warm and well.

We hung our clothes in front of the fire to dry. Bob put a kettle on the fire. We did not dress. I could not have dressed, except in a towel, or in Bob's clothes which I would have burst. Bob made tea. He put some whisky in it. It was very nice. We sat on the bed, side by side, naked, drinking tea. Not much light came in through the one little window, but there was plenty of light from the fire.

Bob said that the nets and sticks were for catching partridges. He had snares for pheasants and hares and rabbits, and different nets and traps for other birds. He said the best snares were made of horsehair, and the best horsehair came from his own pony's tail.

"'At's why a-ben an' botten thicky poany," he said, "for t'get they hairs o' the tail."

He asked me about Io. I was surprised that he had seen her. He said he had seen her shopping in the village before I came to the caravan.

"I don't know who she is," I said. "She won't tell me."

I put my cup down on the table. My hand was shaking. I looked down, between Bob's legs. I wanted him again. His legs were crossed, so that it was completely hidden. I could only see the curling hairs at the bottom of his hard, flat white stomach. I touched the hairs. I stroked them. They were silky, like Io's.

Bob grinned. He kept his legs crossed, as though to tease me. He asked me more about Io. I don't know what I told him. I was distracted. I wasn't thinking about Io. I answered his questions without thinking at all.

He uncrossed his legs at last. It was still small and soft. But, as I watched, it began to swell and straighten. I took it in my hand. I felt it grow in my hand, grow and grow, harden, arch upwards from the hair at its base.

He still held his teacup. I took it from him.

This time I heard myself scream when the climax came. I had never in my life done that before.

I lay beneath him afterwards. The softening thing was inside me. I had not the slightest envy of Jasper or Io. I had no interest in what they did. I was luckier than either of them. I had Bob. Bob was lucky too. He said so. He was as happy to be inside me as I was to have him there.

He wanted to know more about Io. I could tell him no more. I didn't understand his curiosity. He said it was just curiosity.

"A bloke in Ziren were asken," he said. "A Lunnon bloke."

"Asking after the girl?"

"A'ter yer painten bloke, but 'twere the lass a-were seeken."

"What sort of man?"

"Dunno. A Lunnon man."

I wondered about this. But with him still softly inside me I didn't wonder very hard. An army of London men could get as far as Cirencester and still not find the caravan.

The rain stopped.

"I must go," I said. "I must cook for the others."

"Nay. Stay wi' I."

"I must go, dear Bob."

"Came yere t'morrow, then?"

"Yes."

I went the next day, and every day after that. I went for two or three or four hours at a time. The weather was colder. The rain sometimes stopped for a little while, but it always started again. There was always a glorious big fire in Bob's cottage. He lent me an oilskin coat so I could go from the caravan to the cottage without getting soaked.

Bob always had time for me, plenty of time. He said there was no carting to be done in the wet weather. Nobody wanted themselves or their belongings to get soaking wet. He was busy at night, instead. He caught lots of young pheasants in the woods in the night or the dawn. He said it saved them from being shot. He sold them in Cirencester. I never knew how he caught them or where he sold them.

Jasper and Io mostly stayed in the caravan. Neither of them had any clothes for wet weather. Io had no shoes. Jasper did some drawings of Io, but he spent most of his time sitting in his bunk playing his bagpipes. The caravan was very stuffy. It was too cold without the stove and too hot with it. It was impossible to keep it clean and tidy with Jasper and Io always lying about inside. I was glad to get out.

They never seemed to wonder about me. I said I was going to the farm or to the village. They didn't ask why I went shopping every day, so much more often than before. Or why I sometimes came back without milk or eggs or any other food. They left all that to me. They didn't care what I did, as long as the meals appeared regularly.

I don't mean that they were selfish, or thoughtless. Only that they were both used to being waited on hand and foot.

There was no chance for me to make love to Io—Jasper was always there, sitting up in his bunk. Besides, I had Bob. I only wanted Bob. I knew I'd go back to wanting Io or another girl, for the change. But for the moment I wanted to be filled up by Bob. The day would come when I would want a little tongue and little fingers and soft breasts, but for the moment I wanted a big hard ram to sink deep inside me and fill me up.

Bob had that, but he had much more. He was still mysterious to me, not at all like anyone I had ever met before. He was something out of an old painting, out of one of the Breughels Jasper had taken me to see. Everything about him was strange—his clothes, his voice, the words he used, the way he lived. He was like someone from a foreign country, and from long ago in a foreign country.

There was never a speck of dust in his cottage. His clothes and his body were always clean.

He did not talk much. We did not need to talk much. We were relaxed together, like old friends. That was strange. I liked it very much. It was strange because we were not old friends and we came from different worlds. It was very nice. I felt very comfortable in Bob's cottage. I felt relaxed and happy.

Even when we were just sitting by the glorious fire, I felt happy with Bob. When he touched me, stroked my skin, kissed me, I felt on fire, like the fire itself. I'd never known anything so exciting as the touch of his fingers. They stroked me, every part of me, as delicately as Io's little fingers.

And there was his big hard club for me. I loved it. I needed it. I used to kneel and kiss it, for love of it. I used to take his balls in my two hands and kneel, kissing his ram, while he stroked my head.

He told me it was hard for half an hour before I arrived, if he was expecting me. I was the same. I wanted him so badly, day after day, that I felt wet between my legs as I walked to his cottage through the rain.

Io said she was running short of money. We had spent most of the cash she had.

I was appalled. I had wanted to go back to London. Now I wanted to stay. I wanted to stay as long as possible, as long as I could make Jasper stay. I did not want to leave Bob. I needed him. I loved him. He did more for me than any other man, more than Jasper ever did for me.

I need not have worried. Io was still determined to stay, to hide. As long as she had money, Jasper would stay with her. The rain would stop and he would paint again.

We all agreed that we must stay. The others did not ask me why I wanted to stay. Io thought it was because of her. Jasper thought it was because of him and his art.

I did not understand how we could get more money, but Io said she could get all we needed. She had to find a branch of Parsloe's Bank. She had a letter, hidden in a safe place, that she could take to the bank. I was surprised by this. It was extraordinary to me that a young girl could have such a power—that she could walk into a bank with a letter, and get all the money she wanted. But it was normal to her. She took it for granted, like so many other things.

I told Io I would ask in the village if there was a Parsloe's Bank in Cirencester. I asked Bob. He had no idea. He had never been inside a bank in his life.

"A-ben goen t'Ziren t'morrow, for t'sell they pheasantsies," he said.

"Can you ask about the bank?"

"Ay."

"And tell me when you get back?"

"Ay. Y'ben goen t'Ziren, Es?"

"Oh no. I can't wave letters in a bank and get money."

"Painter bloke ben goen?"

"No. If he waved letters in a bank he'd probably be arrested."

"'Tes the young maid?"

"Yes, of course."

"Ah. How d'she plan t'cover they long miles?"

"I suppose she'll take our horse."

"Nay. Thicky harse ben lame. A-seed un goen hoppity."

Bob said he would take Io to Cirencester, either behind him on his pony or in the cart, if there was a branch of Parsloe's Bank in the town.

There was. Bob told me so two days later. He said he would take Io the day after that.

Io was alarmed about going. She stayed clean after I first scrubbed her —I heated water for her every day—so she was frightened of being recognized.

"You'll have to be recognized in the bank," said Jasper, "or you won't get a penny. How will you establish your identity?"

"I'll just tell them who I am," said Io.

"In those clothes? Barefooted? Will they believe you?"

"They can telephone to Mr. What's-his-name. The manager in London. I can easily prove who I am."

"Then your London bank manager will know where you are."

"Yes. Oh God. He'll tell Mamma, and Cousin Dorothea, and—"

There had been a man asking after Jasper in Cirencester. A London man. Looking not really for Jasper but for Io.

"This caravan is a long way from the bank in Cirencester," I said.

"Yes," said Io. "But suppose somebody follows me here?"

"They won't follow Bob if he doesn't want to be followed."

"Who is Bob?"

"Your coachman."

Of course Io had never heard of Bob, or seen him. I had not mentioned him. She had been nowhere near the tiny cottage in the other wood. I had to describe him now without giving anything away.

"I've naturally met him on my way to and from the village," I said. "As he's a tranter."

"A what?"

"He drives a cart."

"Suppose there's a reward," she said, looking anxious. "He might tell them where I am."

"Tell who, darling?"

"Anybody who's looking for me."

"If he says he won't he won't."

"How do you know?"

"I just know."

"But—"

"We've got to have that money," said Jasper. "Or it's back to London, much as I should regret it. If I'm going to starve, I insist on doing it in comfort. Besides, this filthy weather is getting on my nerves."

"*No, no,*" said Io passionately. "We must stay here."

"Then you must be off to the bank, little Io."

"Yes."

Io's little face was pinched with anxiety. I wanted to take her in my arms and comfort her. But Jasper was there. Luckily the rain stopped. A watery sun tried to come out. Jasper said he would go for a walk. I comforted Io. It was sweet. But I was thinking of Bob. I did love Io, and she did everything to me that I did to her. But I did not really want her little tongue, or her teeth on my button, or her fingers inside me. I wanted Bob's hard inches sliding into me. It was sweet with Io, and she was comforted, but it was Bob I wanted. I couldn't lose myself with her. I had to pretend, which I'd never done with her before.

Io found the letter she needed for the bank, which she had hidden. I read it when she was not looking. I found out for the first time who she was.

I was startled. I had never met a Ladyship before.

I was surprised that a Ladyship should behave as she did with Jasper and with me. I was surprised that a Ladyship, a great aristocrat, should want to hide.

It poured with rain the next day. But Jasper insisted that Io must go to Cirencester. Otherwise there was not enough money to buy him any more whisky.

I took Io to meet Bob in the lane below the wood. He had harnessed his pony to the cart. He was wet. Io was going to get very wet, too, but I did not want to lend her my oilskin coat.

Bob had promised me that he would say nothing to anybody about Io and Jasper and the caravan. He seemed shocked that I even asked him to promise. I knew that Io was safe with him.

They were still not back in the early evening. Jasper was getting fretful. His whisky bottle was almost empty. He was in a bad temper. He had done some crayon drawings which were no good. He wanted Io. He would have had me, as a substitute, but I refused. I had never done that before. But I could only think of Bob in that way.

Jasper made the caravan uncomfortable with his bad temper. I put on my oilskin coat and went out. The rain was teeming down. It was beginning to get dark. I was worried about Bob and Io. They should have been back long before.

I went to Bob's cottage. I saw that his pony was grazing in its field. When I got to the cottage I saw that the cart was here. There was light in the little window, and smoke coming out of the chimney.

I thought, Bob is back, but something has happened to Io.

I tried the door. It was locked. I looked in through the window. I saw them in the firelight. Bob had made a glorious big fire, as he always did when I came to him. Their clothes were drying on a chair. Io was sitting on a little low stool in front of the fire. Bob was standing behind her, drying her hair. He was using one of his big clean towels. He had a towel round his waist. She had one wrapped round her, under her armpits, covering most of her, the way I'd worn my towel when I first came to the cottage. Her shoulders were bare, and her legs below the knee. She looked very beautiful in the firelight. He was drying her hair with the gentleness I knew so well.

I felt sick.

He stopped drying her hair. He stroked the damp, tangled hair back from her face. I couldn't see her face; she turned it away from me and looked towards the fire. He hung the towel over the back of a chair, and went round in front of her. He knelt down on the bit of hearthrug in front of her. He slid his hands between her knees, and pushed her legs apart. He wasn't pushing hard. She didn't resist. He shuffled forward on his knees so that he came closer to her, and closer and closer, his trunk between her knees. He came right up to her. He was kneeling up, and she was sitting on the low stool, so their faces were just on a level. Their faces came together. I couldn't see, but I supposed he was kissing her. I imagined the kiss. I didn't want to but I couldn't help it. I felt sick.

Her arms went round his neck. I saw his arms come round her. I saw his left hand unfasten the towel she wore. It dropped away. She was sitting naked on the towel, on the stool. He pulled his own towel off himself and tossed it away. Her legs were spread wide open and he was between them, kneeling. I couldn't see his club—she was in the way—but it must have been pressed up against her stomach. I knew that feeling so well—his big hard club pressed up against my own stomach. Now it was pressed up against Io's soft little stomach.

I began to cry at the thought. My tears got all mixed up with the rain on my face.

He moved his hands down to her buttocks. He slid them under her buttocks. She was sitting on the palms of his hands. Her arms were tight round his neck. Slowly he got up from his knees. He stood up, carrying her with him. Her legs were wrapped round his waist and her arms round his neck, and he was holding her up with his own hands under her behind. Io and Bob were clamped together, with her breasts in his face.

His club stuck out horizontally between her buttocks and below them. I could see the big pink tip sticking out between his hands. It wasn't sticking upwards but pointing straight out because her bottom above it was nudging it downwards. I knew she'd be feeling it there, nestling against her just where her two legs met. Oh sweet Christ, I'd felt it there myself.

He carried her over to his bed, she clinging like a monkey with her arms and legs wrapped round him, he with his hands cupped under her buttocks and his club sticking out in front of him.

I turned away. I couldn't bear to watch what came next. I turned back. I couldn't bear not to.

I expected him to lay her down on her back on the bed. But instead he sat down himself. Her legs and arms were still wrapped round him. He pushed her away from him a little, sliding her buttocks backwards along his thighs. The tip of his club disappeared from below her. I knew it must be stuck up between them now, resting against her stomach as it had so often rested against mine.

He spread his knees, sitting on the edge of the bed. Clearly in the firelight, below her little pink rump, I saw his balls dangling.

My loves. My playthings.

She took a hand away from his neck. She slid it down between their bodies. I imagined her fingers on his club. Then I saw her fingers, like tiny white fish, groping down between her own legs and his, and playing my games with his balls.

She'd relaxed her hold with her legs now. Her legs were opened wide, as wide as they would go, like a dancer doing the splits, each side of him, her bottom on his legs and her feet on the bed. Her hand disappeared from his balls. It was busy somewhere else, out of my sight. I knew where it was. Her bottom began to wriggle there on his thighs. She was wriggling herself towards him, closer and closer. He was wriggling too. I saw the trembling of the muscles of his legs, and the swinging of his balls hanging down between them.

She pushed his club into her slot. She was jamming herself onto it. He was wriggling to help it in.

I thought he'd lie back, with her on top. Instead he stood up again. He was holding her under the buttocks as before, and she was clinging to him with her legs round his bottom and her arms round his neck. He was inside her, all the way he could go. She was clinging to him that way too, clinging to his ram with her slot. I couldn't see his face because her hair was all over it. I couldn't make out why he stood up. Of course she was so little and light a dwarf could have carried her.

He walked slowly across the room towards the fire, carrying her like that, with his club jammed right up inside her. Her buttocks were wriggling in his hands. She was wriggling her slot on his club. I knew that wriggle she did. She did it on my fingers. She did it to excite herself, to help things along. She was trying to get there, to finish the journey.

I thought with despair what sensations she must be giving him, wriggling like that as he carried her across the room. He couldn't have carried me like that, with my size and big bones.

He laid her down at last on the hearthrug, his club still stuck fast inside her. He began to pull in and out. He pulled so far out I thought the tip would pop clear. But he kept it in, just the knob at the tip, and then sank deep again. When he pulled backwards, I saw the glisten of her wetness on his club. The firelight caught it so that the moisture shone.

I couldn't see his face. It was buried in her hair. I could only see his buttocks and his back, and every other second the glistening tube of his club.

He went in deep and stayed in. I could see the trembling of his bottom. I knew that he'd done it, that he'd unloaded it all inside her.

I couldn't see her face. Her legs were trembling. I knew that tremble of her little knees and thighs.

I was sick with disgust and misery. Physically ill, all my lunch and tea spewed out on the sodden ground as I stood outside the cottage in the teeming rain.

In the morning I went to Cirencester, not with Bob but with another carter in the village. Io gave me money for the carter and for some shopping. She had plenty of money now.

I asked the way to Parsloe's Bank. I went in and asked to see the manager.

17 ❀ *Her cheeks all wet*

> Look how he can, she cannot choose but love;
> And by her fair immortal hand she swears,
> From his soft bosom never to remove,
> Till he take truce with her contending tears,
> Which long have rain'd, making her cheeks all wet;
> And one sweet kiss shall pay this countless debt.

VENUS AND ADONIS

It wasn't really true, what I told Es. They called me Tranter because I sometimes drove a cart and pretended to make a living out of it. Of course I had a name, like anybody else. Robert Showers. I didn't use it when I could avoid, because too many people knew it. The police and the magistrates and the wardens in Cirencester Gaol. They knew it from when I was first caught, pinching from the stalls in the market. The magistrates said it was terrible, a little lad of seven stealing to eat. I said I was seven years old, and hungry. Truly I was eleven, and not hungry at all. It got me off though, that time, that and the voice I used. They could hardly understand me, I spoke so broad, like some of the old women in the village. Of course no one of my age spoke that broad, not in the normal way. I was brought up to speak genteel, but the other was better, most times, for getting me into good spots and out of bad ones.

I used to pretend I couldn't read or write, too. People took pity. They said I couldn't be blamed, being a natural, being so backward. Truly I was the best scholar in the village school. I won the reading prize and the writing prize. I could have been a clerk. God forbid.

I saw beardy and the maid when they first came to these parts. I saw them in the village. Of course I thought they were gips, with that old cart. He might have been a gip, with long black hair. It looked greasy. He looked a bit greasy all over. The maid was dirty too, but she was no gip. Not with hair and eyes that colour, and that skin. I was curious about them, so I followed them. I saw them go into Dogleg Wood and put their horse in the four-acre and light a fire.

They were lucky, picking that spot. It all belonged to Sir Edwin Maltby, that part, eight hundred acres. He lived in Italy. There was an estate manager, but he never bothered. It was a scandal—half the land fallow year after year and the woods not preserved. Else they couldn't have stayed there, nor grazed their horse. (The same with me. There should have been a gamekeeper in my house, but the estate manager pocketed the wages.)

Gips would have had a dog. These two didn't. I made sure of that, first thing.

I was up early, the morning after they stopped in Dogleg, seeing to my snares. I went to look at them and their cart. I kept hidden. I always do. It saves bother. I hate bother. I saw the maid trying to make a fire and cook a meal over it. A right mess she made of it. I thought of coming up out of the bushes to help. But there wasn't any profit I could see in that. There might be a profit other ways, something in the cart, money or watches. I was best to stay hid until I knew more about these people.

Beardy got up and joined the maid. There were a funny pair, him twice as tall as her, his voice ten times louder. I listened to them talking. She was gentry, and him not far off. I was used to the sound of gentry voices, from Sir Edwin, and the magistrates, and parson, and the doctor. I couldn't make out what gentry folk were doing in a gippy cart in Dogleg Wood. I guessed they'd run away together. I thought there was bound to be pickings in the cart for such as me.

I understood a sight better when beardy began to paint a picture. He painted a picture of the maid. I'd seen this often before, mostly ladies with little water-colours like we had in the village school. I won the painting prize one year, as well as the reading and writing.

I started to creep away. There was no profit to me in watching beardy paint a picture. But before I did, that saucy maid pulled off her clothes and sat to be painted as bare as a pollywog.

To be painted, so I thought! Not a bit of it. Two minutes later he was bare, too, and pleasuring the maid like a Jersey bull. I was envious. She was as pretty as paint and as saucy as a stoat. It went funny with her gentry voice, the things she did.

It was funny, watching them. Of course I'd watched others, a many times, peeping through windows in the village. It's when they're busy pleasuring upstairs, you can nip in downstairs for the spoons. That's peeping for profit. There was no profit in Dogleg for me, not at that moment, with them so near the cart. I peeped for diversions, purely, with eight dead pheasants in my bag.

I got into their cart two days later. The maid was walking to Bridge Farm to buys eggs for six times their value from that fat thief Reuben Davy. Beardy was making a painting of brambly bushes at the edge of the wood.

I thought I'd lief not live in that cart, nor even go into it. It was a proper pigsty, and smellier than most sties. About like Reuben Davy's dirty old sty. Even Reuben wouldn't sleep in such a place.

There was nothing in there worth the pinching. Only all beardy's painting clobber, which was no good to me. I knew they had a bottle of whisky, but beardy had that with him. I knew they had a bit of money somewhere, buying Reuben Davy's eggs and milk at his prices. I thought maybe the maid had that with her. I wondered about getting it off her. But she'd see my face. That meant knocking her on the head, like a pheasant poult in a snare. I could do it easy enough, but I didn't fancy the idea. I'd only done it twice, both times with a knife. One was a bloke who found me in his house at midnight, one was a gamekeeper. I didn't like to kill a pretty maid. It was vexing, though, to think of her carrying money.

Another thing was vexing. They were making a pigsty all round about their cart, as well as inside it. Broken glass, flies, smell. It was horrible to see.

It made me wonder if knocking them on the head was such a bad idea.

Next time I saw them was early in the morning. The maid was picking mushrooms in the four-acres. That was a third vexing thing. I wanted those mushrooms, but she picked every one in the field. He was doing a painting as she did it.

Then he painted her sitting on the ground with nothing on but a skirt. She was as pretty as paint but she was getting terrible dirty. Then he painted her bare again, two places. I liked looking at her. The paintings weren't as pretty as she was, but you could see they were paintings of her.

I never saw such a pair for pleasuring. Sometimes I watched them at night, by the light of their lamp, through the window of the gippy cart. Sometimes in the dawning, when I was on my way back from my snares. Sometimes right out in the open in the noontide, out on the bare ground like puppy dogs. She got to looking more like a gip, did the maid, as the dirt darkened all over her.

I wouldn't have lief touched her myself, the state she was in, for all her bare body was so fetching. I like a clean lass.

I saw one a fortnight later—another from London. She was a fine big lass with black hair. She was a grand shape, and she had eyes like a cow, not too clever. (I like a clean lass but not a clever one.) She was looking for beardy, so she said to Jem Tripp at the Red Lion. It was my beardy she wanted—the painter bloke. They'd seen him at the pub, but they didn't know where the cart was hidden in Dogleg Wood.

Liking the look of the big clean lass, I told her I'd take her to the painting bloke. I talked very broad when I spoke to her—made myself ridiculous, truly, just for the diversions of it.

I wondered how they'd get on—one man and two lovely maids in that little dirty cart.

Mary was atween the shafts all ready, so we set off straightway for Dogleg. She had a bag of many more clothes than the others put together. I guessed she'd keep them clean, too.

I told her I didn't have any name, being an orphan. (It was doing no hurt to Mother and Father, in the almshouse in Ciren, to tell it so.) The less Robert Showers got mentioned, the longer I stayed out of gaol.

I admired her as we went. I liked what I could see, and I liked what I could guess at. She said she'd been travelling all day, in trains and such, and she felt all dirty. She looked a sight cleaner than the little maid in the wood. I betted her drawers were clean. So were mine, when I wore them. The little maid never wore any. A good job, too—her drawers would have given the vomits to a tinker.

In the morning Es scrubbed out the cart. (That was her name, all I could be troubled with. The whole of it was as long as a stallion's pike at covering time.) She was one for a clean home. She was a fine strong lass, too.

She looked a draggle when she'd finished, and no wonder, the work she'd done. She got soap and needfuls and went off to wash in the stickleback pool. I followed after, walking sly. I was happy for a sight of Es washing herself. She came to the pool and I hid behind a hazel bush. She took off every stitch. It was better than I'd hoped. She was a lovely lass bare, with a sort of ripe colour to her skin, and the finest tits I ever saw. She soaped and scrubbed herself all over, the way I do myself. I would have liked to come out and help her, but I thought it best to stay peeping.

Still as bare as a pollywog, she started to scrub the clothes she'd taken off. That gave me funny views. She was kneeling on the bank of the pool, her legs apart for to steady herself, scrubbing at her skirt. Watching from behind, all I could see was arse, with the tuft of black hair peeping down between. It was like the hair on her head, thick and black, and just as clean. I knew that, I'd watched her scrub it.

The little maid came up with a basket of mushrooms. (Mushrooms I would have had.) She looked no bigger than a kiddy, in beardy's shirt. She looked all the smaller beside Es, who was a sight bigger than me.

All of a sudden, Es got hold of the little maid, pulled her clothes off, and pulled her into the stickleback pool. The fish never saw anything like that before. Nor did I. Es scrubbed the maid till her skin went from brown to white. The maid fought like a cat being drowned in a waterbutt, but Es was ten times stronger.

Es dried her, very gentle. I could see the maid liked that. She dried her little tits, like I would have done. The maid reached up for Es's big tits, like I would have done.

I never had seen this before. I had heard tell of it, but I never could truly believe they did such things. In our parts, there's people are funny with animals, and sometimes a man with boys, but I never knew a case of two lasses.

It was funny to watch. They were holding each other, the maid sitting and Es kneeling behind. Then Es felt the maid. Then she crawled round and squatted atween the maid's legs, and kissed her right there on the females. She stuck out her tongue and pushed it in like a pike. I never saw such a thing. The little maid was pleasured. I could tell by the look on her face and the way she bounced.

Then they were the other way about. Es cooed like a cushat dove and bounced like a football. She was pleasured, too.

I thought it was an awful waste, but I was interested to have seen it. I couldn't hear what they said to each other because of the gurgle of the water at the tail of the pool. After, they lay like a man and a woman do, the maid's head on Es's breast.

I waited till they went away, then went away myself. I knew the maid pleasured beardy as well as Es. I wondered if Es would pleasure a man, as well as the maid. I guessed not. She seemed that passionate about the maid, kissing her and feeling her like a man would, as I would. I guessed that was what she liked, better than any man, as Joe Metcalf likes a pig better than any girl. There's no accounting.

I had to go away for a few days to see Doris my wife in the hospital in Swindon. She'd fallen off the cart after a few too many of rough cider at harvest time and split her head open. They'd stitched it up, but she had to stay quiet. I was quite glad to see her. She was getting better. I was glad, but I didn't want her better too quick.

When I got home, I went straight to Dogleg to see how the party was. I had another startlement. Beardy was doing a painting of the maid, away by the stream. The maid was bare, and pretending to wash her clothes as Es had done. I didn't get the same view of her that I had of Es—beardy had her placed different. She looked right sweet and lovely, all bare, kneeling by the river bank.

Es was all alone by the cart. I nearly went up openly, to make greetings, but I stayed to peep for a moment. I was glad I did.

Es had a small cucumber. (Probably bought for six times its worth from Reuben Davy.) She rubbed it with a pat of butter. I thought—that's a funny way to go about frying a cucumber. If you ever did such a thing, you'd surely slice it, but I never heard of anybody cooking a cucumber anyway.

She had no intentions of frying, or any sort of cookery. She laid herself on the ground, holding that buttery cucumber. She picked up her skirt, and wriggled her arse to make way for it, and pulled it up to her waist. No drawers today, like the maid. That big bush of black hair was all open to the sky. She played with it with her fingers, pinching and stroking very delicate. Then she raised up her knees and spread them open, exactly like a man was coming down on her from heaven. I couldn't rightly make out what she was up to.

Till I saw her take that old cucumber, and slide it up the hole. Six or seven inches it went in, I do believe. She moved it in and out, slow. She rubbed herself with it, faster. She was working hard at it. I never saw such a sight. There was plenty of room there for the old cucumber. It pleasured her. She mewed like a kitten and shivered like a pleasured lass does.

So there was a question answered, likely. Beardy being occupied with the maid, Es had to make do with a cucumber. One of Reuben Davy's! It was probably worth the money to Es, even at six times the proper value.

This wasn't the moment to meet her, but I decided to meet her, all by happenchance, the first good moment.

They caught me that night, unfortunately. The night watchman at

Deverill's caught me in the livery stable. I hadn't taken a thing—I hadn't had time—which was a bit of luck. But the hour of the night was against me, three in the morning. And previous convictions was against me. I got fifteen days without the option.

Cirencester Gaol was no different. I met some old friends and made some new ones.

One day they brought me up out of the cell to a little room with a high barred window and a pine table. There was a man waiting for me there. I thought there was a mistake, but it was me the man wanted to see. He was seeing a lot of people, and I was one of them. He was a tall thin man with a thin red face and a billycock hat. His name was Mr. Brunton and he came from London.

The warder said I was to answer the gentleman's questions, or I'd be done over rightly. The warder left me alone with Mr. Brunton, but I knew he was just outside the door.

Mr. Brunton was something called a Private Detective. I never heard of such a thing before, but it seemed they had them in London. He was try-ing to find a man. He had a client who was paying him to find the man. He didn't say who the client was, or how much he was paying. It seemed a funny sort of job to me, and still does, knowing what I learned after.

"The man we are looking for is an artist, a painter," said Mr. Brunton. He faithful described my old beardy, even to his dirty old coat. "We be-lieve he may be in this area."

"Why?" I asked, wondering how they got so close with the whole of England to pick from.

Mr. Brunton told me, because he was proud of having been so clever. "He has an associate, a young female. His model and, herm, mistress. We discovered her identity from his friends in London, though she uses an alias. We traced her to her sister's residence in Essex. She had left there on receipt of a letter from our quarry. She travelled to Cirencester, to this city."

"There ben a heap o' country hereabouts," I said.

"Yes. Far too much for my organization to search."

"They policemen baint seeken?"

"It is not a police matter."

"Ah. Painter bloke ben done nuthen wrang?"

"That is not established. Nor is it any of your concern. I have been in-structed to proceed with the utmost discretion, if you know what those words mean."

I knew well enough. I was a scholar, one time.

"I am asking you about this matter, Showers, because of information given to me by the police. I understand that you are a, herm, night worker, and that, like myself, it is your habit to proceed with the utmost discretion—from different motives, of course, different motives. The person I have described is known to have purchased a gipsy caravan, and may still be occupying it. If he has passed through your, herm, territory, or is still camped in the area where you, herm, carry on your trade, it seems probable that you would be aware of it."

"Herm," I said, thinking it was a useful noise. "He ben on his own, thicky painten bloke?"

"He was, and possibly still is, accompanied by a young lady."

Mr. Brunton described the young maid. He'd never seen her, let alone seen her as I'd seen her, so he didn't do her half justice.

"If she is in the man's company," said Mr. Brunton, "the young lady is in moral and probably in physical danger."

I saw by that it was the maid they were looking for. They only wanted beardy as a way of finding her.

"Our man may also," said Mr. Brunton, "have been joined by a second female, the associate to whom I referred."

He described Es. He didn't half do her justice, either. Of course he never would see what I'd seen.

"If your information leads to our discovering the persons referred to," said Mr Brunton, "there will of course be a substantial reward."

I'd been wondering when he'd come to the interesting part. Till I knew about that, I couldn't make my mind up about anything. If the little maid was running away from something, then good luck to her. I'd done some running in my time, and I'd liefer not help the hounds catch a puss.

Besides, I had my hopes of Es.

Still, a lot of money is a lot of money. A married man has no right to turn such a thing down.

"Ah," I said, cautious. "Herm. A reward, eh?"

"Five pounds," said Mr. Brunton solemnly. "Five whole golden sovereigns."

I almost laughed in his face. I had over three hundred saved up, hidden where even I could hardly find it. I wasn't going to bring misery to the little maid for a fiver, nor yet give up my hopes of Es.

"Ay," I said, putting on a face of desperate misery. "A-ben joyful t'gain a sight o' golden coins. But a-baint seed thicky bloke wi'beard an' coaten, nor yet they maidies neither. A-ben right sorry, sir."

Ten pounds, now, that would have been a different matter.

When they let me out of the gaol, I picked up my pony in the village and started riding home. It was raining like I never saw. I was looking forward to my fire and my drink. I decided to seek Es the next morning, if they were still in Dogleg Wood. Likely they'd moved off, with the weather broke.

We came round a corner and there she was! Mighty wet, but still a fine lass. Her wet clothes stuck to her tits, very pleasing for to see. I showed I liked looking at her, and I saw she liked me looking at her. I thought there'd be no problems. I thought I'd do better than that old cucumber of hers.

I asked her back to my house for to get warm and dry.

She said yes, quick as a trout in a puddle. We got her up behind, on Mary's quarters, and she took hold around and about my middle. It was a pleasure for to feel those gripping arms, remembering things I'd seen them do with the maid.

I lit the fire the minute we got in. It was needful.

That rain was a godsend, truly, giving us a reason for to take our clothes off. They'd have come off anyway, but the rain gave a reason. It saved time and talk and bashfulness. We had towels, to be decent.

She'd started things properly going by the stickleback pool by drying the maid with a towel. It seemed like a good way to begin. I dried Es's foot while she sat on the bed. She tickled me up with the foot! Then both feet! It was funny, being felt by those feet. Her feet were a bit cold for to squeeze my pike with, but it was a pleasure even so. She pulled away my towel that I had around and about me for decency. I showed her I was as good as any old cucumber.

Since she tickled me up with her foot, I tickled her up with mine. It's not a thing I ever did before. It's not a thing I ever thought to try. I won't be making a habit of that.

She wanted it all terrible bad. I never knew a lass wanted it so bad. I knew what she liked, from watching by the pool, so I did the things she did to the maid, and the maid did to her. It was funny, all that licking. It's another thing I never thought to try before. I knew Es was a clean lass, or I wouldn't have cared so much for the licking. I was a long time playing about before I properly went in. That's a good thing, to delay. I never did believe in scurrying, not with pheasants or trout or silver spoons or lasses. When I properly did it, old pike slipped in as easy as that buttery cucumber. I never knew a lass so slippery.

I knew what to expect, having seen her with the maid and with the cucumber.

When the fish did jump, it was more than I expected. It was grand. I opened the bung in the barrel at the exact same time. It's lucky, that, and it doesn't happen so very often.

She was that grateful. I felt almost a sort of guilt, making a lass feel that grateful. It showed how bad she wanted it, like the cucumber had showed.

She was grand, was Es, but beardy preferred the little maid. I wondered, as I lay there with Es, why he did. It struck me the maid must be something wonderful, if beardy liked her better than Es. That gave me ideas about the maid. I thought about her while Es was fingering of my old soft sausage after we came out from inside.

I made tea and asked Es about the maid. Es couldn't tell me much. She didn't know the maid's proper name, even, or where she came from. I thought that was funny. The maid was very rich, and higher than gentry. She was used to being looked after, to having maids and servants. She was frightened of something and stayed hiding. That was why she was living there in the gippy cart. She pleasured beardy whenever he wanted because she had to stay there hiding. It didn't come right for her with beardy; she didn't truly finish. Es didn't say so, but I saw that was why she pleasured with Es. Es could make her finish, with fingers and such, while beardy couldn't with his pike.

Es told me more than she meant to, because she wanted it again. I could see her tits getting harder, like, and her tummy going in and out with her breathing. She began to stroke my old bush, like it was a kitten. She wanted to look at old sausage again, so I let her pull my legs apart. Of course it took heart, did old pike, and began to stand up like a soldier. Specially when she took and gripped it.

We did it much quicker the second time. She was already jumping when I stuck it into her. She gave a scream. She almost strangled me. My, she did want it bad. It was a grand way to spend a morning just out of gaol, ramming a big clean lass in front of the fire.

I told her about Mr. Brunton, not mentioning names. This was for a roundabout way of giving warnings.

The more I thought about it, the more I thought the maid must be extra wonderful that beardy liked her better than Es. It gave me ideas.

Es came and saw me every day after that, morning or afternoon. She was fine. She treated my old pike right worshipful, she was wanting it so bad. She cuddled it like a lass with a young baby. It was funny.

I still had my ideas about the maid, specially after what Es told me. I went and spied, there in Dogleg, but there was no profit. The rain came down all the time, and the maid stayed inside the cart with beardy. I couldn't so much as get to talk to her, leave alone more. I lived in hopes, though. It seemed they were stuck there permanent.

I was glad I kept quiet to Mr. Brunton. It was lucky, truly, that he didn't offer me a tenner.

Es asked me one day if there was a Parsloe's Bank in Ciren. She said the little maid had to go there to get more money. I saw my chance, same like an open window in any empty house. I said their old horse was lame. (Truly he was as sound as a pippin.) It came out, as I knew it would, that I'd take the little maid to the town.

I took her, on a rainy day.

Es said she was called Eye-oh, or it might have been I.O. I thought that was truly ridiculous, but the maid told me, in a little high gentry voice, that it was right. I knew it wasn't her real name. It was like Es being called Es, or me Tranter Bob. It made no odds what she was called, as far as I could see.

I talked genteel to Eye-oh. The old village-woman voice didn't seem right for her. I couldn't talk gentry-voice like her. I don't understand how they make those noises. Their mouths must be different inside from ordinary folks'. But I was a sight more genteel than with Es. It seemed the right thing.

We didn't talk much on the way to Ciren. It was raining plentiful, and we both got wettish. I didn't feel free to talk to Eye-oh as I did to Es, about borrowing pheasants and partridges, and other things on my mind. Es wasn't truly gentry, leave alone higher—the game in a preserve meant nothing to her. But Eye-oh was a different kind of trout altogether. Her family was apt to be friendly with Sir Edwin or Lord Bathurst or the Duke of Beaufort. She'd be as down as they were on a poor man with a snare in his pocket. They stick together, do that lot. So, as far as Eye-oh knew, I made my living as a tranter.

She went into the bank looking like a scarecrow in a sheep-dip, and came out a full hour later. It was funny to see a little draggledy maid with no shoes go into that big red bank. She came out still like a scarecrow, but drier. She carried a packet in a piece of oilcloth. I knew they were bank notes or golden sovereigns.

All the way home I thought about that packet, more even than I thought about Eye-oh. It was a terrible temptation. But I didn't much want to bash Eye-oh on the head, like a pheasant poult or a trout. Wet or dry, she was as pretty as paint. And Es, and beardy too, knew full well that Eye-oh was with me. If she didn't get back, there'd be questions. All the same, it was a terrible temptation.

Of course I took her back home to get warm and dry, like I did Es. I lit the fire and found the towels, like with Es. The rain made things easier, like with Es. It gave us a reason to strip off. I said to Eye-oh she must, or she'd catch her death or rheumatics. She was shivering, too, pitiful to see, by the time we got back. That was a cold rain, that tide. She was better by my fire than in that gippy cart of theirs, warmer and more comfortable.

When I said she must strip her clothes off, she gave me a look. Ah, I said to myself, that's why they call you Eye-oh.

We went a funny way about things, me and Eye-oh that tide. It was her being so dainty and light made a lot of things possible. I like to try something new, and her being so light gave me chances. I always do believe in taking my chances when they come. So I did what I never thought of previous, which was walking round the cottage with a lass skewered on my pike. It was grand.

But getting it in there took a sight of doing. Old pike, he slid into Es like a greased ferret in a rabbit-hole. She was that ready and anxious, always. And being she was a fine big lass, her females was big by nature. Little Eye-oh was a mite beside Es. I never felt such a tight fit. Too tight, truly—I felt like a cork in the neck of a bottle.

It wasn't only she was small by nature, it struck me. She wasn't truly ready when she took and skewered herself on me. She thought she was but she wasn't. She wasn't going to be, neither. She was tense, all tightened up and tense inside like a lurcher before the coursing. When a maid's to get her pleasures rightly, she's got to be happy about it, relaxed like. Eye-oh was more like doing it because she must. It's ridiculous, truly, but it was like she felt a sense of duty. She was deep serious. Her face was as solemn as a Magistrate. That's no spirit for pleasuring.

A laugh would have helped, I do believe. If she could have laughed, right loud and cheerful, that might have pushed away the tenseness. That little hole might have gone softer. I do believe that. I should have made her laugh, if I could. But maybe I never could, a gentry maid with that voice. Likely she'd find other things funny.

I wanted to delay, like I always if I can. But with that tight fit I knew there'd be no holding the barrel-bung. She did wriggle too, like a little speckled trout. She was trying to give herself the tickles, that I knew, but she gave me the tickles. The natural tight fit and the tickles and the tenseness, between them they had old pike bursting quick. There was no stopping it.

Well, it was grand for me. You can't always be doing things perfect for a lass.

I could understand how beardy liked Eye-oh better than Es. That little white body was as pretty as a flower, and her face, too, and that golden hair. And that tight fit! Her wriggles were grand, too.

She put on her clothes the moment they were dry. I wanted it again, that tight fit like a hand squeezing. But she said she hadn't time. Beardy needed money for to buy whisky. I lent her a coat for her back. She said goodbye like all I'd given her was tea.

Es didn't come the next day or the next. The day after that, at noon, I went to Dogleg Wood for to see what was up. I went sly. There was tanglements ahead, unless I was careful.

It was another wet day, the rain coming down cold and hard. I did have to drive myself from my own fireside to go out into that. But I was wondering about Es, what kept her away. I wanted to see Eye-oh, too. I was going to try to make her laugh. Then maybe she'd relax, and get her pleasures rightly. I wanted them both, truly. I wanted to arrange that they both came, different times.

I liked the thought of Es in the forenoons and Eye-oh in the afternoons, but backsyfore was all right. It made no odds, truly.

In the lane below the wood was a big motorcar. We didn't see many of them hereabouts, though Ciren had aplenty. There was nobody in it or near it. I thought it was a funny place to leave a motor, miles from anywhere.

I went up through the wood, going sly. It was a sight wetter than the bottom of a beer-mug.

I got nearer to the car, standing all forlorn in the drippings from the trees. It was still only half painted in new colours. Smoke came out of the stove-pipe. I came near, going sly.

I heard a scream, so, "No! No! No!"

It was Eye-oh's voice. Even screaming I knew it. I thought beardy was strangling her, maybe, after too much whisky. I ran to the cart, but still sly, and spied through the window.

Eye-oh was there, standing up, dressed like always, one hand to her mouth. Nobody was strangling her, but a man had hold of her wrist. Es was there beside Eye-oh, standing up, dressed a bit warmer for the weather, with a hand to *her* mouth. Beardy was there, sitting down, dressed like always, with a hand to *his* mouth. Es looked funny, kind of grim. Beardy looked truly amazed. Eye-oh looked like a baby rabbit in the jaws of a stoat. Frightened to death, hurt, near crying.

The other man was a stranger. He was thin, with a thin face. His face was as pale as Eye-oh's tummy, smooth white skin like that. He was dressed up in grand London clothes, with a dark coat and a London hat.

If Eye-oh was like a baby rabbit gripped by a stoat, this London stranger was that stoat. He had the eye of a stoat and the smile of a stoat. He was a bad man. I'm a bad man myself, I always was, and I can tell.

"Oh yes, dear little Camilla," he said to Eye-oh. "I have so many things planned for you. I told you about them, you remember, when we met in Pimlico. At least, I gave you an intriguing hint of them."

Eye-oh was near to fainting. He called her Camilla, which didn't sound any more likely to me.

He had a voice like the Magistrate who sent me to Ciren gaol that last time.

He seemed to be Eye-oh's owner. That's ridiculous, truly, but it was the air he had. He held her like he owned her, like a man holding the lead of his dog.

"How did you find us?" said beardy suddenly.

"It was tedious but not really difficult, my dear Whittingham," said the stranger. "I heard that you had left London, unexpectedly and mysteriously, at the same time as our wayward nymph here. I was aware that you had met at Moreys. I went to your studio, and there interviewed a slatternly female in a curious hat. She reported a visitor to you, a girl who answered my description of silly little Camilla. She showed me some drawings, unmistakably yours, unmistakenly of Camilla. Good. It was at least possible that it was you we should look for. I talked to a number of your Bohemian friends who reported that you had been boring them all summer with tales of a gipsy caravan you wanted to buy. Good. It was possible that it was that we should look for. I knew you had no money. I knew Camilla could command unlimited money. I went to see her bank manager. From what he told me, I was able to formulate a theory of how you financed the purchase of the caravan.

"He also told me about a letter which, at Camilla's request, he had sent round to Berkeley Square by messenger. I called on old Lady Hale in Berkeley Square. She showed me that letter. It was on paper of curious shape, as though shortened. It had been shortened. The top had been cut off, leaving a certain irregularity. I compared it to another letter, also shown to me by Lady Hale as having a possible bearing on Camilla's disappearance. This was an interesting exhibit. It was on the same paper, but complete with the address. And it was a dinner invitation from a lady who does not exist. I called on that imaginary lady's grandson, but he was away. His landlady, however was able to describe both yourself and your new protégée. I saw the letter you left for Matthew Alban. I am intrigued, incidentally, that you are to paint him. He has an excellent face, the strength concealed yet discernable. But I digress. I engaged a company of private detectives, and they and I have been engaged in unremitting search for you ever since.

"Learning of Miss Brumby here, whose face is so familiar to me from many of your paintings, my dear Whittingham, we discovered upon inquiry that she had a sister. We interviewed the sister in a deplorable little house in Ongar. That brought my sleuths to this area. But we drew these coverts blank, as my fox-hunting friends would say. I will not conceal from you that I began to despair. I had spent an immense amount of time and money, both of which I bitterly grudged, to no avail. I shall not forget, dear little Camilla, the expense and inconvenience you have caused me.

"Then I heard from the manager of Parsloe's Bank in Pall Mall. He had been required to identify Lady Camilla Glyn by telephone. He was able to do so by asking her questions to which only she could know the answer—as, what hat she was wearing when she came to his office before disappearing. I understand it was a bizarre confection.

"I was contemplating, with distaste, the thought of personally conducting a search through this countryside when I received another message from my ally at the bank. He had himself heard from his colleague in Cirencester. A person had visited the latter and had given him precise directions for finding this quaint conveyance. As soon as I could, I presented myself in Cirencester and received those directions. They were admirable, and I am grateful to whichever of you supplied them. You may think it foolhardy of me to have undertaken this mission alone. I think not. You need my good offices, my dear Whittingham. You know that as well as I. This idyll is terminated, and you will be wise to accept the fact."

I understood. It was Es had told them in the bank where Eye-oh was to be found. It must have been. I'd seen beardy about the place, but not here that day. She didn't come to me that day. Nobody else knew where the cart was. It must have been Es. But her face didn't show anything.

I didn't think Eye-oh had listened to the stranger, truly. A baby rabbit in a stoat's jaws doesn't wonder how the stoat found him.

"I can't let you take her," said beardy loudly. "I won't."

"Do you want to paint any portraits ever again, my dear Whittingham?

If you do, I counsel you not to interfere. I may add that you could yourself be subject to criminal charges, after your abduction of my fiancée."

Beardy had started to stand up, but he sat down again. Painting portraits was more important to him than Eye-oh. He didn't want criminal charges.

"Help me, Jasper!" said Eye-oh, in a voice like a bird in the birdlime.

But I could see he wasn't going to.

"Maybe I can help," I called in through the window.

It wasn't what I expected, truly. I never meant to interfere. The words just rushed out, like lurchers when they slip them for the coursing, faster than I could stop them.

They all jumped, Eye-oh and Es and beardy and the stranger. They hadn't expected a voice through the window, and they hadn't expected my old face peeping in.

I couldn't make out Es's face. I couldn't make out what she was feeling. Beardy looked as blank as a beech tree—of course he'd never seen me before. The stranger looked a bit vexed, like a parson interrupted in a sermon. Eye-oh looked suddenly hopeful. It was grand to see that sudden hope in her face. I was glad then that I'd spoken.

She reached out towards me, towards the window, with the hand the stranger wasn't gripping. She cried out, "Bob darling, help me!"

She struggled to get away from the stranger, but he held her fast. They swayed and staggered about. There wasn't truly room for them all. They were tripping over beardy's legs, and bumping into Es. It was a sight too small, that cart, for dancing like they did. They were packed in together like fish in a bass, the four of them. There was a proper jumble of people.

Es picked up a whisky bottle. It was full, a new one. I thought she wanted a drink, she was feeling that upset. She took it by the neck and lifted it up. Funny way to drink, I thought. At that moment Eye-oh knocked into her and the stranger knocked into her, and both of them tripped over beardy's legs, and beardy was shouting and Eye-oh was screaming, and Es brought that bottle down like a club. She was a fine big lass, as strong as a man, and she truly brought it down like a club. She hit that old stranger bang on the nob. The bottle burst and so did his head. There was whisky and blood everywhere. It was like a slaughterhouse in a distillery, or the other way about.

The stranger went down with blood all over his face and whisky all over his coat. Eye-oh sat down, weeping like the rain I was standing in. Beardy sat with his mouth open, as though he'd been conked on the nob too. Es began to weep as loud as Eye-oh.

I managed to get in there, though they filled the place so a mouse would have had to move edgeways. The lasses were just about hysterical, truly, and beardy was stunned. I took a look at the stranger.

He was bad. There was a deep gash on the side of his neck, and blood was gushing out of that like beer out of a barrel. I couldn't rightly see how a bash on the head made a gash in the neck, till I understood he'd cut himself when he'd fallen on a bit of broken glass that got to the floor before he did.

That made it an accident, truly, but the Magistrates wouldn't see it so.

He wasn't dead, nor knocked out for more than a moment. His eyes opened and he blinked at me. I saw the cleverness and the wickedness in them, hurt as he was. I'm clever and wicked myself, so I know the signs.

"Ah," he said, "the unexpected face at the window. The witness of this assault."

His voice wasn't like Magistrate's now. It was still teachy, like, but fainter, more like the old vicar in the days when I had to listen to vicars.

He tried to sit up. But he was weak because he was losing so much blood. I helped him with a hand behind his shoulders. His blood made a terrible mess of my coat. I propped him against the bed and let go. I didn't want more blood on my coat. It's terrible stuff to get out, and if you don't get it out there's questions. I do hate questions.

"Broken glass," he said faintly, looking at the mess all round. "Was I smitten with a bottle? How crude. The large female aimed the blow? I fancy so. My little Camilla was powerless, Whittingham was obeying the commands of self-interest, and the small delinquent who alone seems prepared to assist me was outside the caravan. Leaves the voluptuous charmer, by process of elimination. How ironic. I have been hit by many tools or weapons, sometimes at my own instance and no inconsiderable expense, often by ladies not dissimilar to you, my dear, but never before with a bottle. My neck is painful—Little Camilla, you look quite shocked. Well you may. This is your doing. What a naughty child you are. You are the sole cause of this ridiculous situation. You will have to be punished, little one. I will not afflict you with a bottle, but with a strip of rawhide I acquired some years ago in Africa. It inflicts an exquisite pain, sharper and more terrible than that of any other whip."

I was amazed, truly. The stranger was bleeding to death, and all he could think about was whipping poor Eye-oh for punishments.

It's ridiculous, truly, but he seemed to grow happy, thinking of his whipping of Eye-oh. He was a bad man.

I could have stopped the bleeding, maybe, but I didn't have a mind to.

Es and Eye-oh and beardy, they couldn't lift a finger. They were that shocked. They were like frozen meat come over from the Argentine, a-hanging in a butcher's in Ciren.

More and more blood came a-pumping out of stranger's neck. The mess in the cart was terrible to see. Even Es would have a job getting things straight, so it struck me.

"We will not revisit those premises in Pimlico, little Camilla," stranger went on, weaker and weaker in voice, but still propped against the bed. "The tenant suffered an accident, for which I was in part responsible. He made an impertinent demand. We shall go abroad, little one, for our honeymoon. We shall go to a remote place, among discreet people, because I think you will scream. Loud and often, my little love, very loud and very, very often . . ."

Yes, I was amazed. He was getting very weak, was stranger, and his face had the look of death. I'd seen it often in animals. Yet all he'd talk about was the way he'd make Eye-oh scream. It gave him his pleasures, it came to me. He was a bad man. I truly believe he was worse than me, some roads.

"Is this blood?" he said sudden. It seemed he noticed it for the first time, though it covered him and all the cart round. "My blood? Whittingham, be so good as to fetch a doctor."

"Too late," I said.

I couldn't have beardy scampering off to the village, coming back with doctors and policemen and such. Nothing but disagreeables could come of that. Besides, the whole Ciren hospital, where Doris my wife lay, they couldn't save stranger now. When he first fell we could have saved him, maybe, but not now.

It was funny, truly, that he had so much blood. He looked like a man with no blood, or blood the wrong colour. But it was as red as a Christian's, and there was buckets of it.

"There is hempen stitching along the edges of my rawhide, dear little Camilla," said stranger in a very thin voice, like a little wind in the old withies by the stream." It is the stitching which really hurts . . ."

That was the last word he said. "Hurts" was the last word he said. He was still propped up and his eyes were open, but there wasn't any sight in them. They were like the eyes of a fish on a fishmonger's slab. He went from life to death quite gentle, in the moment of saying "hurts."

The others woke up a bit when they saw he was dead. It did ease the strain.

"What are we going to do?" said Es, her face all adabble with tears.

"Ben 'at his motorcar, down t'lane?" I asked her, using the voice I used to her.

"I suppose so. Yes, it must be."

"Put this bloke in, tip motorcar over, an' set fire to un."

"Oh God. Oh God."

"Ye'd best help me, sir," I said to beardy, "t'get lady out o' bothers."

"Oh God. Oh God," he said, same exact as Es just did.

It was awful to see the waste of that good whisky all over the floor of the cart. There was no saving any, though, it was that mixed up with the blood.

Beardy wasn't much help with the stranger. He seemed incapable. He didn't want to look at it nor touch it. Eye-oh wouldn't look at it and Es wouldn't look at it. Mostly I had to get the meat out by myself, with beardy whinnying like my old pony and flapping of his hands like a duck with its head cut off. It was awkward, getting the stranger out in the tight space, the lasses in the way and weeping, and beardy in the way.

It was still pouring with rain. That washed some of the blood off the stranger and off beardy and me. I don't know how it was that so much blood got all splashed about in the cart. It was everywhere, with whisky and bits of the broken bottle.

We dragged the stranger down through the wood to his motor. I knew nothing about motorcars, nor beardy neither. But we took and pushed it so it went into the ditch, half turned over. Then we took and pushed the stranger into the seat. Beardy hated that bit. He was no help at all. My idea was, it would look as though he'd driven into the ditch, and bashed his head when it stopped. I busted the glass in the front, the piece like a window. That was to explain away the broken glass mixed up in the stranger's busted head.

Then I set fire to it all, which wasn't easy in the rain. Rain or no, it burned right merry once it started. The rain did hiss on the flames and the flames did hiss on the stranger.

Back at the cart, the lassies had recovered wonderful.

Eye-oh said she was off away home. There was no need to hide any more, she said. Es said she was off away to London. She didn't like it in Dogleg any more, she said, looking at me. Beardy said he'd go to London too, if Eye-oh was off, because he couldn't stay without money.

Es said, "What do we do about the caravan? It's all blood. If anybody sees it they'll think—"

"Ay," I said, in my voice for Es, "we ben bes' t'burn un."

"But my canvasses!" said beardy. "I can't take them out into the rain."

"Can you bring your cart here, Bob?" said Eye-oh, not so much asking as giving commands.

"Ay," I said, "for the price."

So we loaded my old cart with beardy's paintings and Es's clothes and the other clobber they had, and covered it up with a tarpaulin. Then we burned their old cart. It went up grand, for all the rain hissing on it. I believe they were all three glad to see the last of it.

I took them to Swindon. It was a terrible long road for my pony, but Eye-oh was paying me handsome.

She gave beardy money too, for to get back to London. Beardy and Es got on a train. Es never did say goodbye, which was hurtful.

Eye-oh went off into a shop for to buy clothes. She came out looking so different I didn't hardly dare to talk to her. But she was grand. She gave me money and she kissed me goodbye. Then she took a train herself, to Christ knows where. It made no odds to me where she went. I'd liefer she'd stayed for a piece, for that tight grip she had.

I went to visit Doris my wife. She was moderate glad to see me.

One thing was funny. There was one thing Eye-oh never realised, and beardy never realised. When Es brought that whisky bottle down like a club, it wasn't the stranger she was trying to hit. It was Eye-oh. Because she'd called me "darling." Es was that jealous. But it worked out tidy.

18 ❊ *Her fire must burn*

> Never did passenger in summer's heat
> More thirst for drink than she for this good turn.
> Her help she sees, but help she cannot get;
> She bathes in water, yet her fire must burn.

VENUS AND ADONIS

I felt happy in the gipsy woman's clothes. I liked Jasper's shirt, too. I felt free in those things. I felt disguised. When Jasper and I finally got to the middle of that Gloucestershire wood I felt safe.

I could see that the wood had been let go. Nothing had been done about clearing or culling for a long time. The timber was going back and the rides were choked. It was not preserved, either, and it would not be shot. So there was no harm in our being there, and no one would see us. It was the same with the field where I put Bluebell. It had not been cut or grazed. It was bad, sour pasture, full of weeds. It was wasteland, really, and it would have been silly to waste it. There was water, and enough grass for one horse.

I was terribly grateful to Jasper for coming with me, even though it was what he wanted to do. That was one of the reasons I pulled his shirt off after breakfast that first morning in the wood. Another reason was that if we were going to do it, I thought we should do it at once. The longer we put it off, the more embarrassing it would become. The third reason, the biggest reason, was that there was still something I was looking for. I had done it to myself, countless times, but Henry Clinton had not done it, and Desmond Dacre had not done it. They had both cheated me. I wanted it not only from my own finger but properly. I wanted what Mamma got with Uncle Gareth. I wanted it very badly and I thought Jasper would do it.

He did not. He was too quick. He was finished and useless before I was ready. It was exciting, but I was terribly disappointed.

I tried and tried. As often as he wanted to. It never worked, not really. not for me, not as my fingers worked. It was lovely for him. He said so, and I could see that he meant it. I had to be content with that.

I began to think there was something wrong with me.

I thought so all the more after Esmerelda came.

I was not sure about getting into Jasper's bunk with Esmerelda in the other one. It should be a private thing. One cannot be entirely quiet. It is boring to try. Jasper certainly could not be entirely quiet. I tried to forget Esmerelda, lying a few feet away, but it was difficult. It was impossible. Even though it was pitch dark, it was like having an audience. It put me off, and made the whole thing worse than usual. I could not relax. So it hurt, which generally it had quite stopped doing.

Then there was that business with Esmerelda in the morning.

The first thing that struck me when I saw her naked, washing her clothes, was how beautiful she was. She was like Mamma, but of course much younger and firmer. I liked it when she pulled off my clothes and scrubbed me. It was going back to childhood, to my earliest memories. I was back in the nursery at Moreys, being scrubbed by Nana. It made me feel very safe and protected. I struggled and screamed, but that was part of the game, part of being a baby again.

When she began to stroke me, I found that I was expecting it. That did surprise me. I had read about girls who made love to each other, in those boring books in the locked bookshelf in the library at Moreys, but I never imagined that I would become one of them. But fighting with Esmerelda in the water, both of us naked, was a kind of lovemaking. When she dried me, she was being my nurse and my lover at the same time.

It was love without risk, without pain, without talk, without men, very gentle and comforting. I was very excited. And it worked. Esmerelda did what none of those men had done. Her tongue and fingers were magical. I had never felt anything so beautiful. I had never forgotten myself so completely. I liked doing it for her, too. It was a strange feeling, a sort of masculine, masterful feeling, to do it all to her and to see it working. There was a great satisfaction in that.

But, of course, it made me suspect there was something wrong with me.

I went on doing it with Jasper, whenever he wanted it, but nothing happened to me. There was no magic. I never felt as much as I did with my own fingers. I went on doing it with Esmerelda, whenever either of us wanted it, and everything happened to me, every time.

She was a commonplace sort of person, really, but she was very kind to me, and her body was magnificent, and she did lovely things to me. I became very fond of her.

Sometimes I felt guilty about letting her do all the work of housekeeping. But she did it much better than I would have done it. We were all much more comfortable after she came. What was more important was that it was what she herself wanted. She liked looking after Jasper and me. She liked feeling responsible. She needed to be needed. She was that sort of person. I suppose it is a good sort of person to be, like a nurse in a hospital. I am not really like that. At least, I was not very much like that then.

Once or twice I had the horrors, nightmares about Whitewater. Esmerelda was wonderful to me then. I felt beautifully protected, with her arms round me, like a baby held by a good mother. At those times she was a much better mother to me than Mamma had ever been. I used to feel warm and safe, and then I realised I was excited too. It was all joined up. Her breasts were a haven but they were exciting at the same time. The warmer and safer I felt, the more I felt that warm dampness between my legs.

I knew it was important to Esmerelda, too—she liked making me feel safe. She was a good sort of person. In many ways I wished I was more like her.

When we ran short of money, Esmerelda produced a man called Bob, with a cart. As soon as I saw them together, I realised there was something between them. Esmerelda said she had just met the man going to the farm or the village. But it was obvious that they were much closer than that. Jasper never noticed—he noticed very little, except as a painter—but it was obvious to me. It was the tone of voice they used to each other, like old friends, and the way they looked at each other.

That made me realise two important things. One was that Esmerelda could enjoy it both ways, with me and with a man. At least, with that man. If she could, I thought, I could. Perhaps there was nothing wrong with me—I had just been unlucky. I was very anxious to know the truth about this. When you are young, and face a whole lifetime ahead, you are anxious to be reassured about things like that.

The other important thing was that the carter, perhaps, was better at it than Jasper was. Jasper was better than Henry Clinton or Desmond Dacre, but he was not good enough to make it work with me. Bob the carter might be better. If so, it would be a good idea to try with him. Then I should know whether I was really odd and strange and wrong.

He took me into Cirencester in pouring rain. He was a criminal, really, but I liked him. He reminded me of one of the underkeepers at Moreys who was sent to prison for poaching. That man was actually poaching the coverts he was supposed to be guarding. It was rather treacherous, but it was impossible not to like the man.

I must admit, though it may sound discreditable, that the first thing I liked about him was that he was so interested in me. He said our Bluebell was lame, so that he would have to take me into the town. Bluebell was not lame at all. I had ridden him round the field, bareback, the day before, and he had gone perfectly sound. It was a lie, an excuse. It was quite good enough for Esmerelda and Jasper, but I had been brought up with horses.

Well, it was more comfortable to be taken to Cirencester in a cart than to ride old Bluebell all the way. And it was flattering.

You can tell when someone looks at you with admiration. He looked at me with lots of admiration. One cannot pretend that that is unpleasant. But he only looked at me when Esmerelda was not looking at him.

He was attractive himself, too—very graceful in his movements, very neat and clean. That made a change from Jasper. I was quite fond of Jasper, but he was not graceful or clean. Bob spoke better than one would have expected, too, more like a bank clerk than a carter.

Another interesting thing about him was that he *was* a criminal, a thief and a poacher. That was obvious. I do not know why that should have made him more attractive.

Another thing still which attracted me was something which I hardly like to admit. He was Esmerelda's. I do not know why *that* should make him more attractive, but I am afraid it did. She was so beautiful, so much more opulent and spectacular than me, so much more experienced; but I was sure that he was very interested in me, and it was a kind of triumph.

I am not at all proud of having felt like that.

I thought it was possible that, even though he liked me, he might want to steal my money. So I put all the money in the turned-up hem of my skirt, and carried an old newspaper wrapped in oilskin in my hand. Getting all that ready was why I was so long in the bank. In the event, Bob did not try to steal my money, but it did seem sensible to be prepared.

We got terribly wet on the way back, so I went to Bob's hut to get dry.

I knew exactly what was coming, and I felt ready for it and excited about it.

Immediately afterwards, I was a bit surprised that I had given myself to a funny little poacher in his funny little hut. (It was a nice hut.) But when I thought about it later, I thought I understood my reasons. I was anxious about myself, I wanted to be reassured about myself. He had satisfied Esmerelda, judging by the way she looked at him, which made it an experiment I had to try. And he was nice to look at, with a sort of elegance, and a nice face. And he had the fascination of being a criminal. And he was Esmerelda's, and I was winning a sort of secret war by having him myself.

Anyway, I was a gipsy living in a gipsy caravan off the edge of the world. I might as well behave like one. I was free. I might as well enjoy my freedom.

Altogether it was impossible to resist. He was impossible to resist.

I thought it was going to work. He was lovely in the early part, the exciting getting-ready part. Far better than Jasper, more like Esmerelda. But it was no good. He was too quick, like Jasper. I was cheated again. He was soft and useless inside me before I was ready.

I thought: I was using him. But he was using me. I suppose it serves me right for trying to use people.

So I still did not know the answer about myself. Or rather, I was becoming convinced that I was wrong, that I could only achieve the beautiful ultimate sensation by myself, groping squalidly at myself with a finger, or with another woman. That was what I thought, walking back to the caravan through the rain.

I did not blame Bob. I liked him, as I liked Jasper. The fault was mine, not theirs. They were not cheating me. I was cheating myself—the thing that was wrong with me was cheating me.

I was very depressed about this. But I thought that, at least, it was a good thing to face the truth about myself.

A day or two later the thing I most dreaded happened. All my very worst nightmares came true.

Maurice Whitewater walked into the caravan and said he had come to take me away.

I have only a blurred memory of what happened next. I think Jasper would not save me, or could not, or at any rate did not. Bob somehow appeared. I think I appealed to him. I do not know what happened after that. My next clear memory is of Whitewater lying covered in blood on the floor.

It was a long time—minutes or hours, I have no idea—before I fully realised what had happened to me. I was free, I was saved. Mamma and Uncle Gareth were saved.

I was sorry to see the caravan burn. It was the right thing to do, because of the blood, but I felt sentimental about it.

We went to Swindon. I gave Jasper and Bob some money. I wondered about giving Esmerelda some, because she had been so good to me, but I thought she might be insulted. The middle classes are very odd about these things. I am still not sure if this was right.

I got home to Moreys in the evening after an exhausting journey, changing trains at Reading and at Basingstoke. I got a cab all the way out from Salisbury station to Moreys. The horse was the one that looked like Miss Fordham, Mamma's secretary.

It turned out to be a Wednesday, which I had not known. Mamma was consequently in London. Someone sent her a telegram to say that I was safe. The servants were all in an uproar, having thought I was dead or a white slave in South America.

Mamma came down first thing the next day, arriving in time for a late lunch. It was not reasonable to expect her to get up much earlier than usual. It would not have been fair on the servants at Bulbarrow House to upset their routine.

"Camilla!" screamed Mamma. "Where have you been?"

"Away," I said. "Quite safe. With friends."

I would say no more, then or later. (It took me weeks to persuade Mamma, and all the rest of them, that I would say no more.)

Mamma looked pretty well, I thought. She said she had been terribly worried about me, and I was sure it was true. She was selfish but not unnatural. There were more lines about her mouth and eyes. Somehow I had expected her to be transformed, which was silly after only a few weeks. I expected myself to have been transformed, too, but when I put on my own clothes in my own bedroom, with my own maid Grace looking after me, I looked exactly the same.

"I saw Maurice Whitewater a few days ago," said Mamma at tea time. Suddenly she did look different—haggard and frightened.

"You won't see him again," I said. "He was killed in a motor accident yesterday."

It took as long for Mamma to grasp all the implications of this as it had taken me. She ate a macaroon, looking ten years younger.

I felt closer to her than I had ever felt before. Liberation united us. We could be happy together. We were. She embraced me.

She pressed me against her magnificent bosom, emotionally, weeping. It was very like being hugged by Esmerelda, but not so nice, and of course not at all exciting. I missed Esmerelda.

That evening, I found I missed someone else. I missed Emmy. I was no longer sick with anger when I thought of her. It was a long time since I had felt like that. I understood better about a lot of things. I knew now that people's feelings are what they are, as people are what they are, and it is no good becoming angry because people do not feel as you wish they would, or do feel as you wish they would not.

I felt guilty about Emmy. She had been pitched out into the world without a character and without even a home. I had acted in fury and I had acted cruelly and wrongly.

I did not feel guilty about any of the other things I had done (although I felt distinctly embarrassed when I thought of some of them). But I felt bitterly guilty about my treatment of Emmy.

No one at Moreys or in the village knew what had become of her. No one had heard from her, or heard news of her.

I remembered that Maurice Whitewater had spoken of engaging private detectives to find me. I asked Mamma who they were. She did not know, but Uncle Gareth found out from Whitewater's lawyers or servants or somebody. I wrote to them with a description of Emmy.

I thought it would be impossible to find one orphan servant girl in the whole of England, but it turned out to be easy.

The very day I ran away with Jasper, a man was murdered in a room over a shop in Pimlico. Nobody ever found out who did it, but the man was apparently a black-mailer, and it was assumed one of his victims did it. That was all I heard about it from my detectives, and all I wanted to hear about something so nasty. Anyhow, Emmy was somehow linked to the murdered man, and gave evidence at the Coroner's Inquest. As a result of this, her name was in the newspapers. She was befriended by some charitable people. The police knew all about her, so my expensive detectives had no trouble at all. In fact, I really hadn't needed them—I could simply have asked the London police.

I wrote to Emmy at the hostel where she stayed and where she earned her board in Battersea. I said I was sorry I had treated her so badly and I wanted her to come back.

She came back. She looked exactly the same, plump and rosy, with bright dark eyes like Victoria plums, and a figure like Esmerelda's. She came into my schoolroom where I was reading. She looked happy. Her face was pink from running up the stairs. She curtseyed, but I held out my arms and we hugged each other.

I was so happy to see her again. I begged her pardon for my cruelty. We hugged each other for a long time, laughing and crying. Immediately she was my maid again. Poor Grace was upset. I hugged her too, but that was not at all what Grace wanted.

That evening I had my bath, as usual, and Emmy as usual brought me hot towels from the airing cupboard.

"Last time I saw you in that there bath, m'lady," said Emmy, looking down at me in the water with a funny smile on her face, "you was soaping your little bust so I thought you'd pull them off."

"Oh," I said, suddenly remembering. "I didn't think you saw."

"Best to be clean," said Emmy. "They could do with a soaping now."

"I'm so tired. I'm too tired to wash myself properly."

"You're nothing but a babby, m'lady, if I may make so bold. You'd best be washed like a babby."

"You'll do it much better than I would, Emmy," I said faintly.

She rolled up her sleeves. Her arms were plump and round with a tinge of rich colour under the skin, like Esmerelda's arms. She picked up the cake of soap and rubbed it into a lather. She began rubbing me with her lathery hands. Her hands were slithery with the lather in the hot steam of my bath. I gave myself up to the luxury of being lathered by those smooth, slithery, soapy hands.

Emmy lathered my legs and arms and shoulders. Her face was very pink. Her mouth was slightly open, and her underlip was caught in her teeth.

"You're getting all wet, Emmy," I said. "Either I must come out or you must come in."

"I haven't properly finished with my scrubbings, m'lady," said Emmy. "I don't want you out of that bath just yet."

"Then you'd better join me."

"Dressed up like this? Then I will be wet, and no mistake."

"If you think I need scrubbing, Emmy," I said, "you'll have to get in and scrub. And if you don't want to get your clothes wet, you'd better take them off."

So dear Emmy took off all her clothes and got into the bath with me. It was a big bath—there was room for us both. We soaped each other. We soaped every bit of each other. It was not at all like my struggle with Es-merelda in the stream. It was much warmer and more comfortable. It was just as exciting. She had a lovely plump body, with big rounded buttocks and deep breasts and dimpled arms and legs. We slithered against each other like fish, covered in soap, in the warm water and steam.

I found myself kneeling above her, my knees each side of her chest, caressing her with soapy hands. She was panting with pleasure. Her face was scarlet in the steam. She was soaping over my behind and between my legs and over my fleece. Then one soapy finger slid, like an eel, into the hole I have in front, and another soapy finger slid into the hole I have behind.

Well, it seems there is a nerve inside one's behind, inside the little rude hole itself, and if you rub that you produce the most intense and fantastic sensation of all. It is true. Emmy told me later that she was taught about the nerve by a Portuguese doctor. I felt one soapy finger sliding in and out behind, and one soapy finger sliding in and out in front, and between the two of them I was nearly screaming with joy.

We sent half the bathwater over the floor of the bathroom.

Ladies'-maids do differ. So do ladies.

Emmy said later that she was sick of men. She was sick of being used. She'd felt like a piece of meat, often, just a thing to be stuck into, just a piece of meat for the man to rub himself against as though he was doing it with his own hand. It didn't mean any more than that, Emmy said, and somebody else got most of the money.

What it all did, of course, was confirm my suspicions of myself.

I accepted it, a bit drably. I was thankful to have Emmy. I tried not to feel bitter about being perverted.

I accepted it until, in the spring, I got a letter from Sir Matthew Alban. What memories that name brought back! Of Sir Matthew himself I only remembered nice blue eyes.

He said in his letter (what memories that writing paper brought back!) that he had an urgent and confidential matter to discuss with me. He would entrust the message neither to paper nor to a messenger. He would not discuss it on the telephone. If I expected to be in London, could he call at Bulbarrow House? If not, might he call at Moreys?

Mamma, as puzzled as I was, asked him to stay.

As soon as I saw him, I felt I was joining an old friend. Actually I had never exchanged one word with him. I had never heard his voice. He had *very* nice blue eyes. I liked everything else about him, too—his face and hair and clothes. I knew he was very popular, in a quiet way, and I could immediately see why. He was clever without being pretentious, simple without being stupid, fashionable without being foppish, gentle without being effeminate, masculine without being boorish. Uncle Gareth had told me all this about him months before, and it was most evidently true. I formed a very high opinion of him while he talked to a group of people in the drawing room.

I revised it as soon as we were alone.

"I must tell you, Lady Camilla," he said, "that I have become the owner of a number of paintings by Jasper Whittingham. I visited his studio three weeks ago, saw the paintings, and bought them all. They are paintings of you. They are all excellent likenesses."

"Oh," I said, wishing the parquet floor would split open and swallow me up. I had forgotten about those paintings. I remembered them now with the most excruciating embarrassment. "Not . . . ?"

"One shows you lying on your back beside a campfire. One sitting on the shafts of a gipsy caravan. One washing clothes beside a stream. That is, I think, my favourite, but they are all delightful. There are several others. Whittingham wants to hang them in the Chenil Gallery, where he is having a one-man exhibition next month. I thought you might have objections. My instinct is to burn them all, but I cannot bring myself to do so. They are really very good, and they give me enormous pleasure. What shall I do with the pictures, Lady Camilla?"

19 ✿ *Love keeps his revels*

> Art thou ashamed to kiss? then wink again,
> And I will wink; so shall the day seem night;
> Love keeps his revels where there are but twain;
> Be bold to play, our sport is not in sight:
> These blue-veined violets whereon we lean
> Never can blab, nor know not what we mean.

VENUS AND ADONIS

I came back from Ireland to my lodgings in Jermyn Street to a number of surprises.

The first was, perhaps, to find myself in London at all, instead of on my beloved western seacoast. But there were many friendships I had made that I wanted to pursue, many conversations that I wanted to continue, many things to see that I had not seen.

I knew also, from London newspapers I had had sent to Albanstown, that Lady Camilla Glyn was to "come out" this spring—the Tennysonian fairy princess who had filled a good many of my thoughts and dreams. This alone, I think, would have brought me back to Rivvy Trench and Mrs. Huxtable and the cushioned treadmill of the London Season.

The second surprise was the immense pile of invitations waiting for me on my writing table.

The third, told me within minutes by dear old Rivvy, was that Maurice Whitewater had been killed in a motor accident in Gloucestershire in the autumn. I had missed this in the newspapers. Whitewater's car had caught fire, Rivvy told me, but it and the body had been identified. I was not as sorry as I should have been. He had called on me the previous summer, far more often than I wanted him to, bringing me all kinds of books to look at and even to keep. He was interesting and well informed, but he was not an endearing personality. I heard a number of rumours about his private habits, but I saw no trace of that side of him. His heir, a distant cousin, lived in Australia.

The fourth surprise was thoroughly disquieting. Lady Camilla Glyn had suffered from a serious and mysterious illness for several weeks in the autumn which caused her to be kept in complete seclusion at home. This was never mentioned in any of the society journals. Rivvy picked it up from gossip among valets in one of the West End public houses. He loved that sort of gossip. His relish for oddments of news about the great was undiminished. He thought I would be concerned about Lady Camilla, and I was. However, she was reported to have made a full recovery and was expected to take her place in London society in the summer.

The fifth surprise was a letter, propped on my mantelpiece, from an artist I admired but had never met—Jasper Whittingham. From the letter, it appeared that I had suggested that Whittingham should paint me. It had never occurred to me to have myself painted. I was not a politician, a successful general, or the chairman of a great public company. The idea was absurd.

I found out where Whittingham's studio was, and went round there. I was intrigued to know what odd misunderstanding had given birth to that letter. He was out, but busy in the studio was an attractive dark girl whose face I recognized from a number of Whittingham's pictures I had seen. She was his favourite model, and I could see why. She was an amiable creature, and kept me amused until Whittingham came back.

He was a delight—a full-blooded Bohemian with a big black beard and an infectious roar of laughter. I showed him the letter he had written me. At first he denied all knowledge of it—at least all memory of it. Then recollection flooded back, apparently, and he laughed until he cried. It was impossible not to laugh with him, though I was more and more astonished.

He explained the circumstances. He had needed writing paper embossed with a respectable address for a complicated reason involving an assignation with a young lady. The letter to me was an excuse for a visit to my chambers and the abstraction of some of my writing paper.

"I've still got a couple of sheets," Whittingham said to me. "Of course I ought to return them to you. I suppose I ought to pay for the ones I used, but—"

"But you've spent the last of Io's money, and you haven't any more," said the girl.

I was a good deal amused by Whittingham's story, and I admired the ingenuity of his scheme.

"Why *not* have your portrait painted?" said Whittingham.

"Not I," I said.

"Well then, buy a landscape. A dozen landscapes."

Before I could protest that Albanstown already housed many more pictures than I could hang, he began pulling stacked canvasses away from the wall and propping them against chairs and table legs. Some were better than others, but I was not enormously impressed. I thought his portraits were better.

The girl was helping him display the pictures to me. She turned one round, but he quickly turned it back again. But not before I had seen it, briefly but quite clearly. It utterly astounded me. It was a portrait, an exquisite portrait, of Lady Camilla Glyn. It was a true speaking likeness. There was no mistaking those big soulful grey eyes, that cloud of curly golden hair, the delicate solemnity of that face. What was startling was that it was a nude. Whittingham had painted her sitting, in the nude, on the shafts of a gipsy caravan.

"Hold on," I said.

"No no, you can't look at those," said Whittingham.

"Those? There are several?"

"Certainly not. Work of imagination. Valueless."

"We must eat, Jasper," said the girl.

"They're not for sale," said Whittingham.

"Oh yes they are," said the girl. "You've sold a dozen of me."

We argued for a long time, she and I against Whittingham. Her arguments were the ones that carried weight. Whittingham had not a penny, and needed many pence to settle an abundance of pressing debts.

I bought eight pictures for seventy-five guineas each.

Neither Whittingham nor the girl would say anything about the model —they stuck to the alias "Io" when they mentioned her. They would not say anything about the circumstances, about how those astonishing pictures came to be done, or when, or where.

I studied them when I got them home to Jermyn Street. I gazed at them, each of them, for hours, behind locked doors.

They had taken some time to do. Eight pictures were not the work of a morning. They were rural scenes, all of them, showing Lady Camilla posed against trees, fields, streams. The colours were those of the landscapes I had not liked—autumnal hues, the leaves turning, berries in the hedgerows.

They were painted from life. Of that I was certain.

Had Lady Camilla been kept in a secluded sickroom in the autumn? If so, how came Whittingham to paint her somewhere in the countryside? How in God's name came he to paint her, eight times, in the nude or seminude?

I was absolutely baffled and intensely curious.

Nobody must be allowed to see the pictures. That was very clear. Yet they must not be destroyed. They were works of very great merit, great charm, delicately sensuous, beautifully composed and painted. They reminded me of Renoirs I had seen in Dover Street, but I preferred the Whittinghams. Certainly I preferred Whittingham's model. These were the best things I had seen of Whittingham's, and I knew I had got them cheaply. But I could show them to no one. They could never be hung, except in a room which no one entered.

More than anything else, what struck me was the breathtaking beauty of the subject. It was a body out of a fairy tale, almost unreal, almost too perfect to be possible. I had guessed, seeing Lady Camilla herself, at a slim delicacy of figure which was very much to my taste; but I think no one could have dared to guess at the slender miracle which Whittingham had painted.

I felt a sort of guilty excitement, gazing at my purchases. I felt a peeping Tom. No normal man could have looked at those pictures without excitement, without racing pulse and physical yearning.

The pictures gave me great joy. They gave me an awesome responsibility. And they gave me a marvellous excuse for a meeting with their subject.

She blushed crimson when I told her. I had not supposed that any improvement was possible to that little marble-white face; but the blush was adorable.

It was adorable. She was adorable. I adored her. I was in love with her.

I had seen her briefly, here at Moreys, a year before. We had been talking for two minutes. It was impossible that I should be deep in love with her, but I was.

"I will give you the pictures," I said, "on two conditions."

"What?" she whispered.

"First, that you do not destroy them. Second, that I may come and see them, and you."

"You have seen me," she said painfully. "In those awful pictures, you've seen me . . ."

For some reason, I found myself blushing as hotly as she was. I felt as though I had been caught peeping through the keyhole of her bathroom.

And then, for some reason, we both burst out laughing. I could not then imagine why we did such a thing; I cannot now. The tension between us vanished, blown away by our laughter. There was happiness and trust in that beloved little face. I took her hand, and she let me hold it.

Then we went for a walk, in great content. After swearing me to secrecy, she told me some of her adventures.

I was at Moreys constantly after that. I did not think Lady Bulbarrow would have invited a nobody like myself quite so often, had not her daughter persuaded her. I had an ally also in Sir Gareth Fortescue, who was often there and always kind to me.

My courtship of Camilla was conventional, even demure. It was magical and unbearably exciting. When I first kissed her I trembled so I hardly could stand.

"I am beginning to believe," she said, after that first chaste kiss, "that I am not so very odd after all . . ."

"Why, darling Camilla?" I said in a shaking voice. "I have never met anyone so right in every way. Why, just looking at some pictures which I have locked up in London—"

She blushed, and put a hand over my mouth.

"I am praying," she said. "I am praying to God that, with you . . ."

I did not know what she meant, and she would not tell me. She had secrets from me. She was right to have them. I knew I would never understand her completely. I did not want to. Life is a voyage of discovery, and so is every important relationship.

Our engagement was announced at the end of May. For the rest of the season, Camilla was a fiancée as well as a debutante. Among men, I was the most hated man in London.

We had a prodigious London wedding, in St. Margaret's, Westminster, of which I remember nothing. Through my head, throughout, kept pounding the absurd litany: "The flowers in the church alone have cost over a thousand pounds. The flowers in the church alone . . ."

The reception, of course, was in Bulbarrow House. All the presents were displayed in one of the saloons, an incredible treasury in number and value according to the ostentatious custom of the time. (The display, I think, was designed to please the givers of expensive presents. Comparison was invited and inevitable.) There were speeches. I was obliged to gargle a few words myself in reply to the speech proposing the health of Sir Matthew and Lady Camilla Alban.

I imagine I wore a fixed, silly grin all afternoon.

An electric car took us to Waterloo Station, and we giggled like children as we shook the confetti and rose-petals out of our clothes. Our luggage was already at the station. A train took us to Dover and the first night of our honeymoon.

I had engaged a suite—a large bedroom, a smaller one, a sitting room and a bathroom. I could not imagine that we should make much use of the sitting room during one night unless things went miserably wrong.

Which was possible, agonizingly possible.

I was not widely experienced, but I was by no means ignorant. I knew that with a young bride, great patience and tact were necessary. She could be disgusted, frightened, hurt. It would be difficult for her to relax, to throw herself uninhibitedly into perilous waters into which she had scarcely as yet put a toe.

At least, I thought not. Of all the girls I had ever seen, Camilla was the most delicately virginal to look at. Whittingham had painted her in the nude. Any experiments they had made together had been, I understood, unsatisfactory. Camilla was not communicative about all aspects of her adventures. Though naturally full of curiosity, I had forborne to press her with questions. She would tell me anything that she wanted to tell me, or that she thought I ought to know.

This attitude was, perhaps, unconventional at the time. Other husbands would have demanded, as of right, a full history. I did not feel that I had any such right. I had had my own adventures, made my own experiments, and I was not bent on describing them in detail to Camilla. That would have been unseemly and unhelpful. Could I not accord her the privilege of reticence which I awarded to myself?

She was my Camilla, my unique Camilla. She was what she was, and that was what I loved. What she was, was composed in part of what she had done. If I loved her, I loved what she had done, because it was part of her. So my mind ran. It was unconventional to think thus; but I believed I was right, and I believe so still.

Meanwhile there had been little that was physical in our courtship. I had held her in my arms to kiss her, but gingerly, as though she might break. She seemed to me so fragile; I was terrified of bruising her.

She did not seem to have developed a repugnance for the physical. She did not at all recoil from my kisses. But I knew that the night that we faced—the physical act that we faced—loomed large and perhaps menacing in her mind. Many scraps of unfinished sentences had told me so much. This put a huge and daunting responsibility on my shoulders. When the time came, late, in the dark, after dinner, I must subdue my own excitement—must set myself to lay whatever ghosts troubled her spirit.

When we arrived, I followed Camilla upstairs, after a word with my servant and with the affable manager of the hotel. I thought it right to give her five minutes, and spun out this time in an atmosphere of winks and nods and goodwill.

She was not in the sitting room of the suite. I put a hand to the door of the larger bedroom. Was I to knock? I was her husband, though I was not yet used to this astonishing fact. But only her husband of four hours. I must tread gently. I must be considerate and respectful. A confident intimacy would follow, in time, when we were used to one another.

I knocked.

After a pause she called, "Who is it?" in a muffled voice.

"Your husband."

"Come in, darling."

The room faced west. It was so full of bright evening sunlight that for a moment I was dazzled.

Then, what I could see, I was still more dazzled.

Camilla was on her knees by the bed, in an attitude of prayer. She had just raised her head from her hands. She had been praying.

She was naked.

Jasper Whittingham had not flattered her. Neither his brush nor any other could do justice to Camilla's body. Slender as a bird, yet womanly, fragile yet firm, milky-white with a froth of secret gold, unexpectedly moving in that humble and graceful attitude of prayer.

She looked up at me gravely, her eyes wide. A sudden smile, brief yet brilliant, came and went across her face, as when a gap opens in clouds above the sea and a shaft of radiance kindles the waters to fire.

She was blushing.

I fell on my knees beside her and put an arm about her little shoulder. Kneeling, we kissed. It was our first truly passionate kiss. I felt her mouth open under mine. I was delirious to feel, under my hands, the silky bare skin of her back.

"Now," whispered Camilla fiercely into my cheek.

She pulled herself away from me and lay on her side on the bed, her back to me. Her back, hips, legs were beautiful beyond imagination. I leant to kiss the small of her back. I felt a hand like a moth on my hair. I wondered how I could have the brutality to force entry into so fragile a shrine. My own blood pounded in my head and my loins.

Now. In the full glare of the evening sun. The milky pallor of her skin rosy in the warm sunlight.

With fingers that scarcely functioned, I began to pull off my clothes, dropping them on the floor in my haste.

She rolled over onto her back, into the position in which Whittingham had painted her by a campfire.

"After all," she said faintly, "you've already seen me like this."

Nevertheless, she was blushing.

I struggled with my clothes. An intolerable number of clips and straps and buttons, as though tailor and shirtmaker had conspired to drive me mad with frustration. A certain embarrassment at the unequivocal urgency of my own flesh, which I could by no means conceal.

I felt my own cheeks burning. And, as I gazed at her, waiting for me on her back on the bed, I was a battleground between embarrassment, desire, love, lust, concern for her, concern for myself . . .

I struggled with a small final button, my fingers trembling so that I could *not* get it undone. They were idiotically designed, those drawers. And the silk in front was thrust outwards in the most grotesque and unseemly way.

Camilla watched me, solemn as a little owl.

In the front of my drawers there was, of course, a slit, of the necessary kind common to all male undergarments. My fumbling efforts with the bottom of the waistband dislodged my erect member so that, in the most disgraceful way, it popped out through the slit in the front of my drawers and flaunted itself like a flagpole.

I was aghast. I had not meant her to see it, naturally. It was awful, not merely obscene but also ugly.

Camilla stared at it, blinking.

I gaped at her, my hands uselessly twitching at the button.

And then that happened which had happened to us once before—and which had sent us on the road which led to this room and this bed. We both burst out laughing.

Nothing could have been more utterly unexpected. Nothing could have been better.

Camilla laughed, lying on her back, so that her firm little breasts shook. I laughed, standing beside the bed, so that my shameless member shook. Laughing, she gestured me onto the bed. Laughing, I scrambled onto it beside her. She undid the recalcitrant button and pulled off my drawers.

We were still laughing when I took her in my arms. I felt all her body along all my body, and both bodies were vibrating with laughter.

Laughter pressed us together. Laughter made our diaphragms caress each other. Laughter mingled our breath as we kissed. Laughter banished embarrassment, constraint. Laughter sent us wholeheartedly into this marvellous physical moment. We were relaxed, because we were laughing.

I had been intensely determined that, in spite of overmastering excitement, I would delay the moment of abandon as long as I possibly could, so that she might share the magic of fulfilment. I knew it would be difficult, perhaps impossible. But laughter helped. Laughter distracted my mind from the mounting sensation in my loins, when she blindly, gently, accepted me into her body.

I could see and feel her own mounting excitement. I could no longer control my own. Try as I might to stem it, the exquisite climax of sensation opened the floodgates and emptied the reservoirs of passion.

She lay afterwards, clamped to my side, her arms tight round me, her head under my chin. I felt wetness on my chest. She was streaming with tears.

"Oh my darling," I muttered, aghast.

I had not laid the ghosts. She wept with misery and disgust. I had failed.

"I am crying with happiness," said Camilla.

She twisted her head so that we could look into each others' faces. She smiled at me, through her tears, with such radiant intensity that I knew that what she said was true.

She hiccupped and sniffed, like a child. I loved her, if possible, even more desperately because of her childish hiccup and sniff.

Speaking with difficulty, through happy sobs, she said, "You see, I thought—only by myself, or with Esmerelda or Emmy— But you, my darling magician—I understand at last. We must always laugh a great deal. Will you promise me to laugh a great deal. And it is love. That makes a great difference. I ought to have known that, but I have only just learned it. Isn't that silly?"

It was laughter, it was love; it was also, in some small measure, my own determination to control my own avid body. By those happy tears I was rewarded a million-fold.

"We," said Camilla, sniffing, "are going to live happily ever after."

And we have.